Steps
selected fiction and drama

Also by Gabriel Josipovici

FICTION

The Inventory (1968)
Words (1971)
Mobius the Stripper: stories and short plays (1974)
The Present (1975)
Four Stories (1977)
Migrations (1977)
The Echo Chamber (1979)
The Air We Breathe (1981)
Conversations in Another Room (1984)
Contre-Jour: a triptych after Pierre Bonnard (1984)
In the Fertile Land (1987)

THEATRE

Mobius the Stripper (1974)
Vergil Dying (1977)

NON-FICTION

The World and the Book (1971; 1979)
The Lessons of Modernism (1977; 1987)
Writing and the Body (1982)
The Mirror of Criticism: selected reviews (1983)
The Book of God: a response to the Bible (1988)
(ed.) The Modern English Novel: the reader, the writer
and the book (1975)
(ed.) Selected Essays of Maurice Blanchot (1980)

STEPS

Selected Fiction and Drama

GABRIEL JOSIPOVICI

CARCANET

First published in Great Britain in 1990 by
Carcanet Press Limited
208-212 Corn Exchange Buildings
Manchester M4 3BQ

British Library Cataloguing in Publication Data

Josipovici, Gabriel *1940-*
   Steps – selected fiction and drama
   I. Title
   828.91409
   ISBN 0-85635-873-8

The publisher acknowledges the financial assistance of
the Arts Council of Great Britain

Typeset in 10½pt Garamond by Bryan Williamson, Darwen
Printed and bound in England by SRP Ltd, Exeter

Contents

Note

One writes what one would like to read but cannot find written by anyone else.

One writes what seems impossible – until it is done.

Of course impatience, lack of imagination and insufficient skill frequently lead to failure. But that is the aim.

It is not an abstract aim. Autobiographies and most novels bore me because they are only too possible. Anyone who can write a letter can write an account of what happened to them or invent a story and tell it. Why add to the sum total of such accounts, such stories?

What excites me is the sense of something impossible to imagine and yet – given enough luck and hard work – something which it might just be possible to *make*. At the end of the process something will perhaps have entered the world which could not have been conceived before it appeared. And yet, once there, it will be equally inconceivable that it should ever *not* have been.

Once a piece of work is satisfactorily completed, however, once the impossible, that which one dreamed of reading but could never find in print, has been made actual, there is absolutely no desire to re-read it. In fact re-reading, for the purpose of correcting proofs for example, is not only tedious but painful. While one is at work the lure of the impossible drives one on but once it is done one's whole relation to it alters. Because one has made it oneself it lacks otherness, and otherness is an essential element in the response to art. That is why artists cannot be the best judges of their own work. They tend to judge it by the glow engendered by the process of making; or rather, by their memory of that glow. This can hardly be a reliable criterion. Borges meant something like this, I think, when he said that artists judge others by their achievements, themselves by their intentions – a hard saying, but true.

In the following pages therefore I have not tried to include

what I imagine to be the best of my earlier work, only what
has left the warmest glow. Even so, the volume is less a *selection*
than *a* selection: on another day I might well have chosen
differently.

Some writers think of short stories as novels that failed to
develop. I don't. One can do things in two pages which one
could not do in two hundred (and *vice-versa* of course). Nor
do I think of plays, for stage or radio, as essentially different
from novels and stories: all are explorations, steps on the way
– the constraints of each medium merely push one forward. I
have thus chosen two novels, my first, dating from 1968, and
my sixth, published in 1981; ten stories which span a twenty-
one year period, from 1963 to 1984; and three plays, written
in the 1970s. I hope the individual items will give pleasure,
and that any constants that emerge will seem less like compul-
sive repetition and more like the shadowy outline of that secret
signature Proust suggests all artists are unconsciously in the
process of signing in the course of their working lives.

Lewes
14.iv.90

1
THE INVENTORY

For my mother

I

'You need a holiday,' she said.

'I need you,' he said.

'I can't hear you,' she said.

'What have I done to you?' he asked her.

'I just don't want to see you,' she said.

'Complete strangers,' he told her, 'have more pity on me than you do.'

'What's that?' she asked.

'Complete strangers have more pity on me than you do,' he said. 'One of them writes here that if I really need him he'll meet me here at nine.'

'I can't hear you,' she said.

'I'm simply reading what it says here,' he said. 'If you really need me I'll –'

'Go to hell,' she said.

'I'm simply reading –'

'It's no good, Joe,' she said.

With a small, one-bladed penknife he began to scratch her initials over the mirror: SH. Gothic script.

'There are still things,' he said. 'About the inventory. To discuss.'

'I can't hear you,' she said. 'There's something wrong with the line.'

H is easy, but what do you do with a wiggle like S?

'I said there were still one or two things I wanted to ask you. About the inventory.'

'The inventory's over and done with,' she said.

'There are still things,' he said. 'I've been typing it for Stout and there are still things.'

'What?'

'Things I wanted to ask you.'

'No,' she said.

'Susan, please. It's only a few odds and ends to clear up. It

11

won't take long. Dinner, maybe, or lunch tomorrow if you prefer, or just a drink, or –'

'Ring Gill,' she said. 'She'll be delighted to help you.'

'It's you I want to see, not Gill,' he said.

The trouble with Gothic is it needs the illuminations. The snakes sliding down the esses, the monkeys balancing on the crossbars of the aiches and ayes, and all those gorgeous palaces and cloud-capped towers in the cees and oes. But who has the time or the patience to write like that today? To paint in all those worlds nestling in the folds of an S?

'The inventory's over and done with,' she said. 'You need a holiday, Joe.'

'I need you,' he said.

'I can't hear you,' she said.

'Oh no no no,' he said. 'Not that again.'

'What?'

'Why is it,' he asked her, enunciating slowly and very clearly, 'that I can always hear you perfectly well and yet you can never seem to hear me?'

'Perhaps because I don't particularly want to,' she said.

'Oh my god, my god,' he said. 'Don't you realize that *I'm* the one who's supposed to say that?'

'It's no good, Joe,' she said. 'Really, I don't ever want to see you again.'

'The world's a small place,' he said. 'People are constantly running into one another. Long-lost friends. Chaps you knew at school. The man you directed to the only decent hotel in Port Said. It's not easy not to see people ever again these days, what with places and trains and ships and cars and –'

'It's no use threatening me, Joe,' she said.

'I'm not –'

'Goodbye,' she said.

Consider the difference between an S and an H. The one cunning, slippery, giving you nothing to grip, nothing to hold on to; the other solid, serious, standing almost ponderously on heavy legs. But what can you do with a penknife anyway? A single-bladed penknife with an aluminium body. It's hopeless without the right tools, the proper equipment. Palette. Brushes of varying sizes. Scrapers. The lot. And even then who knows? Everyone's so restless these days somebody's bound to foul it up. Cover it with their personal variations. And why not? Considering the price of paper nowadays.

The girl on the next stool studied Joe with interest.

'You a student?' she asked.

'No,' said Joe.

'You look like a student,' she said.

'Do I?' he said.

'Oh yes,' she said. 'Definitely.'

'And you?' he asked.

'Well,' she said. 'Back home I studied a while at a college in Minnesota.'

'Is that so?' said Joe.

'It was a kind of general course we did,' she explained.

'Oh yes?' he said.

'Psychology, music, political science, drama, geography, painting. A kind of mixed course.'

'How very interesting,' said Joe.

'That's really why I'm here,' she explained. 'I've been wanting to come over for a long time. You know how it is. You want to see for yourself, don't you? All these things you read about in books, it makes you want to come over and see for yourself.'

'Naturally,' said Joe.

'The official tour only starts tomorrow. But I've been here a week already, looking round.'

'Oh yes?'

'There's so much to see,' she said. 'I landed at Southampton last Monday, around seven-thirty in the evening. The boat was delayed outside the harbour so it was about seven-thirty in the evening. Maybe a bit after. I was pretty tired with having been in that big monster of a ship all that time so I went right to bed and didn't see anything of Southampton that evening or the next morning either, because I caught the eight-thirty-four to London and I had a job getting up to catch that! But my friend tells me I didn't miss much.'

'No,' Joe reassured her. 'You didn't.'

'Tuesday afternoon,' she went on, 'I went to see the Tower of London, and in the evening I went to see *King Lear*. On

Wednesday morning I went to the National Gallery and in the afternoon to Kew Gardens, and I ended up with *The Black and White Minstrel Show* in the evening. Thursday morning I went to the Tate Gallery and to Windsor in the afternoon, and then I stayed nice and quiet in my hotel in the evening – I think you need to give yourself a break once in a while, don't you? Then Friday I went to Oxford and Blenheim for the day and in the evening I saw *The Mousetrap* by Agatha Christie. On Saturday I went to the Victoria and Albert Museum in the morning and to Hampton Court in the afternoon, but there were too many people, and in the evening I went to a very *avant-garde* play at the Earls Court, and on Sunday I went to Cambridge all day and got back too late for anything and today I've been to the British Museum and the National Portrait Gallery and here I am.'

'There won't be much left for you to see when the official tour starts,' said Joe.

'Oh I don't know,' she said. 'I think it's always a good idea to see things twice if you can.'

'Yes, yes, of course,' said Joe.

'Then after England,' she said, 'we spend two days in Belgium and Holland, because there's not all that much to see in those two countries, and then five days in France and seven in Italy, and we end up with three in Germany before flying back.'

'You pack a fair amount in,' he observed.

'You get so you can take in a good deal,' she said.

'I suppose you do,' he said.

'Actually,' she confided in him, 'I'm only in this place tonight because I'm due to see a play at the National Theatre at seven-thirty.'

'Oh yes?'

'My friend suggested I go with her to a genuine old London pub, and I was tempted, but I felt I really ought to see this play at the National Theatre. I've seen a good bit of these Jacobean plays back home and I want to see how these boys tackle it.'

'But you're in a genuine old London pub now,' he told her.

'I am?'

'Sure,' he said.

'A genuine old London pub?'

'So you see,' he said, 'you've killed two birds with one stone.'

'But that's marvellous,' she said. 'Are you quite sure this is a genuine old London pub?'

'Oh yes,' he said. 'Quite sure. There's another just round the corner and one down the street and two more behind the station.'

'But this part of London's full of them!' she exclaimed. 'No one ever told me.'

'Every pub in London is a genuine old London pub,' he said.

'Really?' she said. 'No one ever told me.'

'These things don't get into the guide-books,' he explained.

'No,' she said doubtfully. 'I suppose they don't.'

They drank in silence, each digesting the information the other had given.

'Hey!' she said. 'Are you going to this show too?'

'No,' he said. 'I live here.'

'Here?'

'In the neighbourhood.'

'You're not an actor by any chance?'

'No, no,' he said.

'You've got the handsome looks of an actor,' she said.

'I'm a lawyer,' he said.

'A lawyer? But how interesting!'

'It's dreadful,' he said.

'You can't say that,' she protested. 'Why, it must be chock full of human interest, being a lawyer.'

'What's your job?' he asked her.

'I'm a telephonist,' she explained. 'That's pretty full of human interest too. Better than sitting in an office all day long taking down shorthand. Of course it's not quite people. Voices.'

'Look,' he said. 'There are just three subjects I prefer to avoid. The first is telephones. The second is my job. The third is human interest.'

'Oh,' she said bleakly. 'That doesn't leave much.'

'No,' he agreed. 'It doesn't leave much.'

'It's funny,' she said, getting off the stool. 'You look like you're a student. Or an actor.'

'Well I'm not,' he said.

II

'Mr Stout?' said the woman who opened the door.

'Hyman,' said Joe. 'Mr Stout's on holiday. In Corsica.'

'Gill said it would be Mr Stout,' said the woman doubtfully. Joe shrugged.

'They could at least have sent one of their permanent staff,' said the woman.

'I am one of their permanent staff,' said Joe.

'You look like a student,' said the woman.

'As a matter of fact,' said Joe, 'and if you want me to be quite precise, I *am* their permanent staff.'

'You'd better come in,' said the woman.

'Thank you,' said Joe.

'I'll lead,' said the woman. 'Close the door behind you and give it a push or it won't stay shut.'

'I'm afraid,' he said to the woman, 'I stepped on something which gave a kind of squeak.'

'What kind of squeak?'

'Well...sort of high-pitched, I suppose.'

'Don't worry,' she said. 'That was probably one of Mick's toys. He leaves them about everywhere. I hope you broke it.'

'I rather think I felt it move,' he said.

'Some of them even do that,' she said. 'But it may have been Oscar.'

'It felt more like Oscar,' he confessed.

'Poor thing,' said the woman. 'He's having a rough time. He doesn't know what's happening to him, with us pulling everything open and those brats teasing him or just running about and shouting. He slinks from corner to – This is my cousin Gill Clemm, this is her Baby Choo.'

'Howdodo,' said Joe.

'This is the man from Davey, Stout and Son,' said the woman.

'*How*dodo,' said Gill Clemm. 'You haven't come down that dreadful corridor in the dark, have you?'

'Yes,' said Joe. 'I'm afraid we have.'

'Susan, you said you'd get a bulb put in there before you did anything else,' said Gill Clemm.

'Well I haven't,' said Susan.

'I'm afraid, Mr...?'

'Hyman. Joe Hyman.'

'...Mr Hyman, that you find us in the middle of a simply dreadful chaos, everything is in such frightful confusion here ...But that's what you're here for, isn't it?'

'I beg your pardon?' said Joe.

'Well, I mean you're here to put things in some sort of order, aren't you, to inventory everything and tell us exactly what there is and all the rest of it...?'

'He's the man come to disconnect the gas,' said Susan.

'But...?' said Gill Clemm. 'I thought you said he was from Davey, Stout and Son? I don't understand...I thought...'

'That's right,' said Joe. 'Davey, Stout and Son.'

'Then you're not...?'

'No.'

'The gas...?'

'No,' said Joe. 'I've come to do the inventory.'

'Why did you say he'd come to disconnect the gas then?'

'It was a joke,' said Susan.

'Oh,' said Gill Clemm. 'I see. A joke. It doesn't seem very funny to me.'

'It was the best I could do,' said Susan. 'Gill does the cleaning and the tidying,' she explained to Joe. 'She and the children. I make the coffee.'

'I thought,' said Gill Clemm, 'it was Mr Stout who was supposed to come?'

'Mr Stout is on holiday,' Joe explained. 'In Corsica.'

'You will forgive me, won't you, Mr Hyman, for not getting up,' said Gill Clemm. 'But as you see I'm trying to sort out these bills and old postcards and bits of paper, there's so much junk here, so much that's all out of place and mixed up with other things, letters, little mementos, odds and ends that one doesn't know what to do with, which is why you find me like this in the middle of the floor, I –'

'Please,' said Joe. 'Don't worry about me. Just go on with whatever you're doing.'

'I expect Susan's gone to make the coffee – Mick will you stop unzipping my dress – she spends her time making it and then drinking it, I really can't keep up with her, I sleep badly enough as it is – go and play with Oscar – I've never been a heavy sleeper, Mr Hyman, and of course since I had Baby... Do excuse the children, Mr Hyman, just don't pay attention ... I find it so exhausting, physically and mentally exhausting, to work in a mess like this, which is why I felt I just had to put a little order into it all, try and get the flat just a little bit tidier and get rid of the smell, that awful musty smell, that's what really drives me round the bend, I hope you don't mind, I mean I hope it isn't illegal or anything, I just thought it might help, make it easier for you and the flat was so filthy it –'

'But of course,' said Joe. 'It's quite natural. It's always done.'

'I mean,' said Gill Clemm, 'one doesn't want to put oneself on the wrong side of the law, does one?'

'Oh,' said Joe, 'the law, you know...'

'I always feel,' said Gill Clemm, 'that if you are getting the benefits of living in a certain community you should make a point of abiding by its laws, however absurd some of them may be.'

'I wonder,' said Joe, 'if I could have a look round?'

'But of course,' said Gill Clemm. 'There's not much to see. This is all there is, in fact. Two rooms, kitchen, bathroom, corridor. Not exactly luxurious, but enough for one man and a cat, though it must have been a tight squeeze when Sam was living here too.'

'I didn't realize... ?' said Joe.

'His son Sam lived here with him till a couple of years ago,' said Gill Clemm.

'And where is he now?'

'He vanished one day, just like that. The next they heard of him he'd died in Amsterdam. He and the old man used to quarrel I gather, and he was always threatening to go away. The old man never really tried to find him, I think he knew that when he'd gone it was for good. But it's Susan you must ask about all that. She saw quite a bit of them at one time. I'm something of an outsider here really, I – Brigid, how many times have I told you that it's rude to whisper? Besides, I can't hear a word you're saying.'

'I put milk and sugar in the coffee,' said Susan. 'It's a bad habit of mine. I hope that's how you take it.'

'Actually,' said Joe, 'I take it black, without sugar.'

'I'm sorry,' said Susan. 'You don't have to drink it.'

'Oh,' said Joe. 'Once won't hurt.'

'What?' exclaimed Gill. 'Again? It's those sweets you stuff yourself with. It's got to stop, do you understand? Or else I'll have to take you to see Doctor Rillier and you know you don't like that.'

'How long is it going to take?' asked Susan.

'It's difficult to say.'

'Mr Stout didn't tell you what to expect?'

'Mr Stout,' said Joe, 'is on holiday. In Corsica.'

'Yes,' said Susan. 'You've told us that already.'

'But it's true,' protested Joe. 'He is.'

'Didn't he leave any instructions, details...?'

'He didn't know Mr Hirsh would die.'

'Well, you've looked around. Can't you tell?'

'Three or four days,' said Joe. 'Maybe a week. It depends on the small things.'

'Here am I,' said Gill Clemm, 'wearing myself out trying to make this place look presentable, and what do my children decide to do but be sick all over the floors.'

'It's those sweets she stuffs herself with,' said Susan. 'I told you this would happen.'

'I know, I know,' said Gill Clemm. 'But what can I do?'

'If you'll excuse me,' said Joe.

'You haven't drunk your coffee,' said Susan.

'Oh, no,' he said. 'How stupid of me.'

'I wouldn't drink it now,' she said. 'It'll be cold.'

III

'Black,' said Joe. 'Without sugar.'

'The sugar's on the table, sir,' said the waiter.

'I said without sugar,' said Joe.

'That's up to you, sir,' said the waiter. 'To put in or not. It's on the table for those who want it.'

'Can you clear away the rest of this mess then?' asked Joe.

'We're terribly busy, sir,' said the waiter. 'Two of our staff are ill and –'

'Sure, sure,' said Joe soothingly. 'I'm not asking you to stand on your head. Just clear all this so that I can put down some papers without being afraid that when I pick them up again I'll be putting the remains of my own and godknowswho else's dinner in my pocket with them.'

A martyred expression on his face, the waiter obliged.

'Is that wiped and cleaned to your entire satisfaction, sir?' he enquired when he had finished.

'Perfect,' said Joe.

'And here,' said the waiter, 'is your coffee, sir. Black. Without sugar. The sugar is on the table.'

'I don't take sugar, thank you,' said Joe, as he smoothed the sheets out on the newly-wiped table.

One (1) Turkish carpet, 21′ x 18′ – worn & damp.
One (1) pair maroon velvet floor-length curtains – worn; one with large stain.
One (1) small fireside rug – dirty.
One (1) ladder-back chair – rush seat broken.
Five (5) walnut dining-chairs – one with leg chipped; upholstery worn on seats.
One (1) round polished dining-table – badly scratched surface.
One (1) camphor-wood chest – foot loose; lock broken.
Contents: see Rider 3 (linen).

'Baby Choo, Baby Choo, whatever shall we do with you?' sang Brigid in a high toneless voice.

'It's ridiculous,' said Susan. 'It's not even as though most of the furniture was theirs in the first place.'

'What do you mean?' he asked.

'They bought most of it with the lease. Curtains and fittings. Only in this case it was a good deal more than is usually meant by the term. Look at it all, third-hand third-rate stuff that's been sat on and eaten off by God knows who!'

'Baby Choo, Baby Choo, whatever shall we do with you?' sang Brigid.

'Didn't they have anything of their own?' he asked.

'The old man sold most of it just so that they could go on living,' she said. 'There are a few pieces I suppose, the book-case, the mirror, one or two others, but –'

'Baby Choo, Baby Choo,' sang Brigid, 'whatever shall –'

'For goodness sake shut up, Brigid!' said Susan.

'It's a lullaby,' said Brigid.

'Go and sing it somewhere else.'

'Mummy said to sing it in here.'

'Well I say to sing it somewhere else.'

'Mummy said I'm always to obey her.'

'And I say you're always to obey me.'

'Mummy's stronger than you are.'

'But Susan's stronger than you are,' said Joe.

'Baby Choo, Ba –'

'Hell hell hell,' said Susan.

'It's only a lullaby,' protested Brigid.

'Gill!'

'Who's misbehaving now?' Gill wanted to know.

'It's only a lullaby,' said Brigid.

'What on earth is that?' exclaimed Gill.

'What?'

'That. On your head.'

'It's a scarf,' said Susan.

'Don't be silly,' said Gill. 'I can see that. Where did you find it?'

'In there,' said Susan.

'In there? With the rest of those things on the bed?'

'Yes,' said Susan. 'Why?'

'You found it in there and you put it on?'

'That's right,' said Susan.

'I'm going to drop Baby,' announced Brigid.

'Like that?' said Gill. 'Their property? You found it in there and you put it on?'

'It's mine,' said Susan. 'I gave it to Sam because he liked it. He saw me wearing it and he said he liked it. So I gave it to him. I like it too. So now I've taken it back.'

'But you can't do that,' said Gill. 'It's not yours any more, you can't do things like that, it's illegal, it's ... Mr Hyman ... ?'

'Strictly speaking,' said Joe, 'the law –'

'Bugger the law,' said Susan.

'Susan!' exclaimed Gill. 'The children!'

'I'm going to drop Baby now,' warned Brigid.

'Don't be a nuisance, dear,' said Gill.

'Hullo! Hullo!' said George Clemm. 'Anybody at home?'

'Give Baby to Daddy,' said Gill.

'I say!' said George Clemm.

'Give Baby to Daddy,' repeated Gill.

'That's a bit much!' exclaimed George Clemm.

'He's yours too, isn't he?' said Gill.

'I sincerely hope so,' said George, 'but –'

'Don't worry,' said Gill. 'He's got all your charming characteristics.'

'All the same,' said George Clemm. 'To be handed wet Baby first think after work is more than most husbands would put up with.'

'But not more than mine will,' said Gill sweetly, putting up her cheek to be pecked.

'It's my good nature,' said George. 'You trade on my good nature.' He pecked.

'George, this is Mr Hyman from Davey, Stout and Son. He's doing the inventory.'

'Howdodo.'

'Howdodo.'

'Things getting under control?'

'It's a slow business.'

'But I expect you're used to this sort of thing?'

'However often I do it I never get used to it,' said Joe.

'But lawyers are supposed to be such patient people,' said

George. 'I'd have thought this would have appealed.'

'Lawyers are all sorts of people,' said Joe.

'He's been wonderfully patient with the children,' said Gill. 'They've been absolute pests.'

'Why don't you leave them at home, darling?' asked George. 'It can't be much fun for them being cooped up here all day.'

'If you'll stay at home and look after them, darling,' said Gill. 'I don't ask better.'

'Can't they go and play with friends?' asked Joe.

'None of their friends want to play with them,' said Susan.

'Couldn't Susan take them out for a walk once in a while?' asked George.

'I wouldn't touch your children with a bargepole,' said Susan.

'I don't blame you!' laughed George Clemm, showing white teeth.

'Nine seconds,' said Susan.

'What?' asked Gill.

'The laugh,' said Susan.

'The what?'

'Skip it.'

'I think we ought to go,' said George Clemm. 'Mustn't keep the kiddies up past their bed-time, must we?'

'Oh, darling,' said Gill. 'Brigid was sick again today. On the sofa this time. We really must take her round to see Doctor Rillier even if the old ogre does frighten the wits out of her.'

IV

If you drop a threepenny piece into the Thames from the exact
centre of Waterloo Bridge on a clear night you can, if your
eyes are good enough, watch it fall right into the water. If your
ears are sharp enough you can hear the plip it makes as it enters.
If you've got a strong enough imagination you can drop with
it through the cold black water, still a little salty even this far
up, till it lies small and dull on the muddy bottom. Even then
it probably hasn't finished its journey, for the tide pulls and
tugs and who can say where it will end up?

My sight is going to the dogs, thought Joe. My sense of
hearing is all fouled up; and I've always had a lousy imagination. What the hell am I doing throwing coins over Waterloo
Bridge in the middle of the night?

'You're early,' she said.
'I'm a hard worker,' he said.
'How very commendable,' she said.
He shrugged his shoulders.
'Close the door behind you and give it a push,' she said.
'With all this anti-draught tape they've stuck round the frame
it keeps swinging open.'
'Tell me if I'm likely to step on Oscar this time.'
'He's in the kitchen eating,' she said.
'Why don't you get a bulb for the corridor?' he asked her.
'For godsake don't you start nagging too.'
'I'm sorry,' he said. 'But it is rather long and dark.'
'Will you have some coffee?' she asked him.
'I've just had breakfast.'
'I'm making some for myself.'
'In that case,' he said.
'It's practically ready.'
'Your cousin not here yet?' he asked.

'No. She has children to look after, a husband.'

'They tend to go together.'

'Sometimes,' she said. 'It annoys her not being able to get here before me.'

'Why?'

'I make a mess, you see, unless she's after me. Then all her lovely work is wasted.'

'She brings the children with her every day then?'

'Every day, Mr Hyman.'

'They seem to be nice children,' said Joe. 'A bit undisciplined perhaps, but –'

'They're monsters,' she said.

'Oh, I wouldn't say that,' said Joe.

'But I do,' she said.

'It must be very trying for them, cooped up all day in this flat, it –'

'I thought you'd come early so as to get on with the inventory?' she said.

'I don't follow you,' he said.

'It's just that you seem to spend an awful lot of time standing around and chatting.'

'You offered me some coffee,' he protested.

'I wonder,' she said. 'Would Mr Stout have stood around chatting instead of getting on with his job?'

'Since he has always struck me as having exceedingly good manners,' said Joe, 'I should think the answer to that is yes.'

'People are getting so polite these days,' she said. 'They are even prepared to tell you what your opinions are.'

'Look,' he said. 'I don't like doing this any more than you do. But it's my job. I didn't ask to come here.'

'Here's your coffee,' she said smiling at him.

One (1) mahogany bookcase, glass doors with ogival glazing-bars.
Books – see Rider 1 (books).
One (1) small octagonal coffee-table – top badly scored & marked.
One (1) small Regency desk-chair – upholstery torn.
One (1) large oil-lamp – shattered.

'And anything that wasn't scratched or broken or too dirty ever to get clean again has been receiving the full treatment from Mick and Brigid,' said Susan.

'They've broken things?'

'You've seen what they're like.'

'Yes but –'

'They're monsters.'

'A bit wild perhaps but –'

'They disgust me,' said Susan. 'The whole lot of them. I was just telling Mr Hyman,' she said to Gill, 'that you disgust me, the whole lot of you.'

'Yes, we are pretty disgusting,' agreed Gill.

'Oscar scratched me, Mummy,' said Brigid.

'Serve you right.'

'But I'm bleeding, Mummy!'

'You shouldn't tease him. I've told you.'

'Baby Choo, Baby Choo, whatever shall we do with you?' sang Brigid.

'Don't be tiresome,' said Gill.

'It's a lullaby,' said Brigid.

'It's Mick I'm really worried about,' said Gill.

Brigid dropped Baby Choo.

'Haven't I told you never to drop him like that?' said Gill.

Slap slap.

'Mick's reached such an impressionable age,' said Gill. 'He's always trying to unzip my dress.'

'I'd have thought he'd be past that stage,' said Joe. 'Isn't he rather backward?'

'He's big for his age,' explained Gill.

'I'm going to kill that Baby Choo,' said Brigid.

'I won't have you talking like that,' said Gill. 'All his teachers say that he's very *advanced* for his age, Mr Hyman.'

'In that case,' said Joe.

'Very advanced,' said Gill.

One (1) parchment lampshade.

Four (4) electric bulbs.

One (1) inlaid needlework table – compartment piece broken. Contents: 1 travelling alarm clock – broken;

1 penknife – rusty; 1 small Kodak camera – broken; 3 small ivory elephants; 17 toy soldiers; 5 pencils; 1 ball of string; 1 roll of sticky tape; 1 pr. pliers; 1 small packet 'Oxo' cubes; 28 French centimes; 1 white stone; 1 book of stamps – 2/9 left; 3 sea shells; 400 envelopes.

'Bang! Bang!' shouted Mick.

'I'm something of an outsider here really,' said Gill Clemm. 'My mother, you see, was David Hirsh's second cousin whereas Susan's father was his half-brother, but –'

'Bang!' shouted Mick. 'You're dead! You're dead! Bang! Bang! Bang!'

'But we were never much of a family for family feeling,' said Gill Clemm. 'It's not so much that there were any great family rows as that –'

'You're dead! You're dead!' howled Mick, and launched himself at Joe's shoulders.

'Out!' shouted Gill. 'Out of this room at once! It's not so much that there were any great family rows as that no branch of the family ever seemed to be interested in what any of the other branches was doing. So that as a child I never saw anything of my cousins, and I gather they didn't see much of each other. Of course I was a little older than both Sam and Susan, but I do think it's a pity, I –'

'Mummy, when is Daddy going to buy me a new rifle?'

'I don't know,' said Gill. 'Why don't you ask him?'

'He says it's a secret.'

'I do feel that the family is a *natural* unit, don't you, Mr Hyman?'

'Mummy!'

'That's really why I went out of my way to see something of Susan. I'm sorry to say that Sam and his father tended to keep to themselves even more than the rest of us, though I know Susan saw something of them at one time.'

'When, Mummy? When is he going to give it to me?'

'I don't want you to think I don't respect people's privacy, Mr Hyman, but I do think that if families kept together more, some of the things we hear about would –'

'You're not recounting our boring old family history to Mr Hyman, are you?' asked Susan.

'Why not?' said Gill. 'It helps to put him in the picture.'

'He doesn't want to be put in the picture,' said Susan. 'I remembered this time,' she said to Joe. 'No sugar.'

'But you put milk in,' said Gill.

'Bang! Bang! Bang!' screamed Mick, and leapt on to the table.

'Get off that table!' shouted Gill, and beat at his legs.

'My God, what children!' said Susan.

'You're dead Mum you're dead Mum!' chanted Mick. 'You can't talk to me 'cos you're dead, you're dead, you're dead!'

'Mr Hyman doesn't take milk in his coffee,' said Gill.

'Go and play in the kitchen, for chrissake,' said Susan.

'Leave me alone,' said Mick.

'As I was saying,' said Gill, 'we were never much of a family for feeling. We –'

'Please, Gill,' said Susan. 'We're not interested.'

'No no,' protested Joe. 'It's most interesting.'

'You're too polite,' said Susan.

'You don't have to listen,' Gill told her. 'I'm sure Mr Hyman likes to be put in the picture. After all, it can't be much fun going through the possessions of people one has never known, can it?'

'More fun than going through those of people one has,' said Susan. 'Anyway, I don't expect he thinks of his job as being fun. He told me so himself.'

'All this has been rather upsetting for her,' said Gill. 'She's not usually like that. And she genuinely likes the children I think, although she pretends to loathe them – but one couldn't be *so* outspoken if one meant the things one said, could one, Mr Hyman?'

'No,' agreed Joe. 'I'm sure one couldn't.'

'But I *do* mean the things I say,' protested Susan. 'Only you won't ever believe me.'

'It's so difficult,' said Gill, 'with three children to look after, and one of them a baby.'

'Is that water over there?' asked Susan.

'Where?' asked Joe.

'And of course,' said Gill, 'I would never dream of employing a nurse. I think children should be brought up by their own parents and by no one else. I always feel that if you're not

prepared to devote yourself to bringing them up you shouldn't
have children in the first place.'

'Yes,' said Joe. 'It looks like a stream of water.'

'I know it's old-fashioned of me,' said Gill, 'but I do think –'

'They're breaking up the house!' screamed Susan. 'Your children are flooding the house! They –'

'What? Where?' cried Gill, looking wildly round. 'What's
happening?'

'Look . . . the bathroom . . .'

'Oh my God!' shrieked Gill. 'Oh my God, they've drowned
him! Mick! Brigid! Where are you? Oh my God, they've
drowned my Baby Choo!'

'I can't stand this, I can't stand this, I can't stand this,' said
Susan very quietly standing in the centre of the room.

'It's all right!' shouted Gill from the bathroom. 'Everything's
all right! Mick just forgot to turn the taps off! But I was going
to wash the bathroom anyway, so everything's for the best!'

'I was going to wash the bathroom anyway!' said Susan
bitterly.

'You're early,' she said.

'I'm a hard worker,' he said.

'How very commendable,' she said.

He shrugged his shoulders.

'Close the door behind you and give it a push,' she said.
'With all this anti-draught tape they've stuck round the frame
it keeps on swinging open. Inquisitive neighbours would peer
in on their way up the stairs.'

'Tell me if I'm likely to step on Oscar this time,' he said.

'He's in the kitchen, eating.'

'This corridor really does need a bulb,' he said.

'For chrissake don't you start nagging too,' she said.

'I'm sorry,' he said. 'But she does have a point.'

'She always has a point,' said Susan. 'Will you have some
coffee?'

'I've just had breakfast.'

'I'm making some.'

'In that case,' he said.

'It's practically ready,' she said.

'You sleep here?' he asked her.

'No. I come early to look after Oscar.'

'Wouldn't any of the neighbours...?'

'I'd rather look after him myself.'

'What happens to him when all this is over?'

'The inventory? I don't know. I suppose in the end I'll take him.'

'In that case why don't you take him now and save yourself the bother of coming so early?'

'I don't know,' she said. 'I'm afraid of his trying to find his way back here and getting run over. He's lived here for most of his ten years. You know what cats are like about moving.'

'What about the flat?'

'The flat?'

'What happens to it?'

'There's still a couple of years' lease to run. What do you do in a case like that? Gill can decide.'

'She's not here yet?'

'She's got children to look after – A husband.'

'They tend to go together,' he said.

'It annoys her not being able to get here before me.'

'Why?'

'I make a mess, you see, unless she's after me. Then all her lovely work is wasted and she has to start all over again.'

'Does she bring the children with her every day then?'

'Every day, Mr Hyman.'

'They seem to be very nice children,' said Joe. 'A bit undisciplined perhaps, but –'

'Here's your coffee,' she said, smiling at him.

'I take it black,' he said.

'Oh,' she said. 'I'm sorry. I thought it was without sugar you took it.'

'Black,' said Joe, 'and without sugar.'

'Once won't hurt you,' she said.

'I'll be sick on the sofa,' he said. 'You wouldn't like that, would you?'

'It's so difficult breaking yourself of a habit,' she said. 'Everything was always in such a mess I was lucky if I could find one spoon, let alone three, and the milk jug leaked and taking it from the bottle meant spilling half of it on the table,

so I used to prepare it all in here and stir with whatever I could
lay hands on and then bring it out to them.'

'I meant to ask you,' he said. 'The son. Sam. What happened
to him exactly?'

'One day he disappeared,' she said. 'And never came back.'

'Your cousin told me he died in Amsterdam.'

'Birmingham,' she said. 'Gill always thinks she knows everything but she always gets her facts wrong. He died last year
in a hotel in Birmingham.'

'Susan, meet me for lunch tomorrow.'

'I've told you, Joe. I don't want to see you again.'

'Just once. Please.'

'You've been overworking. You need a holiday.'

'It's you I need, not a holiday.'

'I can't hear you.'

'All right, all right.'

'What?'

'Susan, I've only got money for four more calls. Don't force
me to make them. You know how I hate the phone.'

'I shall disconnect the damn thing.'

'Then I'll have to come round and see you.'

'I'll call the police.'

'For some inexplicable reason I dropped one from Waterloo
Bridge just now. I thought –'

'One what?'

'Threepenny piece.'

'Serve you right.'

'No, no. You don't understand. On purpose. To see how
far down I could see it fall.'

What do you say to a dead telephone?

One (1) corner cupboard: Contents: 3 small willow-
pattern plates; 1 glass candlestick; one glass fruit-bowl –
chipped; one street map of Marseilles; one curved china
spoon.

Three (3) cushions – dirty.

One (1) bed-divan.

One (1) embroidered cover – dirty, stained.
One (1) gilt-framed rococo convex mirror.
One (1) oak-framed mirror, 3′ 6″ sq. – backing scratched and broken.
One (1) Malay kris in sheath.
One (1) small wooden Japanese dragon.

'George doesn't seem to worry,' said Gill. 'But I've reached the stage where I feel something's got to be done, no matter what.'

'It's only a phase,' said Joe.

'But that's what everybody says,' said Gill. 'It's so embarrassing. And now he's taken to doing it at school and the parents of some of the girls have started objecting. Luckily the headmistress is fearfully forward-looking and she explained to them that it was just a phase he was passing through, I explained to them Mrs Clemm, she told me, I explained that it was just a *phase* your Michael was passing through, just a phase and nothing more.'

'Why don't the girls wear buttoned-up dresses?' asked Susan.

'Oh, he undoes buttons as well,' said Gill. 'He prefers zips but he undoes buttons as well.'

'That rather puts paid to my theory,' said Susan.

'And what was that?'

'That he's simply mechanically-minded. Theoretically interested in how zips work. But buttons aren't for the mechanically-minded. I'm sure they despise them.'

'Mummy,' whispered Mick.

'Don't whisper,' said Gill. 'It's rude.'

'Brigid has dropped Baby,' announced Mick.

'You dropped Baby?' said Gill. 'After what I told you.'

'I was dead,' said Brigid. 'Mick shot me and I was dead. So I had to drop Baby.'

'I told you never to drop him. Do you understand?'

Slap slap.

'Mick shot me! He kicked me because I wouldn't die! So I had to die!'

'Liar! I never kicked you!'

'Yes you did!'

'No I didn't!'
'Yes you did!'
'No I didn't!'
'You mean you kicked her? While she was holding Baby?
Are you mad?'
Slap slap.

One (1) brass rubbing, 3' x 1' 2" – knight in armour.
Three (3) glass vases – one cracked.
Two (2) Malay rice pictures.
One (1) 'Fyrside' paraffin stove.
One (1) cat basket & blanket.
Five (5) ashtrays – 2 glass, 2 pewter, one china.
One (1) eighteenth cent. celestial globe.

'What's this doing here?' asked Joe.
'It's Oscar's bowl,' she said.
'It seems a bit big for that.'
'Sooner or later everything in this flat was converted into
either a bed for Oscar to sleep in or a bowl for him to eat out
of. Sam always –'
'I wanted to ask you,' he said. 'What did you mean by saying
that he disappeared one day?'
'He just disappeared,' she said. 'No one knew where he'd
gone to.'
'But why?' he said.
'He just did,' she said.

One (1) cat's bowl (?) – china.
Two (2) portraits, gilt frames – one damaged.
   i. Gent with beard.
   ii. Dark woman in red dress – caption: 'Madame
      Carmen'.
Seven (7) lustre jugs – perfect condition.
Nine (9) green and yellow stones – various sizes.
Four (4) coloured tiles – one chipped.
One (1) jade lizard.
One (1) wicker waste-paper-basket.

'I can't imagine where all this dust comes from,' said Gill. 'You'd think that on a first floor things would stay relatively clean, but here I seem to spend all my time scrubbing and sweeping, and as soon as I've finished it's got to be done all over again.'

'It's this building going on all round us,' said Susan. 'You can't breathe in the streets.'

'It's not as bad as that,' said Joe.

'Oh but it is,' said Susan. 'It is in this part of London anyway, even if the air is clean and fresh where all you smart people live.'

'I suspect it's mainly taking things out of drawers that haven't been opened for months if not years,' said Gill. 'I always try to take my time and make sure I don't spread the dust that's accumulated in there all over the flat, but –'

'Meaning that I don't,' said Susan.

'Well, you are rather untidy, aren't you, dear?'

'The phone,' said Joe.

'It's for me,' said Gill. 'It must be George.'

'I'm rather untidy,' Susan told Joe.

'Haven't you got any idea why he disappeared?' Joe asked her.

'I told you I don't know,' she said.

'But you must have some idea,' he said. 'People don't just disappear like that.'

'Look, Mr Hyman, why don't you just get on with your job and leave us alone?'

'I'm sorry,' he said, 'I –'

'It seems to me you've taken long enough about it already.'

'What's the matter with you?' he said. 'You've been consistently rude from the moment I arrived, you've gone out of your way to make me feel I've barged in on something I wasn't meant to, that –'

'You have,' she said.

'Thanks,' he said.

'It's not your fault,' she said. 'It's your job. If it hadn't been you it would have been someone else.'

'Aren't you being a bit melodramatic?' he asked.

'You don't understand,' she said. 'You're in the way. Gill and I know what we think of each other, and we know how to keep off each other's toes though you might not think so at times. You confuse the issue. You're in the way.'

'I'm sorry,' he said. 'I –'

'There's nothing to be sorry about. It's your job, as you once told me. All I'm suggesting is that you get on with it and leave us alone.'

'Thanks,' he said again.

One (1) china pig – snout chipped.
One (1) brass mortar and pestle.
One (1) brass table-lamp – Victorian.
One (1) enamel vase – cracked.
One (1) ivory paper-knife.
Poker, tongs, and shovel set.

'You mustn't pay attention to Susan,' said Gill Clemm. 'Of course she's upset by this, but then aren't we all, to some extent? And to tell you the truth, Mr Hyman, I'm never quite sure whether Susan feels more than she shows, or rather less than she tries to make out she's not showing, if you see what I mean.'

'Perfectly,' said Joe.

One (1) small Yugoslav stool.
One (1) bronze paper-weight.
One (1) 'Philips' portable gramophone – broken.
Thirty-eight (38) records – 32 l.p.'s.
Two (2) metal book-ends.
Two (2) pipes.
One (1) tobacco-pouch.
One (1) Victorian rocking-chair – upholstery worn.
One (1) green sofa – arm broken.
One (1) large armchair – upholstery very badly torn.

V

'If I could have a word with you, young man?'

'I'm afraid I really haven't got time,' said Joe.

'It won't take a minute of your time, young man. Everybody's in a hurry on a cold night like this, bitterly cold it is for this time of year, but it's a foul summer we've had, and what with my wife in hospital and five children to look after and the doctors not giving me more than a year to live at the very most, it's my bones you see, my bones are just rotting away, young man, and what's to happen to these children when I'm gone? I was wondering if maybe you could spare half a crown, young man?'

'I don't have half a crown,' said Joe. 'All I have is a bloody inventory running round and round inside my head.'

'A bloody what?'

'All right, all right,' said Joe. 'Here.'

'Thank you, young man, thank you, that's more than one life you've saved by this kind act if you only knew it, thank you...'

Whichever way you look at it it's a weakness. Strong you either give or you don't. Weak you hesitate and then give. At first I was always giving, she said, but they weren't interested. They didn't want anything. Just to be left in peace to sit here in this room over-crowded with junk, smoking their pipes and looking into space. It's nice of you to call, Susan, the old man would say, and then they'd go on smoking, what do you do I ask you what do you do if you don't smoke a pipe? I'd run out of cigarettes in an hour and then there was nothing to do but sit and look at them or at Oscar or into the fire. They didn't mind my being there, in a way it might have been better if they had, at least it would have meant that I made some impression, impinged somewhere upon their consciousness, but this! You can't understand what it was like, I simply wasn't there to them, each one sitting in his place, the old man in the rocking-chair and Sam opposite in the big armchair, even Oscar always slept just there on the rug in front of the fire, never any further to the right or the left, you can see the mark, there, not quite in the middle, it was a funny thing about this flat, as soon as you entered it was as though your individual freedom to do this or that or the other simply disappeared and then everything, the hour you came and left, where you sat, even what you said, was determined by what you had done or said the first or second time, it was as though it had been fixed once and for all and there was never any question of departing from the pattern, never –

'Why are you telling me all this?' he said.

'Why – ?' she said. 'I don't know, this last week cooped up here with Gill and the children, it's been hell. Going through their things in this empty flat, only the cat left and those children everywhere, yelling, squabbling, crying.... And there's so much of it, so much, I suppose when a place is lived in you don't notice, it all seems necessary, you never question, but all this lying about, unused and useless, toothbrushes, ink-bottles, shoe-horns, ivory elephants... You begin to feel it's too much, it's crushing you, I don't know.... It's so absurd seeing it all lying there, slowly being translated into your neat list, one useless item after another, curtains, carpets, chairs, tables, ash-trays, knick-knacks, why do human beings surround them-selves with so much, why do they need all this, all this...?'

'You're tired,' he said. 'You need a rest, to go away some-where.'

'No, no,' she said. 'You don't understand. You don't under-stand at all.'

One (1) oak sideboard & dresser – Georgian (?)
Eight (8) soup-plates – two cracked – one chipped.
Five (5) large plates.
Seven (7) medium plates.
Eleven (11) dessert plates – two chipped.
One (1) soup-tureen.

'When Susan got divorced,' said Gill Clemm, 'she decided she needed an education.'

'I didn't know she'd ever been married,' said Joe.

'So she took an external degree in philosophy at one of the London colleges,' said Gill.

'Hadn't she had an education before, then?' asked Joe.

'Not higher,' said Gill. 'Not higher.'

'I see,' said Joe.

'She thought,' said Gill, 'that it would help her to cope with life better.'

'It's a point of view,' said Joe.

'It's a point of view all right,' said Gill. 'But not one with which I myself have much sympathy – will you stop teasing Oscar! Especially when you consider what modern philosophy is like.'

'I'm afraid I don't know anything about modern philosophy,' said Joe.

'To be quite frank I don't either,' said Gill. 'Not what you'd really call knowing. But it does seem to be so niggling, doesn't it? He'll scratch you and serve you right.'

'Give him to me,' said Joe.

'Leave me alone,' said Mick.

'Don't talk like that,' said Gill.

'Leave me alone,' said Mick.

'I mean,' said Gill, 'this idea that all our problems are really problems of language, it's got its point, of course, but I do feel it's been a bit overdone.'

'Who was her husband?' he asked.

'Oh,' said Gill. 'He was a dear. He was in carpets. Terribly interesting. He – leave that cat alone!'

Slap slap.

Six (6) Pyrex soup-plates.
Six (6) Pyrex plates – large.
Six (6) Pyrex dessert-plates.
One (1) stewing-pot – Danish.
Four (4) Pyrex dishes.
Three (3) egg-cups.
Nine (9) assorted dishes – three chipped.

'It's ridiculous, all these plates,' Susan said. 'They ate so little. The old man always insisted on cooking, I don't know why, because he never stopped grumbling all the time he was doing it. I suppose it kept him occupied, not that he ever seemed to be bored even when he was doing nothing at all, that was a capacity they had, never to look bored and yet spend their time doing nothing at all, but the food was so bad, so bad, you have no idea. The first time I came he cooked the meal and I struggled and struggled with it, doggedly chewing the lumpy meat and tasteless mash, I was determined not to show what I thought of it, or even that I was having to fight to get it down at all, and I was so busy struggling I didn't see that they'd both of them left most of it on their plates, and then Sam said, You don't have to eat it all you know, but it was too late, I had. I learned later that they never bothered to eat more than a few mouthfuls, why he cooked such quantities I can't imagine, most of it had to be thrown away or given to Oscar, but even he turned up his nose at it usually, not that he's a difficult cat, when he's hungry he'll eat most things but not those potatoes, never those. The old man seemed never to have heard of salt or butter, never to have grasped the fact that if macaroni cooks too long it gets soggy and if rice cooks too little it stays hard, and he always bought the cheapest ingredients, partly because they were so hard up, but more because he had theories, oh endless theories, about diet and the evils of cheese and the need for food to be cooked in its natural juices, what he called its natural juices, what could be more natural than butter and salt? I would ask him, and he'd stare at me for a while in a way he had and then puff himself out and say sententiously so that you never knew if he was serious or joking, it made me so angry but it was impossible to tell and he never gave you a clue, sometimes I wondered whether he knew himself, anyway he would puff himself out and say, Everything, you, me, this cabbage, contains *within itself* all that is necessary for it to cook as the Lord meant it to be cooked, have you ever heard of a cannibal who cooked men in anything but plain water? And you're not going –'

'But I don't understand,' said Joe. 'Why did you go, why – ?'

'The first time,' she said. 'The first time he came up to me at a concert. I hadn't seen him since we were children, and then only twice, our parents never got on, ours was never much of a family for family feeling, I remember I was bigger than he was and he had a scout belt which I coveted and a sulky expression. I sat on his head because he wouldn't give me the belt and he bit my behind, not the sort of memory on which lasting friendships are built, I didn't recognize him when he came up to me at that concert, you know how it is with people you haven't seen for a long time, you go on seeing them in your mind, whenever you think about them, you go on seeing them as they looked the last time you saw them, as if time had stopped for them, had frozen them into just that age and attitude, which is absurd when you think about it, because it certainly hasn't done the same to you, but it's as if your unconscious or whatever it is doesn't know the meaning of time, is unaware of its existence, so that even with the testimony of your mirror always in front of you you often find yourself surprised that you no longer look like the little girl you feel you are, anyhow, when he came up to me at that concert I didn't know who he was but he seemed to be quite sure, You're Susan, he said, and I must have looked quite blank because he laughed and explained, but you see the most ridiculous part of the whole thing was that he thought we liked the same sort of music whereas I was only there because of one of the cellists, but I didn't tell him that at the time, there wasn't any reason to, and afterwards it was too late and we never cleared it up, so that whenever he remembered that I was actually in the same room as they were during those interminable evenings he would put some Elgar or Strauss on the gramophone and I would have to pretend I liked it at least I did at first so as not to hurt his feelings, but afterwards I took to saying I was off music or something equally silly and he wouldn't insist because he really preferred to sit there in silence, smoking his pipe with the old man, while I sat on the sofa, trying to make them out or leafing through a book or trying to interest Oscar in a game, they didn't seem to mind what I did and that only made it worse, at least if they'd got angry or something, but no, they were always pleased to see me they said, anyway, that first night I went to dinner I didn't know he lived with his father, and he opened the door, it was the night after the concert, and said The old man's in a flap, the meal's not going too well, and I said What old man? And he, Surely you haven't forgotten your Uncle David, he certainly hasn't forgotten you, he was quite excited when I told him you were coming, this is quite an occasion, quite an occasion, we don't often have people to dinner, you'll have to prepare yourself for the worst, he's not the world's best cook but he insists on doing it all himself, and I said Oh really? or something equally fatuous, I had no idea what to expect, I'd got married you see and been abroad and divorced and thought I was in love with a cellist and I didn't really know why I'd come at all except to be polite and I suppose I must have been just a little bit curious....'

'Susan Hirsh, this is the voice of your long-lost lover come to claim you.'

'Go away.'

'I've started giving away all my money now.'

'I don't want to know.'

'Soon I won't even have enough for the fare to Putney.'

'I don't want to see you or speak to you again.'

'Do you realize what that means?'

'It means I'm fed up with you.'

'No no. What it means is that soon I won't have enough money left to pay for the tube.'

'Please, Joe.'

'It means I'll have to walk. Arriving about five in the morning, since I am a notoriously slow walker, unlike cousin Sam.'

'I'll call the police.'

'Especially when there is so much to ponder and so little reason to hurry since —'

'Joe?'

'Yes?'

'What do you want from me?'

'The truth, the whole truth, and nothing but the truth. I love you, Susan.'

'I have my doubts about that.'

'You have?'

'I've been thinking about it, Joe. I think you're in love with them.'

'What?'

'It's the only explanation.'

'You're too modest, Susan. Much too modest.'

VI

At the corner of the street Joe Hyman bumped into a young man in a brown suit.

'I wonder,' said the young man, holding out a small and dirty piece of paper, 'could you direct me to this address please?'

'No,' said Joe.

'You could not?'

'No,' said Joe.

'You live in London?' asked Brown.

'Yes,' said Joe.

'Yet you cannot direct me?'

'No,' said Joe.

'You are Cokenay?' asked Brown.

'No,' said Joe.

'How you live in London and you are not Cokenay?'

'I come from Ruritania,' said Joe.

'Ruritania?'

'Albania, Serbia. One of those places. Poland.'

'But Poland I have visited,' said Brown enthusiastically. 'The Polish girls, you have seen them, yes? Gold hair and brown bodies, all day they spend in the swimming-pool and at night dancing. It is lovely country.'

'So they say,' said Joe.

'I can give you addresses, names...' Brown dug into his pocket; remembered; stopped. 'This address, you really do not know?'

'Really,' said Joe.

'It is a pity,' said Brown sadly. 'It is a great pity. It is night-club. Very recommended by knowledgeable man, my friend. Perhaps we go together, yes?'

'No,' said Joe.

'You are busy perhaps this evening?'

'That's right,' said Joe.

'It is a pity,' said Brown. 'Always it is better two than one. My friend, my knowledgeable friend, he would come with me, only he has somewhat broken his leg.'

'He has?'

'It is the sanitation of Paris,' explained Brown.

'Oh yes?'

'Yes yes,' said Brown. 'My friend, you see, he is big man, fat. He cannot be kneeling always. Not kneeling. How you say...? Crouching. He cannot be crouching always. It is a big effort for his ankles.'

'It is?' said Joe.

'Then comes the water,' said Brown. His hand swept forward. 'Like a torrent it comes rushing. To escape you must have practice. He has no practice. He is not used. He is fat man. He is crouching. He pulls. The water it comes rushing. He makes movement to jump – crack! His leg is somewhat broken.'

'Bad luck,' said Joe.

'Paris is bad luck,' said Brown. 'It is insane city.'

'Look,' said Joe. 'This is very interesting, but I've got some phone calls to make and –'

'But that is excellent,' said Brown. 'I will seek the way and you will telephone. Then we will go together.'

'Well, actually,' said Joe, 'I –'

'Yes yes,' said Brown. 'That is good arrangement.'

They didn't want anything. Just to be left in peace to sit here in this room overcrowded with junk, smoking their pipes and looking into space. It's nice of you to call, Susan, the old man would say, and then they'd go on smoking, what do you do I ask you what do you do if you don't smoke a pipe? I'd run out of cigarettes in an hour and then there was nothing to do but sit and

'Black,' said Joe. 'Without sugar.'

'Anything with it?'

'One of those sweet things. What do you call them? A flapjack.'

You're Susan he said and I must have looked blank because he laughed and explained, but you see the most ridiculous part

of the whole thing was that he thought we liked the same sort
of music whereas I was only there because of one of the cellists
but I didn't tell him at the time, there wasn't any reason to,
and afterwards

'And a flapjack,' Joe reminded the waiter.

I had no idea what to expect, I'd got married you see and
been abroad and divorced and thought I was in love with a
cellist and I didn't really know why I'd come at all except to
be polite and I suppose I must have been just a little

'It is not clear to me that we should meet here,' said Brown,
sliding into the bench opposite Joe. 'It is five minutes walking
from the telephone. At the beginning I wait. Inside there is a
man. I think it is you. I wait. Then he comes out and I see it
is not you. I ask him the direction. He does not know. Then
I think perhaps you have other business this evening. I walk.
I am sad. I think I will come inside here and ask direction. I
come inside, and I see that you are waiting for me. What joy.'

'What joy?' asked Joe coldly.

'Pardon?'

'Never mind.'

'What is this that you eat?' enquired Brown, after a pause.

'It's called a flapjack.'

'Flapjack?'

'Flapjack.'

'It is good?'

'I can recommend it.'

'Oh yes?'

'Unreservedly.'

'Pardon?'

'Unreservedly.'

'Unreservedly?'

'Yes.'

Brown dug into his pocket. 'Look here. This address. You
don't know it at all?'

'No,' said Joe.

'Perhaps I will not eat,' said Brown. 'You have finished. We
will go now.'

'I'm only going across the road for a drink,' said Joe.

'That is a good idea,' said Brown.

'What will you have?' asked Joe.

'Tomato juice please,' said Brown.

They didn't mind my being there, in a way it might have been better if they had, at least it would have meant that I made some impression, impinged somewhere upon

'I go and ask him the direction,' said Brown.

'He doesn't look quite the type to me,' said Joe.

'I go and ask him,' said Brown.

made some impression, impinged somewhere upon their consciousness, but this! You can't understand what it was like, I simply wasn't there to them, each one sitting in his place, the old man in the rocking-chair and Sam opposite in the big armchair, even Oscar always slept just there on the rug in front of the fire, never any further to the right or the left, you can see the mark, there, not quite in

'I go and ask him,' said Brown.

'What?'

made some impression, impinged somewhere upon their consciousness, but this! You can't understand what it was like, I simply wasn't there to them, each one sitting in his place, the old man in the rocking-chair and Sam opposite in the big armchair, even Oscar always slept just there on the rug in front of the fire, never any further to the right or the left, you can see the mark, there, not quite in

'Excuse me,' said Brown.

see the mark, there, not quite in the

'Excuse me,' said Brown. 'This gentleman. He is called Arrinoks. He wishes to speak with you.'

'With me?'

'This is my friend, Mr Arrinoks.'

'This guy a friend of yours?' asked Arrinoks.

'No,' said Joe. 'Definitely not.'

'He *says* he's a friend of yours,' said Arrinoks cunningly.

'He can say what he damn well likes,' said Joe. 'I've never set eyes on him before.'

'I know your game,' said Arrinoks. 'I seen you come in together. I don't like people takin liberties with me.'

'Mr Arrinoks,' said Joe, 'no one is taking any liberties with you.'

'Harrynokes,' said Arrinoks.

'Mr Harrynokes,' said Joe. 'No one is taking any liberties with you.'

'I'm going to bust you filthy perverted cunts,' said Arrinoks, and showed Joe a hairy red fist of enormous dimensions which he had been hiding behind his back.

'Belt up, Arry,' said a second man, who had appeared at his side.

'Keep out of this, Squinty,' said Arrinoks.

'Letimavitarry,' said a third arrival on the scene.

'Keep out of this, Beaky,' said Squinty.

'Keep out of this, Squinty,' said Arrinoks.

'Trouble, boys?' asked a large and genial young man who had added himself to the group.

'Keep out of this, Shorty,' said Arrinoks.

'Keep out of this, Arry,' said Squinty.

'Keep out of this, Squinty,' said Beaky.

'The lads been making suggestions to you?' asked the young giant, sadly shaking his head and clicking his tongue.

'I'm doin all the talkin, Shorty,' said Arrinoks.

'No no, Mr Nokes,' said Shorty. 'I like a little chat with civilized gentlemen once in a while.'

'Not in here,' said Squinty. 'Not in here.'

But it was too late. Even as he spoke Shorty gave Arry a friendly tap on the chest, a gesture which the other immediately reciprocated. Shorty replied by patting his companion gently on the head, while Arry placed the fist he had held up for Joe's admiration tenderly in the other's midriff. Squinty, unwisely attempting to come between the two friends, found himself pushed back into the open arms of the waiting Beaky, who proceeded to pulverize with extreme care a large dish of potato crisps on the good Squinty's balding and vein-festooned head.

Many friends and supporters of both parties had meanwhile gathered, and the cheering was loud and fervent. Much as he enjoyed the spectacle of a contest between two opponents so evenly matched and both so clearly at the height of their powers, Joe reluctantly decided that it was incumbent upon him to depart. Looking round for Brown, he realized that the foreigner, in whom the sporting instinct was no doubt less strongly developed, must have long since left the scene.

VII

Ten (10) silver knives – large –   initialled P.H.
Seven (7) silver forks – large –   "   "
Eight (8) silver spoons – large –   "   "
Four (4) silver forks – small.
Six (6) silver spoons – small.
Twelve (12) silver oyster forks.

'What are these funny things?' he asked.

'I don't know,' she said. 'They never used half of what's in here. They never entertained. The idea's ludicrous. If you'd known them you'd see what I mean.'

'They're oyster forks,' said Gill.

'Oyster forks?'

'Haven't you ever seen an oyster fork before?'

'I can't stand oysters,' said Susan.

'Yes but surely –'

'No,' said Susan.

One (1) silver gravy spoon – initialled P.H.
One (1) silver cake-knife – no initials.
Six (6) silver fish-knives.
Two (2) silver fish-forks.

'Sometimes,' she said, 'Sam would suggest we go for a walk. Suggest is the wrong word. Suddenly, quite suddenly, he would be off. One minute he would be sitting there as though he never intended to move for the rest of his life, and the next he would be on the stairs with his scarf and his overcoat already on. He walked very fast so that I had to run to keep up with him, and his scarf was enormous and brightly coloured, and hung down his back almost to his knees no matter how many times he twisted it round his neck, and he wasn't small, not by any means small. He would swing up the hill and out on to the Heath, past the lake and the Windmill to Wimbledon Common, always the same route, no matter what the weather was like nor what the time of day or night. In the summer they serve tea at the Windmill, but in winter it's deserted. Once we saw a swan flying over the trees, he must have come from the river down below. Once –'

'But what did he do?'

'Do?'

'For a living,' said Joe.

'He worked in an insurance firm, something like that,' she said.

'Oh,' he said.

'He didn't talk about it. It wasn't important. It may not have been insurance, but something similar. The old man stayed at home and cooked. He looked after the house.'

'They couldn't afford a daily?'

'There was that,' she said. 'But I think he enjoyed doing it.'

Rider 1: Books.
The Good Life, by Gore.
Kiss Me Deadly, by Spillane.
The Mystery Omnibus.
3 vols. of Byron's *Works*, 1st. ed. 1832 – one with cover missing; one ink-stained.
European Morals, by Lecky.
Old Possum's Book of Practical Cats.
The Seven Pillars of Wisdom, by Lawrence.

'They never read anything,' she said.

'And these?'

'They look as though they came with the rest of the furniture,' she said.

'But they must. . . . Books are such personal things. . . .'

'They never read anything,' she said.

'But what did they do?' he asked her.

'Do?'

'Yes, do. Did they write, paint, anything?'

'I don't think so,' she said. 'They seemed to be quite happy just to sit there, evening after evening, smoking their pipes. . . .

It was so peaceful, they seemed so calm, so unanxious, it's a
silly word but I don't know how to describe –'
   'Every evening?' he said. 'You came here every evening?'
   'It was such a cold winter,' she said. 'There had been a thaw
in January and all the buds started to come out, and then the
ice set in and the real cold weather so that everything was
muffled by the snow and the cold, sounds, feelings, everything.
I used to come here after school, you can't understand the
feeling of peace, of calm, to be here, with them, with Oscar
in this room, the fire cracking and no one saying anything or
expecting you to say anything sometimes I would look up into
that mirror, there, over the fireplace, that round convex mirror,
and see us all reflected in it, smaller and slightly distorted,
Oscar there on the carpet and the two of them on either side
of the fire, and me here on the green sofa with the broken arm,
and when I looked up it seemed to me it's silly but it really
seemed to me that time had just stopped or been abolished or
slipped round the walls of the house, and this was paradise,
some sort of paradise, just the three of us and Oscar and the
silence except for the fire and Oscar's snores and –'
   'I don't think I would include Oscar's snores in my idea of
paradise,' he said.
   'It wasn't a question of thinking,' she said. 'They were just
there. I can't imagine it without them.'

The Turn of the Tide, by Bryant.
Vanity Fair, by Thackeray.
Teach Yourself Swahili.
4 vols. of Plato's *Works* – Loeb library.
The Woman of Rome, by Moravia.

   'Take Moravia,' said Gill Clemm.
   'I beg your pardon?' said Joe.
   'Some people,' said Gill, 'think he's merely a dirty writer.
Even quite intelligent people. There was a friend of George's,
a university lecturer, who actually referred to him as "that
dirty writer". Isn't that extraordinary?'
   'I –' said Joe.
   'Surely,' said Gill, 'surely what is important about Moravia

is his compassion, his extraordinary compassion, and not the fact that he is frank about the details of sexual passion, wouldn't you say, Mr Hyman?'

'I'm afraid,' said Joe, 'that I haven't read Moravia.'

'Oh but you should,' said Gill. 'You really should. He's a writer of major importance I would say. Absolutely major importance.'

Gordon Craig on Theatre.
Middlemarch, by Eliot.
African Witchcraft, by Eliot.
The Thirty-Nine Steps, by Buchan.
Sons and Lovers, by Lawrence.

'It was such a big scarf,' she said. 'I kept tripping up on it even though he wound it round and round his neck so many times you wondered how he could breathe, but even so it hung down way below his knees. He used to tie it round both our necks and we would walk over the heath like that, falling into ditches and getting up and falling back, until he was forced to untie it and release me. I don't know where he had got it from, I never saw him go out without it.... Once he noticed one of mine and liked it and I gave it to him but he never wore it, he still put on the big one, I don't know if –'

'When is Daddy going to give me a rifle?' asked Mick.

'I don't know,' said Gill. 'What do you want another rifle for anyway?'

'This isn't a rifle!' said Mick contemptuously, and flung it down on the floor.

'Pick it up at once,' said Gill.

'It's only an old piece of wood,' said Mick. 'Daddy promised me a real rifle with real bullets, to kill real people with.'

'I don't know anything about that, dear,' said Gill.

'But he promised!'

'If he promised he'll give it to you. Now be a good boy and go and play somewhere else.'

'He promised!' said Mick.

Napoleon, by Ludwig.
Constitutional History, by Maitland.
Alexander Werth in Paris.
Complete Theological Works of Dorothy Sayers.

'He would put his hands round the tea-pot as soon as I brought it in,' said Susan. 'The old man would grumble You'll only make the tea cold, but he would sit there and smile without saying anything, his hands round the pot and the old man would say Come on, come on, I want my tea, sometimes it would break out into a quarrel and one or the other of them would go off into the other room, but usually he would pour out and the old man would sip his noisily and be happy, that's why I always made it in the earthenware pot, it keeps the heat better than metal or silver and there isn't the risk of burning yourself against the sides, it makes better tea too, in fact I've never understood why people ever use anything besides earthenware, it seems to me that –'

'You always made the tea?' he asked.

'I cooked all their meals for them,' she said.

'But you said he always insisted on doing it himself, the old man?'

'He wasn't so old,' she said. 'I don't know why we called him that. And he didn't look old either, not at the time.

'You said he always did it himself.'

'That was at first,' she said. 'It was so bad, so bad, but I didn't like to suggest that he let me, he might have taken offence, felt I was pushing myself forward, but one day Sam brought the subject up himself, I don't blame him, I don't know how they ever survived on that muck, but they did, they even looked quite fit, it's amazing what human beings can put up with if they have to. Anyway one evening he suddenly said I'm sure this plain fare must bore you, perhaps you would like to show us one or two of your special recipes, not that I have any but everything was special after that, and so I got to cooking all their meals for them, but it was they who asked me, I never suggested it though once or twice I really had to hold myself back not to. Of course I didn't cook the old man's lunch, he had that alone, but he only ate bread and cheese then, he'd done that all his life he said, and he'd go on doing it till the day he died, he –'

'Baby Choo, Baby Choo, whatever shall we do with you?' sang Brigid.

'No,' said Susan. 'None of that in here. Out you go.'

'I'm rocking Baby,' protested Brigid.

'I don't care what you're doing,' said Susan. 'Out you go. Come on.'

'You know how to handle them,' he said.

'Like hell I do,' she said. 'You should see me at school. I couldn't control a class of paralytics. I just hang on for dear life and hope the bell will go before a tragedy occurs.'

'Oh, come, come,' he said.

'But you don't know me,' she said. 'How can you tell?'

VIII

Middle East Mission, by Coward.
Ten Years in Tokyo, by Smithers.
The Story of the Greek People.
The Perennial Philosophy, by Huxley.
Complete Works of Wilde.
Fanfare for Elizabeth, by Sitwell.
The Story of the Roman People.

'I've made up my mind,' said Gill.

'Oh yes?' said Joe.

'I'm taking Mick to a psychiatrist on Friday,' she said.

'Isn't that rather a drastic step to take?' asked Joe. 'I mean won't you just be filling him with complexes and things?'

'I know exactly what you mean,' said Gill. 'Now he's naughty but at least he's *natural*. Yes, I absolutely agree with you. After all, if you're not natural at his age, when will you ever be?'

'Quite,' said Joe.

'But I can't have him doing this sort of thing in public,' said Gill.

'Have you tried talking to him?' asked Joe.

'I've told him not to do it,' she said. 'What else is there to say?'

'Couldn't you explain to him...?'

'Explain what exactly?'

'I don't know.... That it's not done.... That there are certain conventions.... I don't know.'

'There's a man at the door who would like to speak to you,' said Susan. 'In private.'

'To me?'

'Yes,' said Susan.

'But what about?' asked Gill.

'I gather,' said Susan, 'that Brigid has dropped or thrown an

53

overripe tomato on this man's head. Her aim to judge by his appearance, is exceedingly accurate.'

'Oh my God!' said Gill. 'Where on earth did she find an overripe tomato?'

The Koran.
Rise of the Dutch Republic, by Motley – 4 vols.
Women of All Countries – 5 vols.
Old St. Paul's.
Dead Souls by Gogol.

'It was so cold that winter,' she said. 'Or perhaps it simply feels cold in retrospect, because in here it was so warm, with the fire always burning in the grate, not logs of course, who can afford logs these days, but coal is almost as good, incomparably better than electricity or gas or ghastly central heating. You don't know what it was like to come here in the evenings, on week-ends, after all those years, I seemed to have spent all my life rushing from one place to the next, from one person to another, I –'

'But –'

'In the evenings we sat here, always in the same places, Sam in the deep armchair, look at the cover, torn to shreds by Oscar, he used to stretch up and pull his claws slowly and deliberately along the arms, and the old man in the little rocker, I don't know how anyone could find it comfortable, and he wasn't a small man by any means, even Oscar had his place, his particular area of the mat to which he always returned. Sometimes we would start a game with him, rolling the ping-pong ball towards him, you should have seen how absorbed they would get in the game, trying to get him to move, but usually he disdained it, he would give the ball a perfunctory smack as if to humour them and then settle back in front of the fire, though occasionally he'd forget his age and dignity and start chasing it round the room, crouching down to wait for it to roll out from under the sideboard and launching himself at it, he –'

'He looks rather past that sort of thing now,' Joe said.

'Two years makes a lot of difference at his age,' she said.

'But he didn't look any different then, I should think he's always been fat and lethargic-looking, but you should have seen him hit that ball when he really got going.'

'There's one thing,' said Joe. 'One thing that I don't –'

'Have you seen Baby Choo?' asked Gill.

'Do you want some more coffee?' asked Susan.

'It's all so silent,' Gill said. 'I wonder where they are.'

'As you can see,' said Susan, 'they are not in here. Do you want any coffee? I'm just going to make some.'

'It's all so silent,' said Gill. 'I'll see if I can find them first.'

'There's one thing I don't understand,' said Joe. 'What made him go away if you were so happy?'

'What?'

'You haven't told me,' he said.

'I've told you,' she said. 'I don't know.'

'But –'

'Mick has put Baby Choo in the bath,' Brigid announced.

'In the bath?'

'He put him in and turned on the taps,' Brigid explained. 'I told him Mummy would be angry.'

'Baby Choo, my Baby Choo!' howled Gill. 'They've drowned my Baby Choo!'

'It's all right, it's all right,' said Joe. 'He's quite alive, only very wet.'

'My little Baby Choo,' moaned Gill. 'They've drowned my little Baby Choo.'

'I told him not to do it,' said Brigid. 'I told him you wouldn't like it.'

'Liar! You told me to do it!'

'I did not!'

'You did!'

'I did not!'

'You did! You promised me all your sweets if I did!'

'Liar! You drowned him! I told you Mummy wouldn't like it!'

'My little Baby Choo,' crooned Gill. 'My poor poor Baby.'

'It's all right,' said Joe. 'It's really quite all right. Don't upset yourself. Nothing fatal has happened.'

'What are they going to do next?' said Susan. 'What on earth are they going to get up to next?'

'George,' moaned Gill. 'Ring George. Fetch the doctor, the ambulance, the –'

'Don't upset yourself,' said Joe. 'Just dry him thoroughly and wrap him up warmly. We don't want him to catch cold.'

'What have I done to deserve such children?' moaned Gill. 'Dear God, just tell me what I've done?'

Carlyle, by Welsh.
The Long Goodbye, by Chandler.
Complete Works of Jane Austen – 5 vols.
The Book of Birds and Beasts.
La Peste, by Camus.
Great Short Stories of the World.
Treasure Island, by Stevenson.
Ten Little Niggers, by Christie – torn.

'But you must have some idea,' he said.

'Sometimes,' she said, 'when I came in, he would be lying on his bed in the corner of the main room, the old man slept in the bedroom and he slept on the bed in here, it was a sort of extra sofa in the day time, though no one ever sat on it, they would never have dreamed of sitting anywhere except the chairs they always used, and I got into the habit too, there was something about this flat, you only had to enter it to adopt their habits, rituals almost you might call them, and I would sit here on the green sofa, always on this side because of the broken arm, I don't know when it had got broken, it was like that when I came that first time, they would never have thought of having it repaired, they simply used things till they fell apart and even then they didn't throw them away. Sometimes, though, when I came on a Sunday morning he would be lying on his bed in the corner there, not in it, just lying on it, it had been made and the cover pulled over it, and then he would stand on his head and wave his legs in the air and –'

'He would what?'

'As a sign of greeting,' she said. 'He would stand on his head and wave his legs in the air.'

'Wasn't that rather an odd thing to do?' he asked.

'It seemed natural enough at the time,' she said.

'But –'

'I should have been a bird, he used to say. One of those ducks that go through elaborate pantomimes at mating time rather than talk. That would have suited me fine, to be one of those ducks.'

'What a funny thing to say,' said Joe.

'Look,' said Mick.

'Go away,' said Joe.

'Look,' said Mick.

'What is it?' asked Susan.

'I don't know,' said Mick.

'It looks like a scorpion to me,' said Joe.

'A scorpion?'

'Yes,' said Joe. 'They kill themselves by pricking themselves with their own tails.'

'With their own tails?'

'They've got a poisonous sting on the end,' Joe explained. 'If they feel they're going to be killed they prefer to sting themselves to death.'

'Oh,' said Mick.

'What does it do?' asked Susan.

'It jumps,' said Mick.

'Jumps?'

'On the wall. Like that. You wind it up here and then you put it on the wall and it jumps and –'

'Goodness!' exclaimed Susan.

'It's meant to stay on the wall,' explained Mick. 'But some-times it jumps off and you've got to get out of the way.'

'Does it jump on the floor?' asked Susan.

'No,' said Mick. 'I wish it did. But it only jumps on the wall. Can you pick it up please?'

'Can't you reach it?' said Joe, 'It's – ouch! It pricked me!'

'Ha ha ha!' laughed Mick. 'It's got a prick in its tail. If you pick it up when it's wound up it pricks you. Ha ha ha!'

'It seems a very foolish toy to give to a young child,' said Joe. 'Particularly to you.'

'Ha ha ha!' laughed Mick.

Trilby, by du Maurier.
The Boy's Book of Sport.

The History of Europe, by Fisher.
The Letters of T.E. Lawrence.
The Kiss of Death, by Steer.

'He didn't do anything? Except stand on his head?'

'His hands never trembled,' she said. 'He could put things on top of one another, the most unlikely things, first a glass and then a book and then an orange and then a saucer, very calmly and deftly. On the saucer he would put another glass and on the glass another book, always very calm and deft. Every now and again he would pause to study the situation, but his hands, when once he had come to a decision, never trembled. On the book he would place an egg-cup and on the egg-cup the salt-cellar. At the very top the ping-pong ball. His hands never –'

'I don't understand,' said Joe. 'What happened to him? What happened?'

'Happened?'

'In Amsterdam. Birmingham. Wherever it was. You know what I mean.'

'He died there.'

'And no one knew where he was?'

'The old man didn't try. He didn't try to trace him after he disappeared.'

'But why did he disappear, what was he after, what –'

'I don't know,' she said.

'But you must –'

'I don't know,' she said.

'If you were in love, so happy, the calm, I don't –'

'I don't know,' she said.

IX

Thirteen (13) assorted glasses.
Seven (7) assorted glass bowls.
Two (2) salt-cellars.
One (1) plastic butter-dish.
Three (3) metal toast-racks.
One (1) milk-jug – handle broken.
One (1) china teapot.
One (1) metal teapot.
One (1) coffee-pot.

'Baby Choo, Baby Choo, whatever shall we do with you?'
sang Brigid.
'You don't find it gets monotonous, saying that like that
over and over again?' asked Joe.
'It's a lullaby,' said Brigid.
'Even lullabies have more than one line,' said Joe.
'It's to rock Baby,' explained Brigid.
'Don't you think Baby would like a change of lullaby?' asked
Joe.
'No,' said Brigid.
'Perhaps we could make up some more lines?' suggested Joe.
'What more lines?' asked Brigid suspiciously.
'More lines after that one.'
'There aren't any more lines after that one.'
'Bang! Bang! Bang!' shouted Mick, and jumped on to Joe's
back.
'You'll wake Baby,' said Brigid.
'No I won't!'
'Yes you will!'
'Get off my back, Mick, there's a good boy,' said Joe.
'You're dead!' shouted Mick in his ear. 'You're dead!'
'Yes you will!' shouted Brigid.
'Promise you'll be dead if I get off.'

'I can't promise,' said Joe. 'I'm not dead.'

'Baby Choo, Baby Choo, whatever shall we do with you?' sang Brigid.

'All right, I promise,' said Joe.

'Lie down on the floor,' ordered Mick.

'Baby Choo, Ba —'

'You promised!' cried Mick. 'You promised to be dead!'

'But now I've come alive again,' said Joe.

'Leave him alone, both of you,' said Gill.

'But he promised!'

'Baby Choo —'

'Stop it or I'll murder you!' screamed Gill.

'I'm going to drop Baby,' announced Brigid.

'I've had enough of you,' said Gill.

Slap slap.

'Bang! Bang! Bang!' shouted Mick in her ear.

'I've had enough I tell you!' screamed Gill. 'Enough! Enough! Enough!'

Slap slap.

'I hate you,' said Mick. 'You never keep your promises. Any of you.'

'One of these days,' said Brigid, 'I'm going to kill that Baby Choo. And trample on him.'

One (1) gravy dish and spoon.

Six (6) semi-circular salad plates – one cracked.

One (1) wooden salad bowl.

One (1) wooden salad fork and spoon.

Five (5) assorted cups and saucers – two chipped.

'The first evening,' she said. 'When I came to dinner. I was nervous enough when he told me the old man was in a flap about the meal. I didn't know what to expect, I'd been married you see and gone abroad and divorced and I thought I was in love with a cellist, I didn't really know why I'd ever come except out of politeness, and I suppose I was just a little bit curious. And then trying to get through all that food, it was so tasteless, so dry, it stuck in my throat, every mouthful of potato that I took and there I was trying to pretend I was enjoying it with the old man grumbling away to himself and leaning across and trying to be very polite but you see his heart wasn't in it, and then in the middle of all that Oscar stalked in. He came right up to me and stared up at me in silence for a long time, summing me up, then a sick expression crossed his face and he turned and ran for the door. Not very flattering. Afterwards, when I started to come every evening, he seemed to forget that first impression and quite took to me though Sam said it was only because skirts provide a more comfortable lap than trousers, but that first time it was –'

'I'm sorry,' he said. 'I can't drink this coffee.'

'Don't apologize,' she said. '*I* should. But it's so difficult breaking yourself of a habit and you always insist on my not making any more, you –'

'You'd only put the sugar in again,' he said.

'They were so helpless,' she said. 'After a while I got to cooking all their meals for them and then there were never any spoons when you wanted them and what there was was dirty.... They asked me, it was they who suggested it, I didn't want to push myself forward but Sam brought it up, I'm sure you'd like to try one or two of your recipes on us he said to me one day, out of the blue, and I must say I –'

'Wasn't it natural?'

'Natural?'

'If you came every day. That you should cook for them.'

'What were they,' she said, 'but three old bachelors living together? And the old man, who'd been married after all for fifteen years, you tended to forget that but he had before his wife died or ran away with someone else, I had been told once but could never remember and they never mentioned her, Sam's mother, and I couldn't very well ask a question like that so I still don't know though I think she died, but not before they'd been married for fifteen years, it's a long time but he was the worst of the lot. In many ways poor neutered Oscar had the most sense. At least he didn't try to impose his fads on other people. But the old man... He had a peculiar aversion to giving his clothes out to the laundry and he wouldn't dream of taking them to a launderette because he said the soap they gave you ruined good material. He insisted on washing everything himself in the bath and then he wouldn't put them in the airing-cupboard or hang them up on the line outside, oh no, he said the clothes smelt damp and hot when you wore them if you did that, or just got dirty again hanging outside, so every three weeks, thank God it wasn't more often, every three weeks he would tie an old rope above the front door and to that nail at the end of the corridor and hang those dripping and badly washed things up there, with all the movable fires in the flat lining the walls and all the windows firmly shut so that in no time at all the whole flat was like a turkish bath, you could hardly see yourself for the steam and then the only refuge was outside on the heath and off we'd go for hours and hours, Sam way ahead and the two of us trudging after him, but when you got back there was still all that steam to face and –'

'But –'

'They couldn't do a thing for themselves,' she said. 'Not a thing. They had to ask me here to look after them, that's what I was, a housekeeper, that's all, when you come right down to it, cooking and looking after them and –'

'But I don't understand,' he said. 'You said –'

'Have you ever tasted pity?' she said. 'It makes you sick and fills you up but once you've tasted it you can't stop eating. You –'

'I don't understand,' he said. 'You told me –'

'Don't you see?' she said. 'Don't you see? He was in love with me, in love with me. And what was I? I was sorry for him, for them. You couldn't help but be sorry. How could I tell it would end like that? How could I tell?'

'What do you mean?' he said.

'The last evening,' she said. 'The old man had gone to bed. He did sometimes before I left. He slept in the bedroom and Sam in the main room, on the bed in the corner, in the day-time they used it as an extra sofa though I never saw either of them sitting on it, they each had their own chairs and they never used any others, and it was the same with everything, they never deviated from a pattern that had been established a long long time before I ever came on the scene. Anyway, the old man slept badly, he woke up at three or four in the morning and couldn't go to sleep again so he would get up and sit by the window and watch the dawn coming up over the city, he said it was the best part of the day watching the dawn like that from his chair by the window and for all I know he may be right, I'm not in a position to tell because the only times I've been awake at that time I haven't been in any state to appreciate the dawn, anyway he'd gone to bed and left us, I was here on the sofa and Sam in his armchair, you can see the marks Oscar made on the sides and arms, he used to come and scratch at it when Sam was sitting there and he wanted his dinner or to be fussed over, usually the latter, he would eat anything but he wasn't a greedy cat, even now he'll eat what you put in front of him but he isn't greedy, and all of a sudden I couldn't stand it any more, even pity has its limits, I said I'm going away, I'm not coming back, and I could see him thinking and puffing, not saying anything, just puffing at that pipe, then he said You know we like having you here, you know that, Susan, but I was fed up, fed up with all the mess and the dirt and the confusion, I felt they were stifling me with that flat and the silence and their dependence. Just to cook for you and look after you? I said, and he said No, we like having you here, and I said Thank you very much but I don't like being here and I got up and went away.'

'When I got divorced,' said Susan, 'I decided I needed to get an education. So I enrolled as a philosophy student at one of the London colleges.'

'You hadn't had an education then?' he asked.

'Not higher,' she said. 'Not higher.'

'I see,' he said.

'I thought,' she said, 'that I would be able to cope with life better after that.'

'It's a point of view,' he said.

'It's a point of view all right,' she said. 'But not one with which I am myself any longer in sympathy.'

'Baby Choo, Baby Choo, whatever shall we do with you?' sang Brigid.

'What,' asked Gill, 'is that?'

'This idea,' said Susan, 'that all our problems are really problems of language, it –'

'That,' said Gill, 'on your head.'

'Baby Choo, Baby Choo, whatever shall we do with you?'

'It's a scarf,' said Susan.

'Don't be silly,' said Gill.

'Baby Choo, Ba –'

'Stop that at once,' said Gill. 'Where did you find it? Wasn't it –'

'Yes.'

'I'm going to drop Baby.'

'Like that? Their property? And you put it on?'

'I gave it to Sam. He –'

'But you can't.... It's illegal...Mr Hyman...?'

'Actually the law –'

'Bugger the law!'

'Susan! The children!'

'Hullo! Hullo! Anyone at home?'

'Give Baby to Daddy.'

'I say –'

'Give.'

'That's a bit.'

'George this is...'

'How...'

'But lawyers are supposed to be...'

'Lawyers are all sorts of people.'

'But how long will it take?'

'It depends on'

'Didn't Mr Stout...?'

'On holiday. In Corsica.'

'Look around.'

'Three or four days, maybe a week. It depends on the small things.'

At first I was always giving but they weren't interested. They didn't want anything. Just to be left in peace to sit here in this room overcrowded with junk, smoking their pipes and looking into space. It's nice of you to call, Susan, the old man would say and then they'd go on smoking, what do you do I ask you what do you do if you don't smoke a pipe? I'd run out of cigarettes in an hour and then there was nothing to do but sit and look at them or at Oscar or into the fire. They didn't mind my being there, in a way it might have been better if they had at least it would have meant that I made some impression, impinged somewhere upon their consciousness, but this! You can't understand what it was like, I simply wasn't there to them, each one sitting in his place, the old man in the rocking-chair and Sam opposite in the big armchair, even Oscar always slept just there on the rug in front of the fire, never any further to the right or the left, you can see the mark, there, not quite in the middle, it was a funny thing about this flat, as soon as you entered it was as though your individual freedom to do this or that or the other simply disappeared and then every-thing, the hour you came and left, where you sat, even what you said, was determined by what you had done or said the first or second time, it was as though it had been fixed once and for all and there was never any question of departing from the pattern, never

His hands never trembled. He could put things on top of one another, the most unlikely things, first a glass and then a book and then an orange and then a saucer, very calmly and deftly. On the saucer he would put another glass and on the glass another book, always very calm and deft

A man Muriel recommended. Very nice but nondescript in appearance

never quite sure if Susan feels more than she shows or rather less than she tries to make out she's not showing, if you see what I mean.

You don't understand. You're in the way. Gill and I know what we think of each other, and we know how to keep off each other's toes though you might not think so at times. You confuse the issue. You're in the way.

X

One (1) mincer.
One (1) pepper-mill – broken.
One (1) coffee-grinder – broken.
Two (2) frying pans.
Eight (8) assorted saucepans.

'You mean,' said Joe, 'he disappeared because he was in love with you?'

'I suppose I was sorry for them,' she said. 'They were so absurd, so clumsy and messy and unable to do a thing for themselves. The old man used to do all the washing himself, in the bathtub, and then hang the clothes up in the corridor to dry, just imagine, in there, with all the fires on as high as they could go so as to do the job quickly, of course the place filled up with steam so rapidly the only thing to do was to get out, and even then you had to come back eventually, usually to find that the door had swung open and a group of inquisitive neighbours would be peering in to see if there was a fire or something, and trying to make out what strange monster was swinging on a rope all the way down the corridor. They –'

'But you told me,' said Joe, 'you told me you were in love, those evenings, those walks...'

'I was wrong,' she said.

'But –'

'At first I was sorry for them,' she said. 'I thought they needed me. I thought they liked to have me there to help them out. Then it dawned on me, from the way he looked at me, the things he did, but he never spoke, never really gave anything away, so how could I tell, how could I tell for sure? One day by the Windmill we saw a swan flying over the trees, he must have come from the river down below, and when he'd gone Sam tied his scarf, he had an enormous coloured scarf which he wound round and round his neck and even then it was so long it hung down his back to his knees, so that when he walked very fast, which was always out there on the heath, and when the wind blew, which was most of the time it's so exposed the wind seems to cut right through you, then his scarf would fly straight out behind him and slap me in the face as I ran to keep up with him, I've never seen anyone change so fast from total stillness to furious activity, it always had to be either one or the other with him and that day, when we saw the swan, when it had gone, he tied the scarf round my neck as well as his own and we both fell into a ditch and I tore my stockings, that's how he was, instead of saying anything he would do things like that, I should have been a duck he used to say, one of those ducks that go through elaborate mimes at mating time, if it was his idea of elaborate mime I could have done without, thank you very much.'

'I don't –'

'How could I tell he'd react like that?' she said fiercely. 'I was fed up, fed up, there comes a point when even pity has to end, when –'

'She's broken my rifle,' said Mick.

'It's no use coming to me for sympathy,' said Susan.

'She jumped on it and broke it,' said Mick, and burst into tears.

'Go and tell your mother. I'm not interested.'

'It's Mummy who broke it!' sobbed Mick.

'That,' said Susan, 'is the limit.'

One (1) carving-knife & fork.
One (1) bread-knife – handle loose.
One (1) cakeknife – blade bent.
One (1) corkscrew.
One (1) ladle.
Three (3) tin-openers.
One (1) bottle-opener.
Four (4) tin spoons.

'You can't blame yourself,' said Joe.

'Can't I just,' she said.

'It's not your fault,' said Joe. 'You couldn't stop him falling in love with you.'

'You don't understand,' she said.

'There was absolutely nothing you could do about it,' he said.

'I don't know,' she said. 'I keep thinking, if I'd done this or not done that, if —'

'Look at the mess the place is still in,' said Gill. 'I don't know where on earth these old curtains have come from, I—'

'I found them in the cupboard in the corridor,' said Susan. 'I thought you might want to have a look at them.'

'But I haven't started on the corridor,' said Gill.

'I was only trying to help.'

'It was very sweet of you,' said Gill. 'But I've still got all the linen and the bathroom things to go through. I wish you'd stick to making coffee, Susan.'

'Hullo! Hullo! Hullo! Anybody at home?' shouted George Clemm.

'Daddy! When are you going to give me that rifle?'

'Come on,' said George. 'I'm in a hurry.'

'We're not ready,' said Gill. 'You're never as punctual as this.'

'A real rifle, Daddy, you promised me, with real bullets to kill real people!'

'Come on,' said George, 'I'm in a hurry.'

'Well you'll just have to wait,' said Gill. 'We're not ready yet.'

'I'm sorry I can't stay and chat,' said George.

'Daddy, you promised!'

'That's quite all right,' said Susan. 'We'll resign ourselves to that.'

'You must come to dinner one of these days,' said George. 'And you too, Mr Hyman. We can't have you slaving away here without some reward, can we dear?'

'Here's your reward,' she said.

'You cook divinely,' he said.

'Don't be silly,' she said.

'I mean it, Susan,' he said.

'It's impossible to cook on this stove the way he's let it go.'

'One old man alone, what do you expect?'

'But there was no need to let the place get like this. He used to do all the cleaning anyway, and though the place wasn't tidy, far from it, it wasn't positively dirty. It's so much, I don't know, so much as though he was deliberately doing it to accuse me, to –'

'Don't be silly. One doesn't look after things so well when one is alone. There's no real incentive.'

'When I heard that he'd gone I came straight round here. I wanted to talk to him, to ask him. There was only Oscar here when I arrived, so I walked around and smoked and tried to contain myself in patience, as they say. Then he came in – the old man – I didn't recognize him for a second, he didn't seem to be the person I'd known, there was an image running about inside my head, a stupid image but it seemed to fit, the image of an orange that a child had sucked dry and that has just shrivelled up, collapsed into itself, his face was like that. We looked at each other. There was nothing to say. I went away.'

'Give Oscar some more,' he said.

'He's had enough. He'll get too fat.'

'What do you think he is now?'

'That's not fat. He's just a large cat. Well-built.'

'Well-built! He's grossly over-weight.'

'He's a big cat. But I've got to watch his waistline. Gill is always feeding him tit-bits when I'm not looking. She's under the impression I'm starving him.'

'She doesn't object?'

'Object?'

'To your using the kitchen like this, to entertain your men friends?'

'I look after Oscar, even if I don't do it as well as she might, and that's one burden off her long-suffering shoulders. Of course she doesn't like me digging around in drawers, turning over what she's stacked so neatly all ready for you to put down in your inventory: two dark suits, one dirty; seventeen ties; five shirts; eight vests; one sports jacket; two scarves; one pair corduroy trousers; one –'

'You're not very nice to her.'

'I don't like her.'

'That's no reason.'

'Don't start moralizing, for godsake. If she took my dislike a little more seriously I might like her better.'

'She's very fond of you. She treats you like a younger sister.'

'Thank God I was never that. I'd have died. She thinks I've messed up my life.'

'Have you?'

'No more than other people.'

'Don't throw him off the table like that.'

'He's acquiring bad habits. Those children are corrupting him.'

'No one could corrupt him. He's a gentleman.'

'I suppose in his way he is.'

'Will you take him then?'

'We'll play with Oscar, he used to say, and then dig the ball out from under the bed or the sideboard. I think it's then I realized he was in love with me, when I saw him looking at me, creeping about the floor after that ball that Oscar would dutifully punch, after all, he seemed to be saying, if they want a game I suppose I'll have to humour them, creeping around after that ball and looking at me, even before that day, on the heath, when we saw the swan, I must have known before then but I didn't admit it to myself, or perhaps I was flattered or –'

'When do you go back?' he said.

'Back?'

'To school?'

'Middle of the month. I can't complain,' she said.

'Why don't you move in here with Oscar?'

'I might,' she said. 'I don't know. We'll see when all this is over.'

'Susan.'

'Go away.'

'You've got to listen to me.'

'I don't want to hear anything you have to say.'

'Susan, you must. We can't just leave it at that.'

'But we can.'

'Just once.'

'You tire me, Joe. You make me tired. I don't want to see you or hear your voice again. Can't you understand that?'

'I'm coming to see you, Susan. We've got to talk. You can't shut out things like that.'

'We've talked too much already, Joe.'

'How can I make you understand?'

XI

Five (5) tin forks.
One (1) toasting-fork.
Eight (8) tin knives – all bent.
Two (2) vegetable knives.
One (1) cooking-knife.
One (1) kitchen table – top badly scratched.
Two (2) kitchen chairs.
One (1) 'Electrolux' refrigerator.
One (1) 'Super' gas stove – filthy.
One (1) crockery cupboard – broken in several places –
one shelf missing.

'How old is Baby Choo?' asked Brigid.
'You should tell me that,' said Joe.
'I don't know,' said Brigid.
'Do you like Baby Choo?' he asked her.
'He's my baby brother.'
'Yes. But do you like him?'
'Most of the time I like him,' said Brigid.
'But not all of the time?'
'Sometimes I want to kill him,' said Brigid.
'Why is that?' asked Joe.
'He can't do anything for himself. He has to be carried
around everywhere, or sung to. He can't talk.'
'But you couldn't talk at his age,' said Joe.
'I could talk right from the moment I was born,' said Brigid.
'Don't tell such lies, darling,' said Gill.
'Yes I could. Ever since I was born I could talk and before
that too.'
'You remember that time?'
'I could talk in my mother's tummy.'
'You must have been a very clever little girl,' said Joe. 'And
Mick could do that too?'

'Mick's stupid,' said Brigid. 'He has to go and see a doctor because he's so stupid.'

'Liar!'

'I'm not! Mummy told me!'

'You are!'

'I'm not!'

'You are!'

'Get out!' screamed Gill. 'Get out of this room at once! Both of you! I'm sick to death of you!'

'They're restless,' said Joe.

'Don't make excuses for them,' said Gill. 'They can put up with this for a few more days if we can. After all, they have the whole flat to play about in.'

'It's not that,' said Susan. 'They're not my children. But I would have thought you could have brought them up to be a bit more interested in things, in...'

'I know, dear, I know,' said Gill. 'Of course you're right, but what can I do? I come home an absolute wreck after a day here and then there's still George to look after and the children to put to bed.... But that's only making excuses of course, I have brought them up badly though goodness knows I've tried hard enough.... But what can I do? I do my best, what –'

'A noble sentiment,' said Susan.

'Oh, you can laugh at me,' said Gill. 'But wait till it comes to you. I'm just not made for this sort of thing, I can't cope. If there are two possible decisions to come to I'm bound to opt for the wrong one, if there are two possible courses of action to be followed I'm bound to follow the wrong one, if –'

'All right, all right,' said Susan. 'Stop feeling sorry for yourself. Back to work.'

'She won't even let me feel sorry for myself,' said Gill. 'What is there left for me to do?'

Three (3) toothbrushes.

One (1) tube toothpaste.

One (1) tube shaving cream.

One (1) Gillette razor.

One (1) packet Gillette stainless steel blades.

One (1) packet cotton-wool – unopened.

'Why should he have done it except to attract attention?' she said. 'His hand was steady but not to the extent of succeeding every time. And why put a second orange when it was already difficult enough with one? And the glass! So that if it fell there'd be a mess and we'd have to keep Oscar from walking there till every fragment had been found. . . . Or walking about on his hands in that overcrowded room, what's the point of walking about on your hands and every now and then he would rest against a wall, the door, not straighten up but rest like that, upside down against a wall, he –'

'Why are you telling me all this?' he said. 'Why are you making it all up? What's the matter with you?'

'What do you mean?'

'Can't you forget them, Susan?' he said.

'You don't understand,' she said.

'You can't go on blaming yourself,' he said. 'It's not your fault if he went and killed himself every time a girl turned him down, it –'

'Shut up!' she said.

'I'm sorry,' he said, 'I –'

'Why don't you get on with your job and leave us alone?'

'You still haven't got a bulb for the corridor,' said Gill.

'Why don't you get one if you're so keen about it?' said Susan.

'I'd have got one ages ago if you hadn't said you would,' said Gill. 'That's what's so annoying. You say you'll do something so I forget about it and then you never do. At least if you said from the start that you had no intention –'

'Oh stop it,' said Susan.

'It's most annoying,' said Gill.

'And don't you think there are things about you and your children I can't stand?' asked Susan.

'There's no need to take that line,' said Gill. 'I was merely making an observation.'

'You've driven her into the bedroom,' remarked Joe.

'Driven her! She couldn't wait to get in there and start tidying up, putting everything in order, getting rid of the smell, any life this place ever had, any –'

'Calm down,' he said. 'Calm down.'

'Oh for godsake!' she said. 'You don't understand. You're

in the way. You confuse the issue. Gill and I, we'd settled down nicely here. We'd got to know the tender spots where just a small prick hurts, and the larger areas of thick hide where no matter what anyone does or says you feel nothing at all. We'd learnt to co-exist. You confuse the issue. You're in the way.'

'I'm sorry,' he said. 'I –'

'There's nothing to be sorry about. It's your job, as you once told me. All I'm suggesting is that you get on with it and leave us alone.'

'Thanks,' he said. 'Thanks very much.'

One (1) packet of sticking-plaster.
One (1) bottle after-shave lotion.
One (1) bottle aspirin.
One (1) bottle meths.
One (1) box with assorted pills, etc.

'You know,' said Gill. 'You mustn't let Susan worry you. She does tend to be melodramatic. Of course she's upset by all this, but then aren't we all?'

'Of course,' said Joe.

XII

'The same again,' said Joe. 'And twenty Players.'

'You a student?' asked the girl on the next stool.

'No,' said Joe.

'You look like a student,' said the girl.

'Oh, it's you,' he said.

'Hi,' she said. 'I didn't recognize you.'

Joe shrugged.

'Say,' she asked, 'is this a genuine old London pub?'

'Uhuh,' said Joe.

'It is?'

'There's another just round the corner,' he told her. 'And two more up the street.'

'But this part of London is full of them!' she exclaimed. 'No one ever told me.'

'Every pub in London's a genuine old London pub,' he said.

'Really?' she said. 'No one ever told me.'

'These things don't get into the guide-books,' he explained.

'No,' she said doubtfully, 'I suppose they don't.'

Joe shrugged.

'Have a cigarette,' she offered.

'Thanks.'

'Fancy meeting you again.'

'Fancy.'

'The show was a wow,' she told him.

'It was?'

'Boy, was I impressed. I've seen a bit of this Jacobean stuff back home and believe me it had nothing on these boys!'

'So you liked it,' he said.

'Liked it? It was a wow.'

'You weren't disappointed then?'

'It was great.'

'You didn't feel your evening was wasted?'

'Wasted? You kidding?'

'The thought never entered your mind,' said Joe, 'that your time might more profitably have been employed in some other fashion?'

'I tell you,' she confided in him, 'I've seen a good bit of this stuff back home and this was tops.'

'Have a drink.'

'Thanks. I'll have another whisky.'

'And now,' said Joe, 'I'm going to tell you a story.'

'A story?'

'Yes,' said Joe. 'A story.'

'Fire away,' she said. 'I'm a good listener.'

'You know what an inventory is?'

'An inventory.'

'It's important that you know,' he said. 'To get the point.'

'You can tell me,' she said.

'They didn't teach you that at college?'

'No, I don't think so.'

'You don't think so, but are you sure?'

'I've got a good memory for that sort of thing,' she said. 'I'd have remembered if they had.'

'What sort of thing?' he asked.

'Inventories and suchlike.'

'So you know what they are?'

'What what are?'

'Inventories.'

'No, I tell you I'd have remembered if I did.'

'That,' said Joe, 'sounds vaguely wrong. But just at present I don't feel at my strongest on logic. Or grammar.'

'Well, what is it?'

'You're quite sure they didn't teach you that at college then?'

'Quite sure.'

'But what on earth did they teach you?'

'In the first year,' she said, 'we –'

'No no,' said Joe. 'That was a purely rhetorical question. One that does not require an answer. Cicero was very strong on those.'

'Cicero?'

'One day, he tells us, his son, a growing lad, came to him and begged him (the father) to teach him (the son) the art of public speaking and of eloquence. Cicero Senior was considered,

by himself as well as by other people, to be quite an expert in
the field, and whenever he was sent into exile he would amuse
himself by composing treatises on the subject – and once he
got going there was no stopping him, he didn't let up till the
subject had been wrung so dry a steam-roller couldn't have
got a drop more out of it. Now he was so pleased at this
unexpected break, his own son actually asking him to do something he would have done anyway, without persuasion, just
to please himself, that he promptly sat down and wrote the
whole thing out, over one hundred pages of it in the Loeb
library edition which I own. History does not relate what
expression appeared on the face of Cicero Junior when his
modest enquiry was answered with that massive document,
but I myself often wonder whether Cicero Senior didn't make
the whole story up because he felt guilty at pouring the stuff
out for no reason at all. Now one –'
    'But –'
    'One of my favourite passages,' said Joe, 'is the one where
the father instructs his son in the "suave genus" or charming
style. It will be achieved first, he says, by the pleasing elegance
of a sonorous and smooth vocabulary, and secondly by combinations of words that avoid both rough collisions of conson-
ants and gaping juxtapositions of vowels, and are enclosed not
in lengthy clauses but ones adapted to the breath of the voice,
and that possess uniformity and evenness of vocabulary; then
the choice of words must employ contrary terms, repetition
answering to repetition and like to like, and the words must
be arranged to come back to the same word in pairs and doub-
lets or even more numerous repetitions, and the construction
must be now linked together by conjunctions and now discon-
nected by asyndeton. It will also give the style charm to employ
some unusual or original or novel expression. For anything
that causes surprise gives pleasure, and the most effective style
is one that stirs up some emotion in the mind and that indicates
amiability of character in the speaker himself; and amiability
of character is expressed –'
    'What a beautiful voice you have,' she said.
    Joe held up a hand to silence her.
    '...and amiability of character is expressed either by his
indicating his own judgement and humanity and liberality of

mind, or by the modification of the style when it appears that the speaker, for the sake of magnifying a second party or disparaging himself, is saying something different from what he actually thinks, and that he is doing this more out of good nature than insincerity. But there are many rules for charm that render the style either less lucid or less convincing; consequently in this department also we have to use our own judgement as to what the case requires.'

'What a beautiful voice you have,' she said.

'You really think so?'

'But I do!' she said.

'Have another drink.'

'Thanks. Same again.'

'Cigarette?'

'And you look so young! They told me English boys look young because they lead such healthy lives. Is that true?'

'Well, I don't –'

'I really love the English. They're so kind, so helpful! The other day I went to Blenheim, the home of Winston Churchill, you can still see a lock of his hair in one of the rooms no don't turn your head you've got a lovely profile and the guides were so helpful, so friendly, just this strand of hair that makes all the difference no don't brush it back, there, that's how it should be, and that nice strong neck and those broad shoulders and –'

'Really I –' said Joe backing towards the door. But the young telephonist – for it was she – had so lovingly entwined her arms about his neck that, feet trailing in the dust, she slithered towards the exit in his wake. Thus interlaced they left the scene of their recent conversation.

Joe then suggested that a cup of strong black coffee might awaken them both to a sense of their human responsibilities, but the young telephonist explained to him that she had no responsibilities in the whole wide world except to her own vital organs, and that these required nothing less than immediate gratification. Joe, who was understandably upset by this information, thereupon attempted to impress upon the young telephonist the jeopardy in which her actions might place the whole of the tour which she had so painstakingly planned and to which she had no doubt looked forward for so long. The young telephonist remained unmoved by this eloquent plea. Indeed, his words, reminding her as they did that only three more days remained of her sojourn in this land, days full indeed, but not of Joe, made her only the more eager for them to consummate their friendship there and then. It was only by the exertion of considerable physical pressure that Joe succeeded in achieving his objective.

'Two coffees,' said Joe. 'Strong. Black. Big.'

'I don't want any coffee,' said the young telephonist.

'Is the young lady feeling unwell?' enquired the solicitous waiter.

'She's fine,' said Joe.

'I'm not fine,' said the young lady.

'A touch of the sun perhaps?' suggested the waiter.

'You're joking,' said Joe. 'And where are those coffees?'

'At last I have the luck!' exclaimed Brown, sliding into the bench opposite Joe and looking into his eyes.

'Oh no, no, no,' said Joe, and covered his face with his hands.

'But yes,' said Brown joyfully. 'I find you again, my friend!'

'And it's made your day I suppose?' said Joe.

'Pardon?'

'Who is this guy?' the young lady wanted to know.

'Just a guy,' said Joe.

'I tell you,' said Brown, leaning across the narrow table. 'I tell you. At last I find someone who direct me. So I find the address given by my friend, my knowledgeable friend. It is cellar. There is music. Talk. Women. I go in. At the door I am stopped. What do you want? they ask me. I explain about my friend. I tell them in Paris he somewhat broke his leg jumping in the sanitation to avoid the rushing of water. They throw me out. I am angry. I come back. They tell me now it is private club. The friend of my friend he is in prison, they tell me. It is not nightclub now, it is chess club, they tell me. I am angry. It is not chess club. It is nightclub. Is no music in chess club. I am angry, but I go away. You know what for I go away?'

'No,' said Joe. 'I've no idea. No idea at all.'

'Because,' said Brown, 'when I have been inside I have smelled it. It is not good sanitation.'

'Say, what's your name?' asked the young lady.

'Brown,' said Joe.

'It is everywhere the same,' said Brown sadly. 'Everywhere

you think will be clean and sane and everywhere the sanitation it is no good.'

'I'm Priscilla Glue,' said the young lady.

'You never told me,' said Joe accusingly.

'You never asked me,' she replied coldly.

'England!' said Brown, his voice rising. 'They tell me England is not like Italy, Spain, France – Portugal I do not talk about, I have not been. They say in every house there is bathroom, England is home of sanity, yes, yes, I have heard it, England is the home of sanity! I come here, I see. Everywhere the pipes burst, everywhere something is stopped up. Yes. Everywhere something is stopped up!'

'Say,' said Priscilla, nudging him. 'You know any genuine London nightclubs?'

'See, here I have list,' said Brown, digging into his pocket. 'Nothing on this list is good like what my knowledgeable friend recommend,' he explained. 'Here it is the Ministry of Tourism that recommend. But is something.'

'Sure it's something,' said Priscilla.

'See,' said Brown, 'here is one much recommended called The Hot Potato. It is transformed from tea-room where once the great German poet von Goethe drank tea. It says here.'

'I'm not really meant to be doing Goethe till we get to Weimar next week,' said Priscilla doubtfully.

'Is only tea-room in the past,' said Brown reassuringly. 'Now is nightclub. Is no trace of the great von Goethe.'

'Well...' said Priscilla.

'Some people,' read Brown, 'say that Doctor Samuel Johnson, the famous English wit, frequented this tea-room.'

'He did?' said Priscilla. 'Doctor Samuel Johnson, the famous English wit?'

'Another black coffee,' said Joe weakly, watching them depart. 'The largest you've got.'

XIII

One (1) medicine chest – mirror cracked.
One (1) linen cupboard – see rider 2 (linen).
One (1) bath-mat.
One (1) mop.
One (1) sponge.
One (1) packet 'Lifebuoy' soap – unopened.
One (1) framed reproduction of 'Mona Lisa'.

'The last evening,' she said. 'I didn't know it was the last evening. It was no different from any of the others. The old man had gone to bed, he did sometimes, he got up so early in the mornings, when you get to my age, he used to say, you'll learn that the early morning just before dawn, that's the best part of the day. That evening, I don't know why but suddenly that evening I was frightened. I said Does it annoy you to have me here? and he said No, I don't think so. I suppose I was tired of it all, of all the evenings of silence, of never knowing what they thought of me, whether they only tolerated me out of pity or if they really liked having me there, I said surely it must do something to you one way or the other? and he said Yes, we like to have you here, I've just told you so, we like to see you, and I said Only to cook your meals, that's the only reason, and he said I know what you're leading up to, I don't want to talk about it, Well I do, I said, why did you ask me here in the first place, why did you ask me to dinner or speak to me at that concert? I don't want to talk about it, he said, I–'

'I don't understand,' said Joe, 'I thought he was in love with you, I thought –'

'I didn't sleep much that night,' she said. 'Not much at all. Objects suddenly seemed to swell in significance, words he'd said kept on coming back to me, I kept on seeing the two of them in their chairs under that damned mirror, evening after evening, there seemed to be some sort of riddle to solve in their silences, in the flat, in the things they ate and washed with and put in the dustbin, and just this image of them sitting there so self-contained, and him saying Yes, we like to have you here, we like to see you.... In the morning, Sunday morning, I couldn't stay at home, I thought there was something wrong with me, something that could only be put right by coming here. There was no one in except Oscar which was odd because they never went out in the morning on Sundays, so I wandered round the flat smoking and trying not to think about anything and after a while the old man came in. He wasn't the same person as the one who'd said good-night the evening before, his face had sunk in like an orange a child has sucked dry. I didn't even ask. I just knew. I went away.'

'He wasn't in love with you?' Joe said.

'They were so self-contained,' she said. 'They looked as if they needed nothing and no one in the world. When they sat there, smoking their pipes, they made you feel like an ant crawling over a sleeping person, crawling into the mouth, the ears, the nose, under the eyelids, the armpits, the hollow between the legs.... God how I hated them for being like that! With most people –'

'Susan,' he said, 'listen to me!'

'With most people,' she said, 'there's some attempt to accommodate you, to make things easier. Why did they have to be so different?'

'But why?' he said. 'Why did you go back? Tell me the truth.'

'Don't you understand?' she said. 'Don't you understand anything at all? I was in love with him, that's why I had to keep going back.'

Rider 2: Linen.
Seven (7) prs. linen sheets.
Nine (9) flannelette sheets.
Two (2) eiderdown quilts.
Two (2) bed-covers.
Two (2) large bath-towels.

'I do feel,' said Gill Clemm, 'that Susan tends to take things a little too hard.'

'Oh yes?' said Joe.

'Of course it must be trying for her, but it's not fun for anyone when a relative dies, is it?'

'No, no, of course not,' said Joe.

'She and Sam did I believe have some sort of affair once, but all that's been over for a long time. We all have our troubles, don't we, Mr Hyman, and I don't see that there is any point in bringing them under public scrutiny.'

'No, no,' said Joe. 'No point at all.'

'She's so highly strung of course,' said Gill. 'But I would have thought the best thing she could do was to help me get everything sorted out and cleaned up as quickly as possible, so that we could forget the whole thing. But now she's even talking about moving in here when all this is over.'

'Well, there is Oscar to think about,' said Joe.

'I know,' said Gill. 'I feel very bad about Oscar. But really, with three children to look after and one of them a baby I don't feel –'

'She's used to him,' said Joe, 'he likes her...'

'She could just take him with her, couldn't she? I don't know why she hasn't done so before. He's only in the way here – oh, I know it's not his fault, poor thing, but he is such a temptation to the children, I can't be after them all the time and it's inevitable that they should start playing with him, they don't mean any harm you know, Mr Hyman, but children being what they are they tend to get a bit rough and of course he doesn't like it. I think it would have been much more sensible to take him with her in the first place, and as for this idea of moving in here with him I –'

'But you know what cats are like,' said Joe. 'He's lived here for the greater part of his ten years, he'd be trying to get back and then he'd be bound to get run over.'

'I'm sure you're exaggerating the difficulties,' said Gill.

Four (4) white bath towels.
Seven (7) small Turkish towels.
Six (6) linen face-towels.
Five (5) Victorian tray-cloths.
Five (5) dressing-table covers – embroidered – initialled
C.T.

'There was nothing to grip,' she said. 'Nothing to hold on to. When you spoke to him he laughed. A nice laugh. But he would never answer. You couldn't argue, discuss anything. As soon as you tried to pin him down he stood on his head or put his head between his legs or something funny like that, to show he didn't want to talk, he used to say he should have been one of those birds that dance ritually at mating time, I should have been that instead of a Talker, he would say, You a Talker? I would laugh at him, but he was quite serious then, All human beings are Talkers, he said, but I don't like it. When you asked him a question he'd start taking all those queer shapes, responding like that instead of actually answering, or go on piling things up on the table, one on top of the other, cups and saucers and oranges and glasses. ... After a while I gave up trying, I'd sit there as silent as they were, so that at times I didn't know if I had said anything out loud or not, it was so silent in that room, just the fire cracking and Oscar snoring and the two of them puffing away at their pipes under that wretched convex mirror which reflected me and them and the cat as though we were doomed to remain in just those positions for the rest of time, as though –
'I'm afraid we're closing, sir,' said the waiter.
'Oh,' said Joe. 'I can't have one more coffee?'
'We're closing, sir,' said the waiter.
'Yes, you said that before,' said Joe 'I asked if it was possible to have one more coffee before you closed.'
'Oh no, sir,' said the waiter. 'No more coffee. We're closing now.'
'That's a great pity,' said Joe. 'A very great pity. You realize I hope that you are losing an excellent customer?'
'I'm afraid, sir,' said a second waiter who had joined his colleague, 'we are –'
'Yes I know,' said Joe. 'You're closing.'
'That's right, sir,' said the two waiters in unison. 'We're closing.'
'Do that again please,' said Joe, for they suddenly reminded him of Tweedledum and Tweedledee.
'We-ee-ee-ee-ee're clo-o-o-o-o-sing, si-i-i-i-ir!' sang the waiters.
'Good-night,' said Joe.

'Goo-oo-oo-oo-ood-ni-i-i-i-ight, si-i-i-i-ir!' sang the wait-ers.

'This,' said Joe, holding his head in his hands and gently shaking it to and fro, 'has gone on long enough.'

He kicked an empty tin along the pavement.

XIV

Eight (8) Ceylonese table mats.
Twelve (12) cork table mats.
Six (6) small linen napkins.
Six (6) small natural linen napkins with flowers.
Three (3) tea-cloths – one torn.
Nine (9) prs. curtains: 2 prs. blue; 1 pr. yellow; 1 pr.
flowered; 4 prs. white homespun; 1 pr. velvet.

'Tell me quite frankly,' said Gill. 'Do you think Baby Choo
is very small for his age?'
'I don't really know about babies,' said Joe.
'Mrs Kaplan says he's small for his age. But he's no smaller
than any of the others were at that age, and you wouldn't say
they were dwarfs would you?'
'No,' said Joe. 'Not dwarfs.'
'Just seeing him like that you wouldn't think of him as an
abnormally small baby, would you?'
'No,' said Joe. 'Not an abnormally small baby, no.'

One (1) oak bedstead.
One (1) mattress.
One (1) bedside table.
One (1) table lamp and shade.
One (1) electric fire.
Two (2) bulbs.

'At first it was just habit,' she said. 'It was something to do,
something to hold on to, things had been happening to me so
fast for the last few years that it was nice just to be able to go
there and sit with them in the evenings. And then they asked
me, I didn't push myself forward, it was they who suggested
it, I wouldn't have wanted to offend the old man but they

asked me to cook for them, he did it so badly, so badly . . . And
then –'

'Put that broom down, Mick,' said Gill.

'I'll put your eye out,' said Mick.

'He's going to kill us all one of these days,' said Susan.

'Go and play with Brigid,' said Gill.

'I want to stay here,' said Mick.

'Come and help me with the corridor,' said Gill.

'I want to stay here,' said Mick.

'He would come into the kitchen while I was washing up
or cooking. He used to sit and watch me. He never helped. I
don't think he would have known how to, but he liked to pick
up the plates with one hand, he –'

'With one hand?'

'With the fingers extended round the edges, as you'd pick
up a ball with one hand. He liked to see how big a plate he
could pick up like that. Then he would wrap a cloth round the
plates and see if he could break them clean in two. He –'

'What an extraordinary thing to do,' said Joe. 'Why did he
do it?'

'I don't know,' she said.

'You didn't ask him?'

'You couldn't, somehow.'

'Why not?'

'I don't know. You couldn't.'

'But –'

'You dropped it on purpose!' shouted Gill.

'It slipped,' said Mick.

'I saw you,' said Gill. 'You dropped that broom on purpose.'

'He dropped it on purpose,' said Brigid.

'I didn't!'

'You did!'

'I didn't!'

'You did!'

'Stop it!' shouted Gill.

Slap slap.

Slap slap.

'Why do you slap me? I didn't do anything!' cried Brigid.

'Shut up!' shouted Gill. 'Go down and fetch it at once, Mick!'

'At first it was just habit,' said Susan. 'Then I began to realize it was more than that. When he came into the kitchen like that, when I watched him scrambling after that ping-pong ball I realized I was in love with him. I wanted to go away, never to come back, I didn't want to start again with love and jealousy and pain. But I kept on coming back.'

'I'm sorry,' he said. 'I didn't –'

'He broke it, he broke it!' howled Mick.

'Who broke what?' asked Gill.

'That man! He broke my broom!' sobbed Mick.

'What man? What are you talking about?'

'Downstairs,' sobbed Mick.

'He tried to knock the man's hat off with the broom,' explained Brigid. 'So the man broke the broom.'

'You mean you were using the broom to knock off the hats of people passing in the street?'

'I wasn't!'

'Yes, you were!'

'I wasn't!'

Slap slap.

Slap slap.

One (1) white-wood wardrobe cupboard.

One (1) mirror – oak frame broken.

One (1) icon – saint with scroll.

One (1) small painted wooden cow.

One (1) wooden chair.

One (1) armchair – upholstery completely worn.

One (1) box shoe-cleaning equipment.

Two (2) shoe-horns.

'As soon as you advanced he retreated,' she said. 'He wouldn't argue, discuss. At times I thought he was in love with me only too shy to say so. At times I thought he hated me and didn't want to see me any more. He –'

'Why did he disappear?' said Joe. 'I don't understand why he disappeared.'

'I drove him away,' she said. 'My being in love with him drove him away.'

'Don't be silly, Susan.'

'You don't understand,' she said.

'No,' he said. 'I don't. Why don't you try explaining?'

'How can I explain,' she said, 'when all that's left is this flat, this furniture, the things they owned, they lived with? It doesn't mean anything any more, all these objects, just names in your inventory, one oak bedstead, one electric fire, one bedside table, one lamp and shade, one small painted wooden cow.... And the other rooms, there in your list, don't they make you want to cry? One Turkish carpet, 21' x 18' – worn and damp; one pair maroon velvet floor-length curtains; one camphor-wood chest, lock broken; one inlaid needlework table – what did they want a needlework table for anyway? It's not even something they went out and chose because it was beautiful or something handed down from father to son or anything like that, it's just a piece of third-rate junk they bought with the lease. That's a nice little table the old man would say, I like that little inlaid table.... And look at the contents: a broken clock, a rusty pen-knife, some string, some foreign coins, 400 envelopes – where did they all come from? What did he want with all those envelopes? To invite all his cronies to the funeral? What –'

'You're not explaining,' he said. 'You're just working yourself up.'

'I'm trying,' she said. 'I'm trying to explain.'

Two (2) ash-trays – china.

One (1) Chinese rosewood screen.

One (1) small desk with drawer. Contents: 3 pencils; one packet playing-cards; one quill pen; one scout knife in sheath; box of letters and postcards.

'When I was a little girl,' said Gill, 'I was madly in love with him.'

'Really,' said Joe.

'I had never set eyes on him but I was madly in love with him Isn't that funny?'

'How was that?' asked Joe.

'My mother used to talk about him. She didn't approve of him. They were cousins, you know, but they never got on,

I don't think any member of that family ever approved of or
got on with any other. But then I didn't approve of my mother
at the time, so I built him up into a wonderful romantic figure,
he was the younger brother, you know, and reputed to be a
great rake though I later found out that most of the stories
about him had no factual basis whatever. I had dozens of other
uncles and cousins, all on my father's side, but they were terribly
dull, Susan's father no one talked about for some reason. . . . I
used to write him poems. I never sent them of course. I didn't
even know where he lived, he was just a mysterious cousin
David who existed in some fabulous world of imagination.'

'How old were you?' asked Joe.

'Oh, eleven or twelve at the time. Then I met George and
it passed.'

'You did what?'

'Didn't you know George was a childhood sweetheart of
mine? It's really a very moving story. Especially as he isn't
even my first husband.'

'He isn't?'

'No,' said Gill. 'George isn't Brigid's father. Hadn't you
noticed how different she and Mick are in features and colour-
ing? But George and I were childhood sweethearts, isn't that
touching?'

'Very touching,' said Joe.

Rider 3: Clothes.
Two (2) dark suits – one dirty.
Seventeen (17) ties.
Five (5) shirts.
Eight (8) vests.
Six (6) pants.
One (1) sports jacket.

'As soon as you advanced he retreated,' she said. 'He
wouldn't argue, discuss. At times I thought he was in love
with me only too shy to say so. Once, on the heath, by the
Windmill, we saw a swan flying high over the trees, he must
have come from the river down below. We stood there looking
at him as he disappeared leaving only the echo of his wings

behind, and then I don't know what took me but I caught hold of his scarf and tied it round my neck so that we were both of us tied up in it, he tried to jerk away but all that happened was that we fell into a ditch, he was –'

'Why are you telling me all this?' he said. 'Why are you making all this up?'

'I'm not –'

'You're in love with a ghost, Susan,' he said.

'What do you mean?'

'You make things up as you go along. You invent him as you talk. You're in love with a man who never existed.'

'But don't you understand?' she said. 'Don't you understand anything at all? That's what he was, a man you had to invent as you went along. That's what he demanded of you.'

XV

'When George came out of the army,' said Gill Clemm, 'the first thing he said to me was: You look just like my mother. Have you ever heard anything like it?'

'Have some more wine, Mr Hyman,' said George.

'Joe,' said Joe.

'Joe,' said George.

'What a thing to say when you haven't seen someone for over a year!'

'It was the truth,' said George. 'It only struck me then, but it was the truth. That's obviously the reason why I married you in the first place.'

'You should have seen his mother, Mr Hyman.'

'Joe.'

'Joe.'

'She was a beautiful woman,' said George. 'Prime Ministers were among her admirers.'

'Prime Ministers these days,' said Gill, 'are not exactly made in the mould of Adonis.'

'Dukes have wooed her.'

'And a banker married her.'

'There's nothing wrong with bankers,' said George.

'She was hideous,' said Gill. 'An old hag.'

'Come on, darling.'

'But it's true. An old hag.'

'Surely she wasn't always like that?' said Susan.

'She was never like that, Susan dear,' said George. 'She was, how can I put it? Ephemeral. Spiritual. Preraphaelitish.'

'Well I ask you! Do I look like that?'

'But you did, darling! That day, when I saw you on the platform. Like a Rossetti maiden.'

'My!'

'You never believe what I say, darling. You've never looked so beautiful.'

'Now there,' said Gill, 'is a man who really knows how to
pay a woman a compliment. I've never looked so beautiful,
he assures me, as when I looked like his old hag of a mother!'

'But it's true, darling!'

'Thank you.'

'No no. I mean about Rossetti and all that.'

'And how,' asked Joe, 'is poor Baby Choo after his wet-
ting?'

'He's fine,' said George.

'I took Mick to a psychiatrist this afternoon,' said Gill
defiantly.

'You did what? You never told me you were going to.'

'I knew you disapproved, darling.'

'I don't exactly disapprove,' said George, 'but I do think it
makes children attach too much importance to these things.
Who did you take him to?'

'A man Muriel recommended. He wasn't at all as I had
imagined him.'

'What was he like?' asked George.

'How had you imagined him?' asked Susan.

'Well,' said Gill, 'he was very nice but nondescript in appearance. Characterless somehow.'

'He's probably so busy bolstering up other people's disinteg-
rating characters,' said George, 'that he hasn't any time to
spend on his own.'

'How exactly had you imagined him?' asked Susan.

'I don't really know,' said Gill. 'Anything but nondescript.'

'What did he say?' asked George.

'He loved him.'

'He loved him? He must be crazy!'

'Who loved whom?'

'The psychiatrist. He loved Mick.'

'He must be crazy,' said Susan.

'And Mick too. He loved the psychiatrist.'

'So everyone loved everyone else.'

'He said to me afterwards: I love your little boy, Mrs Clemm.
He is a lovely little boy. We understand one another, he and
I. And all that you tell me, Mrs Clemm, do not upset yourself,
it is quite natural at his age.'

'Natural? To drown his baby brother?'

'No, dear. I didn't go to him about that. To keep unzipping people's dresses.'

'He called that natural?'

'He said that with a balanced home life like his Mick ought to grow into a fine healthy, human being.'

'What does he know about his home life?'

'I told him, darling.'

'How much did he charge?'

'Don't be mercenary, darling.'

'I'm not being mercenary, but I have to pay for him, don't I?'

'That's what you always say, darling.'

'But I always do.'

'Are you taking him back at all?' asked Susan.

'Well,' said Gill, 'Dr Enzenburger sug –'

'Is that his name?'

'Of course it's his name. I wouldn't call him that if it wasn't his name, would I?'

'It sounds very suspicious to me,' said George.

'It's his name anyway,' said Gill. 'Whatever it sounds to you.'

'What did he say?'

'Well, he rather suggested –'

'No,' said George.

'He said that if the children were at all peculiar, if, that is, we felt at all worried about them –'

'We don't,' said George.

'But it's not you who's got to look after them, darling, is it?' said Gill.

'Have some wine, Joe.'

'Thanks.'

'Susan?'

'Thanks.'

'In fact he did rather suggest that it might be a good idea if you went along to see him yourself.'

'Me?'

'He thought a chat with the father might help.'

'But I don't want to help him. I want to hinder him as much as I possibly can.'

'Don't be tiresome, darling.'

'I don't want to have anything to do with him.'

'It would help him make up his mind,' Gill explained.

'He needs help to do that?'

'About Mick. He needs all the available data.'

'Do you mean he wants to psychoanalyse *me* so as to understand what's wrong with Mick? But the thing would never end! He'd have to go on to psychoanalyse my father and his father before him and –'

'Not psychoanalyse you, dear. Just have a friendly chat.'

'What's the difference? Didn't he just have a friendly chat with Mick?'

'Informally, I mean. Not a real session or anything like that.'

'Darling, you must be crazy.'

'But why? It's quite natural. He wants to have all the available data.'

'And you? What about you?'

'What do you mean what about me?'

'Are you having one of these informal chats too?'

'No. He didn't seem to feel I was the real source of the disturbance.'

'The real source – ? So he felt I was the real source of the disturbance, did he? What disturbance, anyway? I thought you said there was nothing wrong with Mick, that he was a lovely little boy and that his behaviour was quite natural. Those were his very words, as reported by you to me just three minutes ago, a lovely little boy and his behaviour was quite natural.'

'Yes, darling, you're quite right, but he did go on to say that the natural behaviour of little boys was in itself unnatural – or could be unnatural – and that if we really wanted to get to the root of the matter the only way was by having a chat with you, not with me, although we had already had something of a chat when I outlined the situation to him in the first place. With you, he said, he felt he might be able to get to the root of the matter, to understand the causes of this unnatural behaviour and –'

'But you said it was natural?'

'Natural to little boys but unnatural in itself. Surely you can see the difference?'

'I'm damned if I can,' said George.

'Would you go around drowning your brothers and sisters?'

'N-no, I suppose not.'

'And unzipping your mother's dress?'

'No. Definitely not.'

'There you are then.'

'But if I was a little boy I might.'

'Did you?'

'No. But then there weren't any psychoanalysts about in my childhood.'

'You don't know what you're talking about, George. I really do think you'd better see Dr Enzenburger, it would do you the world of good.'

'I don't –'

'Oh for chrissake,' said Susan.

'We're boring you,' said Gill.

'Not at all,' said Joe.

'Yes,' said Susan.

'Let's change the subject,' said Gill.

'You brought it up in the first place,' said George.

'I was only telling you about your own children. One would have thought a father would evince a little more interest in the subject.'

'I'm quite interested enough in my children without having to send them to a psychoanalyst,' said George.

'You don't know what you're talking about, dear,' said Gill.

'I don't –'

'Oh for –'

'Are you quite worn out, Mr Hyman?' asked Gill.

'Joe.'

'Joe.'

'No no. This is all very interesting. I once thought –'

'Don't be so polite,' said Susan. 'She meant the inventory, not the conversation.'

'Oh, the inventory,' said Joe.

'The children have been absolutely unbearable,' said Gill.

'They always are,' said George. 'It must be the way you bring them up.'

'George! How can you say that!'

'What other –'

'Are you saying I don't know how –'

'Don't start again, please,' said Susan.

'Worn out,' said Joe.

'What?'

'The inventory. It's wearing me out.'

'It's these good ladies' conversation that's wearing you out,' said George. 'I don't know how you can put up with it day after day like that.'

'It really was rather inconsiderate of Mr Stout to take his holiday just now, wasn't it?' said Gill.

'Wasn't it inconsiderate of Uncle David to die just now?' asked Susan.

'I suppose it was,' said Gill.

'Have some coffee, Mr Hyman.'

'Joe.'

'Joe.'

XVI

One (1) pr. Corduroy trousers.
Two (2) waistcoats.
Eight (8) pullovers.
Three (3) scarves.
Five (5) hats.
One (1) beret.

'It was as though we were frozen there,' she said. 'Sometimes I would panic, I would shout to them Wake up! Wake up! You can't go on like this! And he would say What are you talking about, Susan? and I, I can't go on like this I can't... saying all this to myself, the words jumping about like rabbits in my head, it was no use talking to them, arguing, but sitting there in that room under that mirror I would panic and then I didn't know if I spoke out loud or just to myself, whichever it was they paid no attention, they were always so calm so polite and solicitous, it would have been better if they'd got angry, yelled at me, told me never to come back, at least it would have meant that I made some sort of impact, impinged somewhere upon their consciousness, at least –'

'Can't you forget them?' he said. 'Just forget them.'

'Even when they quarrelled, which they did frequently, but not open quarrels, no shouting and slamming of doors but only this feeling of tension under the surface, even then they didn't say anything, at least not in my presence but I don't think ever, though I could feel their antagonism as if it was another person in the room, there, with us, they –'

'Stop it!' he said. 'Stop it, Susan!'

'You couldn't argue with them,' she said. 'You couldn't make them talk sense or do things the right way. The old man with his crazy ideas about cooking food in its natural juices, and then he wouldn't give his clothes to the laundry or let me take them to the launderette, he said they smelt damp if he

hung them out in the garden or put them in the airing-cupboard,
I'd like to know how they smelt after he'd hung them on that
old rope in the corridor with all the fires in the house turned
on so that the steam invaded the rest of the flat and then the
only thing to do was to go for one of those interminable walks
over the heath with Sam rushing ahead and his scarf slapping
into your face and then when we came back the door would
have swung open and the steam and smoke would have invaded
the stairs and the neighbours would be peering in to see what
was happening, trying to make out those weird things hanging
silently in the corridor and –'

'You've told me this before,' he said. 'What are you trying
to do?'

'There was nothing to hold on to,' she said. 'Nothing to
grip. Even when they were on the floor playing with Oscar
they were so absorbed in the game they didn't notice you or
try to include you or…or…As soon as you made up your
mind that he was like this or like that he did something to
show you he wasn't…like the furniture they went out and
bought, coming home one day with that mirror they'd spent
eighty pounds on or the sideboard dresser which –'

'But you said they belonged to them! That they were the
only pieces they'd got left, that –'

'I said that?' she said.

'Can't you talk to me, Susan?' he said. 'Tell me the truth.
What happened in this flat? What are you trying to do?'

'Understand,' she said, suddenly tired. 'I'm trying to understand.'

'But what? What?' he said angrily.

'Leave me alone,' she said. 'Go away. Leave me alone.'

'You've got to tell me,' he said.

'Leave me alone,' she repeated. 'Get on with your job and
get out of my hair.'

'Thanks,' he said. 'Thanks very much.'

'Get out,' she said. 'Get out of here for godsake.'

There are one thousand four hundred and sixty-three (1463)
telephone booths in Greater London, including thirty-four
(34) at Victoria Station, sixteen (16) at Paddington, twenty-two

(22) at Waterloo, and no less than forty-eight (48) at King's Cross. A generous estimate of one hundred and twenty-seven (127) telephones out of order will leave one thousand three hundred and thirty-six (1336) from which to choose.

'Can't you understand plain English,' she said. 'I don't want to speak to you.'

'Susan, I have scratched your beautiful name into the red paint of seven telephone booths already, in a variety of scripts ranging from the small unostentatious secretary hand to the flowering uncials of the Burgundian court. Any minute now the police will be on your trail.'

'I don't give a damn what you've done,' she said. 'And if the police come here it will save me having to summon them.'

'You have no mercy, have you?' he said.

'Why on earth should I have mercy on you?' she said. 'Do you have any on me, ringing up at all hours of the night like this?'

'It's different this time,' he said. 'I've been thinking it over and I've come to the conclusion that you're right, Susan, absolutely right. I see that now. I won't pester you any more, I won't –'

'Don't then,' she said, and rang off.

Some people walk better in cities than in the country. The gay lights and the shop windows keep them going. Others walk better in the country than in cities. The springy turf and the fresh air keeps them going. Some people can't walk at all, in city or country, their feet are bad or they just can't see the point. Others, however, will cover miles on foot in any conditions – and that's not counting professionals such as marathon runners or tramps.

Joe did not belong to either of the two latter categories. But to which of the others did he then belong?

Seven (7) prs. shoes.
One (1) pr. slippers.
One (1) pr. Wellingtons.
One (1) dressing-gown.
Three (3) prs. pyjamas.

'The last evening,' she said. 'I didn't know it was the last evening, but I was restless, I felt something was going to happen. The old man had gone to bed, he did sometimes before I left, he got up so early, he said that the best time of day was between four and six in the morning summer and winter, and he would get up then and sit by his window until the city began to wake up. He'd gone to bed and I must have been smoking the last of my cigarettes, sitting here on the green sofa and Sam in the armchair where he always sat, you can see where Oscar has scratched it all down the arms and sides, he used to go up to it and stretch up and sharpen his claws on it when Sam was sitting there, never at any other time so it can't have been simply the desire to sharpen his claws, there must have been an element of showing-off, the desire to attract attention, and it wasn't simply to ask for food either, he often did it just after he'd eaten, I used to sit there and try to puzzle out just why he did it, see if there was any explanation that would fit all the instances but of course I could never find one, I don't know what got into me then, I felt it was the wrong thing to do but I was fed up and I was in one of those moods where you do what you feel to be the wrong thing with a perverse relish, an active pleasure, Why did you ask me round in the first place? I said, Why do you keep asking me round? Is it out of pity or what? And he, We like having you here. And I, Just to cook your dinner for you? And he, No no we like to see you, Susan. And I, Is that all you can say, is there nothing more than this polite "it's nice to see you"? And he, What more do you want? And I, I don't *want* anything except frankness. And he, It's not politeness, it's the truth, we like to see you. And I, It would be much better if you admitted now that it was out of pity, better for you and for me – you see I couldn't stand it any longer not knowing what was going on in their minds, not knowing whether to keep coming or stay away, not knowing anything at all. Let's not talk about it any more, he said. But we must, I said. I'd rather not, he said, I can see what you're leading up to, I don't want to talk about it, I love you, I said, I love you – I didn't know what I was saying, I kept repeating that, and he drew back into himself straight away, I knew it would have that effect but I couldn't go on like that, then he got up and went into the bathroom. I stayed on for a

few minutes, I didn't understand what was happening, I felt
something was but I couldn't understand what, then I went
home, I went to bed but I couldn't sleep, not all night, it was
as if I had that mirror screwed into my skull and whatever I
did or whatever happened to me it would go on reflecting the
three of us sitting here in this room with Oscar on the mat and
the smoke from their pipes hanging above our heads.... Next
day, in the morning early, I found myself here, there was no
one in except Oscar, lying on his mat as though he hadn't
moved all night, that was unusual, they never went out on
Sunday morning, but I wandered around the flat telling myself
I was being a fool, that nothing had happened, that I had
imagined the whole thing.... Then the old man came in. I
could see by his face. We didn't say anything. I went away.'
    'It's not your fault,' he said. 'How could you help it?'
    'I've still got that mirror in my skull,' she said.
    'It's nothing to be afraid of,' he said. 'Look. It only reflects
an empty room, some pieces of furniture, you and me....'
    'Look at it,' she said. 'It's so pathetic it makes you want to
cry. One broken-down sofa covered in a hideous bright green
velvet that has faded unevenly and registered every blessed
thing that has ever been spilt upon it, one ageless though
extremely comfortable armchair with most of the upholstery
methodically torn to shreds by Oscar, one small Victorian
rocking-chair, one inlaid needlework table with inside it among
numerous other things, nothing less than 400 envelopes. Who
the hell were they so keen to write to? They never corres-
ponded, the idea's ludicrous – or do you think the old man
was sending out appeals for charity and –'
    'Baby Choo, Baby Choo, whatever shall –'
    'For godsake shut up, Brigid!'
    'I'm rocking Baby.'
    'Go and rock him somewhere else.'
    'Mummy said in here.'
    'Well, I say not in here.'
    'Mummy says always to obey her.'
    'Oh for –'
    'Bang! Bang! Bang!' shouted Mick. 'You're dead, all of you!'
    'Baby Choo, Baby Choo, wha –'
    'I said not so much noise!'

'Take Baby,' said Brigid.
'Behave yourself,' said Gill.
'Take Baby!'
'Don't talk to me like that!'
'I'll drop him then.'
'Don't you dare.'
'I hate that Baby Choo,' said Brigid.
'Bang!' shouted Mick, and hit Brigid on the head with his
rifle. Brigid screamed and dropped Baby Choo. Gill screamed
and slapped Brigid. Brigid screamed and kicked Mick. Mick
screamed and butted Brigid in the stomach. Brigid screamed
and kicked Gill. All three fell on top of Baby Choo.

Eight (8) prs. socks.
Three (3) belts.
One (1) pr. braces.
One (1) mackintosh.
One (1) duffel coat.
One (1) windcheater.
Four (4) prs. gloves.

'It was Sam who suggested it,' she said. 'I didn't want to
push myself forward but in the end it was Sam who suggested
it. And the old man wasn't at all put out. I was afraid he might
be, I didn't know how they felt about me, I couldn't figure
out how their minds worked, they never said anything, they
never gave any help, with most people there's some effort to
meet you half-way, some attempt to –'
'Eat,' he said. 'Eat and don't talk.'
'Do you like it?'
'Delicious.'
'But why?' she said. 'Why couldn't they be like other
people?'
'Isn't it always like that,' he said, 'with people one loves?'
'No no,' she said. 'You don't understand.'
'Forget them,' he said. 'It's all over, just try and forget them.'
'You don't understand,' she said.
'There's nothing to understand,' he said. 'It's all perfectly
clear.'

'That's what I mean,' she said. 'You don't understand. I thought you did but you don't. You won't even try.'

'Oh for chrissake,' he said.

'If you did you wouldn't say that sort of thing. All you're concerned about is –'

'I just want to be able to talk to you,' he said.

'But how can we talk,' she said, 'when you won't even try?'

'There's nothing to understand,' he said.

'That's what I mean. You won't try.'

'Oh for chrissake!'

'Leave me alone, Joe.'

'I'll have some more if I may.'

'They were so self-contained,' she said. 'They made you feel like an ant crawling over the body of a sleeping person, your eyes became ants, they did that to you, they –'

'But –'

'I'd get so angry,' she said, 'so nervous and angry, but they didn't notice, they never noticed anything, at times I felt like getting up, never coming back, I –'

'But why? Why did you keep going back?'

'I was in love with him. There was nothing else I could do. It's ironic that it should be that which drove him away.'

'If you'd been in love with him,' he said, 'you wouldn't have got so angry.'

'I don't know,' she said. 'That's how it was. Somehow I resented it. Partly the old man I suppose. I felt shut out, cut off. If I could have found some way to separate them, to pull them apart, but together they were like a wall shutting me out, out of their quarrels, their jokes, their games with the cat, the pipes they smoked, if only I could separate them I might get through to them, see what it was that made them what they were, I kept saying this to myself, I would sit here and watch them and try to work out how I could do it. In the end I did.'

'Did?'

'I worked it out. I succeeded. In the end he went away.'

'I suppose,' he said, laughing, 'it would have suited you better if it had been the old man who had gone away.'

'By that time I didn't care,' she said. 'That seemed victory enough.'

'That seemed what?'

'I was satisfied with that.'

'Satisfied? You mean you actually persuaded him to go away?'

'You don't know what hate is,' she said. 'You don't know how love can change to hate, how love is only another form, a way of possessing, destroying, a –'

'You don't know what you're saying,' he said.

'I couldn't stand it any longer,' she said. 'I started doing little things, setting them up one against the other. They used to quarrel, he would threaten to go away, it wasn't difficult to see once I'd accepted the fact that I couldn't make him love me I was really in control of the situation, I was –'

'Susan, stop it! You don't know what you're saying!'

'I drove him away,' she said.

XVII

Three (3) scrubbing-brushes.
One (1) long-handled broom – broken.
One (1) carton 'Lifebuoy' soap – unopened.
One (1) plastic pail.
One (1) mop.
One (1) automatic mop and ball brush.

'I've been meaning to ask you,' said Gill. 'Do you think some sort of art therapy would do Mick good?'

'I wouldn't know,' said Joe.

'I'm so worried about him,' said Gill. 'I don't feel he's really benefited from Dr Enzenburger, though of course it is a little early to tell yet. But I thought if perhaps he took up some modern painting, you know, threw paint at the canvas or something *active* and at the same time *creative* like that...?'

'I wouldn't know,' said Joe, 'I'm afraid I really wouldn't know.'

'I wish you'd remember to keep the door shut,' said Gill.

'I didn't forget,' said Susan. 'Mick opened it.'

'I didn't,' said Mick.

'Now they're starting to lie as well,' said Susan.

'Everybody's tired,' said Joe. 'Let's not have any more quarrels at this stage.'

'Nobody's quarrelling,' said Gill.

'Oh yes they are,' said Susan. 'They're insinuating.'

'Please,' said Joe.

Two (2) carpet brushes.
One (1) dust-pan.
Three (3) brooms.
Three (3) dusters.

'I drove him away,' she said.

'Don't be silly,' he said.

'I did,' she said. 'And the awful thing is I suppose one half of me really wanted to do it. Half of me did and half of me didn't.'

'People don't –'

'It made them restless, having me here. It was that that set them quarrelling. Oh, they looked calm enough but you could feel it boiling away underneath, they used to quarrel about me, I never caught them at it they were too polite, but I could tell, I could feel it, sometimes it was the old man who didn't like having me there, he didn't like me doing all the cooking and playing with Oscar, and then Sam would take my side, sometimes it was the other way round, I thought the only thing was never to come back, to go away and never come back, oh a dramatist could have made a really nice exciting play out of it, with both of them in love with me or Sam in love and the old man possessive or the old man in love and Sam hurt or embarrassed, the possibilities are endless but it was none of these things – simply that it made them restless having me there, every evening, the best thing would have been to go away, but I had to do something, don't you see, I had to do something, it wasn't difficult to pretend I didn't know what was going on and then –'

'It's all over,' he said. 'Try and forget them.'

'How can I?' she said. 'All the time I'm wondering should I have done this? Or that? Been less compliant? Talked more? Less? How –'

'It's been going round in your head for too long,' he said. 'Leave it alone.'

'You don't really understand, do you?' she said.

'There's nothing to understand,' he said.

'That's what I mean. You won't even try.'

'Oh for chrissake!'

'If you understood you wouldn't make that sort of remark. But all you're concerned with is yourself, your little egotistical self, and whether I pay enough attention to it or –'

'Don't be silly,' he said. 'I just want to be able to talk to you.'

'But how can we talk when you won't even try to understand?'

'There's nothing to understand.'

'That's what I mean. You –'

'Oh for chrissake!'

'Leave me alone, Joe.'

'Susan –'

'I don't want to speak to you. I don't want to talk about it.'

'Thanks,' he said. 'Thanks very much. You talk and talk and talk about it and then when I try to reason with you you tell me you don't want to talk about it. Can't you see you're being silly?'

'Go away,' she said. 'For godsake go away.'

Four (4) tins floor-polish – unopened.

One (1) can 'Transpex' window-cleaner.

One (1) roll red lino.

One (1) 5 gallon can paraffin: empty.

One (1) box of tools. Contents: hammer, chisel, pliers, box of nails & screws, roll of fuse-wire, box of tin-tacks, bottle of glue, pencil-sharpener, rubber.

'She's very highly strung,' said Gill.

'Oh, that,' he said.

'No, no, it's true,' said Gill.

He shrugged.

'Mind you,' said Gill, 'I'm pretty highly strung myself. *And* I've got the children to cope with. And I hope I'm not as snappy as she is.'

'I don't see what right you have to discuss me in my absence,' said Susan.

'You weren't absent,' said Gill, 'if you heard us discussing you.'

'But you didn't know I could hear you, did you.'

'Pull yourself together, dear,' said Gill.

'I am pulled together,' said Susan. 'I don't know what you two are on about. I think it's extremely rude.'

'I think it shows what a lot of concern we have for you,' said Gill.

'Concern my foot,' said Susan.

'You need a holiday,' said Gill.

'Getting away from all this is the only holiday I need, thank you,' said Susan.

'Since that is precisely what you have decided not to do,' said Gill, 'that can only mean getting rid of us.'

'Precisely,' said Susan.

'Ear,' said the policeman.

'Me?' said Joe.

'What are you doing?' asked the policeman.

'Walking,' said Joe.

'Walking?'

'Walking.'

'Funny time of night to be walking,' said the policeman.

Joe shrugged.

'Where,' asked the policeman, 'do you think you are walking to?'

'Putney,' said Joe.

'Why don't you take a taxi if you missed the last tube?' asked the policeman.

'Because I want to walk,' said Joe. 'It helps me to think.'

'I shouldn't be walking around London at this time of night if I were you,' said the policeman.

'I don't often do it,' said Joe.

'You'll do it a lot less often if someone conks you on the head,' said the policeman.

Joe agreed with him.

'All right,' said the policeman, walking round him once as a precaution. 'Get along with you.'

'Thank you,' said Joe.

'I don't see what right you have,' Susan said.

'No right at all.'

'You're extremely rude.'

'Oh for chrissake!' he said.

'You won't even try.'

'What is there to understand?' he said.

'What it was like, all those months when –'

'You can't blame yourself,' he said. 'These things happen. One thinks one does things and then –'

'What things?'

'I don't know,' he said. 'What you told me, I...'

'What you said, what you told me, you make me sick. Try and understand.'

'What?' he said. 'Understand what? Tell me the truth, Susan. What happened here? Why did he go away? Why do you invent all these lies to torment yourself? Why –'

'Go away,' she said.

'I won't,' he said. 'Not till you've explained.'

'I'm tired,' she said. 'Go away, Joe, I'm tired.'

'You've done a wonderful job,' he said.

'I'm glad it's over,' Gill said.

'It's been heroic of you,' he said. 'And with all those children to look after too.'

'Oh,' she said. 'They're not so bad as all that. And it isn't really too difficult to do so long as one has a method and doesn't try to attack all the rooms at once. I must say there were moments when I thought I would never be able to get on top of the chaos, but I think I've really succeeded. I think it needed an absolutely thorough cleaning, if only to get the smell out, and especially if Susan's going to pursue her crazy scheme of coming to live here with Oscar....'

'It's been heroic of you,' he said.

'So you're going through with it?' he said.

'Yes,' she said, 'I was looking for something self-contained anyway.'

'Susan,' he said, 'what happened here? Were you in love with him? Was he in love with you? Did you drive him away? What?'

'Nothing happened,' she said.

'What do you mean?'

'Nothing happened,' she said. 'You heard me.'

'But –'

'Was he in love with me? Was I in love with him? I don't

know. People cheat all the time. They say I love him or he loves me or I hate him, but things aren't like that, there isn't anything solid like love or hate, there are only stirrings, bits and pieces of emotion, nothing you can put down clearly and label, nothing you can talk about, saying I love or he loves or they love, just indeterminate feelings, emotions, as soon as you say: This is what happened, or That is what happened, as soon as you do that it's false, you've added something, taken something away.... You start out saying something and you end up saying something else, words pile up, one on top of the other, and you try to pull them back, to make them mean what you want, but they go on rising higher and higher until you don't recognize them any more or the things they are saying.... How can I explain anything when as soon as I begin it turns into something else, something I never meant to say, but something that I now see could be true, is true, at least as true as any of the things I was going to say and didn't.... Nearly every day for a month, or two, or six, I saw two people. At the end of that time something happened. Why? Was there a reason? Now they are both dead and all that's left is this furniture, their belongings, their *havings*. And what does this tell us about their *beings*? Nothing. Precisely nothing. So what do you want me to tell you? What? What?

'Leave them alone,' he said. 'Leave the whole thing alone. Come and live with me, Susan.'

'Don't be silly,' she said. 'What would happen to Oscar?'

'I mean it,' he said. 'I need you, Susan. Bring Oscar with you.'

'Don't be silly.'

'Why not?'

'I don't want to. I want to live here. By myself.'

'And be free to think about them.'

'Perhaps.'

'Don't you see, Susan? It's not him you're thinking about. You're in love with a man who never existed.'

'No.'

'You make him up as you go along. You're in love with the ghost of a man who never even existed.'

'You don't understand.'

'Let's not start that again.'

'I keep telling you. That's what he was. Always. Not just now he's dead. Always. Even when he was here. So what difference does it make that he's dead? Most people give you a lever, a handle, they're writers, or labourers or bores or idealists or do tricks with bits of string. But with him there was nothing, nothing to hold on to like that. It drove me wild not being able to say he's like this or like that, he stands on his head or breaks plates or thinks only about money or chess or something, but he wasn't like that, every day was new and also monotonously the same so that all that's left is the image of the two of them and Oscar sitting there, evening after evening, just sitting there smoking their pipes.'

'You're twisting things,' he said. 'You're twisting them to suit your own convenience.'

'Doesn't that make more sense than twisting them to suit yours?'

'How can I make you understand?' he said.

'There's nothing to understand,' she said. 'You're not in love with me at all, Joe. You're in love with my memories of them. If you can call that love. What a situation!'

'Please, Susan. Talk sense. And stop talking to yourself.'

'I'm talking to you.'

'No you're not. I'm just there. A convenient wooden figure, a useful prop. While you address yourself. I don't exist for you. All this time you've been talking to yourself, trying to understand, and I thought it was me you were addressing. But don't you see, there's nothing to understand. Nothing.'

'I lived those months, didn't I?' she said. 'Now go away. Please go away.'

But I was fed up, fed up with all the mess and the dirt and the confusion. I felt they were stifling me with that flat and the silence and their dependence. Just to cook for you and look after you? I said, and he said, No, we like having you here, and I said Thank you very much but I don't like being here and I got up and went away

And we both fell into a ditch and I tore my stockings, that's how he was, instead of saying anything he would do things like that, I should have been a duck he used to say, one of those ducks that go through elaborate mimes at mating time, if it was his idea of elaborate mime I could have done without, thank you very much.

But as you see I'm trying to sort out these bills and old postcards and bits of paper, there's so much junk here, so much that's all out of place and mixed up with other things, letters, little mementos, odds and ends that one doesn't know what to do with

Words he'd said kept on coming back to me. I kept seeing the two of them in their chairs under that damned mirror, evening after evening, there seemed to be some sort of riddle to solve in their silences, in the flat, in the things they ate and washed with and put in the dustbin, and just this image of them sitting there so self-contained and him saying

Going through their things in this empty flat, only the cat left and those children everywhere, yelling, squabbling, crying.... Going through their things, there's so much of it, so much.... I suppose when a place is lived in you don't notice, it all seems necessary, you never question, but all this lying about, unused and useless, toothbrushes, ink-bottles, shoe-horns, ivory elephants... You begin to feel it's too much, it's crushing you.... I don't know.... It's so absurd seeing it all lying there, slowly being translated into your neat list, one useless item after another, curtains, carpets, chairs, tables, ashtrays knick-knacks, why do human beings surround themselves with so much, why do they need all this, all this...?

For anything that causes surprise gives pleasure, and the most effective style is one that stirs up some emotion in the mind and that indicates amiability of character in the speaker himself; and amiability of character is expressed either by his indicating his own judgement and humanity and liberality of mind, or by the modification of the style when it appears that the speaker, for the sake of magnifying a second party or disparaging himself, is saying something different from what he actually thinks, and that he is doing this more out of good nature than insincerity. But there are many rules for charm that render the style either less lucid or less convincing; consequently in this department also we have to use our own judgement as to what the case requires.

'Are you mad?' she said. 'Ringing up at this hour of the morning?'

'No,' he said. 'Quite sane. I'm ringing from the tube station just round the corner.'

'You're not coming here,' she said. 'If that's what you want.'

'No,' he said. 'I thought it was what I wanted. But now I'm ringing up to say I don't any more. No, I'm not coming round, Susan, don't worry.'

'You sound pleased with yourself,' she said.

'Susan,' he said. 'Tell me the truth. This is the time of day for the truth. There never was anything between the two of you, was there?'

'I don't wish to discuss it,' she said.

'It's you who went away, isn't it? A long time before he disappeared. You had nothing to do with it, did you?'

'Have you been talking to Gill?' she asked.

'No,' he said. 'No, I haven't been talking to Gill. But that's how it was, isn't it? And that's what hurts?'

'I don't know,' she said. 'I don't know how it was at all.'

'Goodbye, Susan,' he said.

He laid the instrument gently down on its cradle and stepped out into the street. A milk cart clattered past him as the yellow glare of London faded into the dawn. It was at this time that the old man, David Hirsh, liked to sit and look out of his window.

'Yes,' thought Joe, 'I need a holiday. I really need a holiday.'

Clutching the sheaf of papers in his coat pocket he strolled down the street, waiting for the cafés to open.

2

The Voices

When the voices stopped there was only silence.

He thought: Perhaps there was no voice. Suddenly he was afraid. I should have put something down on paper, he thought. For now it was impossible to say if the voice had ever existed. And it was so important to know.

'So important,' he said out loud, the words dancing in the empty room.

How many walls to a head? he wondered. And he felt the house flow through his limbs and sink into the earth beneath him, many many stories beneath him.

Tying him to the earth.

The old woman came, she brought food on a tray. She put on a face and prepared a voice. She held the tray pressed to her stomach.

'There,' she said, and judged the voice right, and the distance between them, so that it fell plop into his ears: 'There.'

Now that she had given him this word, whose precise tone and quality had grown within her on the long climb up the stairs, she gave him the tray.

Then there was nothing more to give him and she began to turn away.

But he said: 'Who was that singing?'

'Singing?' she asked, uncertain – because it was not usual for him to give her words and she did not know what to do with them.

She started to turn away again, but he said: 'Who was that singing down below? It sounded like a boy's voice.'

'Yes,' she agreed. 'A boy's voice. Or an old man's.'

'Or an old man's,' he repeated, assenting.

She kicked the words absentmindedly, her eyes empty, and they disintegrated and disappeared. Pieces strayed under the bed with the sound of dead leaves.

117

'I must sweep up the dead leaves,' she said.

'Yes,' he agreed.

They looked down at the trees spreading below them, an infinity of trees, creaking in the wind.

'What are they saying?' he asked.

'They always leave me out of their conversations,' she said. 'You stand around and wait for one of them to step aside and draw you into their circle, but they are adept at ignoring you.'

He looked at her in silence.

'Oh you wicked trees!' she cried out, and banged the windows shut. Her eyes were red.

'No,' he said gently. 'No. They would only shock you if you could hear what they said. They are better left alone.'

She began to turn away again. They had spoken enough. But he said: 'I started to hear voices today.'

'You always hear voices,' she said.

'When did I begin to hear them?' he asked her.

'You don't begin,' she said. 'They are always with you. At the edges. And you can't hold on to them. Try and they go.'

'Why?' he asked her. 'Why can't you hold them?' He felt cheated. They had spoken for too long.

'It's like that,' she said. 'We are made like that. To hear voices unawares, or in sleep. And if you cheat and try to listen for them you only hear the sounds of your own body.'

'I don't think we are talking about the same sorts of noises,' he said, very dignified. He wanted to cry.

'No,' she agreed. 'Perhaps not.'

Then she left and he ate and she came and took the tray and left again and he was alone again.

The children were playing in the garden.

Maurice said: 'Tell me. Tell me why you looked at that tree like that.'

Maurice said: 'Don't be frightened of a tree, silly.'

Maurice, the elder, pleaded: 'What do you see, what do you see in that tree?'

The children were playing in the rubble, under the trees, at the end of the garden, not far from the house, close to the road, one morning, or afternoon, in winter.

Maurice said, 'It's not fair. I won't ever tell you anything any more if you don't tell me what you see.'

'Spoil-sport,' said Maurice.

'He won't tell us what he sees.'

'Go on,' they chanted. 'Go on. Tell us what you see.'

'Why are you frightened?' Maurice asked. 'There's nothing to be afraid of here.'

'He's frightened of the tree,' one of them said.

'Why?' asked Maurice. 'Why are you frightened of the tree? What's so frightening about an old tree?'

'Look,' Maurice said. 'Either you tell us what's frightening you or we go on playing without you.'

'He won't tell us. He's just having us on.'

So the children played, in the rubble, at the bottom of the garden, by the road, under the trees, one winter morning, or afternoon.

Looking at the trees he was suddenly afraid. His heart slid about inside his body like a live fish in the hand, and he clamped his lips shut to stop it getting out. Words formed in his head.

> Oh, Trees! I loved you once,
> But now no more;
> For you are still old and wise
> And I am still a child

> Oh, Trees! I feared you once,
> But now no more;
> For I am grown old and wise
> Who was then a child.

When the woman came he said: 'I have made a song.'

'I have brought you your food,' she said.

They were silent, not knowing what to say.

'I was sick last night, and today too,' he said. But she could see he wasn't. Just tired, perhaps. And he knew she could see.

They held out the right faces to each other. When you know someone well it does not matter too much about the right face. You can usually count on the other emending it. But they held out the right faces.

'I keep hearing the person in the room below. And someone playing out in the garden.'

She looked out of the window.

'Tell me about him,' he said.

'There is not much to tell,' she said. 'There was a garden with a lake, and trees peering over the lake to look at their reflections waving up at them from the water. In winter they were locked in a prison of ice and could no longer see clearly the outlines of their branches: they only knew that they were imprisoned down below. And when the cold white sun came out they grew frightened of their reflected shapelessness, but they could not turn away. She was a little girl then, and all at once she was frozen in there alongside the trees, looking up at herself bowing down to meet her, vague and formless, but definitely oh quite definitely there. She could not turn away, but only look, while she climbed into herself – and she never grew any more clearly defined.'

'What rubbish you talk,' he said. 'I did not ask about you but about him.'

'It is the same,' she said. 'It is the same for him too. Perhaps you only asked about yourself.'

They looked at the words they had spoken with satisfaction, because the moment of saying them was gone and the words were no longer theirs, and frail, but formed patterns among themselves and would live on with a life of their own.

The woman went away.

Maurice said: 'Don't upset your glass or Grandad will be furious.'

Maurice said: 'I hate you.'

'You've got to tell me,' threatened Maurice. 'Or I won't ever tell you any of my secrets again.'

'I dreamt a funny dream last night,' the Grandfather said. 'That's the way they always start: I dreamt a funny dream last night. And then go on: It was like this, do you see?'

'Like what?' asked the Mother.

'Not like anything,' said the Grandfather.

'I don't understand,' said the Mother. 'It must have been like something.'

'Why?' asked the Grandfather. 'Does everything have to be like something else?'

'No,' she admitted, hesitantly.

'But,' said the Father, 'if it isn't like anything else that we know, how can you describe it to us?'

'And,' said the Mother, 'if it isn't like anything else that you know, how can you know what it is – or even *if* it is?'

'I know it because I dreamt it!' roared the Grandfather. 'I can feel it, like a great piece of cheese lodged in my right breast. It won't go down and it won't come up and it hurts like hell.'

'Oh,' said the Mother.

'At least I didn't dream it,' said the Grandfather. 'I was only telling you how they always start.'

He grumbled to himself. Then: 'Funny dream indeed!' he said.

'Give me that pot of mustard that is right there in front of you,' he said. 'And don't upset your glass, if you please.'

'The glass was upset on purpose,' he said.

'Never mind,' said the Grandmother. 'There was not much water left in it, and none of it has touched you.'

'You have meddled in my life for too long,' the Grandfather told her. 'It is high time you were dead.'

Now he was tired of hearing voices and he wanted to see. The children were playing in the garden and he leant out of the window. But an infinity of trees screened the garden from him.

'Perhaps it is my child she is keeping from me,' he thought. 'Why not?' he said out loud. 'Why not? Is it impossible?'

He shadow-boxed with the words as they came gliding down.

'Words are getting heavier,' he said to the woman, when she came.

'Words!' she said contemptuously. 'How can you think properly if you are always thinking of words? They get in the way.'

'They are getting heavier,' he said. 'They come rolling out of my mouth and slide down my chest on to the floor. They don't give me a chance to look at them, to feel them any more.'

'It's like Grandad was saying about dreams,' she said. 'Words are funny in dreams. They stretch out or bulge like your reflection in those fairground mirrors, and you stop and look at them and they look all funny to hear and you wake up trying to understand what they mean. Because it is obviously important to know.'

'Yes,' he said. 'I heard Grandad.'

'You heard him?' she asked. 'Through all those walls?'

'Didn't you hear him, through all the walls of your head?' he rejoined.

'We didn't talk so much before,' she said after a while.

'No,' he agreed.

'Perhaps,' she said, 'all the time we are only looking for a word, a phrase, that will save us.'

'You are an old woman,' he said. 'You think too much of your salvation.'

'But they are all we have,' she protested.

'They are all that other people have,' he said. 'And the words of other people will not save you. Not ever.'

'I am confused,' she said. 'I have spoken your thoughts and you mine.'

'It is often like that,' he said. 'When two people know each other well.'

The Uncle, with the indeterminate features, the all-too-definite smell, was in the room saying: 'It's the dark you are afraid of. There's always something hidden in the dark. You put on the light and it goes, but put the light out and it's back. They come and comfort you, saying, "Look, there's nothing there, silly. It's only your imagination." But, they don't understand. Not at all. They think because it isn't there when they look that it will never be there. Perhaps, however, they have forgotten how to look. For there is always something there; some of us may learn to forget it, but we can't kid him that we have learnt to get rid of it.'

'Don't try to foist your guilty conscience on to us,' said the Mother. 'Your pet furies may be pursuing you still, but that is no reason for trying to make out that we too are afflicted with them.'

'There's no way of placating them,' said the Uncle, 'except with the gift of one's life.'

'You are frightening the children,' said the Grandmother.

'No,' said the Uncle. 'They are frightening me.'

Playing, playing, at the bottom of the garden.

The rubble? No, not the rubble.

The hedge? No, not the hedge.
The grass? The flowers? No.
The house? No.
The tree? No, not the tree.
Not anything.
Just a feeling, at the edges of the body.
And Maurice there, saying: 'I'll never give it back to you.'
Saying: 'If you don't tell I'll twist your arm.'
There is nothing to tell.
Nothing is changed. Everything is as it has always been: the
house, the hedge, the tree. Only that feeling at the edges of
the body.
More than a feeling. A voice. A shape behind the eyes.
How far behind?
The same distance, always the same distance.
What distance?
Out of reach. Just.
When did this symptom begin to manifest itself?
One day. One day. But it must always have been there.
And now, what are you going to do about it? (If the answer
is not known, leave a blank to be filled in later.)
Later?

'When a man says that he will do something "later",' said the
Father, 'he is using the word to mean "some time between the
present moment and my death". The use of the word "later"
in this way involves the hypothesizing of an indeterminate
future, when the action, which has not been performed at the
moment of speaking, will be completed. But it also implies a
"latest", hidden, it is true, or even suppressed from the mind
of the speaker, but called up nonetheless by the exigencies of
language. What, I ask you, is this "latest"? Is it, for instance,
the first of the Fifteen Last Days, or is it the moment of Judgement itself? Or, more important to us perhaps, is it the moment
of our bodily death, or that in which the strength to perform
the said action leaves us forever? The real, the all-important
question, the question we must truly ask ourselves, is this: "Is
not later too late?"'
Oh admirable preacher! Oh incomparable philologist!
And so the words are spilt, lying at first in isolated fragments

on the floor, slowly forming a carpet upon the boards, tumbling out into the hall, trickling through the cracks in the wall, rising to the height of the table, the necks of the children, drowning the women, drowning the men, drowning the philologists, rising to the ceiling, pushing through to the first floor, the second floor, up and up through the house, until the walls can stand the strain no longer and burst and crumble and collapse – so that where the house stood there is now only rubble.

'My head has burst,' he said. 'There were too many words.'

He was surprised to find it still intact. He still heard the laughter of children coming up through the open window.

When the woman arrived he said: 'Something has burst inside me.'

'It is probably your bowels,' she said. 'You never had much control over them.'

'When am I going to die?' he asked her. 'When?'

'That's not a way to talk,' she said. But he could sense that she was afraid of death.

'Tell me about the boy,' he said. 'What is the song he always sings?'

'You and your boy,' she said.

'There are so many things I don't understand,' he said. 'I am terrified that I will not have understood them by the time I die.'

'That is the artist in you,' she said. 'Who can escape his destiny?'

'It is always difficult to calculate the degree of your irony,' he said.

He thought she had died and would no longer bring him any food. The thought did not disturb him.

When she came he said: 'I thought you were dead and it did not disturb me.'

She went away and he thought of a name for her. But when she returned he could not remember it.

It began to grow dark, darker than it had ever been before. He could see no part of himself, and he felt himself disappearing, the darkness encroaching more and more on territory that had once been his. He longed for the sun, a light, any light, but there was only darkness. He lay in the darkness, following a name that eluded him forever, following it down the stairs and through numberless corridors thinking: Bosch is right and all human habitations are but decaying growths, animal or vegetable, rotting, slowly rotting.

The woman came, and with her a light. Her shadow hung, huge and silent in the room, then went away.

Now everything was shadow, colourless, soundless, meaningless. The shadows joined hands and danced round his bed, silently, on the walls of the room.

The walls began to lean inwards, slowly, until there was no ceiling left, pressing in upon him, as the shadows danced, faster and faster, until they touched him, were part of him, were inside him.

'There isn't a man at the window,' said Maurice.

'There isn't a man dying upstairs,' said the Father.

It is never a nice thing to have someone dying in your own house, upstairs. On your head, so to speak.

'Everything is as it always was,' said the Father.

'I am glad to see that he has been given no water, said the Grandfather. 'Like that there is a chance that he will not spill it.'

They hung out the words on lines across the room.

'Nothing,' said the Mother, 'ever is or was, but thinking makes it so.'

'Ah, Shakespeare!' said the Father. 'He had an answer to everything.'

'Yes,' said the Uncle. 'He always killed his characters off-stage.'

'It's morbid, all this talk of death,' said the Mother.

'It has been clearly demonstrated,' said the Father, 'that Shakespeare was not: happy from 1593 to 1598; depressed from 1598 to 1608; serene from 1608 to 1613.'

'It has indeed,' said the Uncle. 'The laws governing the creation of immortal masterpieces are not to be over-simplified by a naïve psychology. We are wiser, if not older, than our fathers.'

'I would not say that of myself,' said the Mother.

'Children,' said the Uncle, 'are always wiser than their fathers.'

'That too modern psychology has taught us,' said the Father.

'Does it not seem to you suspicious,' said the Grandmother, 'that modern psychology, the child of nineteenth-century psychology, should insist that the child is wiser than the father?'

'Children have a habit of insisting,' said the Uncle.

'No,' said the Fathers. 'It is the fathers who insist.'

'We are talking of different fathers,' said the Grandmother. 'And different children.'

'But we always are,' said the Uncle.

'Is there a man upstairs?' asked Maurice. 'He says he's seen a man upstairs.'

'Why should there be a man upstairs?' asked the Mother.

'He says he saw him,' said Maurice.

'This man,' said the Uncle, 'is not Within, as our eminent novelist has told us, but upstairs, a little behind and above.'

'Do you mean God?' asked the Mother.

'No,' said the Uncle. 'I cannot believe God would peer from an upstairs window.'

'How you talk,' said the Father. 'One almost believes he exists.'

'Who?' asked the Uncle.

'The man,' said the Father.

'I thought you meant God,' said the Uncle.

'That is another question,' said the Father.

'Perhaps,' said the Uncle.

It was very quiet now, and he was no longer frightened of the dark. He wrapped it round him like a cloak and felt along the walls, moving cautiously until his fingers touched the cold door-handle. He felt the stair-carpet, rough and loose under his bare feet. His hand slid down the smooth surface of the banisters. His feet knew the number of the steps, and those which creaked, or groaned. He kept his eyes closed and moved silently down and down.

On the first landing, a cupboard. Here he had kept his marbles, in a tin box tied with string.

But there was no box, no trace of marbles in the empty cupboard.

He had forgotten the dining-room, but it came back to him

when he entered. The heavy chairs with the sagging upholstered seats, the oak table, the flowers in the window. He felt his life flowing into his body from the furniture, but he could not stay.

The gravel cut his feet, but on the side of the path the grass was cool and soft. The tree. Leaning flat against it with his arms outstretched, he could barely encircle half the trunk. It was a tree rarely known in its totality. One branch swung down to form a giant arm, parallel to the ground and only a few feet from it, with, at the elbow, a gentle bend. Nestling in the arm, he breathed with the tree.

He stood there for a long time. But there were other things to be done. Gravel under the feet again, then the dining-room, the stairs, the landing with the empty cupboard.

A door was open and he entered a room. It was dark but he knew who was there. He said: 'I have come to look at you but also to relieve you of your terror. Death alone of all things can only happen once and it does not help to anticipate it in the imagination, for while the actuality is never easy it is always bearable, the imagination on the other hand never encompasses the fact that death alone of all things can only happen once and it does not help to anticipate it in the imagination, for while the actuality is never easy –'

'Stop it!' shouted the woman. 'Don't talk like that.'

'But it is good to talk,' he said, 'And explain.'

'You mustn't talk like that,' she said again.

'I should like to explain it all to Maurice now,' he said. 'Because, really, it is quite simple.'

'Rest,' she said. 'Sleep. Don't talk.'

'But now I am feeling quite rested,' he said.

'Yes,' she agreed. 'That is true. You are looking quite rested now.'

This

– It was when I was walking down to the sea front.
– What time was that?
– In the middle of the day. Some time in the middle of the day. But Sunday, you know what it's like.
– It's like nothing. Sunday in England is like nothing.
– So there was nobody about much. The cold, perhaps, had something to do with it.
– Nobody down on the front?
– This was before the front. When you cross the main road you go through one of those large squares that open out to the sea. From the houses there you can see the sea. But not when you're walking.
– And it was there, in the square?
– I was walking down towards the front, not thinking of anything in particular or looking at anything in particular, and I must have looked up, perhaps there was a movement when he lifted the child –
– Lifted the child?
– When he lifted the child up to the window. To look out. It may have been some movement like that which made me look up, because I did look up, still without thinking of anything in particular, and saw the two of them framed in that window.
– Yes?
– At least framed gives the wrong impression. It suggests centrality. Whereas it was one of those huge windows you get in these Regency terraces and squares, and the two of them, the man and the child, occupied only the lower quarter of the window. They were looking out, each with a different expression on his face, but both with the expression of a human being looking at the world.
– A human being?
– Animals don't look at the world, do they? There is the

128

feeling that they exist in the world, and that is the end of it. That is why it is so upsetting to see an animal in pain. Because he seems unable to understand how something as alien as pain could have penetrated his world. But with a human being it is different. Most of the time people exist with their gaze averted. Not so much from each other as from the world. They don't want to see. Because it's painful or because there is just too much which they don't understand and would rather know nothing about. But sometimes they are taken off their guard, and then they look and it is as if the world filled their eyes and they could not have too much of it. This is what I meant when I said that they were looking out, the man and the child, with the expression of a human being looking at the world.

– I wonder if even now I understand.

– The man had grey hair and wild eyebrows. The child smiled and looked in a different direction. They only occupied the lower quarter of the window.

– And the rest?

– In the rest of the window, out of the opaque distance, the sky and parts of the square emerged. Branches. A formation of clouds. Roofs.

– And when you saw them, the man and the boy, you stopped?

– I am still there.

– You stopped?

– I cannot remember. There was not much more than one moment that I looked at them and caught the look in their eyes. He must have lifted up the child to see.

– Yes?

–

– You are thinking about it?

– I am thinking that it moved me because it was an image of ourselves, that their position, the pane of glass, and the walls, somehow reflected accurately the way each one of us relates to life, and that there is something unbearably pretentious in putting it like that.

– Perhaps, and yet...

– Do not misunderstand me. I am not saying that we are each one of us living in a glass cage or anything as sentimental as that. I am only trying to understand and help you to understand, why the image of them framed in that large ground-floor window, looking out, affected me as only the few really important things affect one. It is not just a matter of the glass, but of that in which it is set. Not only a frame, but a wall, the inner side of which is a part of a room, in which, as in every room, people are happy and grow old and feel fear. And remember that the pane not only divides, but brings together. We choose to live in houses, and not only to protect ourselves from the world. The pane allows me to relate to the world and the nearest thing to a window is perhaps language, which also separates in order to bring together.

    – As the three of you were brought together in that moment?

    – Though people are free to walk as they wish, I suppose, thinking their own thoughts, and especially on Sundays.

    – As the three of you were brought together in that moment?

    – I do not think that we were brought together. For they were not looking at me but at the world. And I was perhaps not only looking at them but at the reflections in the window.

    – The square. The clouds.

    – It was not a pure reflection, you understand. Because of the light on the window, because of the peculiar formation of the clouds, it was more like a reflection in smoked glass, more like the swaying of weeds at the bottom of the sea, when one is no longer sure which is the sky and which the water.

    – And you saw all that as you walked by?

    – There must have been a movement. Perhaps he lifted the child up to the window or himself only appeared at that moment, so that his appearance, framed there between those flower-like columns, coincided with mine, walking past.

    – Thinking, as you say, of nothing in particular.

    – The feel of the cool against the forehead. Is it my forehead, I wonder?

    – And not stopping even after you had seen, but taking it in all in a moment.

    – And what does 'my' mean in a context like this? Only that I am privileged to feel it.

    – But continuing your walk down to the sea front, though no part of that walk, either before or after, remains in your memory.

    – And then, by extension, only that I am privileged to look

out at the clouds the sea the square made emptier now by the presence in it of one human being, turning, holding up that object, a box, a camera, of course a camera.

– Though in itself you say there was nothing to distinguish this particular moment from any other, no thunder, no lightning, no manifestation of the Deity.

– David.

– Describe the window to me.

– Along either side, some five inches from the window, a narrow pilaster, fluted, running vertically, framing the frame, framing the man and the boy, framing the horizontal line of the sash above them, the trees and roofs emerging out of the smoky clouds.

– Did they smile when they saw you looking?

– Their eyes were fixed elsewhere, though the man and the child were not looking in quite the same direction.

– So that they failed to see you staring up at them from the pavement?

– I was not staring. They were only some fifteen feet away from me, and perhaps a yard or two above me. I turned away almost immediately. Perhaps if I had looked at them longer the image would not have remained so deeply etched.

– Perhaps, indeed.

– They were not father and son. I would guess there was a generation between them.

– And you sensed that in the one moment?

– David. Remembering it later. When I am gone. The cool of the pane against his forehead. Perhaps a moment for him too.

– Who knows?

– But what sort of moment? What does one mean by the word? And where is it, this moment, now? Perhaps they were posing, carefully settled into position by the photographer before he stepped outside to snap them?

– That too is possible.

– So that all our imaginings go for nothing.

– Not nothing.

– No?

– No. Because imaginings.

– Explain.

– Because imaginings, therefore something. A possibility realized. Like the other.

– The other?

– Your careful photographer, setting them in position. Smiling. Glancing back. Emerging. Examining them from the other side. Returning. Altering the line of an arm. The tilt of a chin. Emerging again. Signalling to them that all is well, that they are not to move. Taking his picture.

– A good picture.

– Yes. Since it has led to this.

– Just a small piece of paper on the table between us. And look at the imaginings to which it has given rise.

– A possibility realized. Like us.

– Us?

– You. And me.

– A possibility?

– It would be tedious to explain. Let me say only that the you who is here is only one of innumerable possibilities, and that goes for me as well. And the fact of our being here and talking in this way is of course itself only one possibility realized out of an infinite number.

– So that it could be that you would not have been here?

– Tortuously put, but there is that possibility.

– Or that I would not have been here.

– Indeed.

– Or the photograph.

– Or, as you say, the photograph.

– Because, perhaps, no photographer walked through the square.

– Or posed them with deliberation.

– Nobody walked through the square.

– Or looked out of a window.

– David, will you remember?

– And remember. What power has remember?

– Who can tell?

– Indeed, who can?

– And where then does it all belong, that picture so suggestively framed? What point in time does it occupy? And in space what point? Is it in my mind? Or in yours? And I mean: this, now.

Mobius the Stripper

a Topological Exercise

No one knew the origins and background of Mobius the stripper. 'I'm not English,' he would say, 'that's for certain.' His
language was an uneasy mixture of idioms and accents, jostling
each other as the words fell from his thick lips. He was always
ready to talk. To anyone who would listen. He had to explain.
It was a need.

'You see. What I do. My motive. Is not seshual. Is metaphysical. A metaphysical motive, see? I red Jennett. Prust.
Nitch. Those boys. All say the same. Is a metaphysical need.

I first heard of Mobius the stripper from a girl with big feet
called Jenny. She was one of those girls who make a point of
always knowing what's going on, and in those days she was
constantly coming up with bright and bizarre little items of
information in which she tried to interest me. Once she dragged
me to Ealing where, in the small and smoke-filled back room
of a dingy terrace, a fakir of sorts first turned a snake into a
rope, then climbed the rope and sat fanning himself with a
mauve silk handkerchief with his greasy hair just touching the
flaking ceiling, then redescended and turned the rope back into
a snake before finally returning the snake to the little leather
bag from which he had taken it. A cheap trick. Another time
she took me to Greenwich, where a friend of hers knew a man
who kept six seals in his bath-tub, but the man was gone or
dead or simply unwilling to answer her friend's urgent ring at
the doorbell. Most of all, though, Jenny's interest centred on
deviant sexuality, and she was forever urging me to go with
her to some dreary nightclub or 'ned of wice' as she liked to
call it, where men, women, children and monsters of every

To strip. To take off what society has put on me. What my
father and my mother have put on me. What my friends have
put on me. What I have put on me. And I say to me: What
are you Mobius? a man? a wooman? A vedge table? Are you
a stone, Mobius? This fat. You feel here. Here. Like it's folds
of fat, see. And it's me. Mobius. This the mystery. I want to
get right down behind this fat to the centre of me. And you
can help me. Yes you. Everybody. Everybody can help
Mobius. That the mystery. You and you and you and you.
You think you just helping yourself but you helping me. And
for why? Because in ultimate is not seshual. Is metaphysical.
Maybe religious.'

When Mobius spoke other people listened. He had presence.
Not just size or melancholy but presence. There was something
about the man that demanded attention and got it. No one
knew where he lived, not even the manager of the club in

---

description did their best to plug the gaps in creation which a
thoughtful Nature had benevolently provided for just such a
purpose. Usually I didn't respond to these invitations of
Jenny's, partly because her big feet embarrassed me (though
she was a likeable girl with some distinction as a lacrosse player
I believe), and partly because this kind of thing did not greatly
interest me anyway.

'But it *must* interest you,' Jenny would say. 'They're all part
of our world, aren't they?'

I agreed, but explained that not all parts of the world held
out an equal interest for me.

'I don't understand you,' she said. 'You say you want to be
a writer and then you *shut* your mind to experience. You simply
shut your mind to it. You live in an ivory bower.'

I accepted what she said. My mistake was ever to have told
her I wanted to be a writer. The rest I deserved.

'Did Shakespeare have your attitude?' Jenny said. 'Did
Leonardo?'

No, I had to admit. Shakespeare had not had my attitude.
Neither had Leonardo.

'Well then,' Jenny said.

Notting Hill, behind the tube station, where he stripped in public seven nights a week.

'You want to take Sundays off?' Tony the manager asked when he engaged him.

'Off?' Mobius said.

'We allow you one night a week,' the manager said. 'We treat our artists proper.'

'I doan understand,' Mobius said. 'You employ me or you doan employ me. There an end.'

'You have rights,' the manager said. 'We treat our artists proper here. We're not in the business to exploit them.'

'You not exploitin,' Mobius said. 'You doin me a favour. You payin me and givin me pleasure both.'

'All right,' the manager said. 'I'm easy.'

'You easy with me, I easy with you,' Mobius said. 'Okydoke?'

'You're on at six this evening then,' the manager said, getting up and opening the door of his little office.

Sometimes, at this point, I'd be sorry for Jenny, for her big feet and her fresh English face. Mobius. Mobius the stripper. I could just imagine him. His real name was Ted Binks. He had broad shoulders and a waist narrow as a girl's. When he walked he pranced and when he laughed he.

'Well then,' Jenny repeated, as if my admission made further discussion unnecessary. I sighed and said:

'All right. I'll come if you want me to. But if we're going to go all the way across London again only to find the door closed in our faces and the –'

'That only happened once,' Jenny said. 'I don't see why you have to bring it up like this every time. Anyway, it was you who wanted to see those seals. As soon as I told you about them you wanted to see them.'

'All right,' I said, resigned. 'All right.'

'It's yourself you're doing a favour to, not me,' Jenny would add at this point. 'You can't write without experience, and how the hell are you going to gain experience if you stay shut up in here all day long?'

Indeed, the girl had a point. She wasn't strictly accurate,

Mobius wanted to kiss him but the manager, a young man
with a diamond tiepin, hastily stepped back behind his desk.
When the door shut behind Mobius he slumped back in his
chair, buried his head in his hands, and burst into tears. Nor
was he ever afterwards able to account for this uncharacteristic
gesture or forget it, hard as he tried.

Mobius arrived at five that afternoon and every subsequent
afternoon as well. 'You need concentration,' he would say. 'A
good stripper needs to get in the right mood. Is like Yoga. All
matter of concentration.'

'Yes,' the manager would say. 'Yes. Of course. Of course.'

'With me,' Mobius explained to him, 'is not seshual, is
metaphysical. A metaphysical motive. Not like the rest of this
garbage.'

But they didn't mind him saying that. Everybody liked
Mobius except Tony the manager. The girls liked him best.
'Hi Moby,' they shouted. 'How's your dick?'

---

since my mornings were spent delivering laundry for NU-nap,
the new nappy service ('We clean dirt' they modestly informed
the world in violet letters on their cream van – I used to wake
up whispering that phrase to myself, at times it seemed to be
the most beautiful combination of the most beautiful words
in the language), and my evenings kicking the leaves in the
park as I watched the world go by. But not quite inaccurate
either, since I recognized within myself a strong urge towards
seclusion, a shutting out of the world and its too urgent claims,
Jenny included. And not just the world. The past too I would
have liked to banish from my consciousness at times, and with
it all the books I had ever read. As I bent over my desk in the
afternoons, staring at the virgin paper, I would wish fervently,
pray desperately to whatever deity would answer my prayers,
that all the print which had ever been conveyed by my eyes to
my brain and thence buried deep inside me where it remained
to fester could be removed by a sharp painless and efficient
knife. Not that I felt history to be a nightmare from which I
wanted to awake etcetera etcetera, but simply that I felt the
little self I once possessed to be dangerously threatened by

'Is keeping up,' he would reply. 'How's yours?'

They wanted to know about his private life but he gave nothing away. 'We're always telling you about our problems,' they complained. 'Why don't you ever tell us about yours?'

'I doan have problems,' Mobius said.

'Come off it,' they said, laughing. 'Everyone's got problems.'

'You have problems?' he asked them, surprised.

'Would we be in this lousy joint if we didn't?'

'Problems, problems,' Mobius said. 'Is human invention, problems.'

But they felt melancholy in the late afternoons. far from their families, and in the early hours of the morning when the public had all departed. 'Where do you live?' they asked him. 'Do you have a man or a woman? Do you have any children, Moby?'

---

the size and the *assurance* of all the great men who had come before me. There they were, solid, smiling, melancholy or grim as the case might be, Virgil and Dante and Descartes and Wordsworth and Joyce, lodged inside me, each telling me the truth – and who could doubt it was the truth, their very lives bore witness to the fact – but was it *my* truth, that was the question. And behind that, of course, another question and another: Was I entitled to a truth of my own at all, and if so, was it not precisely by following Jenny out into the cold streets of Richmond or Bermondsey or Highgate that I should find it?

At other times I'd catch myself before I spoke and, furious at the degree of condescension involved in feeling sorry for Jenny – who was I to feel sorry for anyone? – would say to her instead: 'Fuck off. I want to work.'

'Work later.'

'No. I've got to work now.'

'It's good for your work. You can't create out of your own entrails.'

'There are always excuses. It's always either too early or too late.'

'You want to be another of those people who churn out

To all these questions he replied with the same kindly smile, but once when he caught one of them tailing him after a show he came back and hit her across the face with his glove so that none of them ever tried anything like that again.

'I doan ask you you doan ask me,' he said to them after the incident. 'I have no secrets but my life is my own business.' And when Tony came to have a talk with him about the girl's disfigured cheek he just closed his eyes and didn't answer.

'If it happens again you're out,' Tony said, but although he would, in his heart of hearts, have been relieved had this in fact occurred, they both of them knew it was just talk. For Mobius was a gold mine. He really drew them in.

Alone in his little room, not many streets away from the club, he sat on the edge of the bed and stuffed himself sick on bananas. 'Meat is meat,' he would say. 'I'm no cannibal.' Bananas he ate by the hundredweight, sitting with bowed

---

tepid trivia because it's the thing to be a writer? Why not forget that bit and live a little for a change?'

Dear Jenny. Despite her big feet – no, no, because of them – she never let go. She knew I'd give way in the end and if she'd come to me with the news in the first place it was only because she hadn't found anyone else to take her anyway. Jenny had a nose for the peculiar, but she was an old-fashioned girl at heart and felt the need of an escort wherever she went.

'Look,' I said to her. 'I don't want to live. I want to be left in peace to work.'

'But this guy,' she said. 'The rolls of fat on him. It's fantastic. And the serenity. My God. You should see the serenity in his eyes when he strips.'

'Serenity?' I said. 'What are you talking about?'

'It's like a Buddha or something,' Jenny said.

'What are you trying to do to me?' I said.

'Am I one of those people who fall for Zen and Yoga and all the rest of that Eastern crap?' Jenny said.

I had to admit she wasn't.

'I'm telling you,' she said. 'It's a great experience.'

'Another time,' I said.

shoulders and sagging folds of fat on the narrow unmade bed, staring at the blank wall.

Those were good hours, the hours spent staring at the wall, waiting for four o'clock. Not as good as the hours after four, but good hours all the same. For what harm was he doing? If you don't pick a banana when it's ripe it rots, so again, what harm was he doing? Who was he hurting?

Sometimes the voices started and he sat back and listened to them with pride. 'Who's talking of Mobius?' he would say. 'I tell you, everybody's talking of Mobius. When I walk I hear them. When I sleep I hear them. When I sit in my room I hear them. Mobius the stripper. The best in the business. I've seen many strippers in my time but there's none to beat Mobius. I first met Mobius. I first saw Mobius. I first heard of Mobius. A friend of mine. A cousin. A duchess, the Duchess of Folkestone.

Cheltenham hadn't prepared her for this. Her eyes popped.

'Another time,' I said again.

'You mean – you're not going to come?'

'Another time,' I said.

'Wow!' Jenny said. 'Something must be happening to you. Are you in love or something?'

'I just want to work,' I said.

'You always say that,' Jenny said, suddenly deflated.

'I'm sorry,' I said, and I was. Desperately. What sort of luck is it to be born with big feet? 'Another time,' I said. 'O.K.?'

'You don't know what you're missing,' Jenny said.

True enough, but I could guess. Mobius the stripper, six foot eight and round as a barrel: 'That time Primo Carnera was chewing my big toe off, I couldn't get a proper grip on the slimy bastard so I grope around and he's chewing my toe like it'll come off any minute and then I find I've got my finger up his nostril and.' Yes. Very good. He was another one I could do without.

After Jenny had gone I stared at the virgin sheet of paper on the table in front of me. When I did that I always wanted to scream. And when I left it there and got out, anywhere, just out, away from it all, then all I ever wanted to do was get

We had been childhood friends. I remember her remarking that Mobius the stripper was the most amazing man she ever knew. I hear them all. But what do I care? That too must be stripped off.' Give him the choice and he preferred the beautiful silence. The peace of stripping. But if they came he accepted them. They did him no harm.

He flicked another skin into the metal waste-paper basket and bit into another banana. When it was gone he would feel in the corners, between the molars, with his tongue, and sigh with contentment. How many doctors, wise men, had told him to pack it in, to have a change of diet and start a new life? But then how many doctors had told him he was too fat, needed to take more exercise, had bad teeth, incipient arthritis, a weak heart, bad circulation, bronchitis, pneumonia, traces of malarial fever, smallpox? He was a man, a mound of flesh, heir to all that flesh is heir to. Mobius sighed and rubbed the folds of

---

back and start writing. Crazy. In those days I had a recurrent nightmare. I was in my shorts, playing rugger in the mud against the giants. Proust, languid and bemonocled, kept guard behind the pack; Joyce, small and fiery, his moustache in perfect trim, darted through their legs, whisking out the ball and sending it flying to the wings: Dostoyevsky, manic and bearded; Swift, ferocious and unstoppable; Chaucer going like a terrier. And the pack, the pack itself, Tolstoy and Hugo and Homer and Goethe, Lawrence and Pascal and Milton and Descartes. Bearing down on me. Huge. Powerful. Totally confident. The ball kept coming out at me on the wing. It was a parcel of nappies neatly wrapped in plastic, 'We clean dirt' in violet lettering across it. I always seemed to be out there by myself, there was never anyone else on my side, but the ball would keep coming out of the loose at me. It always began like that, with the ball flying through the grey air towards my outstretched arms and then the pack bearing down, boots pounding the turf as in desperation I swung further and further out, knowing all the time that I would never be able to make it into touch or have the nerve to steady and kick ahead. There was just me and this ball that was a parcel of nappies and all

his stomach happily. It was a miracle he had survived this long when you thought of all the things that could have happened to him. And if so long then why not longer? 'Time,' he would say, 'she mean nothing to me. You see this? This fat? My body she my clock. When I die she stop.' And after all he had no need of clocks, there was a church the other side of the street and it sounded for him especially for him, a particular peal, at four o'clock. Then he would get up and make the bed ('You got to have order. Disorder in the little thing and that's the beginning of the end'), wash his teeth and get his things together. No one had ever known him to get to the club after five ('You need time to meditate if you do a show like mine. Is like Yoga, all meditation').

When Tony the manager took his annual holiday in the Bermudas he locked up the place and carried the keys away with him. Mobius, a stickler for routine and with a metaphysical need to satisfy, still got up at four, made his bed, emptied the

---

of them coming at me. Descartes in particular obsessed me. I would wake up sweating and wondering how it was possible to be so sure and yet so wrong. And why did they all have to keep coming for me like that, with Proust always drifting nonchalantly behind them, hair gleaming, boots polished, never in any hurry but always blocking my path? What harm had I done any of them except read them? And now I wanted to forget them. Couldn't I be allowed to do that in peace? You don't think of it when you look at a tempting spine in a library or bookshop, but once you touch it you've had it. You're involved. It's worse than a woman. It's there in your body till the day you die and the harder you try and forget it the clearer it gets.

I tried aphorisms:

'If a typewriter could read what it had written it would sue God.'

'He is another.'

'The trouble with the biological clock is it has no alarm.'

No good. They weren't even good enough to fit end to end and send in as a poem to the *TLS*. In the streets Rilke walked

banana skins into the communal dustbin in the back yard, cleaned his teeth, packed his things, and went on down to the club. He rattled on the door and even tried to push it open with his shoulder, but it wouldn't give and he wasn't one to be put off by a thing like that. 'I got my rights, same as you,' he said to the policeman who took him in. 'Nobody going to shut a door in my face and get away with it.'

'That's no reason to knock it down,' the policeman said, staring in wonder at Mobius.

'I got my rights,' Mobius said.

'You mean they don't pay you?' the policeman asked.

'Sure they pay me,' Mobius said.

'I mean in the holidays.'

'Sure,' Mobius said.

'Well then,' the policeman said.

'I got my rights,' Mobius said. 'He employ me, no?'

---

beside me and whispered in my ear. He said beautiful things but I preferred whatever nonsense I might have thought up for myself if he hadn't been there. In the mornings I drove my cream van through the suburbs of west London and that kept me sane. I screamed to a halt, leapt out with my neat parcel of clean nappies, swapped it for the dirty ones waiting on the doorstep in the identical plastic wrapper, 'We clean dirt' in violet lettering. 'Like hell you do,' said a note pinned to the wrapper once. 'Take it back and try again.'

I took it back. They weren't my babies or my nappies and I didn't give a damn but my life was sliding off the rails and I didn't know what in God's good name to do about it.

'Why don't you come and see Mobius the stripper?' Jenny said. 'It'll change your ideas. Give it a break and you'll all of a sudden see the light.'

'That's fine,' I said, 'except I've been saying just that for the last fifteen years and I'm still in the dark.'

'That's because you don't trust,' Jenny said. 'You've got no faith.'

I had to admit she might be right. Unto those who have etcetera etcetera. But how does one contrive to have in the

'If it's a holiday why not go away somewhere?' the police-man said. 'Give yourself a break.'

'I doan want a break,' Mobius said. 'I want my rights.'

'I don't know about that,' the policeman said. 'You've com-mitted an offence against the law. I'm afraid I'll have to book you for it.'

'You doan understand,' Mobius said to the policeman. 'This is my life. Just because he want to go to the fucking Bermudas doan mean I got to have my life ruined, eh?'

'Are you American or something?' the policeman asked, intrigued.

'You want to see my British passport?' Mobius said.

'Stay at home,' the policeman advised him. 'Take it easy for a few days. We'll look into the matter when the manager returns.'

The next time Tony took his holiday he gave Mobius the key of the club, but without the audience it wasn't the same,

---

first place? There was a flaw somewhere but who was I to spot it?

'All right,' Jenny said. 'Make an effort. Anybody can write *something*. Just put something down and then you'll feel better and you can come out with me.'

Something. Mobius the stripper was a genial man when in the bosom of his family. Etcetera. Etcetera etcetera. 'Oh fuck off,' I said. 'I told you I didn't want to be disturbed.'

'It'll do you good,' she said, standing her ground. The worse the language I used the more she responded. She had a lot of background to make up for. 'Besides,' she said, 'it's all good experience.'

'I don't need experience,' I said. 'I need peace and quiet. And, if I'm lucky, a bit of inspiration.'

'He'd give you that,' Jenny said. 'Just to look at him is to feel inspired.'

'What do you mean just to look at him?' I said. 'What else are we expected to do?'

'Go to hell,' Jenny said.

'Tomorrow,' I said.

and after a day or two he just stayed in his room the whole time except for the occasional stroll down to the park and back, heavily protected by his big coat and Russian fur hat. But he wasn't used to the streets, especially in the early evening when the tubes disgorged their contents, and it did him no good, no good at all. Inside the room he felt happier, but the break in the routine stopped him going to sleep and he spent the night with the light switched on. The bulb swung in the breeze and the voices dissolved him into a hundred parts. I first saw Mobius at a club in Buda. In Rio. In Albuquerque. A fine guy, Mobius. Is he? Oh yes, a fine guy. I remember going to see him and. I first heard of Mobius the stripper from a kid down on the front in Marseilles. From a girl in Vienna. She was over there on a scholarship to study the cello and she. I met her in a restaurant. In a bar. She was blonde. Dark. A sort of dark skin. Long fingers. A cellist's fingers. There's nobody like Mobius, she said.

'You said that yesterday.'

'Nevertheless,' I said. 'Tomorrow.'

Jenny began to sob. It was impressive. I was impressed. 'Just because I have big feet,' she said, 'you think you can push me around like that.'

'Jenny,' I said. 'Please. I like big feet.'

'You don't,' she sobbed. 'You find them ridiculous.' When she sobbed she really sobbed. Nothing could stem the tide.

'In men,' I said. 'I find them ridiculous in men. In women I find them a sign of solidity. Stability.'

'You're just laughing at me,' she said. 'You despise me because of my big feet.'

M.E. the foot fetishist. He was a quiet man, scholarly and abstemious. Everyone who ever met him said he was almost a saint. Not quite but almost. Yet deep inside there throbbed etcetera etcetera.

'But I don't,' I said. 'You've no idea what I feel about feet. I can't have enough of them. That's just what I like about you, Jenny. Your big feet.'

She stopped crying. Just like that. 'You're despicable,' she said. 'You're obscene.'

Mobius smiled and listened to the voices. They came and
went inside his head and if that's where they liked to be he
had no objection. There was room and more. But he missed
his sleep and he knew bronzed Tony had a point when he said:
'Mobius, you look a sight.'

That was the day the club re-opened. 'Why don't you take
a holiday same as everyone?' Tony said. 'You must have a tidy
bit stacked away by now.'

'A holiday from what?' Mobius asked him.

'I don't know,' Tony said. Mobius upset him, he didn't
know which way to take him. Maybe one of these days he'd
cease to pull them in and then he could get rid of him. 'Just a
holiday,' he said. 'From work.'

'Look,' Mobius said to him. 'That the difference between
us, Tony. You work and you spit on your work. But for me
my work is my life.'

'Look Jenny,' I said. 'I'll come with you. I'd love to see this
chap. But tomorrow, O.K.?'

An incredible girl, Jenny. A great tactician. 'You promise?'
she said before I had time to draw breath.

'You know I'd love to go,' I said. 'I just don't want to be a
drag on you. And if I'm sitting there thinking of my work all
the time instead of being convivial and all I –'

'You'll see,' Jenny said. 'You'll love him. He's a lovely man.'

Lovely or not I didn't think I could face them, either Jenny
or her stripper, so I locked the door and went out into the
park. Walking around there and kicking my feet in the leaves
and seeing all those nannies and things kept the rest of it at
bay. Had Rilke seen this nanny? Or Proust that child? Had
Hopkins seen this tree, this leaf? So what did they have to
teach me? They were talking about something else altogether.
They were just about as much use to me as I was to them. And
if it's eternity they wanted, why pick on me? There are plenty
of other fools around for them to try their vampire tricks on.
I can do without them, thank you very much. And if it's this
tree I want to see they only get in the way. And if it isn't what
use am I to myself? Their trees they've already seen.

'O.K.,' Tony said. 'I'm not complaining.'

'Is there a holiday from life?' Mobius asked him. 'Answer me that, Tony.'

'For God's sake!' Tony said. 'Can't you talk straight ever? You're not on stage now you know.'

'You just answer me first,' Mobius said. 'Is there a holiday from life, Tony?'

'I don't know what you're talking about,' Tony said, and when Mobius began to laugh, his great belly heaving, he added under his breath: 'You shit.'

At home he said to his wife: 'That guy Mobius. He's a nut.'

'Is he still drawing them in?' his wife asked as she passed him the toast.

'I don't know what they see in him,' Tony said. 'A fat bloody foreigner stripping in public. Downright obscene it is. And they roll in to see him. It makes you despair of the British public.'

After a while, though, I felt the urge to get back in there and sit down in front of that blasted sheet of white paper. What use is this tree even if I do see it? No use to me or to the world. And even if it is, who says I *can* see it? When I sit down in front of that sheet of paper I have this feeling I want to tear right in and get everything down. Everything. And then what happens? He was a small man with a. I remember once asking Charles and. Gerald looked round. Christopher turned. When Jill saw. When Robert saw. Elizabeth Nutely was. Geraldine Bluett was. Hilary McPherson wasn't exactly the. Everything is the enemy of something, and when my pen touches the paper I go blank. Stories. Stories and stories. Mobius the stripper sat in his penthouse flat and filed his nails. Sat in his bare room and picked his nose. Stories and stories. Anyone can write them. All you need is a hide thick enough to save you from boring yourself sick. Jack turned suddenly and said. Count Frederick Prokovsky, a veteran of the Crimea. Horst Voss, the rowing coach. Peter Bender, overseer of a rubber plantation in. Etcetera etcetera. This one and this one and this one. When all the time it's crying out in me (Henry James was much

'Try the blackcurrant jam,' his wife said. And then: 'You hired him. You couldn't go on enough about him at first.'

'It makes you sick,' Tony said. He pulled the jam towards him. 'Bloody perverted they are,' he said. 'Bloody twisted.'

But when Mobius said it wasn't sexual it was metaphysical he had a point. Take off the layers and get down to the basics. One day the flesh would go and then the really basic would come to light. Mobius waited patiently for that day.

'You reed Prust,' he would say. 'Nitch. Jennett. Those boys. See what they say. All the same. They know the truth. Is all a matter of stripping.'

'You talk too much Moby,' the girls said to him. 'You're driving us crazy with all your talk.'

'You gotta talk when you strip,' Mobius explained to them. 'You gotta get the audience involved.'

'You can have music,' the girls said. 'Music's nice. Whoever heard of a stripper talking?'

---

obsessed by this but there the similarity between us ends, Good-bye, Henry James, good-bye Virginia Woolf, good-bye, good-bye) crying out in me to say *everything, everything*.

They keep peacocks in the park. I don't know why. But they do. One of them was strutting about in the path in front of me. With big feet like Jenny. Who was I to say if big feet are attractive or not? And why ask me anyway? Think of the stripper Mobius with his nightly ritual, slowly getting down to the primal scene and after that what? Why do men do things like that and do they even know themselves etcetera etcetera? All the stories in the world but you've only got one body and who would ever exchange the former for the latter except every single second-rate writer who's ever lived? And they still live. Proliferate. And believe in themselves, what's more. Why then the daily anguish and the certainty that if I could only start the pen moving over that sheet of paper my life would alter, alter, as they say, beyond the bounds of recognition? Because I've read them all? The Van Gogh letters and the life of Rimbaud and the Hopkins Notebooks and the N. of M.L.B. Have they conned me even into this? It was possible. Everything is

'O.K.' Mobius admitted. 'Perhaps I do like to talk. Like that I talk I feel my essential self emerging. Filling the room.'

Outside the club, though, Mobius rarely opened his mouth. Certainly he never spoke to himself, and as for the voices, if they wanted to settle for a while inside his head, who was he to order them away? He sat on the bed and stared at the wall, eating bananas and dozing. I first saw. I first heard. I remember His Excellency telling me about Mobius the stripper. In Prague it was, that wonderful city. I was acting as private secretary to the Duke and had time on my hands. I was down and out in Paris and London. A girl called Bertha Pappenheim first mentioned Mobius to me. Not the famous Bertha Pappenheim, another.

Once or twice he would pull a chair up to the mirror on the dressing-table which stood inevitably in the bay window, and

---

possible. 'Tell me the truth,' I said to the peacock with the big feet. 'Go on, you bastard. Tell me the truth or just fuck off.'

A woman with an unpleasant little runt of a white poodle backed away down an alley. 'Don't you want the truth?' I asked her. She turned and beetled off towards the gates. 'Lady!' I shouted after her. 'Don't you want the truth?'

It's always the same. That's what gets me down. If I can say *anything* then why say anything? And yet everything's there to be said. Round and round. Mobius sat on his bed and ate one banana after another. But did he? Did he?

The bird had gone and I sat down on a bench and looked up at the sky through the trees. Jenny would have been and gone by now. Or perhaps not been at all. I sometimes wondered if Jenny knew quite as many people as she said she did. Wondered if perhaps there was only me she knew in the whole of London. Otherwise how to explain her persistence? Unless those feet of hers kept perpetually carrying her back over the ground they had once trodden. Myth. Ritual. An idea. More than an idea. A metaphor for life. 'It is!' I shouted, suddenly understanding. 'It is! It is! A metaphor for life!'

A little group of people was standing under the trees some way along the path. One or two park wardens. A fat man with

stare and stare into his own grey eyes. Then he would push
the chair violently back and go over to the bed again.

'For what is life?' he would say. 'Chance. And what is *my*
life? The result of a million and one chances. But behind chance
is truth. The whole problem is to get behind chance to the
TRUTH!' That was when the jock strap came off and it brought
the house down. But Mobius hadn't finished with them. Sitting
cross-legged on the little wooden stage, staring down at more
than his navel, he let them have the facts of life, straight from
the chest:

'Beyond a man's chance is his necessity. But how many find?
I ask you. You think this is seshual thing, but for why you
come to see me? Because I give you the truth. Is a metaphysical
something, is the truth. Is the necessity behind the chance.
For each man is only one truth and so many in the world as
each man is truths.'

Mobius, staring into his own grey eyes in the little room in

---

one of those Russian fur hats. My friend the poodle woman.
I waved to them politely. They seemed to expect it. One of
the wardens stepped forward and asked politely why I was
chasing the peacocks and using bad language. The man was
preposterous. Couldn't he see me sitting silent on the bench?
I'd chased Pascal down a back alley once, but peacocks? What
am I to peacocks or they to me? I asked the man.

'I saw you,' the poodle woman said. 'Chasin and abusin.'

'Don't be more absurd than you can help,' I said to her.

'Don't you dare talk to me like that, young man,' she said.

What would Descartes have done in my place?

'Chasin peacocks and usin abusin language,' she said.

'Are you going to stand there and listen to this woman's
grotesque accusations?' I asked them.

'It is an offence under the regulations,' the warden said, 'to
chase the peacocks.'

'But I love those birds,' I said. 'I love their big feet.' For
some reason I was still sitting there on that bench and they
were standing grouped together under the trees staring in my
direction. 'What would I want to go chasing them for?' I said.

Notting Hill, occasionally sighed, and his gaze would wander
over the expanse of flesh exposed and exposable. Sometimes
his right hand would hover over the drawer of his dressing-
table, where certain private possessions were kept, but would
as quickly move away again. That was too easy. Yet if you
talk of necessity how many versions are there? His hand
hovered but the drawer remained unopened.

'These girls,' he would say, 'they excite you seshually. But
once you seen me your whole life is change.' He had a way of
riding the laughter, silencing it. 'For why? For you learn from
me the difference between on one hand clockwork and on
other hand necessity. Clockwork is clockwork. One. Two.
In. Out. But Necessity she a goddess. She turn your muscles
to water and your bones to oil. One day you meet her and
you will see that Mobius is right.'

He went home after that session more slowly than usual. If
he was going to give them the truth where was his truth? His
heart heavy with the weight of years he opened the drawer and

---

How could they be expected to understand? Or, understanding, to believe? Had I a beard like Tolstoy's? A moustache like
Rilke's? 'Gentlemen,' I said. 'I apologize. Good evening.'

'He's going away,' the woman said. 'You can't let him go
away like that. He insulted and abused me.'

'In that case, madam,' the warden said, 'I suggest you consult
a lawyer.' Bless his silver tongue. The first thing I'm going to
do when success comes my way is give a donation to the wardens of the London parks.

I was shaken, though. And who wouldn't be? Examples of
prejudice are always upsetting. Upsetting but exhilarating, too.
They make you want to fight back. Something had happened
down there inside me in those few minutes and now I couldn't
wait to get back. This was it. After all those years.

There was no message from Jenny on the door. Not even a
single word like 'Bastard!' or 'Fuck you!' or any of the other
affectionate little words we use when we are sufficiently inti-
mate with a person. Well fuck her. I could do without her.
Without them all. I was sitting at my desk with this white

took out his little friend. Cupping it in his hand he felt its weight. There was no hesitation in his movements now and why should there be? If his life had a logic then this was it. The weight on his heart pressed him to this point. When you have stripped away everything the answer will be there, but if so, why wait? Easy to say it's too easy but why easier than waiting? As always, he did everything methodically. When he had found the right spot on his temple he straightened a little and waited for the steel to gather a little warmth from his flesh. 'So I come to myself at last,' Mobius said. 'To the centre of myself.' And he said: 'Is my necessity and my truth. And is example to all.' He stared into his own grey eyes and felt the coldness of the metal. His finger tightened on the trigger and the voices were there again. Cocking his head on one side and smiling, Mobius listened to what they had to say. He had time on his hands and to spare. Resting the barrel against his brow

---

sheet of paper in front of me and suddenly it was easy. I bent over it, pen poised, wrist relaxed, the classic posture. It was all suddenly so easy I couldn't understand what had kept me back for so long.

I looked at the white page. At the pen. At my wrist. I began to laugh. You have to laugh at moments like that. It's the only thing to do. When I had finished laughing I got up and went to the window. What I couldn't work out was if I had actually believed it or really known all along that today was going to be no different from any other day. That between everything and something would once again fall the shadow. Leaving me with nothing. Nothing.

I turned round and sat down at the desk again. At least if Jenny had been there it wouldn't have been so bad. We could have talked. I looked at my watch. There was still time. She might still come.

I picked up the pen and wrote my name across the top of the sheet, for no reason that I could fathom. And then, suddenly, out of the blue it started to come. Perhaps it was only one story, arbitrary, incomplete, but suddenly I knew that it would make its own necessity and in the process give me back

and smiling to himself in the mirror as the bulb swung in the
breeze over his head, Mobius waited for them to finish.

---

my lost self. Dear Jenny. Dear Mobius. Dear Peacock. 'Gone
out. Do not disturb.' I scrawled on a sheet of paper, pinned
it to the door and locked it. Then I sat down and began to write.

3

Dreams of Mrs Fraser

MRS FRASER
JOHN REDBOLD

The play clearly owes much to Sidney Nolan's paintings of the Mrs Fraser story. The contemporary ballads of which I make some use can be conveniently found in Michael Alexander's *Mrs Fraser on the Fatal Shore* (Michael Joseph, 1971). In my attempts at *bricollage* I have lifted several lengthy passages from Claude Lévy-Strauss's *Totemism*, in the translation by Rodney Needham, published by The Merlin Press.

The stage is divided into two roughly equal areas, each with a set of its own. Set A: a large gilded cage. Set B: a table, two chairs, a bed with feather quilt. When one is lit the other should be in total darkness.

There are two characters plus a tape. The auditorium should be wired so that the voice on tape is whispering in the audience's ears rather than coming at it from the stage area. When Mrs Fraser is in the cage she is naked, showing tattoos; when in set B she is clothed in a long loose gown. (If it is difficult for the same actress to move from one set to the other at the speed required by the play, two actresses should be employed.)

There are 30 scenes, to be played without a break, the pauses between them to be of equal length.

1

(*Blackout.* MRS F's *voice, very low, on tape:*)

MRS FRASER: Not... again.

2

(Sound of toy drum being beaten, military style. Lights come up to reveal set A. MRS F., *naked and tattooed, stands in the cage. Outside, beside the cage,* REDBOLD, *in bright costume, somewhere between nineteenth-century military uniform and Pierrot's dress. He is beating the drum.)*

REDBOLD: Roll up! Roll up! Come and see the tattooed lady! Come and see the tattooed lady! Roll up! Roll up! Only sixpence! Sixpence to see the tattooed lady! Come and hear in her own words the incredible story of her amazing adventures among the man-eating natives of the Australian jungle! Roll up! Roll up! Only sixpence to see the tattooed lady! *(Silence. He looks round. Silence. A roll on the drums. He announces:)* Mrs Fraser!

MRS FRASER: *(She stands upright in the cage, staring straight ahead of her, silent.)*

(BLACKOUT)

3

(As in 2)

REDBOLD: – the tattooed lady! Come and hear in her own incredible words the horrib story of her adventures among the man-eating natives of the Australian jungle! Roll up! Roll up! Come and hear the last survivor of the *Stirling Castle* tell her amazing story in her very own words! *(Silence. He looks round. Silence. A roll on the drums. He announces:)* Mrs Fraser!

MRS FRASER: *(She stands upright in the cage, staring straight ahead of her, silent.)*

(BLACKOUT)

4

(As in 3)

REDBOLD: *(A roll on the drums. He announces:)* Mrs Fraser!

MRS FRASER: *(Without intonation:)* We were two days out to sea bound for Singapore from Sydney on the *Stirling Castle* when we struck a reef and had to abandon ship. We were in the long-boat twenty-seven days. *(Silence. She shouts suddenly:)* The baby! The baby!

(BLACKOUT)

5

(Set B. MRS F., *fully dressed, lying on the bed.* REDBOLD *sitting at the table, drinking.)*

REDBOLD: *(Wheedling:)* I'm a John too you know. *(Silence. He drinks.)* I'm a John too you know. *(Silence. He looks round at her.)* Do you want a drink? *(Silence. He ponders. Then pours her a drink and brings it to her. Tenderly:)* Here, Eliza, it'll do you good.

MRS FRASER: *(She begins to laugh, not moving. He stands helplessly.)*

(BLACKOUT)

6

(Blackout. Tape.)

REDBOLD: Here, it'll do you good. *(Speeding to a gabble:)* Good good good good good good good.

7

(Set A. MRS F. *upright in cage.* REDBOLD *to left of cage.)*

MRS FRASER: The forests were so large. They covered the world. The trees. The swamps. We fell in the swamps. Under the trees, in the darkness under the trees. We fell in the swamps. I saw the stripes. Convict clothes. I saw the stripes in the water. We lay in the water. The mud. *(Pause)* The mud.

(BLACKOUT)

8

(Same as 7)

MRS FRASER: I laughed at him. Convict clothes. I laughed. *(She is silent.)*

REDBOLD: *(Beating drum, trying to generate enthusiasm:)* Roll up! Roll up! Only sixpence to see the extraordinary Mrs Fraser, the naked tattooed lady! The only survivor of the *Stirling Castle*! *(He sings:)*

> Ye mariners and landsmen all
> Pray list while I relate
> The wreck of the *Stirling Castle*
> And the crew's sad dismal fate!

(He hands a flute to MRS F, who now accompanies him:)

> The *Stirling Castle* on May 16th,
> From Sydney she did sail,
> The crew consisting of twenty
> With a sweet and pleasant gale.
>
> Likewise Captain Fraser of the ship,
> On board he had his wife,
> And now, how dreadful for to tell,
> The sacrifice of human life.
>
> Part of the crew got in one boat,
> Thinking their lives to save,
> But in a moment they were dashed
> Beneath the foaming waves.
>
> And Mrs Fraser in another boat
> Far advanced in pregnant state,
> Gave birth unto a lovely babe,
> How shocking to relate!
>
> And when they reached the fatal shore,
> Its name is called Wide Bay,
> The savages soon them espied,
> Rushed down and seized their prey,

And bore the victims in the boat
Unto their savage den;
To describe the feelings of those poor souls
Is past the art of man.

This female still was doomed to see,
A deed more dark and drear,
Her husband pierced was to the heart,
By savage with his spear.

She flew unto his dying frame,
And the spear she did pull out,
And like a frantic maniac
Distracted flew about.

The chief mate too they did despatch,
By cutting off his head,
And placed on one of their own canoes,
All for a figure head.

Also a fine young man they bound,
And burnt without a dread,
With a slow fire at his feet at first,
So up unto his head.

MRS FRASER:
When you read the tortures I went through,
'Twill grieve your hearts full sore,
But now thank Heaven I am returned
Unto my native shore.

I always shall remember,
And my prayers will ever be,
For the safety of both age and sex,
Who sail on the raging sea!
(She is silent, staring straight ahead of her.)

(BLACKOUT)

9.

(Set B. MRS F. *and* REDBOLD *at the table.)*

REDBOLD: Please. Please tell me.

MRS FRASER: *(She looks at him without speaking.)*

REDBOLD: Please. Go on. Please.

MRS FRASER: *(After a silence:)* So small. A bundle. They took it from me and threw it in the sea.

REDBOLD: Go on. Go on. And then? After that? In the jungle? Creeping away into the jungle?

MRS FRASER: *(She looks at him blindly.)*

REDBOLD: *(Getting up, miming it playfully, but anxious underneath:)* The Captain, stiff in his blanket, snoring up to heaven. The stars shining down on forest and beach. And Eliza, my little Eliza, creeping away. Into the jungle. Creeping towards the warmth of another fire.

MRS FRASER: Leave me alone!

REDBOLD: So, in the night, when all were asleep, you crept away, into the forest. *(He smiles.)* Towards another warmth.

MRS FRASER: *(Violently:)* It wasn't warm!

REDBOLD: And the marks?

MRS FRASER: *(She stares at him. He stares back.)*

(BLACKOUT)

10

(Blackout. Tape. The voice of Bracefell:)

BRACEFELL: Is that a promise? Promise? Promise?

11

(Set A. MRS F. *in cage.* REDBOLD *beside it.)*

MRS FRASER: Look at me, ladies and gentlemen? Look at the marks. Do you know what they are? Tattoos. Tattoos imprinted on my flesh by the horrib savages! Look. Here. And here. And here. *(Pause)* They marked my body.

REDBOLD: *(Putting on Eagle mask:)* She became a member of the Eagle clan. *(He hops about stage with mask on.)*

MRS FRASER: They marked my body. I belonged to the earth. I became a member of the Eagle clan.

REDBOLD: *(With mask:)* The term totemism covers relations, posed ideologically, between two series, one *natural*, the other *cultural*. The natural series comprises on the one hand *categories*, on the other, *particulars*; the cultural series comprises *groups* and *persons*. All these terms are arbitrarily chosen in order to distinguish in each series two modes of existence, collective and individual, and in order not to confuse the series with each other. At this preliminary stage any terms can be used, provided they are distinct. Thus: NATURE: Category: Particular; CULTURE: Group; Person. There are then four ways of associating the terms, two by two, belonging to the different series, that is, of satisfying with the fewest conditions the initial hypothesis that there exists a relation between the two series. *(He removes the mask, beams at the audience, bangs on his drum and shouts in his 'public' voice:)* Roll up! Roll up! Only sixpence to see the tattooed lady! Only sixpence for the naked tattooed lady! Roll up! Roll up!

(BLACKOUT)

12

(Set B. MRS F. on bed, REDBOLD standing, hesitant.)

MRS FRASER: *(She begins to laugh, shaking on the bed.)*

REDBOLD: That's what one says, isn't it? That's the way one calls, isn't it? – 'Roll up! Roll up!' That's it, isn't it?

MRS FRASER: *(She goes on laughing.)*

REDBOLD: Isn't it? Isn't that what one says?

(BLACKOUT)

13

(Blackout. Tape.)

SCREECHING OF A BIRD
BRACEFELL: Promise? Promise?
SCREECHING OF A BIRD

14

(Set A. MRS F, *in cage.* REDBOLD *beside it.)*

MRS FRASER: *(Monotone:)* When the baby was born it was dead. I hardly noticed. They wrapped it in a cloak and threw it overboard. We had been without water for five days. I was thirty-seven. We had been married for eleven years. My husband was captain of the boat. When it struck the reef he had the men to save. He had his task to do. When he saw the baby was dead he blew his nose and said: 'Throw it overboard. There's no point in keeping it on the boat.' He had the men to think about. He was captain of the boat.

(BLACKOUT)

15

(Blackout. Tape.)

MRS FRASER: How could I give you up? To them. After all you've done for me.
BRACEFELL: *(Laughing:)* You could. It's easy.

16

(Set A. The empty cage. Tape.)

REDBOLD: *(With flute accompaniment:)*
        And when they reached the fatal shore,
        Its name is called Wide Bay,
        The savages soon them espied,
        Rushed down and seized their prey.
    (Silence)

MRS FRASER: *(Very faint:)* Not... again.

(The empty set. Seven seconds.)

(BLACKOUT)

17

(Set A. MRS F. *in cage.* REDBOLD *beside.)*

MRS FRASER: *(She stares out over audience, silent.)*
REDBOLD: Tattoo.
MRS FRASER: *(She stares out, silent.)*
REDBOLD: *(Petulant, beating drum:)* Tattoo!
MRS FRASER: *(With effort:)* They made the marks. It took them three days. When I shouted they laughed. After that I belonged to them.
REDBOLD: *(Putting on kangaroo mask:)* There are four ways of associating the terms, two by two, belonging to the different series, that is, of satisfying with the fewest conditions the initial hypothesis that there exists a relation between the two series, viz., NATURE: Category: Category: Particular: Particular; CULTURE: Group: Person: Person: Group. To each of these four combinations there correspond observable phenomena among one or more peoples. Australian totemism, under 'social' and 'sexual' modalities, postulates a relation between a natural category (animal or vegetable species, or class of objects or phenomena) and a cultural group (moiety, section, sub-section, cult-group or the collectivity of members of the same sex). The second combination corresponds to the 'individual' totemism of the North American Indians, among whom an individual seeks by means of physical trials to reconcile himself with a natural category. As an example of the third combination we may take Mota, in the Banks Islands, where a child is thought to be the incarnation of an animal or plant found or eaten by the mother when she first became aware that she was pregnant; and to this may be added the example of certain tribes of the Algonquin group, who believe that a special relation is established between the new-born child and

whatever animal is seen to approach the family cabin. The group-particular combination is attested from Polynesia and Africa, where certain animals (guardian lizards in New Zealand, sacred crocodiles and lions and leopards in Africa) are objects of social protection and veneration; it is probable that the ancient Egyptians possessed beliefs of the same type, and to such also may be related the *ongon* of Siberia, even though there they concern not real animals but figures treated by the group as though they were alive. *(He takes off his kangaroo mask. Beneath it there is a lizard mask. He shouts:)* Yippee!

(BLACKOUT)

18

(Set B. MRS F. *and* REDBOLD *sitting at the table.)*

REDBOLD: Tell me. Go on. Please tell me.

MRS FRASER: What is there to tell?

REDBOLD: I'm a John too you know. John Redbold. John Bracefell. *(Pause)* Some people even call him John Graham.

MRS FRASER: What is there to tell?

REDBOLD: *(Getting up, miming:)* The forest. The swamps. Did you sleep together in the swamps, Eliza, you naked and he in his striped convict suit? How long did it take you, walking the forests back to civilization? *(She is silent.)* How long, Eliza? How long? Tell me, Eliza. Tell me. Please. What did he say? What did he look like? What did he do when you said nothing? *(She is silent, looking straight at him.)* Was it frightening? Was it fun? Tell John. Tell your Johnny Redbold. What did the Captain say when he saw you again? Did he twirl his moustaches and hum?

MRS FRASER: *(Shrieking:)* The cage! I want my cage!

(BLACKOUT)

19

(Blackout. Tape.)

MRS FRASER: *(Whispering:)* You should have seen his face. When I turned away.

20

(Set A. MRS F. in cage. REDBOLD beside. As she talks he pulls on a striped yellow and black convict suit over his clothes.)

MRS FRASER: When I had been three years with the aboriginal tribe the convict found me. *(Pause.)* It took us seven months to get back to civilization.

REDBOLD: Seven months, ladies and gentlemen! Seven months! And look what they did to her body before that!

MRS FRASER: At first there was fear. We ran through the trees. We waded through the swamps. The birds sat on the mud and watched us. The damp drifted down from the trees.

REDBOLD: *(He mimes their journey, frequently changing masks.)*

MRS FRASER: John Bracefell was his name. Others call him John Graham. We ate roots. We ran. There was blood in our mouths. But they didn't come after us. What eagle comes into the silent woods?

REDBOLD: What eagle comes into the silent woods? *(Laughs.)*

MRS FRASER: Then we were tired. My body was tired. The animals smelt us out. The wombat. The dingo. Black swans spitting in the marshes. The kookaburra with its hideous voice. The blue-tongued lizard. Slugs crawled along the branches, lifting their bodies at the smell of flesh. The goanna fell on us with all its disgusting weight out of the trees.

REDBOLD: The wombat. The dingo. The goanna with all its disgusting weight.

MRS FRASER: But he loved life!

REDBOLD: Bracefell loved life!

MRS FRASER: We slept under the trees. The rain never stopped in the forest. I was thirty-seven. When the baby was born they pulled it out from between my legs and threw it overboard. At night we drew the striped suit over us and slept. In the morning we ate roots. He asked me once: 'When you get back you won't give me up?' He said: 'You'll speak up for me and say what I've done for you?'

REDBOLD: It is well known that the word *totem* is taken from the Ojibwa, ladies and gentlemen, an Algonquin language of the region to the north of the Great Lakes of northern America. The expression *ototeman*, which means roughly, 'he is a relative of mine', is composed of: initial *o-*, third person prefix; *-t-*, epenthesis serving to prevent the coalescence of vowels; *-m-*, possessive; *-an*, third person suffix; and, lastly, *-ote-*, which expresses the relationship between Ego and a male or female relative, thus defining the exogamous group at the level of the generation of the subject.

MRS FRASER: He was a gentleman in the forest. I cried when I saw my body with the marks on it. When the skin is dark the marks shine and form patterns. My skin was sad. There was nothing to say. He carried me on his back for seventy days.

REDBOLD: It was in this way that clan membership was expressed: *makwa nindotem*, 'my clan is the bear'; *pindiken nindotem*, 'come in clan-brother', etc. The Ojibwa clans mostly have animal names, a fact which Thavanet – a French missionary who lived in Canada at the end of the eighteenth century, ladies and gentlemen, – a fact which Thavanet explained by the memory preserved by each clan of an animal in its country of origin as the most handsome, most friendly, most fearsome, most common, or else the animal most usually hunted.

MRS FRASER
REDBOLD } *(Duet:)*

For seventy days	Usually hunted
For seventy days	Usually hunted
He carried me on his back	Or else the animal
For seventy days.	Most usually hunted.
For seventy days	Usually hunted
For seventy days	Usually hunted
He carried me on his back	Or else the animal
For seventy days!	Most usually hunted!

(REDBOLD canters round the stage and comes back into position for the last line. He bows. MRS F. *does not move. She stares ahead of her over the audience.)*

(BLACKOUT)

21

(Set B. REDBOLD *at table.* MRS F. *on the bed. He pours himself a drink.)*

MRS FRASER: I'm so tired.

REDBOLD: You mustn't overdo it.

MRS FRASER: You think I overdo it?

REDBOLD: *(He drinks, not looking at her.)*

MRS FRASER: You think I overdo it? *(He doesn't answer. She gets up, comes close behind him, suddenly throws the striped 'convict suit' over him. She jumps back and looks at him. He doesn't move. She turns away, facing downstage.)* Seventy days. *(He doesn't move.)* No sun. Can you understand that? All that sun in the sky and nothing but rain in the forest. And that green light.

REDBOLD: *(Getting up, pulling the suit round him like a towel:)* We swam through the swamps.

MRS FRASER: *(Dreaming:)* When I woke you were a butterfly in the trees.

REDBOLD: Naked and white you climbed the tree.

MRS FRASER: You waited for me, a butterfly in the leaves.

REDBOLD: While the kangaroo dogs howled below. *(He puts on dog mask and howls.)*

MRS FRASER: Seven months. What does it mean to walk for seven months? We walked through our lives ten times. *(Pause)* Ten times. *(Pause)* And then?

REDBOLD: I carried you on my back.

MRS FRASER: For seventy days.

REDBOLD: *(Putting down mask – quietly:)* Why did you do it? After all that?

MRS FRASER: *(She turns and looks at him. Suddenly screams and rushes at him.)*

(BLACKOUT)

22

(Blackout. Redbold's voice on tape:)

REDBOLD: *(Quietly, almost humming:)*

Poor Babe! How tempestuous, how stormy thy
    pillow!
Asleep on the surge of the rough mountain billow.
While the world, all around thee, was fearful
    commotion –
So comfortless tossed on life's dreary ocean.

Yet I had a bosom and soft was the pillow
My mother provided far off from each billow;
Her tears and her prayers, and maternal tuition,
Procured me, through grace, all my present fruition.

How brief was thy voyage, how rough was thy
    pillow,
Just launched in the sea and then borne on a billow;
Fit emblem of life, with its ten thousand sorrows,
Through sin and the curse of the world's dreary
    horrors.

How quickly the haven of glory thy pillow,
Received thy blest spirit far off from the billow;
Blood ransomed by Jesus through grace so
    abounding,
The throne of his glory with infants surrounding.

23

(Set A. Stage empty. The cage. Tape.)

REDBOLD: Did you sleep together in the swamps, you naked
    and he in the striped convict suit? *(Pause)* What did he
    look like? What did he do when you said nothing?

(BLACKOUT)

24

(Set A. MRS F. *in cage,* REDBOLD *with drum beside it.)*

REDBOLD: *(Beating drum:)* Roll up! Roll up! Come and see the incredible tattooed lady! Come and hear in her own inimitable words the amazing story of her adventures among the man-eating natives of the Australian jungle! Roll up! Roll up! Come and see the only survivor of the *Stirling Castle*! Sixpence only!

MRS FRASER: *(Too loud:)* They put these marks on my body. What are they for? Tell me. What are they for? You – tell me. What are they for? They won't go away. Look at them. They put these marks on my body and they won't ever go away. *(Quietly:)* That was before.

REDBOLD: That was before her incredible escape through the dank rain-forests. Seven months she and the convict Bracefell, her heroic saviour, struggled through the rain forest. Only sixpence to see the tattooed lady! Sixpence! Only sixpence!

MRS FRASER: *(Screaming:)* Look at me! I'm the tattooed lady!

(BLACKOUT)

25

(Set A. MRS F. *in cage. She stares straight ahead of her, silent.* REDBOLD, *with drum, left. He raises the stick. Tape.)*

REDBOLD: The collective system known as totemism is not to be confused with the belief, held by the same Ojibwa, that an individual may enter into a relationship with an animal which will be his guardian spirit. The only known term designating this individual guardian spirit was transcribed by a traveller in the middle of the nineteenth century as *nigouimes*, and thus has nothing to do with the word 'totem' or any other term of the same type. Researches on the Ojibwa show that the first description of the supposed institution of 'totemism' due to the English trader and interpreter Long, at the end of the nineteenth century, resulted from a confusion between

clan-names (in which the names of animals correspond
to collective appellations) and beliefs concerning guardian
spirits (which are individual protectors). This is more
clearly seen from an analysis of Ojibwa society. These
Indians were, it seems, organized into some dozens of
patrilineal and patrilocal clans, of which five may have
been older than the others, or, at any rate, enjoyed a particular prestige. A myth explains that these five 'original'
clans are descended from six anthropomorphic super-
natural beings who emerged from the ocean to mingle
with human beings. One of them had his eyes covered and
dared not look at the Indians, though he showed the
greatest anxiety to do so. At last he could no longer restrain
his curiosity, and on one occasion he partially lifted his
veil, and his eye fell on the form of a human being, who
instantly fell dead, 'as if struck by one of the thunderers'.
Though the intentions of this dread being were friendly
to men, yet the glance of his eye was too strong, and it
inflicted certain death. His fellows therefore caused him
to return to the bosom of the great water. The five others
remained among the Indians and became a blessing to
them. From them originate the five great clans or totems:
catfish, crane, loon, bear, and marten.

MRS FRASER: Who was he?... It had to be... The distance...
The distance... And me a lady... When they looked for
the boy he was praying... Blue hair on their shoulders
like epaulettes... Let him go... After the baby... And
with those patterns on my skin... With those patterns,
who am I?

BIRD-CRIES: DRIPPING WATER; ANIMAL CRIES; CAT-O-NINE-
TAILS & A MAN CRYING OUT.

(These three layers of sound – REDBOLD, MRS FRASER, forest
sounds etc. – should be superimposed and mixed on tape with
feedback and distortion as necessary. MRS FRASER's phrases
should be frequently repeated, and the whole should fade on
the momentarily clear sound of the lash alone. Then silence.)

(BLACKOUT)

26

(Set A. MRS F. *in cage,* REDBOLD *beside.)*

MRS FRASER: *(She sings:)*
>I shall tell you a story
>A very merry story:
>When I got back the very same day
>I saw the Captain my husband!
>He averted his gaze and smoothed his moustache,
>The Captain my husband!
>(It's always a shock to see your wife come naked
>   and tattooed out of the bush).
>We sailed for England the very next month
>But the Captain wasn't too well;
>We'd barely rounded the Cape of Good Hope
>When he simply laid down and died.
>He simply laid down and died.
>(Oh he left me amply provided. He was a real gentle-
>   man. From the day I returned to the day of his
>   death we never exchanged a word.)

REDBOLD: *(After a silence of some seconds, claps his hands loudly, looks round proudly. Straightens. A roll on the drums.)* Roll up! Roll up! Come and see the tattooed lady! The tattooed lady! Sixpence! Only sixpence to see the tattooed lady, only survivor of the *Stirling Castle*! *(He looks round. Silence.)*

MRS FRASER: *(She opens the door of her cage and steps out to stand beside him.)* I'm so tired. I want to sleep. All I want to do is sleep.

(BLACKOUT)

27

(Blackout. Tape.)

MRS FRASER: So tired... So tired...

28

(Set B., MRS F. *and* REDBOLD *at table.)*

MRS FRASER: Escaped convicts who are recaptured receive five
hundred lashes. There's no mercy.

(BLACKOUT)

29

(Set A. MRS FRASER *in cage.* REDBOLD *beside.)*

REDBOLD: Sixpence! Only sixpence to see the naked tattooed
lady! To hear from her very own lips the incredible story
of Mrs Eliza Fraser of the *Stirling Castle*! Sixpence! *Only
sixpence!*

MRS FRASER: The natives treated me terribly well. They ate
some of the others but they treated me terribly well. They
made marks on my body which you can see to this day –
here – and here – and here – but they treated me with the
utmost politeness. They burned the skin with red-hot
sticks to prepare it for the tattoo, but that's just a custom
with them and they mean no harm. When I escaped with
the convict John Bracefell they didn't even try to follow
us. I promised to intercede for him if he helped me back
to civilization but when it came to it I let them take him
and said nothing. He got five hundred lashes and another
seven years hard labour. That was the normal procedure
in those days. My baby was born when we were four days
in the open boat. It was dead and they threw it overboard.

(Silence. REDBOLD *and* MRS FRASER *stand stiffly, staring out
over the audience.)*

(BLACKOUT)

30

*(Stage lights come up on both sets – the entire stage. It is quite
empty – cage and furniture have gone.* MRS F. *and* REDBOLD
*stand side by side, silent, centre stage front. Tape only in this
scene.)*

REDBOLD: *(And drum:)* Roll up! Roll up! Come and see the naked lady! Come and see the naked tattooed lady! Roll up! Roll up! Only sixpence!
(Silence)

MRS FRASER: The cage! I want the cage! Cage! Cage!
(Silence)
(The lights dim slowly.)

This play was first performed at the Theatre Upstairs, Royal Court (London), 1972.

Flow
FOR CAROLINE BLAKISTON

This is a play for five voices. Two of the speakers, B and D, are female, and three male.

On the stage, five chairs, not too close and not too far apart from each other.

The distinctive characters emerge out of a series of brief phrases which could belong to any of them. I have marked with an asterisk the point at which it seems to me that each character finds his distinctive 'voice'.

E.   Because.

A.   Because what?

C.   And yet?

A.   Because what?

E.   Talking again.

B.   Trying to talk.

C.   Remembering the spring.

D.   Thinking again.

E.   Because what?

A.*   Thinking again. Trying to talk. Recalling at last the time before.

C.   To what purpose?

D.   The time before.

B.*   Remembering the spring.

A.   Recalling at last.

E.   Thinking again. Talking again.

C.   Hoping perhaps.

E.   And yet

C.   Saying it again

E.   And yet

D.   Trying

E.   Because

D.   Turning again

C.	Returning again.
B.	Each little flower. Each little leaf.
E.	Silence.
C.	And yet
B.	Each little leaf. Each little bud. Waiting for the spring. Waiting for the sun. Waiting for it to begin.
C.	And yet
D.	Turning
A.	Thinking again
D.	Turning
C.	And yet
E.	Waiting
D.	Turning
A.	Recalling again, in all its detail
C.	Because I said
E.	Waiting
A.	Recalling again, in all its detail, her face, the rain, the rain on her face, rain on the windowpane, the sound of the engine
D.	Turning
E.	Waiting
B.	Each little leaf. Each little bud. Waiting for the spring.
A.	Rain on the windowpane, the sound of the engine, watching her face, seeing her smile, seeing her tears, the train moving, the rain on the panes, silence.
C.	Turning again.
D.	Waiting
A.	Silence. The empty silence. The hollow silence. Turning away. Crowds on the platform, crowds in the bus, rain on the windowpane, crowds on the pavements, the empty stairs, the empty silence, creak of the door.
D.*	When I turned round he wasn't there.
A.	The empty flat. Rain on the windowpanes.
D.	When I called he didn't answer.
B.	Each little leaf. Each little bud. Waiting for the spring.
E.	Waiting
A.	Rain on the roof. Dripping.
D.	When I looked for him he wasn't there.
E.	Turning.
B.	Each little leaf.

E.   Turning again
A.   Rattle of the spoon against the cup.
E.   Trying to talk.
D.   When I called he didn't answer.
A.   Rattle of the knife against the plate.
B.   Each little leaf.
D.   When I turned
B.   Each little bud
D.   Thinking to see him
B.   Waiting for the spring
D.   Thinking to surprise him
A.   Rain on the windowpane. Silence. The empty silence.
C.   And yet
E.   Waiting for the time
D.   And finding only that he wasn't there.
C.   Because
D.   So that it was driven home to me
A.   Spoon against the cup
D.   That he might perhaps never have been there
C.   Perhaps
D.   And that my sense of his presence
B.   Waiting
D.   And I had a strong sense, had even seen him, or thought
     I had seen him, out of the corner of my eye, as I stood
     looking at the ducks
A.   Rain on the windowpane. The empty stairs. The creak
     of the door.
D.   Observing the drakes
B.   For the spring. The springtime.
A.   The sound of the engine
D.   Sensing his presence, waiting for him to speak, listen-
     ing to the sounds on the grass behind my back
C.   Turning away
B.   The warmth of the sun
A.   Crowds on the platform
D.   Willing him to speak, sensing his presence, even
     noting, out of the corner of my eye, the quality of his
     appearance, the very great quality of his appearance
A.   Crowds on the pavements
E.   Perhaps

A.   Crowds in the bus

E.   And yet

C.   Closing my eyes

E.   Saying it again

B.   The springtime. He said: It is the springtime.

E.   And yet

C.*   Closing my eyes. Repeating it, under my breath. Holding the words. Nursing the syllables.

E.   Trying to forget. Who can tell?

B.   Standing in the grass. Standing in the midst of the flowers. Saying, It is the springtime.

C.   Little syllables, under my breath

A.   Seeing her face

C.   Little words, inside my head

A.   Seeing the tears

B.   The warmth of the sun

E.   Who?

C.   Nursing the syllables, starting again, at the beginning, holding my breath, closing my eyes, moving my lips, uttering, muttering

B.   Lying in the grass. The flowers. Each little leaf.

E.   Why?

A.   When she said she had to go I didn't take her seriously

B.   Each little flower

E.   Why and again why?

C.   Recalling the words, savouring the syllables, starting again, always again, never again

A.   I stopped whatever it was I was doing and gave her a stare

E.   And again why and again why?

A.   When she returned my stare with one of her own I knew things were bad. I kept cool and lit a cigarette, but she didn't budge.

C.   Those words, those days with the words, days by the sea, staring out at the sea, repeating the words, smiling at the sea

B.   Each little bud

D.   Sensing his presence

E.   And yet. Perhaps.

A.   When reasoning proved of no avail I offered to accompany her to the station

B.   Lying there in the grass, in the flowers, watching him lie, watching him say

E.   But why?

D.   I turned round quite suddenly and of course there was no one there.

C.   My face to the sea, staring out at the sea

E.   Why and why and why and why

A.   Later I returned to the empty flat and lay down on the bed.

D.   When I called he didn't answer.

C.   Taking in the sea, closing my eyes, mumbling the words

D.   When I looked for him he wasn't there.

B.   Watching him say: It's the springtime. Laughing.

A.   Closing my eyes, I recalled again in all its detail her face, the rain, the rain on her face, the sound of the engine

D.   So that I wondered if he had ever been there or if perhaps I had imagined it all

B.   Lying in the grass, laughing, feeling the sun on the grass, the warmth on our bodies, seeing his face, the smile on his face

E.   Perhaps not why. And yet

A.   Just as later I was to recall the sound of the spoon against the cup, of the knife against the plate, and recall again

D.   And yet I knew this was not so, that he had been there, had followed quietly, keeping his distance through the trees

E.*   To start. So hard to start.

C.   Mumbling the sea

A.   And recall again the heavy figure on the bed, eyes closed, despair in the heart, seeing her face through the streaming pane, crowds on the platform, the empty flat

E.   And yet to start. The need to start.

C.   Eating the sea.

D.   It was a long time since I had seen him. Indeed, I had not expected to see him ever again.

C.   Eating words of the sea.

B.   Then getting up and running through the grass, the flowers, laughing, my face filled with laughter

C.   Words of the sea

D.   For he had been swallowed up by the city and there was no way of tracing him

B.   That spring we rowed on the river

C.   Slowly munching, slowly chewing, in the old room, eyes closed, words of the sea

E.   The need to start. Yes.

D.   Even if the will to do so had been there.

C.   Eyes closed in the old room, starting again at the beginning, always again, smile on the old face, mumble in the old room, waiting for the end

E.   But where?

D.   The will to look

E.   But how?

D.   When he had gone

B.   Swans on the river, floating past

E.   And yet   And yet

D.   Day following day

B.   Raising their necks, white feathers in the water

E.   Who is to say where is the start?

D.   And night night

E.   The finish

D.   Not adding up

E.   But a start must be made

D.   Never adding up, days and nights, days and nights

A.   Recalling that heavy figure tossing on the bed

E.   A decision is required

C.   Old face in the old room, mumbling old words, light on the old face, smile on the lips, staring at the sea

E.   After which it will be easy

B.   I asked him if he was afraid of the swans but he laughed, showing the muscles on his arms

D.   So that it was a shock, a surprise, a sudden elimination of the empty days and nights to see him walking behind me in the Park

C.   Sea in the face, in the mouth, mumbling the old words, returning again, starting again, light on the face in the old room

B. We drifted past the swans

A. The ring of the knife against the empty plate

D. I did not dare to believe it

B. The sun made spots of light upon the water

E. A closing of the eyes

A. Hollow silence in the empty flat

C. Mumbling the words, turning again, returning again

D. My mind went blank

E. A kind of surrender

B. The grass swayed gently in the breeze

D. I could only walk and half turn, catching sight of him out of the corner of my eye, hurrying on to see if he would follow, noting that he did, that it was he, that he was there behind me, trailing me in the Park, after all those days

E. Out of which

B. We lay in the soft grass

E. Perhaps

A. Spoon against cup, knife against the empty plate

E. Who knows

C. Always there, always the same, the sun on my face, eyes closed, lips moving, mumbling the words

E. Out of surrender

B. Watching the little leaves, the little flowers, unfolding in the spring

A. Sitting at the table, spoon against cup, knife against the empty plate

E. Will come life

B. Watching them open, slowly,

E. A flow

B. Feeling his arm across my body

E. A river

D. I made my way towards the pond. We had often been there together. I did not dare to think.

E. Perhaps a torrent

B. And his body against mine

C. Lips moving, never ceasing, returning again

A. Walking through the flat, thinking of her face at the window, the pane streaming, the crowds on the platform

B.   Laughing and saying: It's the springtime

E.   A torrent of words, a torrent of feelings

B.   It had not always been like that. Nor has it since.

C.   The mist on the sea and the sun on the mist

A.   Thinking of her face

B.   No.

C.   The sea in my face and the words in my mouth

E.   Released at last, after all the striving, all the effort, all the tossing and turning, the hesitations, the uncertainties, the fears and the despair, after...

D.   I stood against the rail, by the pond, waiting for him to talk to me

B.   Although when I question myself about before and after

C.   My lips moving

A.   I asked her what she meant, saying she had to go, but she only shook her head and would not speak

D.   I sensed his presence behind me

C.   In the old room

B.   It is only the springtime I remember

C.   Sitting on the bench looking at the sea

B.   The rest has gone and it is as though I was back in the springtime, watching each little flower

D.   I waited for him to speak to me

E.   The futility of the whole enterprise

D.   To come close to me

C.   Sitting on the bench, thinking of the old room, thinking of the sea

B.   Each little leaf

A.   At first I didn't take her seriously, but when she started to push her clothes into a suitcase I realized she meant business

E.   The baselessness of my confidence

B.   Waiting for the sun, opening with the sun

C.   Of the mist on the sea and the sunlight on the mist

A.   I repeated my request for an explanation but she only sniffed and sat down harder on the lid of the suitcase

D.   I waited for him to touch me

A.   The tears were streaming down her cheeks

E.   The impossibility of my task

D.   I waited for him to touch me

C.   Mumbling

D.   And, touching, to annul those days

A.   Outside it was raining, I hailed a taxi and helped her to get in.

D.   Those weeks

E.   And yet

C.   Never at a loss

A.   Her hands were cold

D.   By a touch

E.   And yet

A.   We didn't speak

B.   The little buds

D.   Waiting

A.   She stood by the window, waiting for the train to move

E.   As they say, as I say

C.   My eyes closed, my lips moving

D.   Turning at last

A.   I said nothing. There was nothing to say

E.   One day

B.   The little buds

D.   Slowly

E.   Perhaps

D.   Very slowly

E.   Perhaps

D.   Expecting to see him there behind me, standing still, against the tree, in the evening

E.   Though where that comes from

C.   Always moving

B.   White birds on the river

D.   The park was silent

A.   The rain streamed down the window. I thought of asking her the reason for her sudden decision and raised my hand to motion her to draw down the window

B.   White swans silently moving

E.   That belief

B.   Sun dancing on the water

E.   That optimistic belief

C.   Never still
D.   No one about
B.   Sun on the mist
A.   Crowds on the platform
E.   Belief that one day
C.   Mist on the water
E.   One fine day
D.   No one behind me
A.   Knife against the empty plate
E.   Just like that
A.   Spoon against the cup
D.   When I called he didn't answer
C.   Sea in my mouth
D.   When I turned. Thinking to see him. Thinking to surprise him
C.   Old room
B.   Silently moving on the silent river
A.   That old body tossing on the empty bed
D.   And finding only that he wasn't there.
E.   Days like that
D.   So that it was driven home to me
E.   They don't make them any more. If they ever did.
D.   Driven home to me
A.   Old mind tossing on the empty waters
D.   That he might perhaps never have been there
C.   Sun in the old room
D.   And that my sense of his presence
C.   Words in my mouth
D.   And I had a strong sense, had even seen him, or thought I had seen him, out of the corner of my eye, as I stood looking at the ducks
A.   Tossing and turning
D.   Observing the drakes
E.   Fond thoughts
B.   Long white necks
E.   Thoughts of such a day
D.   Willing him to speak
C.   Sun in my old face
D.   Sensing his presence
A.   Recalling again

B. I laughed when he showed me his muscles

C. Mumbling

E. When all would begin

D. Even noting, out of the corner of my eye, the quality of his appearance

A. Her face at the window

D. The very great quality of his appearance

C. Waiting

B. And he laughed with me, pointing to the strong necks of the white birds

E. When the past would be behind

C. Waiting for the end

E. And the future in front

D. So that it was driven home to me

E. A day to divide the days

C. So long

B. And laughed in the grass, watching the little buds

E. A stake in the ground

B. The little leaves

D. Driven home

C. So long

E. As though such things were possible

C. Mumbling in the dark

E. Such days

C. In the light

E. Such moments

D. That he might perhaps never have been there

B. Sun warm on the warm buds

A. From the tone of her voice I knew that she meant business

E. Moments to look forward to

A. At first I pretended not to notice, but when she took down the suitcase from the cupboard I decided it was time to intervene

E. To look back to

C. Eyes closed in the old room

A. I asked her what she meant

E. Moments of triumph

D. Though I sensed his presence, saw him even, when I had not expected to see him ever again

A.   I insisted she explain herself

E.   Moments of despair

C.   Lips moving

B.   And he ran, running in the warm grass

C.   Never stopping

E.   Moments of loss

A.   But her lips were pursed and she would not answer

C.   Never still

E.   And of peace

B.   It must be said that my memories of that spring are exceptional

A.   I knew her to be stubborn

E.   But whether of triumph or loss or even despair

A.   But had not expected this cold determination

B.   Other Springs cannot vie with it

C.   Endlessly mumbling

B.   Nor other Autumns, Winters or Summers

A.   This hard antagonism

C.   Eyes closed

E.   But whether of triumph or loss or even despair

A.   This stubborn refusal to answer my simplest question

C.   Words in my mouth

B.   Though they too yield memories, and sometimes rich ones

E.   Or even despair

C.   Sun on my face

B.   Memories of gardens when the frost is out

A.   And found it difficult to know how to react

E.   A point. A place. A line of demarcation.

C.   Mumbling the words, listening to the words

B.   Memories of brown fields when the earth is turned

E.   But where?

A.   However, when I saw her sitting on the suitcase, trying to get it shut, her lips pursed, her face white, I sensed that the time for argument had been left behind

E.   Where are such moments to be found?

C.   Feeling the shape of them

D.   Had not expected ever again

A.   When we got out of the house the rain was fierce

E.   Such lines of demarcation?

B.   Memories of the sea and the mist on the sea

A.   I hailed a taxi and helped her in. She could not keep the tears out of her eyes

E.   Such beginnings?

C.   Large and small, smooth or rough, rolling round the tongue

D.   Accepting the loss

B.   And the sun on the mist

E.   Where?

C.   Mumbling and hearing the mumble

D.   Accepting the silence

B.   Memories of rain and of crowded pavements

C.   Hearing the words

B.   Memories of meetings and partings

C.   Hearing the voices

E.   Where then?

D.   Accepting the empty stairs, the empty room

C.   In my mouth

B.   Memories of crowded platforms

E.   Why not here?

C.   In my ears

B.   Of empty parks

E.   Why not now?

D.   Accepting the silence, the sun on my face

C.   Voices of mothers

E.   At this moment?

C.   Voices of children

D.   The sun on my face

B.   Of empty rooms

A.   Spoon against the cup

C.   Voices of lovers

E.   Why not now?

D.   Walking through the streets

A.   Knife against the empty plate

E.   At this moment

C.   Voices of old men mumbling in empty rooms

E.   This moment

A.   Heavy body rolling on the unmade bed

D.   Sitting in the silent room

E.   This moment

A.   Tossing and turning
C.   Voices raised in anger
D.   Lips moving in the silent room
E.   This moment
A.   Thinking again
C.   Or whispering
D.   Sun on my face
E.   This
A.   Recalling again
D.   Empty room
C.   Arguing
E.   This
D.   Walking in the park
A.   Her face through the pane
C.   Pleading
D.   Looking down at the pond
C.   Begging
A.   Crowds on the pavement
C.   Insistent voices
D.   Sun on my face
B.   Of old men mumbling at the sea
A.   Recalling again
C.   Speaking of spring
E.   Not even this
B.   Of old men eyes closed mumbling at the sea
A.   Recalling again the tears in her eyes, the sound of the
      spoon against the cup, the heavy body on the unmade
      bed
C.   Speaking of flowers
B.   Of old men eyes closed mumbling in empty rooms
C.   Speaking of buds
B.   Of heavy men tossing on unmade beds
C.   Speaking of the sun warm on the warm buds
E.   Not even
B.   Memories? Are these memories?
A.   Recalling again
E.   Not
C.   Speaking of the sun sparkling on the river
B.   Or something else, something other than memories,
      returning again as I turn again, waiting for the spring,

the sun, the little leaves, the little buds

A.   The heavy body

C.   Speaking of trains

E.   Perhaps there has been a beginning

D.   No longer waiting or remembering even

B.   Something other, something else, to be given another name

A.   Sitting up on the unmade bed, feet on the floor and head in hands

E.   And we have not noticed

B.   To be labelled with another label

A.   Feet on the floor and hands on knees

C.   Speaking of rain

E.   A turning-point

A.   Hands on knees and sun on the face

B.   Or not labelled at all

E.   And it has passed us by

B.   Not named at all

A.   Sun on the face and words in the mouth

C.   Speaking of parks and ponds and drakes in the pond

B.   Accepted only

E.   So that it is as though it had never been

A.   Sitting on the unmade bed, feet on the floor and sun on the face

B.   Welcomed even

C.   Speaking of stairs and hollow silence

E.   Though not quite that, since the thought remains that it may have come and gone and not been noticed

B.   Room found for them

E.   So that it might be possible

C.   Speaking of turning

B.   All of them

A.   Eyes closed, words in the mouth

E.   With a little bit of luck

C.   Speaking of turning

A.   On the unmade bed

B.   Though where they live

E.   And some courage

B.   So many together

A.   In the empty room

E.	And a great deal of courage
C.	Speaking of recalling
E.	Or foolhardiness
C.	And remembering
E.	Just possible
A.	Sun through the window
B.	Indeed it is a question
C.	Speaking of beginnings
A.	Mist on the sea
C.	Speaking of endings
B.	A question to ask oneself
A.	Sun on the mist
E.	A great deal of courage and foolhardiness
C.	Speaking of waiting for the beginning
B.	To pass the time at least and in a modest spirit of enquiry
A.	Eyes closed in the old room mouthing the old words
E.	Though I wonder if courage and foolhardiness are the right terms
B.	Those words are not mine
C.	Of waiting for the end
B.	Those phrases are not mine
A.	Spoon against the cup
E.	And if a certain lightness might not better describe the state I imagine
A.	Knife against the empty plate
B.	Float into my mouth
C.	Of an impossible waiting
A.	Heavy body on the unmade bed
B.	Float out again
E.	A lightness of the spirit
B.	Lost, gone, of no importance
C.	And of those things which make it bearable
A.	Tossing and turning
E.	A lightness of the mind
A.	Recalling again
B.	No weight, no importance, beside the memories of the spring and of waiting for the spring
D.	I had not expected to see him again
B.	The little leaves

D.   Had been under no illusion on that score

B.   The little buds

D.   I was not totally inexperienced in the ways of the world

A.   Her face at the window

E.   Doing and it is done

D.   Had always accepted this as a possibility

A.   Rain streaming on the windowpane

D.   Though I had not thought he would vanish so soon

E.   Beginning and it is begun

D.   Not that I wished to hold him against his will

A.   Tears on her cheeks

E.   The burden removed

B.   Sun warm on the warm grass

D.   But that it made me see again in a new light the way he turned, in the room, and turned, eyeing the room

E.   A path opened up

B.   And warm on our faces

D.   Later he explained to me that his disappearance had been necessary and necessary his return, but what could that mean to me after his absence and my acceptance of his absence and his sudden reappearance when I saw him in the park out of the corner of my eye and turned round to find he was not there?

E.   The way clear

A.   Her face set and sorrowful

D.   I knew then that it was finished, when I turned round and he was not there, although perhaps I also knew that some day soon

B.   He showed me the muscles on his arm

D.   Not necessarily the next day

A.   Crowds on the platform

D.   Or the day after that

E.   With a before and an after

A.   The sound of the engine

D.   But soon

C.   Mumbling

A.   Her face set and sorrowful as I helped her into the taxi

D.   One day soon

B.   And laughed so that I had to laugh
D.   One day
C.   Mumbling
A.   I tried to argue with her
D.   Soon
A.   I asked her to explain
D.   He would reappear
C.   Sun on my face
B.   And ran in the warm grass
D.   And he would enter the room and sit
E.   With a start to look back to and an end to make for
D.   As he sits now
A.   I insisted on an explanation
E.   A dream
B.   Never stopping
E.   Grey shadow
A.   But she was adamant
E.   That lightness
D.   Sitting in the room
C.   Sea in my mouth
A.   She would not argue. Would not discuss.
E.   That grace
D.   Talking, explaining
C.   Words of the sea in my mouth
D.   Trying to convince
A.   Anyone could see she had made up her mind
B.   White swans on the sparkling waves
C.   Words washing in my mouth
E.   Where is it?
D.   Insisting that it was still possible to reach an under-
        standing, to forgive and forget
C.   Wash wash wash wash
B.   He showed me the muscles on his arm
A.   Though why she should have done so was beyond me
C.   Why words what words
D.   Forgive and forget
E.   If anywhere
C.   Turning words remembering words
D.   Though what there was to forgive
C.   Recalling words returning words

D.   Forget

A.   Hunt as I might for a reason or a motive

E.   And if nowhere why the shadow of it

A.   Or a stronger reason, more powerful motive than those, and there were plenty, which had not previously led to any action on her part

C.   Yet words because words

B.   I should have known

E.   Haunting

C.   Perhaps words

D.   What there was to forgive

B.   I cannot, try as I may, recall the circumstances of our meeting or its outcome

E.   A shadow

C.   Perhaps

D.   What there was to forgive

C.   Perhaps

D.   Sitting and talking in the room

A.   Or a stronger reason, more powerful motive, than those, and there were plenty, which had not previously led to any action

E.   A shadow

C.   And yet

D.   Sitting and talking in the room when I remembered only the turning and his absence

A.   Which had not led to any action

C.   And yet

D.   Only the calling and his absence

A.   To any action on her part

C.   And yet?

B.   The circumstances of our meeting or its outcome

C.   Because?

A.   Outside there was a fierce rain

D.   And the sense of a death and of an end

B.   Our meeting and its outcome

C.   And yet?

A.   The spoon against the cup

D.   He did not seem to understand

C.   Because what?

A.   Heavy body on the unmade bed

D. Tried to argue and endlessly argue
C. And yet?
D. While I thought of the park and my sense of his presence
A. Heavy body
B. The circumstances of our meeting or its outcome
D. As I turned, expecting to see him
A. Empty flat
D. It was too late
C. No.
D. When I turned he wasn't there
A. Empty bedroom
C. And yet?
B. Recalling again
C. Trying to talk.
E. Perhaps
B. Returning again
A. Empty kitchen
D. When I called
E. Silence.
C. Hoping perhaps
D. Turning
C. Waiting for the end
E. Shadow of a beginning
D. When I called
B. Remembering the spring
E. Shadow of an end
C. Talking
D. Turning
A. Recalling her face and the rain on her face
E. Shadow
B. Each little bud
D. Turning again
A. Hollow silence
E. Shadow
D. So that it was driven home to me that he might perhaps
    never have been there
C. End
E. Shadow
C. And yet
A. Recalling at last

E.	Hoping perhaps
D.	Thinking again
B.	Remembering
A.	Recalling
C.	Because what?
E.	And yet
B.	Because what?
A.	And yet
D.	Because
E.	Because

This play was first performed at the Edinburgh Lyceum, 1973.

Vergil Dying

FOR PAUL SCOFIELD

No one who writes on this subject can fail to be indebted to Herman Broch's great novel, *The Death of Vergil*. Readers of the novel will be aware of how different my own understanding of the theme is from Broch's, but I doubt if I would have had the courage to tackle it in the first place if it had not been for him.

Embedded in the text are numerous quotations, both overt and concealed, from the works of Vergil. For these I have used the fine translations by Cecil Day Lewis of the *Eclogues, Georgics* and *Aeneid*, and the Loeb translation of the minor poems, only abridging and altering here and there for my special purposes. I have also worked into the text a quotation from Ovid and an extended quotation from a letter written by Kafka to Max Brod.

The work was written for Paul Scofield, whose performance of it was broadcast on Radio Three on 29 March 1979.

Brindisi, 19 BC. Vergil has arrived from Athens with Augustus' fleet, bound for Rome. He has caught a chill on the voyage and this has rapidly grown worse. He lies in his room in the royal palace. In one corner of the room there is a metal casket which encloses the MSS of the Aeneid, *which the poet insists on carrying with him everywhere. In another part of the palace, Augustus is giving a banquet to celebrate his arrival in Italy. Outside the room in which Vergil is lying, a fountain plays gently.*

The play is a monologue in seven distinct yet continuous scenes.

I   THE THRESHOLD   (1)

(He groans, tosses on the bed. At first his words are disjointed, mumbled. It is only gradually that they become recognizable)

Mmmmmmm
Mmmmmmm
Where?
Aaaaah
Where?
Aaaaah. Aaaaah. Aaaaah.
Where?
Where are you?
So far.
So far.
Yes.
You are so far.
So far from here.
Where?
And now?
Aaaaah. Aaaaah. Aaaaah.
Always.
Always the labyrinth. Yes.
Inside. Outside.
To get in.
Out.
Aaaaah.
To get...in...
Aaaah!
In...
Always there. Waiting.
And now?
Brindisi. Not Athens, as you'd hoped. That was to be a new start. At last. No more poetry. No more falsehood. Truth. The peaceful study of Truth.
And now? Pah!

(He coughs)

All right. You'll be all right. Slight chill. It'll pass. Always

has. Though they said...
    Nothing. It means nothing. The sun has always risen on you. Fifty-one years. But one day it will rise and you won't be there.

(He claps his hands)

    And so?
    Fool!

(He coughs again)

You wondered what you were doing here. In Caesar's... entourage!
    So far from home.
    And yet...

(He muses. A time)

    What home?
    The farm. The river. The flocks pasturing peacefully on the hills.
    Is that home?
    And yet...

(He muses)

How often have you wanted to get back! Enter the house...
    But you knew.
    All the time. Deep down.

The poet is always on the threshold...
    Waiting...
    Waiting...
    Yes.
    Not outside. Or inside. On the doorstep. The threshold. Waiting.

Always...

Threshold of childhood...
Of marriage
Fatherhood
Power in the state
Yes. He hovers. Waiting. For what?
Even you. The poet of the family. The home. Fields and
farms. Of Rome, centre of the world.
Even you.
And now you wait on another threshold.
(Vehemently) Pah! Rhetoric!
When will you have finished with that?
When will you have done with the old sow?
And yet... Death... It was always there. You have been
waiting for it a long time...

(He muses)

An instinct. Perhaps an instinct kept you outside. All your
life. As though you knew what entering would mean. Loss of
speech. Loss of the power of articulation which is yours alone.
Yes. The loss of the most important thing.
And yet...
And yet...
The poet frees himself from his first Mother. From his childhood, his home, the river running through the green meadows,
the quiet flocks pasturing under the cloudless sky... He frees
himself in order to sing – because he needs to sing, he needs
to! – and then his song expresses only the longing to return!
What is this song, what has it ever been, except for the lament
for the loss of something unimaginably good?

Vergilius.
Spring, you once said, and Truth. Both in the one name.
Your name.
You would sing a new Spring and its content would be Truth.

Pah!

(He coughs)

And yet...

'We flee our fatherland...' That's how it began. The first of the Eclogues, the first poem that you were happy to acknowledge. And Aeneas, how did he begin his tale of woe? 'Homeless I took to the deep sea...'

Homeless...To the deep sea.

Yes. That is the truth of it. Homeless I took to the deep sea. And he cried out. Begged Apollo, begged him: 'Grant us a walled home of our own, a place for tired men, a future, and a continuing city.'

(He groans. Is silent. The fountain plays outside.)

'Now I am swept by the winds through empty space... and through the regions of the underworld.'

'Let me be. Me, vainly seeking rest...'

'Alas, this anguish that will never change!'

Alas. This anguish. That will never change.

(He muses. He recites):

> Matrons and men were there, and there were great-hearted
> heroes
> Finished with earthly life, boys and unmarried maidens,
> Young men laid on the pyre before their parents' eyes;
> Multitudinous as the leaves that fall in a forest
> At the first frost of autumn, as the birds that out of the deep
> sea
> Fly to land in migrant flocks, when the cold of the year
> Has sent them overseas in search of a warmer climate.
> So they all stood, each begging to be ferried across first,
> Their hands stretched out in longing for the shore beyond
> the river.

(He muses)

The shore beyond. Beyond the river.

And Palinurus begging to be buried. Palinurus. Helmsman. My guide. My instinct. 'So that at last I may rest in the quiet place, in death.'

In the quiet place. The shore beyond. Broad-spreading darkness.

Mother.

(Starting suddenly) Are you there?

(Quieter) Was she there? For you? To lead you by the hand? As she led you long ago?

Aeneas too was a wanderer. That is why he moved you. Why you were moved to write about him. Homeless I took to the deep sea. Dido tried to hold him, keep him. He shook her off.

Pah!

A wanderer. Yes. Forced to flee his home. That burning Troy. Longing to found a dynasty. Build another city. And in the end – what? Death. Bloody carnage. And for what? A dream? A dream of home?

They come at him. Always. In the dark. The unburied dead. The helmsman. Dido. Creusa too, his first wife. Go, she said. Go. And he went. Left her in the burning city. Her ghost in the gutted houses. Abandoned her, driven by a dream. A dream of the past. An idea. A vague longing.

And could that lead to such carnage? That?

You wrote of these things. Why? Because he told you to? The quiet one. The smiling one. Set it down for me, he said. For us. So that all may read. And you did.

But was that why?

Was it not rather... to understand? Find out if the dream was true, perhaps? Follow Aeneas until he led you to... yourself?

And now? Are you any nearer to understanding? No. Nearer to the darkness only. You can feel its presence in the room, waiting...

And that dream that all would in the end be clear?

Pah!

Nothing is clear. Except that you are tired.

But you were tired when you started. That is the strangest thing of all, is it not? That you were tired when you started, all those years ago...

Tired to death.

And the days went by so slowly...The years. Fifty-one years on this sun-blistered earth. So many days. So many nights. So many. So many.

You would like to be finished with it all, wouldn't you?
But no. We go on talking. You and I. Old friend.
Old friend.
Longing to enter. Fearing to enter.
Yes...

Athens. That was what you longed for. Athens. Have done with poetry. With words. Stories. Weighing the syllables. But it was as if he knew. The smiling one. As he had always known everything. Philosophy can wait, he said. Come back with me to Rome. We want you to read from the poem. For our birthday. Just a short reading, if you are tired. For our sake. For the sake of Rome. The philosophy can wait. Until my birthday you remain a poet. You belong to us. To Rome. Greece and philosophy can wait.
As if he knew. Knew it was not to be. No peace. No final home in the presence of Truth. Only words. Metre. Stories. Come back, he said. Please. As if you could have refused. Father. Our Father. Though almost young enough to be my son. If I had a son...

(He muses. Then shouts): Let me be!
(Quiet) ...So that at last I may rest in the quiet place...
Pah! Rhetoric!

(He closes his eyes, clenches his fists, groans.)

And yet...How can you rest? Till you have understood?
But where is the understanding to come from?

(He muses)

You move forward. Slowly. You are inside. It is dark. A dark wood. Dark belly of the snake. It winds. It curves. You are inside. But it is not a snake. No. It is your own entrails. You are inside. You look for the light, the entrance, you look for the way out, the way in. You recall the voice, telling you always to turn left, left, left again and again. You look about you for the dove, the branch, you are inside the belly, it heaves, it sways, nothing stays still any more, there is nothing to hold on to, nothing, desert, stone, stone and scrub, stone and scrub, swaying, swaying, moving, inching forward, turning over, turning round, you are inside, outside, inside, outside, nothing, nothing...

Yes. There is nothing at the centre.

No man-faced bull. No father.

There is no centre.

And you – where are you? You call and no one answers. Is it night? Day? What is this room?

Who is speaking in this room?

The blackness rises again inside you, but you go on talking. You know the time has come. You can feel it in the room. Hovering. Waiting. Perhaps it has come and gone and nothing has changed. Perhaps it came long ago, before you started, before you left the farm... Perhaps it has not yet come and will never come and there is only the dream of darkness, of peace, of rest...

You wander through the dark wood. By the broad river. The bank is full of reeds. They bend before you as you walk. Your feet sink into the mud. You turn, you walk more quickly. You are tired. Nothing has changed. The same grey light. The same river with its belt of reeds. The same dark wood. The same voice saying left, turn left, but there is no left, no right, just the heaving desert of stone and scrub and the sun beating like a hammer on your head.

You are inside. The scaly belly moves gently, rhythmically. Where is the throat, the mouth, the passage to the light? There is only the voice, telling you to move, to walk, to turn left and again left and again and again. And now where are you? Where is this voice that says turn left? Where is the voice that says where is the voice?

Where?

Where?

Where?

II ORPHEUS (1)

(A change. He pulls himself together.)

But it's there. In spite of everything. The finished work. Something achieved. Neither the anger of the Gods nor the gnawing tooth of time will be able to undo this. Let the moment come when night closes over you for ever; still your better part shall be immortal far beyond the lofty stars and you will leave an undying name. Wherever Rome's power extends over the conquered world you will be spoken of by men, and if the prophecies of the bards have any truth in them, you will live in fame through all the ages.

The power of song was strong within you, and you bodied it forth to all the world. You have been the Poet. The Poet of Empire. You have outdone Orpheus, Pan. Apollo himself. You sang of the travelling moon and the sun's manifold labours. You sang of Arcturus and the rainy Hiades and the twin Bears. And the reason why winter suns race on to dip in ocean, and what slows down the long nights. You sang of the new Golden Age – and then it came. You sang of the founding of the City and helped Augustus make Rome strong and establish peace over the whole earth. That was something. Why not admit that it was something? You rose above Homer himself who had stood in your way for so long. You gave him the Roman answer.

Yes...

The walls of Thebes were built by Amphion...

Power of the poet...

Power

to consecrate the city
to strengthen the walls
to bless the people...

Such power...

And you used it to the best of the abilities the Gods had given you.

Had you not reason to be proud? Of your calling? Of your achievement?

You never hurried. Time unfolded for you in the way you

always knew it would. From the start you sensed it was an ally and not an enemy. An ally for those content to be on familiar terms with it; an enemy only for those who struggled against it. So that others wondered at the fact that you had come to manhood, almost to the middle of life's span, and still had produced nothing that you would call your own – while they rushed to publish, to bewilder, to impress. But when it was done, when the ten songs of Arcady were completed, when you knew you could not add a line to them because there was nothing more to add or take away – then they were recognised at once for what they were. Are. Perfection. The best that could be done. Something wholly new, accepting, welcoming the conventions, the traditions, but heralding a new dawn, a new Spring. And with them came fame. Everyone talked about you. The songs were recited on the public stage – the songs you had written in the quiet of your study through the long years of your third decade. And Augustus gave you his friendship and his patronage.

Yes...

Others would have let this go to their heads. But your pride was a deep thing. You preferred the satisfaction of silent toil to all other pleasures. Oh, you had friends, you travelled, you were no recluse. But it was the poem that was the important thing. The work on the second great poem. The epic of farming. Factual. Simple. True. And yet wrought in the patterns of art. A simple manual on the tilling of the fields, the keeping of flocks, of bees. But also a song to your own land, to Italy and what is best and truest in her inheritance.

But that was not enough. When it was done the great shadow had to be faced at last. In your youth you had thought to confront it head on and been broken by the effort. Now you knew your own strength. You knew that for Italy too an epic was possible which would vie with the work of Homer. And now you look back. You say with surprise: I was the man who did this. Alone. Yes. Alone you forged the myth for Rome. You. The Mantuan peasant from Andes. Son of the potter. How strange that it should have fallen to you to do this thing...

How strange that you should have carried out the task so silently, so relentlessly, with such certainty that one day it would be done... You...

How strange...
And it is done. There. In the metal box. In this room. With you.
How strange...
Done. A few lines still to get right. A few out of the ten thousand. If he had let you stay in Athens it might have been done by now... But even so... All there... Ten years ago there was nothing. Now it is there...

(He muses)

So much excitement. Some days you thought you would die as you polished the lines, adjusted the balance, went back to the beginning. The excitement was too much. Your heart raced. You felt the blood in your throat. Your hand trembled. But you wrote. You went on writing...
The day you understood what it was you had to do.
The day you began the second book, faced the horror of the destruction of the great city.
The day you conceived the final meeting, down in the shadows, between the proud queen and her lover.
So many days. Such regular hours. Letting nothing distract you. Feeling the breath boiling inside you, your heart pounding in your chest, holding it all, holding, holding... Never hurrying. Confident that you had been born with the right relation to time, to the world, that if you walked in the right path all would unfold before you like a dream.
A dream...

Where did you get that confidence? To do so much. Where? From your mother? Your father? From the land? The winding river, the quiet meadows, the sweet smell of spring, after the winter rains... such peace... such silence...
With your big hands you were made for the plough, not the banqueting table. For the regular routine of daily work, seasonal work... The others never understood. They envied you. Thought it was your learning that raised you above them. Tried to imitate...
They did not have the hands. The confidence in routine. Their breath was too short.

Breath. Breathing. It all comes back to that. The regularity of breathing. Poetry and spirit one. Words...

Bread and wine together. Spirit and flesh together in the word, the spoken word, flesh of the spirit, spirit of the flesh...

Yes...

Orpheus...

When he sang the very winds stood still. No leaf moved in the forest. The animals drew closer. The rivers stopped in wonder, then turned back their courses and flowed towards their springs. The world was caught in a trance, straining, listening, the radiant face of the world turned up in ecstasy towards the orbs of sun and moon.

Silence fell upon the world. Only your voice sang out.

And the silence was your voice, bodying forth the regular breathing of the world.

Orpheus...

(But now the name leads him where he had not expected to go):

Piteous Orpheus...

Bitter his anguish for the wife taken from him. Headlong beside the river she fled. She never saw her death there, deep in the grass before her feet – the watcher on the river-bank, the savage water-snake...

The band of wood-nymphs, her companions, filled the hill-tops with their crying.

And Orpheus? He entered the gorge of Tartarus, the deep underworld. He stepped into the grove where fear hangs like a black fog. He approached the ghostly people. Drew near the King of Terrors and the hearts that are not touched by human prayer. By his song he roused from Hell's darkest depths the flimsy shades, the phantoms lost to light. Mothers and men, the dead bodies of great-hearted heroes, boys and unmarried maidens, the young men laid on the pyre before their parents' eyes...

About him lay the black ooze, the crooked reeds of Cocytus – bleak the marsh that barred them with its stagnant water, and the Styx coiling nine times round penned them in there.

The very home of death was shaken to hear his song, and the

Furies with steel-blue snakes entwined in their tresses; the watch-dog Cerberus gaped open his triple mouth; Ixion's wheel stopped dead from whirling in the wind. And now he's avoided every pitfall of the homeward path and Eurydice, regained, is nearing the upper air close behind him, when a moment's madness catches him off his guard. He halts. Eurydice, his own, is now on the lip of daylight. Alas! His purpose breaks. He looks back. All his labour lost in one moment. The pact made with the merciless king annulled. Three times the thunder pealed over the pools of Avernus, and Eurydice cried out: 'Who has doomed me to misery? Who has doomed us?' she cried. 'Once more a cruel fate drags me away, and my swimming eyes are drowned in darkness. I am borne away. A limitless night is about me, and your hands no longer touch the strengthless hands I stretch out to you!'

Cold, cold she was, voyaging now over the Stygian stream...

And month after month, for seven months alone Orpheus wept beneath a crag high up by the lonely waters of Strymon. Under the ice-cold stars he poured out his dirge. Alone through Arctic ice, through the snows of Tanais, over the frost-bound Riphaean plateau he ranged, bewailing his lost Eurydice, and the wasted bounty of death. In the end the Thracian Bacchantes, flouted by his neglect, one night, in the midst of their Master's revels, tore him limb from limb and scattered him over the land. But even then that head, plucked from the marble-pale neck and rolling down mid-stream on the river Hebrus – that voice, that cold cold tongue cried out: 'Eurydice!'.

Cried: 'Poor Eurydice!' as the soul of the singer fled, and the banks of the river echoed, echoed, 'Eurydice!'

Poor Orpheus. Poor poet. Poor man. Where would he find the confidence to go and not turn back? The words rise in the air and fall back upon themselves...

He sings his loss, and it is this which makes the animals draw close and listen; the rivers cease their movement.

This which stirs the blood of his fellow men. He voices the eternal lament for all that has ever been lost. Even in death the melody rises, floats above the tumult of the busy world, the eternal lamentation of failure, doubt and loss.

Return to the land that bore you, your first mother, Apollo ordered Aeneas. And he did as he was told. But for you that was no longer possible. You had left the farm. The flocks pasturing in the hills, the river winding through the meadows. You had left full of excitement, full of hope. But, once you had turned your back on them there was no possibility of return.

And you abandoned that for what? The City? Fame? Beauty? Is that what you left for?

But what is beauty divorced from daily toil? A mirage.

What fame?

And the City? Is it there you thought to find the answer? All that weight of stone where a man can never catch sight of a tree or a bird or the brown earth? Where he cannot find silence, or darkness, or peace. Where he cannot live as we were surely meant to live. Cannot even die as we were meant to die.

You left for that? A poet's vocation? Meaning what? The dedication to a lifetime's lament? For which the crowd and your close friends praised you? Shallow praise, when what is praised is not even understood. More! they shouted. More! More!

More what?

In truth you lost your way long ago. When you first sought out your own pleasures and called them Beauty, Truth – even Duty. And then you began to write to order – an Imperial lackey!

Is that a man's life?

Dust. Dust. Dust.

(He muses)

Remember how he asked you to do it. How your pride was touched. The poem of Empire. Of peace. Of my new peace, he said. He reminded you of the words you had written, recited them in his quiet voice, tempting, tempting:

> Born of Time, a great new cycle of centuries
> Begins. Justice returns to Earth, the Golden Age
> Returns, and its first-born comes down from heaven above.

Goats shall walk home, their udders taut with milk, and
    nobody
Herding them: the ox will have no fear of the lion,
But snakes will die, and so will fair-seeming poisonous
    plants.
Traders will retire from the sea, from the pine-built vessels
They used for commerce: every land will be self-supporting.
The soil will need no harrowing, the vine no pruning-
    knife;
And the tough ploughman will at last unyoke his oxen.

His voice never rose. He knows that when he speaks other
men will listen. He spoke your own words back to you, fixing
you with his eagle gaze, smiling, always smiling... Gently he
reminded you of your boast, all those years ago:

If but the closing days of a long life were prolonged
For me, and I with breath enough to tell your story,
Oh then I should not be worsted at singing by Thracian
    Orpheus
Or Linus – even though Linus were backed by Calliope
His mother, and Orpheus by his father, beauteous Apollo.

And you, in your pride, were flattered. You succumbed. You
wrote for him the poem of Empire, the poem of Duty.
    And for yourself? Ten years of your life for what? Prop-
aganda?

And yet...
    Is there not something to be said for duty?
    How many men can boast that they have done their duty in
this life?
    Dutiful Aeneas...
    Carrying his aged father on his back. In his father's hands,
on Aeneas's back, the household gods.
    (Violent) The *weight* of the old man!
    (Quiet) The weight...
    Even worse after his death, for then the weight became the
intolerable pointing finger...

How it hurt you to write all that!

You told them you worked slowly because only a masterpiece would satisfy you. But the truth is that at times it was too much. You wanted to scream. Tear up the paper and scream. Have done with all that history, all that order, all that dutifulness!

How it went against the grain to write of that dutiful man, the weight on his back, the pointing finger...

Duty. Carry the old man. At night you woke screaming, clawing at your back, old devil from the sea, clinging there, clinging, whispering in your ear...

When he died Aeneas had to bury him with the appropriate rites. And then – Italy at last! But still he had to venture down and down, into the black depths. And for what? Eurydice? No. That belonged to the carefree age of Greece. Aeneas went down to meet his father. To listen for the last time to the old man. To look where the finger pointed at the long long interminable line of his descendants stretched before them...

Cold. Cold. The coldness of the snake.

He gave up Dido. The warmth of the hall. Of the cave. Of love and peace and the security of her embrace...

For what? Duty?

Pah!

Left his mother: his home. Troy. To carry his father on his back.

Carry his father on his back...

What duty? To Augustus? Rome?

He clung on, the smiling one. You tried to thrust him off. Said you were not ready. But he clung on, talking, cajoling, willing you to meet his bright gaze...

He clung on! He clings on! A part of you!

You accepted the fact that he would not let you go. Bowed your head. Bent over your desk. Every day you wrote. Polished the lines. Wrote what he wanted...

Father!

So it all came to that? The dreams of freedom? Of poetry? Truth?

For Caesar's sake you helped perpetrate a lie. You sang of history as if that was the way it had to happen. And, hearing what you had written, the people believed that it was indeed so. That Aeneas was destined to settle in Italy. That the gods had given them this land.

It is easy to make people believe what they want to believe. To forget the carnage. The slaughter. The deportations. To forget that no one owns any land by right...

You gave history a meaning: Rome, destined to belong to Aeneas and his descendants. But there is no meaning. Except for the iron will of Rome. Of Caesar. Crushing. Crushing. Forcing all into his mould.

And it was you who helped perpetrate that lie. You. Full of good will. Full of virtue. Melancholy. Obsessed by beauty and death. You helped to mould the world to the pattern of Caesar's will.

You did that! It is you they should banish from the city. Much more than Oedipus. At least he dug out the source of the city's pollution, though he had been the cause of it himself. But you helped to pollute the earth, and you have been rewarded with – honour, glory!

Yes. That too is part of it.

Why did you do it? Why did you give in to him?

(He muses)

No. Not that. Not that only. Go deeper. Don't lay the blame on others.

Deeper. Seek out the cause of the pollution...

Bury your nose in it!

III   INTO THE DEPTHS   (1)

Gods...

Deo invicto Julius caused them to write on his statue. To
the invincible god...Both of them – the old man and his
adopted son – both of them had that lust for domination which
is there in all of us to some extent, but never so stark, so
blatant, so...

Gods. Nothing less. This one as much as the other. Neither
willing to conceive of death. They must go on for ever. On
and on. Domination. The power of bronze. Of stone. For ever.

And we love them for that. Julius knew it. Based his life on
it. And Augustus learned it from him. We want to believe
them. To shelter in their shadow. To partake a little of that
immortality of theirs.

We *want* to carry them! To feel the virtue running out of
them into our own shoulders, our legs...

Was it not that which made you set out in the first place?
The pull, the tug, the tickle of immortality? The brown earth
beneath your feet reminded you too strongly of what your
end would be. You fought against it, turned away. For you –
the skies!

And that was the lure of the city. What Caesar promised.
Stay in my shadow. Together we will rise up to the Heavens...

What poetry promised...

Yes. That was the secret plan. Secret even from yourself.
By singing you would master chaos, you would turn all that
was Other into that which was yours. The water would be
turned into the stone of the city and Time would pass away.

The waters of chaos. Of darkness.

Again and again you turned to the depiction of the Underworld, as if by so doing you could exorcise its hold. Again
and again you wrote of the snake of chaos, the soul of the
universe...

To pin it down. Hold it down in words, in metre. Become
a god in your own way...

(He muses)

The snake. Sacred to the peasant. Guardian of the homestead.
Slithering out from the shrine of Anchises, holy, inoffensive,

circling the barrow, sliding between the altars, upon its back
a sheen, a dapple of bluish markings and gold-glittering scales,
like the shimmer of many colours the rainbow lays on the dark
clouds...

And then that other, the helical snake you saw at the very
centre of the cosmos:

> Five zones make up the heavens: one of them in the flaming
> Sun glows red for ever, for ever seared by his fire:
> Round it to right and left the furthermost zones extend,
> Blue with cold, ice-bound, frozen with black blizzards:
> Two zones by the grace of God, and a path was cut through
>   both
> Where the slanting signs might march and counter-march.
> The world
> Rising sharply to Scythia and the Riphaean plateau,
> Slopes down in the south to Libya.
> This North pole's always above us: the South appears
>   beneath
> The feet of the darkling Styx, the deep-down shadow
>   people.
> Here the great snake glides out with weaving, elastic body
> Writhing riverwise around and between the two Bears –
> The Bears that are afraid to get wet in the water of Ocean.

...Form of the unformed. Image of chaos. Holy for that
reason. But the poet pollutes that holiness. By speaking he
betrays. He tries to say the truth and despite himself he is a
conveyor of lies. The black cloud of falsehood covers the earth.
It hangs in the air, the stench!

He thinks to tame the universe. As the city thinks to tame
the ocean. As Caesar hoped to tame the East. He sits on the
back of the world and will not be shaken off!

The world takes its revenge. The dark will not give up its secret...
    Cleopatra dying with the snake at her breast...
    The snake that stung Eurydice...
    The ninefold windings of the river Styx...
    And the two... Yes, the two snakes who came for Laöcöon
out of the sea...

Oh! They stifle me, they strangle me!
Laöcöon...

He was sacrificing a great bull at the official altar, when over
the tranquil deep of Tenedos – yes, they too came out of the
sea! – when over the tranquil deep of Tenedos twin snakes
were seen, with immense coils thrusting the sea together streak-
ing towards the shore: rampant they were among the waves,
their blood-red crests reared up above the water; the rest of
them slithered along the surface, coil after coil sinuously trailing behind them. There was the hiss of salt spray – then they
were on dry land, in the same field – a glare and blaze of
bloodshot eyes, tongues flickering like flames from their
mouths, and the mouths hissing. They went straight for Laöcöon. First, each snake knotting itself round the body of one
of his small sons, hugging him tight in his coils, cropping the
piteous flesh with its fangs. Then they fastened on Laöcöon
as he hurried, weapon in hand, to help the boys. With a double
grip round his waist and neck the scaly creatures embraced
him, their heads and throats powerfully poised above him. All
the while his hands were struggling to break their knots, his
priestly headband is spattered with blood and pitchy venom.
All the while his appalling cries go up to heaven – a bellowing
such as one hears when a wounded bull escapes from the altar,
after it's shrugged off an ill-aimed blow at its neck. Then the
twin monsters glide away, escaping towards the shrine of
Minerva, high up on the citadel, disappearing round the Goddess's shield at her feet there, leaving panic among the Tro-
jans...
...In your heart of hearts you always knew it. Knew that
the snake of darkness, of chaos, must not be touched or it will
turn against you. And yet you did it, you were driven forward,
you bit your lips in excitement, your heart beat faster, you
wanted to explain it all.
But there is no explanation. The poet does not tell the truth.
He weaves an evil spell to protect himself from the dark, to
control, control...
You have tried to bind the world to you as Dido tried to
bind her departing lover to her, calling on the Ethiopian witch
for help...

Near Ocean's furthest bound and the sunset is Aethiopia,
The very last place on earth, where giant Atlas pivots,
The wheeling sky, embossed with fiery stars, on his
   shoulder.
I have been in touch with a priestess from there, a Massylian,
   who once,
As warden of the Hesperides' sacred close, was used to
Feed the dragon which guarded their orchard of golden
   apples,
Sprinkling its foot with moist honey and sedative poppy-
   seeds.
Now this enchantress claims that her spells can liberate
One's heart, or can inject love-pangs, just as she wishes;
Can stop the flow of rivers, send the stars flying backwards,
Conjure ghosts in the night; she can make the earth cry out
Under one's feet, and the elm trees come trooping down
   from the mountains.

What else was the skill of Orpheus? Magic and evil. Magic and
evil. Nothing else.

(He muses)
   But why? You wanted nobody's love. So why did you do it?
   You sang to avoid yourself. To conjure away the thoughts
of death. Of your own death, your very own.
   But death is here. In the room. Nowhere to turn any more.
No words to use any more.

You thought poetry helped you to live, but would it not be
truer to say that it kept you from living? That it perpetuated
this lie, this life? Which of course does not imply that your
life is any better when you don't write. On the contrary, then
it's much worse, quite unbearable in fact, and with no possible
remedy except madness and death.

Yes, creation is a pleasant, a splendid reward, but for what?
These are wages earned in the service of evil. The descent
towards the powers of darkness, the ambiguous contacts, all
that takes place down there and of which nothing is known
while one composes poetry in the sunlight...

Maybe there exists a different kind of creation – you, at any rate, know no other. At night, when anguish keeps you awake, you know no other. And the evil of it all is quite clear to you now. It is vanity and a thirst for pleasure that keeps buzzing round your face... buzzing...

What kind of vanity?

Don't stop. Go on. What kind of vanity?

What children sometimes wish: 'I would like to die so as to see how I will be mourned' – that you achieved at times. Why then this panic dread of death, not necessarily expressed as such, but disguised as fear of change, fear of being torn from your desk, from your quill, from the peace and silence of your room?

There are two main reasons for this fear of death. First, a dread of it because one has not lived. That does not mean that to live one must have a wife, children, fields and cattle. What is required to be alive is to give up seeking satisfaction in oneself, to go into the house instead of admiring it and wreathing it in flowers.

It might be objected that such matters are in the hands of fate and beyond the power of men. But then why does one feel so guilty, why does the sense of guilt never lie down? And why, if guilt does not come into it, the conclusion you always reach in those sleepless nights: You might live and you do not?

The second reason. (But in fact they are one and the same, it is impossible to tell them apart.) The second reason is the following thought: 'The game you played is about to become reality. You have not redeemed yourself with writing. You have been dead all your life, and now you are really going to die. Your life was pleasanter than most, your death will be all the more terrible.' The writer in you will naturally die at once, for such a character has nothing to stand on, the soil under his feet is unstable, it is not even dust, it is only just barely possible for the most ridiculous of earthly existences, it owes the consistency it has to the search for pleasure. But you yourself cannot go on living since you never lived – you are nothing but clay, you have not turned the spark into flame – you have only used it to light up your corpse!

Think of the peculiar funeral which will follow: the writer, that is, something which does not exist, will bring the old corpse to its grave, the corpse which has always existed. And of course you are writer enough to relish the situation with all your being and with total abnegation – for is it not abnegation rather than observation which is the first condition of literary endeavour?

Or rather, which amounts to the same thing, you are writer enough to want to turn the situation into poetry. But that is not possible any more.

And why should we talk only about actual death? Is it not the same while you are alive? Here you are, a little ill, but still comfortable compared to the vast majority of mankind, still comfortable – settled in the easy position of the writer, and having to witness passively the sufferings inflicted on your real self, your poor helpless self...

And what right have you to panic, you who were never at home, at the sight of your house's sudden collapse? Don't you know what led to that collapse? Hadn't you already emigrated, abandoned your house to the powers of evil long ago?

Even this is still a game. You relish playing it even as you denounce it. Nothing will make you stop. Even here, in the proximity of death, you play your old game! You breathe the words of disgust, but does your heart believe them?

As though games could save you!

Can you not see that nothing can save you now? You lost your way long ago. The savour has gone from the earth. Only the dry dust remains. Dust and ashes in your mouth.

Ah, how you like the sound of those words: Dust. Ashes. And you turn, you glance sidelong at the coffer, your heart still stirs when you think of what is there, nestling inside... Still expands with pleasure, with pride... *You* have done this. Alone. You...

After all this! And you still think of it as your salvation? Pah! Pah!

Will you never learn? Not even at the end? The very end?

There. When it comes. Your mouth will still form the phrases. Your mind will still go back over the unfinished lines. You will weigh the words, the syllables...

Even then?

(A time)

It must go. It must be destroyed. Nothing but lies. Pollution. The source of pollution.

A giant stone. A rock. Blocking the way. The way out. Roll it away. Roll it away!

LET ME BREATHE!

IV   THE FINAL ACT

Lucius!
Lucius!
LUCIUS!

(*Silence. No one comes.*)

LUCIUS!
Where are they all? At the feast? But Lucius...?
L U C I U S!

(*He struggles off the couch and across the room towards the coffer. But the fever has weakened him and he falls to the floor. He raises himself and crawls forward. A long struggle. He reaches it, panting with the effort. He pulls it down to him.*)

Key. Where's the key? Damn! Where's the key?
Lucius!

(*Panic. He tries to get the coffer open with his fingers, but fails. He bangs it on the floor in an effort to break it open, but to no avail. He hurls it down, but it remains closed. He tries again and again, more and more desperately.*
Suddenly, the violence exhausts itself. He touches the box. Passes a finger over it. Examines it lovingly. He is very weak.
He holds it close to him – his baby.
The crisis is over. He lets the coffer go.
He crawls back to the bed. Clambers on.
He groans. Mumbles. Falls back on the bed.
He lies still.)

V INTO THE DEPTHS (2)

(The violent action of the last few moments has shaken him badly. He is much weaker.)

Stone. The weight of stone. Can't breathe. The weight.

No earth. No tree. Stone.

Empty. Empty spaces. Can't breathe. So much space. So empty. Oh...

Stars... In that space...

Empty. Empty.

And in the streets. The city. Numberless. Hordes. Lost. Forsaken. No home. No family. Forsaken. Wandering. Numberless. Numberless.

Sea of stone. Labyrinth of stone.

The weight. All that stone. Troy. Carthage. Alexandria. Rome.

No darkness. No silence. No solitude. Hordes everywhere, moving, moving, a sea, a cauldron...

No grass. Stone. The weight. The smell. Numberless...

Bodies. Teeming. Reproducing. Stinking. Dying. No air. No space. Furnace. Burning furnace. In the stone.

Thousands. Thousands. No direction. Always moving. Hungry. Angry. Shouting. Moving. Moving. No direction. So many. Without direction.

Sacred once. Now meaningless the weight. Meaningless the streets. Labyrinth of stone. For ever and ever.

The epithets of the holy city: *illag*, the enclosure; *antiranna*, the forest of Heaven; *ubimin*, the seven regions; *daimin*, the seven sides; *geparimin*, the seven dark chambers.

The enclosure. The forest of Heaven. The seven regions. The seven sides. The seven dark chambers.

Troy. That giant city. Falling. Falling.

Was it not built by magic?
Achilles dragging Hector three times round the walls to break the spell.

The seven regions. The seven sides. The seven dark chambers. That you knew. The old magic. Beyond Homer. Older. Older.

And it was you who sang of the destruction of the city. Stone falling, crumbling. Fire. Fire raging everywhere. The people crushed like ants. Scurrying before the fire. The avenging Greeks.

Troy. Carthage. Alexandria. Rome.

The weight of stone. Crushing weight. Horror. The weight. Stones quarried. Day after day. Slaves cutting. Cutting the stone with soft hands.

The streets. The houses. The temples. No escape. Never. No!

No escape.

(He muses)

And you? Who are you? Tied to me all these years, dying now, in this city of stone...
...putrid corpse...or what?

You rot but there is no burial. The stones will not open. No earth. No soft earth in which to hide. In this labyrinth of stone there is nowhere to hide. You must lie down on the stone and try to sleep, ignore the gaping masses scurrying by. Clasp the old corpse to you and try to sleep.

Let the vermin crawl... Sea of men, crawling...

Flight! Flight! – But the sea of stone is everywhere. Men and women moving in one pulsating mass, one stench, one shriek, one blinding light. No darkness... no end...

Oh...

Look! Animals without heads! Griffins with baby faces! Women with scaly tails and ants crawling on their breasts! Moving. Changing. Nothing stays still any more. They change as you look, grown into trees, rats, fish with giant snouts...

Look! It moves. The walls bubble. They turn green, slimy, rot and fall. Out come the birds, like locusts! The steely wings of the birds of death. Their stinking breath. Bats with women's faces. Beating wings! Beating! Beating!

Silence. No air. The bubbles form.

Aaaaah!

Aaaaah!

(He has struggled off the bed and fallen on the floor as he tries to protect his head and face.
Gradually he grows still. He speaks quietly now.)

And there. There. Everywhere. The cold eye of the snake.
Cold eye of death.
Petrifaction.
Cold eye of Nothing.

You never dared face that before. The cold eye of the snake.

Nothing. The nothing.
Nothing behind...
Silence...

You wrote of the violence. Clawing at the father on your back. The fury of the women reacting to all that weight of stone, of duty, the imposition of order. Allecto the Fury inflaming the Queen with her snaky locks. The women made mad. Crazy with blood-lust, the mania for fighting... As when a fire of wood is stoked up high beneath the belly of the boiling cauldron and the water seethes and dances in the heat, bubbling, spitting up foam, till it cannot contain itself any more...

Mad... mad... As if the weight of stone, the weight of duty, the weight of the Father, had become too much, and they must tear, tear, tear everything to pieces.

– Why could I not have torn up his body and littered the sea with it?... Dido...

Yet Aeneas escaped. Escaped the fate of Orpheus. But he wanted to be torn. One part of him wanted it so badly...

Tearing. Tearing limb from limb. No longer able to live with themselves. Throwing off the weight of the Father. The weight of stone. The weight of history.

Why could I not have torn up his body and littered the sea with it?

Ah!

The keening of the women! Tearing! Tearing!

Like hounds. Dogs unleashed...

Orpheus! Torn!

The gods have abandoned the world. All that is left is the cold eye of death, the labyrinth of stone, and the women tearing...

Tearing.

The heat. The carnage. Opulence of Caesar.

And Orpheus torn! Torn!

I can't –

They come!

Scaly wings!

They tear! Mouths bloody! Hot breath! Ah!

Tearing Orpheus! Tearing out his eyes! His ears! Twisting off his neck!

Yes. Till his limbs float down the river and litter the sea.

Orpheus...

The hounds biting. Sucking. Mouths bloody as the flesh flows from their fangs.

Orpheus...

But even that head, plucked from the marble-pale
Neck and rolling down mid-stream on the river Hebrus –
That voice, that cold cold tongue cried out, 'Eurydice!'
Cried: 'Poor Eurydice!' as the soul of the singer fled,
And the banks of the river echoed, echoed, 'Eurydice!'

Echoed!

(He shouts in the silence) Echoed!

(Silence)

(He shouts again) Echoed!

(Silence)

(He shouts a third time) Echoed!

*(He starts to laugh.
He falls back on the bed in a kind of fit.)*

VI   ORPHEUS   (2)

(He comes out of the fit into a new calm)

Orpheus...
Yes...
The poet. Orpheus. Perhaps... Yes...
Perhaps
       the poet
              must be torn
                    and the voice
                            go on
                                    singing
Perhaps that's it.
The poet must be torn. And go on singing.
Singing of tearing. Yes.
Perhaps singing is a kind of tearing. Tearing loose. Tearing
up the roots. Spreading the fragments over the waters of
silence...
    And the poet sings and tears. Holds down and lets go...
    Silenus, singing of the creation of the world... He will not
sing till the shepherd boys bind him, constrain him...
    And who sang of Orpheus but Proteus, the god of the sea
itself? It is not easy to make Proteus speak, as easy as to make
the sea give up its yield. Entreaties have no effect,

> When you hold him fast in a handhold and fettered, then
> With the guise and visage of various wild beasts he'll keep
>   you guessing;
> Suddenly he'll turn into a bristling boar, a black tiger,
> A laminated dragon or a tawny-backed lioness,
> Or go up in a shrill burst of flame and thus from his fetters
> Escape, or give you the slip gliding off in a trickle of water,
> But the more he transforms himself,
> The tighter must you strain the shackles that bind his
>   body
> Until at last it changes back to the first likeness
> You saw at the start when his eyes were closing down in
>   sleep.

And it was he, Proteus himself, when he was finally caught and held, who sang of Orpheus...

Yes...The poet is Orpheus, but he is also the women who tear him. Proteus, but also the one who holds and fetters him. Dido and the Aeneas who escapes her.

The snake. My error was to put him into the poem. To pin him down in language. But the snake *is* the poem. As the labyrinth is the poem. As both are life itself.

Proteus. Orpheus. The changing sea-god. The ever-changing sea. And the torn head singing.

Homer knew it. He sang of the shield of Achilles. Round the perimeter of the shield, the waters of chaos; in the centre, the labyrinthine dancing-floor of Ariadne.

Yes. Now understanding comes. How the poet, limbs torn and strewn on the waves, sings on.

That is not heroism. He can do nothing else. For there is no song without tearing. No true song. For the tearing is the truth.

And the song is the response. And that too is the truth.

From the rotting flesh emerge the bees. Without the carcase there would be no bees.

Swarming. Swarming.

From the waters, from the snake, comes life itself, destructive and creative. We cannot avoid it.

You did not see all that when you wrote. But you sensed it. And the poem betrays your unease.

Is that a reason to destroy it? Though it hurts to leave it as it is, you know now that that is how it has to be. Once, you might have changed it. You had a dream perhaps of what it might have been. Now it is too late.

Accept. Accept.

Perhaps there was a purpose but you could not fathom it. Who are you to say that you know better?

Accept it all. As it happened. As it is. Accept. Accept.

But the pain of it. Not so much what you did wrong as what you never did at all. The lives you might have lived...The farm...Athens...

And now: nothing more. Nothing possible any longer. Petrifaction.

This room. This bed. Hardest to accept.

And yet... Is that not part of the pattern – the pain of failure, loss?

Perhaps that was really the substance of your poem. That history must be accepted. Recognized and accepted. Not justified. For nothing is ever justified. But recognized.

And the poem must stand. It exists now. It is there. It must be accepted.

Vain now to try and take it away.

My life too. Its failures. No house to enter as my own.

No children. Grandchildren. Dust. Dust.

Accept. Accept that too.

Carry him. Carry the father. The household gods. Carry them on your back...

As Daedalus carried his son

Not as an effort of the will, but out of love...

Because that is what we are: creatures of sympathy...

It is *ourselves* we carry!

And by living... just by living... we perpetuate the line...

The past *and* the future. Accept. Accept.

So hard. And yet...

The city destroyed. The farm left behind. Lost paradise – always an illusion. We are never one with the land, the river, the flocks – with the Mother or the Father.

We have always to set out, to leave the sacred places, the dark wood...

Stone labyrinth...

Be torn be torn be torn!

The power of love!

Daedalus crying for his son... He could not look, could not bear to fashion again the image of those wings...

And had there been no Eurydice, what would Orpheus have sung?

She was there. Existed. That is enough.
Yes...

And can a man love language as I have loved you, my language?
I followed where you led. I did not try to restrain you, only to give you shelter, a place where you could grow in the sunshine and be strong...
The protection of a line, a page...
Where I could nurture you in the warmth...

My language.

And now even you can go. You were not mine, even at the end. I only gave you shelter.
Now you can go.
Gone.
Gone...
Accept.

VII   THE THRESHOLD   (2)

And yet... One last time...

The unconsenting spirit fled to the shades below.

Yes. The unconsenting.

To let go.

Let go of all. Even the name.

Spring and Truth. *Ver* and *Verus*.

What is that sound? That music?

(Lights start to dim. In the background, over the sound of the fountain, a flute has started to play.)

No boundaries any more. Round the city. Round the self.

Gone. Finished.

No Truth. No Spring.

Accept. Accept it all. Sympathy with all.

A fish. A bird.

Bird swimming in the waters of the sea.
Fish flying in the firmament.

The *beauty* of this earth!

Ashes. Warm in the hearth. Warm in the urn.

Yes. At last.

(He listens. Then cries out suddenly): Oh! What? You? Mother?

Venus! Mother!

Must you too be cruel? Must you make a game of your son now with shapes of sheer illusion? Oh, why may we not join hands and talk together? Why this? Why?

Gone.

Gone.

The final folly. Wanting to understand it all. To talk face to face. If only for a moment.

Wanting. Wanting...

At the end. In spite of everything. Wanting to understand the dark. The time before. Before you came into the light of this world. Wanting... to see *behind!*

Mystery. Mystery.

How strange... In all this silence...

Bird in the waters of the world
Fish flying high in the firmament...

Gone. She's gone.

And that's right. Accept that too. Accept. Yes. Accept.

(It is quite dark now. The fountain and the flute still play. He is no longer a body, no longer Vergil. He is a voice, speaking fragments from the work of a poet, Vergil chasing his own echo, but in a kind of game now, no longer in anguish and despair.)

And longer

            longer falls the shadow

Where?

longer falls the shadow cast by the mountain heights

That voice... You? Or you? Or you?

falls

   falls the shadow

                longer falls

                        longer

                            the shadow

(Whisper) AT LAST!

(The fountain. The flute.
The flute fades.
The fountain fades.
Silence. Darkness.)

The author is grateful to Oxford University Press for permission to quote from *The Eclogues, Georgics and Aeneid of Virgil*, translated by C. Day Lewis (Oxford Paperbacks, 1966).

4

The Bird Cage

So you are in the house at last. How well you describe the room. The sea. The window. The bird in the cage. The mirror. And then in the mirror the cage, the window and the sea.

When I read what you say I long to be there, with you, in that room brimming with light and the sea and the bird.

You ask me to come. You describe the way the light fills the room. You describe the way the mirror reflects the light which bounces off the sea. You describe the way the song of the bird mingles with the sound of the waves. I can't wait. I can't wait to come.

I will catch the train this afternoon. In a few hours I will be there. Tomorrow morning I will wake and see the foot of the bed in the mirror and then the cage and the bird and the window and the sea. Last night I dreamed about the bird. About the yellowness of its plumage. You tell me about his song, the sound of his voice, and in my dream it is translated into colours, the colour of his plumage. I wish I knew what that meant. What that dream meant, the transposition in the dream.

I am here now and you are gone. I came and we were together and now you are gone.

I am glad you are not here. I am glad to be able to possess the room myself as you possessed it before I came. I am glad to be able to stand at the window and look into the sea and let the song of the bird fill me up entirely. I am glad to wake alone and look in the mirror and see the foot of the bed and the bird in his cage and the window and the sea outside. I am glad to be able to take possession of it as you took possession of it. In that way I feel I am getting to know you as well as I know myself.

I am glad you have had to go away. I am glad to be alone here with nothing but the sea and the gulls and the bird in the cage. I stand for hours under his cage, looking at the sea. The light reflected off the sea almost hurts. It makes everything in the room seem to splinter into a thousand fragments, as if it could not contain itself, there was so much light. I never draw the curtains. At night I feel myself going to sleep in the middle of the sea. When I wake in the morning I keep my eyes closed for a moment, feeling the light exploding in my body. That's what it does, it explodes in my body. I don't count the days. Sometimes I imagine I have not yet arrived and only have your descriptions to fire my imagination. Sometimes it is almost too much to bear in the present.

I am glad to be here by myself but I begin to miss you. I wonder why you have not yet returned, what it is that is keeping you so long. I have begun to think of how you looked those last few days. I have begun to wonder if you are ever coming back. Yesterday I walked to the farm with the intention of ringing you but when I got there I couldn't do it. Won't you write to me? Won't you tell me when you are coming back?

This morning I walked to the farm and asked to use the phone. I dialled your number but when I heard the phone ringing in your flat I put the instrument straight back. I think I couldn't face hearing the sound of you withdrawing when you learned who it was at the other end. Perhaps tomorrow I will have more courage, be able to go through with it.

I have decided to go away. I have decided that you will not come back here until I go away. I stand at the window and look at the sea and I know I will have to go away. I will bring the bird round to the farm when I bring them the key. Perhaps when you learn that I have gone away you will be able to return.

I had expected an explanation but you have provided none. I had expected the phone to ring in my flat but it was silent. And now you write as though nothing had happened. You write about the bird and the room as you did before. Before I came. As if I had never been and you had never gone and left me there, for a day or two you said, while you dealt with urgent matters in town. What is the meaning of your letter?

You write and ask me to come, as though nothing had happened. I do not know what to make of what you write. You say you are selling the house and want me to see it for one last time. I cannot understand what it is you are asking.

You beg me to answer and let you know if I have received your letters. You tell me the house is sold with the bird and the bed and the mirror and everything else. You say you want to see me and beg me to answer. How can I answer a letter like that?

You write and tell me the owner has allowed the house to go to ruin. You write go to ruin as if that were the most natural thing in the world, and as if the English were correct. Perhaps it is but it feels wrong to me. I would have said fall into ruin, but perhaps it is I who am at fault. You write that you have been back and walked along the beach and pushed open the door because no one lives in the house any more and it is an adventure, to walk along the beach and see this lovely and deserted house right up against the sea which is not locked and climb the stairs which are rotting and enter the bedroom. You write that you would like to buy back the house and restore it. You write that the mirror still stands in the bedroom, reflecting the foot of the bed and the window and the sea. You write that the cage is still there but the bird has gone. I don't know why you write these things to me or what you want of me. You say you do not know if the bird is dead or the owner has found him a better cage. I don't know why you write like this. I remember the light in the room when we woke in the morning and the light of the evening when I stood by myself at the window but most of all I remember how I imagined the room when you first wrote to me about it.

How can I answer your letters? What do you want me to say? I showed my little girl the picture you had drawn, of the mirror and the room reflected in it, and, beyond the window, the sea. She said the bird was singing. I asked her how she knew but she giggled the way children do and wouldn't answer.
   I don't think you understand. I don't think you have much idea what happens to us in our lives. I don't think you see that we are all in cages, but the cages are our lives. You wanted to build a cage around yourself and then you were afraid when

you saw the bars. But there is no need to build. The cages are our lives. When we recognize this we can sing. That is what I think at least.

I say these words to myself: the sea, the window, the bird, the cage, the room, the mirror, and then the room again, the cage, the window and the sea. They are like the bars of my cage. My little girl asks me if I will ever take her to the room by the sea. I tell her: you are there. You are in the room. There is no need to go. She does not hear when I speak. She looks at the picture. The picture on the page. I say: Turn the page. Let us look at another picture. She does not hear. She is absorbed by what is in front of her, as children are. Turn the page, I say. Turn the page and let us look at another picture. But she does not hear.

A Changeable Report

Kent: 'Report is changeable.'
– *King Lear*, IV. vii. 92

I have been dead for five years. I say dead and I am trying to
be as precise as possible. I do not know how else to put it. My
hand trembles as I write but it is comforting to have pen and
ink and paper on which to write things down. It is as if I had
forgotten how to use a pen. I have to pause before each word.
Sometimes I cannot remember how the letters are formed. But
it is a comfort to bend over the white page and think about
these things. If I could explain what happened I might find
myself alive once more. That is the most terrible thing. The
thing I really hate them for. They have taken away my life,
though no court of law would convict them for it. When I
think about that time and what they did to me, my insides get
knotted up in anger and despair and I hate them not so much
for what they did then as for what they are doing to me now,
knotting me up with anguish and hatred at the memory.

I have tried to understand what happened. I thought that if
I could put it all down on paper I would finally understand and
I would be free of them for ever. But when I try I cannot continue. There is a darkness all round the edges. I think that by
writing I will be able to shift that darkness a little, allow light to
fall on the central events at least. But it does not work like that.
It is as though the light follows each letter, each word perhaps,
but no more, and in so doing moves away from the previous
word, which is once again swallowed up in darkness. I pinch
myself to make myself concentrate. I bite my lips and try to look
as steadily as possible at what has occurred, at what is occurring.
But the light moves along with the pen and I can never hold
more than a small sequence in my mind at any one time. So I
give up and wait for a better moment. But there is no better
moment. There is just the urge to seize the pen again and write.

I did not think writing was so important. Till they shut me up. There was no cause. I had been gulled. But they bundled me in and locked the door. They told me I was mad. In the dark I felt about for windows, candles, but there were none. I was afraid of suffocating. I have always been afraid of that. I used to have nightmares about being shut into a basket and forgotten. I could hear them outside, chattering and laughing. I asked for pen and paper. I had to write and tell her what they had done to me. When they finally let me do so she had me released at once. I did not think I had changed then. I did not realize what it does to you to be shut up in the dark without hope or the ability to keep track of time. I vowed revenge on the whole lot of them. As I left I heard him start to sing. I went out into the night.

I had never had much time for his songs or his silly repartees. I do not know why she put up with him. Or with any of them. I need my sleep. I did my work well. I tried to keep them under control. I asked for nothing more. The noise they made. I could not stand that noise, that drunken bawling at all hours of the day and night. I cannot stand the sight of grown men who have deliberately befuddled themselves. It is degrading. Besides, she paid me to keep order in the house and I kept order as best I could. She should never have indulged him. Why put up even with a cousin if he consistently behaves like that? Why keep a Fool just because your father kept one? A hateful habit, demeaning to both parties. Let the Spaniards retain the custom, they are little better than beasts themselves. But that she should do so! And a foolish Fool at that. A knave. As bad as the rest of them, Maria and the cousin and his idiot friend. The noise they made. The songs they sang. Obscene. Meaningless. Vapid. Why did she let them? If it had been me I would soon have sent them packing. Restored some decency to the house. And her still in mourning for her brother.

I thought she had more sense. A page. A mere boy. Get him into bed at any cost. Forget her brother. Forget the injunctions of her father. What kind of life do humans want to lead, what kind of a –

My stomach has knotted up again. I hate them for making me hate in this way. I hate them for doing this to me. When I walked out into the night he was singing about the wind and the rain. I thought I would be revenged on them all. My stomach was knotted with anger. I wanted to scream, to kick and punch them, him especially, the fat cousin, the –

I have said to myself that I will keep calm. I have promised myself that I will control myself and write it all down so that I may understand and be free of the darkness. I am a survivor. I have not survived so long without learning a little about how it is done. I have the will, I have the patience. They think only of the moment. They drink and joke and sing. They did this to me. They tried to make me mad. They tried to persuade me that I was mad. They could not bear to have me there, watching them, I –

At moments, as I write, I no longer know who I am. It feels as though all this had happened to someone else and it had simply been reported to me. I see things in my head. My stomach knots in pain and anger. But I am not sure if my head and stomach belong to the same person.

Never mind. I must use what skills I have and not be deflected. I must be patient. Men have burrowed out of dungeons with nothing but a nail-file. What are five years or ten years when life itself is at stake? I have always been patient. I have my pen and paper and I can always start again. And again and again until the darkness is dispersed and I can emerge into the light once more and live.

I remember the man I was. But he is like a puppet. I do not know what kept him going. Perhaps it was nothing except a sense of duty. I see him bustle. He was a great bustler. I sometimes think I am still there. That I still work there, do what I have to do about the house, take orders from him, from the boy now, while she stands simpering by. I hate her for that, for what she let them do to me and for standing by now and doting on that boy.

But I am not there. I know I am not there. I turned my back on them forever and walked out, vowing revenge. Yet I was not interested in revenge. I only wanted to forget them. To start again elsewhere. But I could not. The song would not let me go. It was like a leash he had attached to me when he saw that I was determined to go. I sleep and it comes to me in my dreams. I wake and it creeps up on me in the daytime. I plotted revenge. I thought I would find my way back there and take

up my post with them again. I would steal her handkerchief
and poison his mind. He would have killed her for that. Killed
her first and then himself. He was capable of it, he went for
Andrew the minute he saw him, broke his head and then lamed
Toby. They would have taken me back. I know how she felt
about me. I would have played on those feelings. I would have
made him kill her and then in despair he would have done
away with himself.

At other moments I thought of other, sillier kinds of revenge.
I would have them all on an island. I would be able to control
the winds and the waves. I would wreck them on my island.
The drunken idiots would be pinched and bruised and bitten
by my spirits, and the others, the others would get their deserts
– the whole lot of them. I would frighten them with ghosts
made of old sheets, I would lead them into swamps and then
reveal myself to them – it would be the silliness of the punish-
ments that would be the most shaming.

Idle thoughts. I am surprised that I can remember them. At
moments they were there, so strong, so clearly formulated.
But I do not think I ever took them seriously. Because it was
as if I had lost the ability to act. As if his song had drained me
of my will. When it flooded through my head I cried. I cried
a lot. There was another music too, unearthly, and fragments
of speeches, but not speeches in the ordinary sense, not
exchanges of information between two people, but somehow
as if their souls had found words. I understood what they said,
but not the meaning of individual words and phrases. In such
a night was the refrain. The names of Cressida and of Dido,
of Thisbe and of Medea came into it. The floor of heaven like
a carpet thick inlaid with patines of bright gold. I remember
that. It was like a music I had never heard before and never
imagined could exist. And then I was in the dark but it was
peaceful, quite different from that other dark, and there was
another song, fear no more the heat of the sun, and home art
gone and ta'en thy wages. It merged with the other voices,
telling of Dido and Medea and Thisbe and Cressida. But when
I tried to hear them more clearly, to focus on them better, they
faded away and finally vanished altogether. I went out through
a door and instead of the garden I had expected there was
desert, dirt, an old newspaper blowing across a dirty street,

decaying tenements. I turned back and there was the music again, but now the door was locked and I could not get in. Why do I know nothing about music? Why have I always feared it? Not just the drunken catches but the pure sweet music of viols, the pure sweet melancholy songs. I fear them all.

I tried to walk then but my feet kept going through the rotten planks. I put my hand up to my head and the hair came away in clumps. I knew this was not so. I knew it was only my imagination. I fought against it. They are trying to do this to me, I said to myself. They want you to think that you are mad. You will not give them that satisfaction. But I woke up dreaming that my head was made of stone and I held it in my lap, sightless eyes gazing past me into the sky. My daughter had betrayed me. She had stolen all my jewellery and absconded with a Negro. There was a storm and women spoke and tempted me. I looked at my hands and they were covered with blood. The storm grew worse and I was on a deserted heath and howling. An idiot and a blind old man held on to me, trying to pull me down, uttering gibberish, but I kicked them off, and then there was that song again, about the wind and the rain. In the rain my daughter came and talked. Something terrible had happened but all was forgiven. She talked to me. She answered when I spoke to her. But I knew it would not last and it didn't, she was dead in my arms, I held her and she weighed less than a cat. I pretended she was alive but I knew she was dead. I walked again and the rotten boards gave way, one leg stuck in the ground, it grew into the ground, and all the time I knew it was not so, that if I could turn, if I could return, and it required so small an effort, so very small an effort, then it would all change, she would be with me on the island and I would rule over the wind and the waves, she had only pretended to run away, only pretended to be dead. But I also knew that I could not make that effort, that I could not go back, that the door was shut forever, hey ho the wind and the rain. I marked the days, the years. I sat at my desk and wrote as well as I could on the white paper. I was determined that they would not make me mad.

It has been like death. Time has not moved at all. Yet it cannot be long before the real thing. I try to put it down as clearly as I can but there is darkness behind and in front.

Nothing stays still. I cannot illuminate any of it. I form the letters as well as I am able, but I cannot read what I have written. It does not seem to be written in any language that I know. The more I look at it the more incomprehensible it seems to be. As though a spider had walked through the ink and then crawled across the page. As though it had crawled out of my head and on to the paper and there could never ever be any sense in the marks it had left.

Perhaps there are no marks. Perhaps I am still in the dark and calling out for pen and paper. Perhaps no time at all has passed since they shut me up. I call for pen and ink and paper but they only laugh and cry out that I am mad. I do not know who I am. Except that I am a survivor. I will go on trying to write something down. This is a pen in my hand. I hold it and write with it. This is me, writing. I will not listen to their words. I will not listen to that music. I will try to be as precise as possible. I will write it all down. Then the darkness will clear. It must clear. The music will fade. It must fade. I will be able to live again. That will be my revenge on them. That I have endured. That I have not let them make me mad.

Death of the Word

Yesterday I talked to my father. He stood in my room with his back to the window, facing the bed, his legs slightly apart, his hands behind his back, in the familiar posture. He has been dead for ten years.

We used to play ball when I was young, my father and I. Not football or cricket or any other known ball game, but simply 'ball'. 'Let's play ball,' my father would say, taking the beach-ball out of the cupboard under the stairs where we kept everything that didn't fit in anywhere else, and we would go out into the yard and begin the game. It started as a simple matter of throwing the ball to each other, backwards and forwards, but soon developed complex and rigid rules of its own, growing more and more violent until I would grab the ball and head for the park with it under my arm and him in hot pursuit. I remember my terror and exhilaration as I ran through the trees, hearing my father's footsteps in the grass behind me and feeling his hot breath on my neck. But nothing else. I remember nothing else. Whether he always caught me or always let me escape has vanished from my memory as completely as though we had never played at all. It is true that sometimes nowadays, while running for the bus or glancing idly out of a train window, I suddenly feel that this last part of the game is about to come back to me, but it never does. Is it that by becoming conscious of its imminent appearance I had somehow chased it away, or do I perhaps grow conscious of its presence before it has quite emerged precisely in order to prevent it from appearing? Whatever the reason, the conclusion of our ball game is lost to me, though I cannot think it can have been particularly traumatic, since we played almost every day and I was a singularly happy and untormented child.

Although my mother later told me that she admired my father greatly for his willingness to spend so much of his time with me, taking part in childish games, I think he enjoyed it even more than I did, and that having a child provided him with a wonderful excuse to indulge in such games with a clear conscience. I sensed this, even at the time, and he too seemed to realize that I saw through his elaborate game of double bluff, pretending to enjoy himself for my sake but actually enjoying it all thoroughly himself. So that we were accomplices in this, against my mother, and, having seen through his secret, I even held him to some extent in my power. Not that I could have acted on this power in any way, for it was intangible, a feeling, a sensation, but it was none the less true that whenever my father said, 'Let's play ball,' he put himself, so to speak, in my hands. And it was this, now I come to think of it, which really formed the mainspring of our game. The ball was only an excuse, a way of controlling and articulating this new and peculiar relationship between us. So that when I picked it up and tucked it under my arm and ran for the trees, I knew deep down inside me that if he caught me he would kill me for what I knew. And I must have known too that, however hard I tried to run, he would inevitably catch and kill me, annihilate me totally so that his secret should remain hidden for ever. And this I now see was what lent the ball-game its ambiguous mixture of pleasure and terror, for is it not what we all most deeply long for and also what we fear above all else, to be annihilated by the father who begot us?

My father was a big man. When he stood in front of the window he blotted out the light. In my memory he leans over me at a dangerous angle, like the Tower of Pisa, and I can chart my growth by his progressive return to the vertical, paralleled by the progressive diminution of his size. In fact I soon overtook him, and by the age of eighteen was able, if not to look down on him, at least to look squarely into his pale blue eyes and know that he would not be able to avoid me. Not that he ever wanted to. We were always having heart-to-heart talks at that time, and he would gaze intensely at me, coming into my room late at night and standing between my desk and the bed, blotting out the light. He was a great believer in heart-to-heart talks, and would hold forth for hours about his own youth in the mountains and his relations with his own father. I never answered him when he started off on this tack, preferring to lie with my hands under my head and look at the halo

of light surrounding him. But my silence seemed to spur him
to greater and greater feats of reminiscence and description,
and he would end by glancing at his watch and clearing his
throat, coming forward and patting me on the head, saying:
'I'm glad we understand each other so well.' I felt then and
still feel that he wanted to talk to me about something but
could never quite bring himself to do so, hoping that I would
ask or that his endless fund of stories would lead naturally in
that direction. But since he was half aware of the problem
himself there could be no question of its coming up naturally,
and as I never asked he never revealed to me what it was. I
think he realized at moments that I was aware of something
and deliberately avoided asking, and he tried to manoeuvre me
into it; but he held the weaker hand and we remained as we
were. I have often wondered what it was that nagged him like
that and whether he would have become a different man had
I allowed him to bring it out into the open, but idly, and
without really looking for an answer. Certainly it was no
'thing' – guilty secret or other banal fact – which could have
been taken out and exhibited or in any way dealt with by
positive action. But there was undoubtedly a core of anxiety
there, and had he managed to talk to me about it it would no
doubt have ceased to trouble him so much – but then he would
have had to be a different person and so would I and the whole
question would not have arisen.

I had a letter the other day from a girl I proposed to ten
years ago and who turned me down, saying that she often
asked herself whether our marriage would have worked and
whether we would have been happy. But what does 'we' mean
in such a context? We are made by our choices. The people
we are today are so different from the people we would have
been had we in fact got married that the question is entirely
without meaning. We are not one self but many, held together
by the memories of a common past registered on our single
body. That is the pathos of memory and of the sentimentality
it engenders, which is the belief that one can have choice without renunciation, that one can be both what one is and what
one might have been. Clearly what I am today was shaped by
the girl's refusal. And yet how much of *me* was there even
behind the question I put to her? I wonder.

My father was incurably sentimental. I think I felt this from quite early on. I was repelled by his constant attempts to hold on to the moment and replay it to himself as it were, with me as the necessary audience. It frightened me, especially – perhaps only – because he was my father. After all, he was there before me. He will loom over me, between my bed and the light, for the rest of my life.

Indeed, it is difficult to see how it could be otherwise. We cannot imagine that what has been there when we arrive will one day cease to exist. It has about it the permanence of the unquestionable. For our parents to die is as unthinkable as that the world should one day disappear. That is why the death of a father is the traumatic event of a lifetime. It pushed Freud into writing *The Interpretation of Dreams*, and one wonders how Kafka's work would have altered if his father had preceded him to the grave. Mourning and melancholia, Freud said, are our two ways of responding to this catastrophic event, but that is perhaps to see the matter in too crude a light (though it must be said in fairness that Freud was as well aware of this as anyone). We are never really in doubt about our own mortality, though we try to suppress the knowledge of it as much as possible, hoping against hope that a miracle will occur and that we, of all the multitudes who have existed since the creation of the world, will prove immortal. Far worse, because so totally unthinkable, is the fact of a father's death. We use thought to protect ourselves from pain; what cannot be thought pierces us where we are weakest and we succumb.

I remember the day my father died. It was the middle of winter. The trees were bare. The snow had come and gone and come again and was now melting in black puddles on the edges of the pavements. My mother rang me up, telling me to come at once, and I put down the phone and walked straight out of the house and up to the station. I don't know how long I waited for the train or how long the train took to get there, but when I arrived he was dead. When I arrived he was dead.

He had a way of lying in bed with his feet sticking up through the blankets which my eldest son also favours. In many ways they are alike, and in my son I seem to see my father, as though they were one and the same person and had no use for me, holding them apart, but would crush me between them and regain their lost unity. It is normal, I believe, for fathers to see themselves in their sons – their youthful selves, hopes unblighted, the world before them. But this is only another instance of sentimentality and I will have no truck with it.

I remember walking with my son along an alley-way lined with trees. It was autumn and the leaves were thick on the ground. It had been a dry summer and they were yellower than honey. My son waved his arms as he talked, driving home his points, each with a gesture, and I thought suddenly that I would always be in the position of listening and watching while others drove home their points. When I wake up nowadays I often have the feeling that we have just emerged from that long alley-way with the autumn trees and the thick carpet of leaves, and that it is impossible for us to turn round and walk slowly back the other way.

The other day I woke up like that, with the sense of that tree-lined alley-way still vivid in my mind and body. It was night. In the distance I heard lorries rumbling through the city. The street-light shone brightly outside the window and patterned the ceiling with unreal colours. The house was silent though someone coughed overhead. It is odd that there are no books on the classification of coughs heard in the night. They are so many and so varied. The unreal sounds of a buried world. I sat at the window and watched the empty street, while the sky changed from yellow to pink and then to streaky blue. When the light in the street went out I returned to bed, careful to make no sound for the springs creak dreadfully and I do not like to advertise my presence to all and sundry.

I was looking out of the kitchen window the day my father died. It was the middle of winter. The trees were bare. The snow had come and gone and come again and was now melting in black puddles on the edges of the pavements. I had switched on the electric kettle to make some coffee and was looking out of the window at the white sky when the phone rang. I went out into the hall and picked up the receiver, leaving the door open so that I could go on looking at the sky. When I heard what my mother had to say I put down the receiver and walked straight out of the house and to the station, forgetting about the kettle. Nothing fused but the kettle was ruined.

The trees were bare. The snow had come and gone. When

I got there he was dead. They had thrown a sheet over him and he lay there as he used to do on Sundays, with his feet sticking up through the blankets in a way my son also favours. In many ways they are alike, my father and my eldest son.

I remember walking with my son along an alley-way lined with trees. It was autumn and the leaves were thick on the ground. It had been a dry summer.

It had been a dry summer. I remember thinking

But why should I go on? Where have they come from, these winters and summers, these autumns and springs, these white skies and yellow skies and streaky blue skies, these gesticulating sons and honey leaves? They have nothing to do with me or with my father.

I sit in my room. Other people move about. Doors open and close as they go off to work. Fortunately I am spared the necessity of doing so myself. I make some tea and tidy the bed. Then I sit in the armchair and look out of the window and think about my father.

Yesterday I talked to my father. He stood in my room with his back to the window, facing the bed, in the familiar posture. He has been dead for ten years. I remember the day he

I remember nothing. No wife. No sons. No autumn days or ruined kettles. And then it must be said: no room either, with bed and chair, banging doors or coughing neighbours. I sit at my desk and write: Yesterday I talked to my father. And then I have to admit: no father either. Oh I must have had one once, but not that kind, not that kind. No ball-game. No heart to heart talks. No secret complicity. No phone call. No death.

But now I have said that I begin to understand. I see that I do after all have a father. He is the first sentence I wrote down: Yesterday I talked to my father. Before today there was yesterday. Before that, another day. Before the first word, another word, making the first one possible. Without that, without my father, a time before, there could be no present, no future. I would suffocate.

My father is the phrase that begins it all and also that against which it is all directed. For now it is clear to me that these so-called memories which have come to me in the wake of that initial sentence have had only one purpose: to oust my father from his pre-eminent position, to annihilate him, to remove him forever from his place between myself and the light.

He was there: framed in the window, black upon white. But now I have succeeded in removing him, first by casting doubt upon his motives, then by casting doubt upon his existence, I find it difficult to go on. Without my father, against whom to push, I cannot continue. If there is no room, no bed, no chair no father blotting out the light, then what am I and where am I? I am only this sentence, hesitating, uncertain, with nowhere to go and nothing to say any more. It is as though the assassination of my father had started my own slow death, since even saying I am this sentence means nothing any more, now that the pretext has gone, body blotting out the light, standing between me and the window, and all that is left is pure light, white page at last, waiting with infinite patience as the sentence vacillates, falters, and I gather myself for one last hopeless cry: Father, father, why have you forsaken me?

5
THE AIR WE BREATHE

For Sophia

And again it came to her, that feeling, overwhelming her, drowning her almost, so that she gasped for air, filled her lungs, opening her mouth wide and closing her eyes with the effort, but the feeling in her chest would not go, the tight knot, the sense of having to say everything, everything, but also the impossibility of ever saying anything, or at least anything he would understand, the flames shooting up in the grate and the crackle of dry wood where had they got dry wood from when everything in this house was so damp where had it lain to acquire that dryness, almost like solidified dust, the sharp bang and the burning embers shooting out into the room, she found them and stamped them out, seeing his face lit up momentarily as she moved, coming back quickly into the orbit of the fire, away from the empty spaces of the large room, from the black uncurtained windows, sitting again, breathing deeply, feeling the constriction in her chest, like the knot on one of those old trees she thought, out on the moors for years and years, grow-ing inwards, never upwards, hardening, tightening, in every kind of weather, every kind of light, not moving or feeling even but just hardening, living, and then one day blown over by the wind, its roots no longer able to hold and lying there white in the moonlight till it rotted and sank back into the bog into the moor became peat or was it coal she could never remember and

– I don't – he said.

– No! she said quickly, before he could go on, before he could get launched, choosing his words, asking, asking, and

– But – he said.

– No! she said again, quickly, and he stopped looking at her, puzzled at the vehemence in her voice

– I only –

– No! she said, and again it came to her that there was no way of starting no way of finishing everything bunching in her

chest, her throat, so that there was no way of saying it but
silence was impossible as well and

– I tried, she said. I tried to –

– What's the matter? he said. What have I said, why are you
what –?

and then it was upon her again and she was struggling in
that narrow room and the smell of smoke everywhere the smell
of trains and soot and dirt and stale cigarettes and then the lift
with its mirrors and those concrete alleyways and then more
trains and

– No, she said, no you don't –

But now she seemed to have been talking all her life she
couldn't remember the time before there must have been a time
before but it was as if her body had suddenly been forced on
her thrust at her and then her life had started and she was in
that narrow room trying to explain they tried opening the
windows he didn't want to but she insisted because of the heat
the smell the lack of air the windows were caked with soot the
smell of trains everywhere she had to get out but she had to
explain as well she had to talk to make him understand about
those fields those trees that house the river the old man sitting
sitting and the others calling and him sitting and the three of
them eating and then the children and the garden and the long
evenings in the summer

– I was one of them, she said. I was one of them.

– But –?

– No, she said, no, how can I say it was me it's only a feeling
a sensation not me like now I came later as if suddenly my
body was thrust at me in that room in that

– But –?

– I don't know, she said, when we went to see them, when
Father took me, just the two of them perhaps he wanted to
play with us he would come he would stand even play but
always by himself never really joining in she didn't know she
wouldn't have let him she had her dignity she was always polite
it was only later when

And now the moonlight shone in on the big brass bedstead,
gleaming on the knobs at the foot, they had put a blanket over
the window at first she had insisted but it had slipped off and
finally she didn't bother any more though she always dreaded

being in a house at night with no curtains on the windows and
the sense of being watched of being vulnerable, there's nobody
for miles, he had said, no one would be crazy enough to go
prowling round in the night she could feel him lying beside
her it was hot they had looked for the radiators tried to twist
them shut opened the window but then the smell of the trains
invaded everything you felt the soot entering, settling on your
face, your lips, inside the nose, the mouth, she had put on the
light again and he had sat up, blinking, surprised, then lain
down on his back again, his mouth open, breathing deeply,
she dressed in the dark there was no point in trying to explain
any more if there had ever been any point it wasn't her life it
would never be her life if he had wanted to live it like that stare
out at the water day after day but perhaps it was not him
perhaps it was her perhaps

Anyway it was too late she knew it was too late the cock
crowed and she heard the whistle of the train as it passed on
the other side of the river, in the distance, as she had heard it
so many nights not sleeping, trying to understand, wanting to
ask him, but she knew it would never be any good, he would
look at her blankly she wanted to reach out to squeeze him to
force him to speak or to touch him and perhaps the other if
he had ever touched ever turned sitting all day by the river not
moving not closing his eyes a rock a stone even they are finally
worn out only the water flows on and

One of the pieces of wood he had put on the fire burst
suddenly and a shower of sparks shot out of the grate but
turned black before falling, so that though she got out of her
chair and pressed her foot down where they had seemed to
land she couldn't be sure of having stamped them all out and
had to sniff, waiting for the acrid smell of burning fibres to
rise to her nostrils and suddenly feeling again the fear shooting
through her and the pain in her chest in the middle just below
her neck, the sense of never being finished, of never having
begun, of everything bunching in her throat so that there was
no way of starting and no way of going on but silence was
impossible too and the train hooting like an owl three in the
morning she knew it passed at three and again at six hooting
so mournfully on the other side of the river in the distance
they had run out she just remembered them all running out,

released from the car, swarming over that house, that garden, that river, there were so many of them the days just went on for ever and then at night the warmth of the bedclothes we didn't think of them we didn't think I suppose that's how one has to put it we didn't think it's not surprising and that time was so happy that's the wrong word more like delirium that's the only way I can describe it like delirium and then when I think of what had been there before and of the old man sitting by that river it was only when I went to see her, started going to see her and even then Father insisted they had lived there before it had belonged to them he insisted we pay her a visit I don't think the others went it didn't mean anything at the time I was bored I wanted to get back I didn't even remember only later when I returned and she talked though why she should have talked to me I don't know, if it was to me and not to herself, I just happened to be there, that's all, she never answered my questions she just spoke her dry voice rasping I just happened to be there that's all and

— But you said —?

— No, she said, no you must let me finish you don't understand you don't —

— But what did the house mean to them? he said. You told me he had bought it, come from the South from the Pyrenees and bought it, so that

And again she felt it overwhelming her like a wave from which there is no escape, as if she would have to speak, to speak for ever, in order to survive, to keep afloat, go on speaking as long as she had breath in her lungs, but without hope of his ever understanding her or of ever coming to an end, watching the fire roaring now in the grate, waiting for the wood to crack and the sparks to fly, no longer turning to him or even trying to see his face, gauge from his expression how much he had grasped what he had

— And his wife? he said. What happened to her? The mother. The grandmother. What

And again the sense of panic invaded her, the constriction in her chest I told you I told you about the village the house the river the silence I don't know when it was after how long I began to hear the cries our cries our shouts the way children scream fear and joy mixed up together the sense of chasing of

being chased of not being able to bear it not any more rushing
through the woods the fields along the river bank the reeds
the willows to hear that screaming against the silence instead
of being inside it inside them just one of the children I don't
know if the others were aware of anything at the time I wasn't
though looking back I can see that there were things there were
signs but one notices and doesn't notice it was only afterwards
only when I saw him again when he talked when we talked
that I realized how it must have sounded to him there had only
been him and his mother and the old man, the sudden flaring
of his mother, shouting at him, at the old man, then her voice
trailing away into silence again and the three of them bending
over their plates, silence, one day after another, like that,
nothing changing, and then to have to get out to be there in
the village on the other side in another house hearing the
screams the laughter he told me he sometimes came to have a
look he stood at the edge of the field behind the house and
peered at us we never saw him I said I had when he told me
but I can't have I'm sure I can't have we were too caught up
in our games you don't stop when you're that age you don't
stop and ask where you are or why there especially when there
are five or six of you we spent all day out in the woods the
fields the reeds by the river right on the spot perhaps it was
right on the spot where he had sat when I think about it now
my heart just jumps right up I feel split in two our shouting
and his silence our shouting and –
  – Where did they bury him?
  – Where?
  – Didn't they bu – ?
  – I don't know, she said, we didn't ask we didn't know there
was a cemetery up the road I suppose they
  And again it came to her the dark kitchen the scrubbed look
the old woman
  – But she wasn't old she can't have been but to us to me
when you're that age anything over thirty seems old though
she may have been forty-five or perhaps it was later it must
have been later when I came back with him we must go and
see her he said after that first time we must go back and see
her perhaps it was then the first time we went back and she
was old then but with the same scarf tied round her head and

the same scrubbed look in that kitchen she couldn't sleep she
would be down at four or perhaps five as soon as it was light
sitting in that kitchen talking in whispers not whispers exactly
but keeping our voices down it was a small house we had the
sense of Claude sleeping upstairs and she said he stopped her
one day and took her arm and asked her where the grave was
and she said what grave and he said his grave and she understood
at once what do you mean she said what grave and he said I have
forgotten I have forgotten where it is where we put his grave
and she began to tremble she told me sitting in that kitchen
we kept our voices down the light was dim still at that time of
the morning what grave she said, feeling the need to bring it
out into the open, what grave what are you talking about I
looked for it he said, I have spent all day looking for it and I
can't remember there's no grave she said there's no grave at all
and he said I thought so, but she saw his expression was strange
what's the matter she said and he said it was the river, wasn't
it, it was the river, and she said what are you talking about
and he said we dropped it in the river didn't we and winked
at her so that she didn't know if he was joking or only pretending to joke or suggesting some kind of complicity or was mad
stark raving mad it was extraordinary his only daughter and
she couldn't tell after all those years she couldn't tell but –
  – What? he said. Couldn't tell what?
  – It got worse, in fact, not better, she said, shaking her head
violently from side to side, trying to shake away his question,
to tell him with her gesture that she didn't want to listen to
his questions, that they had nothing to do with the matter,
that they only showed his lack of comprehension, worse, she
said, as the years went by, as if two people cooped up together
or not cooped because there was plenty of room and they
weren't two but three with Claude but even so two people,
father and daughter, but they got to understand each other less
and less I imagine though she would never say just throw out
phrases, in that kitchen, with Claude sleeping upstairs, throw
out phrases and not explain I didn't try I didn't interrupt she
wasn't talking to me you understand I was there but she wasn't
talking to me just saying things because they had to be said
and if I interrupted if I asked it would look as if I took it
seriously as if I –

– What? he said, took what seriously?

– I mean she said that they had killed him the two of them buried him somewhere perhaps she was talking because she felt guilty I didn't like to ask, where did he go I said once and she shrugged and even smiled I think there was a twinkle in her eye, perhaps the river she said and it was like with her father I didn't know how to take that it wasn't important anyway it was –

– You mean if they killed him or not?

– Wasn't important, she said again, and again the image of the old man sitting motionless staring out at the river overwhelmed her and she gasped at the emptiness the lack of anything to hold on to and then it came back, the old woman's voice, and with it the sense that she was there talking to her in that gloomy scrubbed kitchen with the river not so far away and the train hooting on the other side of the valley six o'clock nine o'clock twelve o'clock three o'clock, lying in bed listening to the hooting and the others breathing quietly round her, getting out of bed and looking out of the window at the moonlight on the water and Jay waking suddenly and starting to scream because her shadow lay across the wall, the old man looking at her, at his daughter, out of the corner of his eye, as she told me later, stopping her in the garden and saying perhaps he is mine perhaps the child is ours after all and her sense of the horror of it the horror of it that never left them there was always the doubt which was why he had this horror this hatred of the flesh Claude I mean I laughed I didn't know how to take it I –

– You mean Claude? he said. He was his child? With her?

– No, she said, no, it was his joke, but once he had said it how could she stop thinking about it how could she put it out of her head she would spend hours looking at him and –

– And she told you that? After you'd married him?

– It wasn't like that, she said, she knew it wasn't true but in another way it was true and anyway I told you she wasn't telling me just speaking not to me not to anyone and –

– And he knew? he said. She'd told him?

– I don't know I –

– She actually went and told him a thing like that?

– No, she said, he –

– And to you? After you and he were – ?

It wasn't like that, she wanted to say, I didn't mean that, you don't understand – but it was too complicated there was too much to explain too much to grasp the train hooting in the middle of the night the river flowing past and the old woman in the kitchen talking talking and she said

– No! No!

– I don't –

– No! she said, and sensed him watching her while the fire flickered now feebly in the grate he had not put any more wood on if you only knew if you only knew she could see the tree outside the window bright in the moonlight the spiky leaves glinting as the breeze moved them gently the meadows spread out round them as though covered by a white tablecloth she could sense him breathing beside her everything silent a cow was that a cow mooing in the distance would a cow moo at that time of night the moon silent above them and the river in the valley below she was tempted to get out of bed to stand in the moonlight looking out of the window at the white hills but that would disturb him he would ask: Are you all right? What's the matter? and she would say, Nothing, and he would sit up and look at her or lie there listening, waiting for her to speak, oh please! she wanted to say, oh please! – remembering those other rooms those other beds the hoot of the engine the soot on the window and then riding down the lift her face reflected finding herself in the underground car-park looking for the exit, stumbling about in the half-dark with just those blue lights high up in the ceiling and the air bad he had met her at the station I can't she had said on the phone I can't I'm coming I can't and he had tried to calm her but she had put down the phone she wanted to forget to put as much distance between her and the village as possible but the further she went the more involved with it she was the more she felt it crushing her oppressing her she watched him combing his hair in front of the mirror in that room with the windows covered in soot it's like that everywhere he said it's like that in all station hotels you wanted to come here it's you who were desperate he spoke to her not looking at her looking in the mirror looking into the room via the mirror listen she said, listen to what I have to say but what did she have to say except listen except to tell

him of this gap this big hole in her body as if it had been fired
into as if it was all black and empty but hurting do you know
what I mean do you understand do –

– I'll get some more wood, he said, and stood up and went
out she could hear him in the shed at the back he returned his
arms full the stocks are low he said there's coal of course he
said but with this wood it's a pity not to

She was shaking her head in the dark he didn't look at her
perhaps he couldn't see her in the dark he knelt over the fire
it flared up again she closed her eyes the chair was hard the
old woman sat upright she was used to it could sit there for
hours never went into the parlour always the kitchen with that
handkerchief over her head he didn't speak she said didn't
speak to us only sometimes he would wink at me or at the boy
or say things like that about the grave or perhaps there was no
father perhaps there were only the two of us at first I laughed
but after listening to that a few times you begin to wonder you
can't trust yourself any more not trust yourself to remember
to recall the past it wouldn't take long he could see me shudder
perhaps he too was afraid I don't know he just sat looking out
at that river sat in the reeds and looked he left the house early
before breakfast sometimes I had to go and fetch him it was
as if his eyes had drawn the river in to them I could see him
as we ate the three of us at that table the river flowing past his
eyes he had drawn it in he wouldn't talk what are you looking
for I said and he would smile but once he said something it
was funny I didn't understand the air we breathe he said he
didn't repeat it I didn't know what he meant Claude looked
at him then he may have spoken to you about it he looked at
him as if he understood once a wooden box passed him on the
river a coffin passed by he said a coffin on the river today he
wasn't part of us any more we were a family once and especially
the two of us but it was as if his eyes had taken over where his
mind was or something human he lived for his eyes I like to
look myself and the Seine is beautiful here but it wasn't beauty
he was after it wasn't a lovely sight it was something else I
don't know when it started it was upon us if you know what
I mean one day it was upon us and then it was difficult to
remember another time the boy never knew him otherwise he
accepted him like that but for me to have him there and turned

away like that after our closeness the air we breathe I turned
that phrase over and over now I think of it sometimes I think
I know what it means what he meant but when you think in
the end

She shivered once, seeing the moonlight on the tree outside
the window, then all of a sudden she had lost control and her
body was shaken with a continuous violent shiver, she caught
hold of the sheet, pushed it between her teeth, bit hard, he
moved once beside her and then settled again, she got up quietly
and went to the bathroom, it was difficult to breathe because
of the smell of dirt and cigarettes they had tried to open the
window earlier when they had first got into the room but the
soot had come flying in he had shut it quickly they had laughed
she had wiped her face it's like that everywhere he had said if
you want a station hotel you must accept the consequences
her face was white in the mirror he stirred once when she took
the suitcase out from under the bed he even sat up but she said
it's nothing I'm looking for something and he sank back she
knew when she lay there she knew she had to go she stopped
at the ground floor but then the sight of the night porter sitting
in his cubicle made her close the lift doors again quickly and
press the button for the basement she couldn't see where the
exit was she felt like a thief it was then she left the case she
didn't want to have to explain to talk to be stopped and dragged
back then she was out in the street a side-street she was walking
away from the hotel she thought of going back for the suitcase
in the end it had been so easy but she couldn't not now not
ever again she was walking fast her footsteps sounding on the
empty pavements she didn't mind she had to walk there were
stars above her she remembered what someone had told her
you couldn't see the stars over a big city at night it wasn't true
they were there perhaps it was an exceptional night perhaps it

– She told you that? he said. When you were married?

– What difference should it make? she said.

– Well, he said, didn't it?

– What?

– Make a difference?

She didn't look at him. He kept his eyes on the road. They
crossed the Severn Bridge and turned off the motorway.

– To have someone telling you the man you've married may

be the product of an incestuous union isn't the best bit of news I'd have thought, he said.

– Why are you so ironical? she said.

– Me?

You don't understand, she wanted to say to him, you still don't understand and I thought you did we've talked so much, so much, remembering again her first glimpse of him in the street and the recognition and his face over lunch you can stay here I've got a spare room how he had looked at her the messages he had left just directions at first how to use the coffee-pot the money for the milkman then little additions little notes left for her to find I hope you have a good day I hope I don't disturb you coming in sitting on her bed and her talking talking it was this need to talk but talk wasn't enough it had to come out all of it she had to say it from the beginning how could she say it where could she start there was always more she could see him stiffen and turn away from her, packing the stones carefully into their case with his little mallet I listen when you talk she wanted to say I listen when you lecture me on glacial formations and mezozoic and all the rest of it why can't you understand when I talk to you why do you have to cut into me like that ask questions like that put on that ironic voice she knew he didn't mean it but she felt the panic mount in her again like nausea, she closed her eyes, her face must have gone white because he asked:

– Are you sick? Shall we stop a moment?

– No, she said.

– If you're sick we can stop. We're making good time.

– No.

– Is it what I said?

– No.

– It just seemed common sense to me, he said.

– What?

– What I just said.

– What did you just say?

– About the shock to you.

– No, she said. It had nothing to do with me. It was what she was saying. She was trying to explain. How the three of them lived.

– How they lived?

    – Of course it wasn't incest, she said. He had a father. The man had lived there. Then he'd gone. I don't know why. If they'd pushed him out or on the contrary they were horrified by his departure. It was just that he'd gone, there was no trace of him, and the old man no longer talking to her, just sitting staring out at the river, getting up at five even earlier in summer, pulling on his thick socks and boots and that old blanket he had punched a hole in and used as a sort of cape or poncho going down to the river she would scream at him sometimes ask him what he saw there what he was doing there he wouldn't answer he couldn't tell her he would sit without moving at least if he had fished she said to me at least if he had done something like other people or if he'd really lost his reason then I'd have known what to do but it was as if he wasn't part of us any more as if he wasn't part of the earth any more it was like a challenge a claim I didn't know what to do I tried to reason with myself if he likes it I thought if he enjoys it it's better than having him round my feet the whole time I should count myself lucky he's out of the way he's happy but I couldn't see it like that it wasn't natural it made me wonder if what I was doing had any value it had that sort of effect of course he always loved water snow ice the sea I'll show you photos of him and Mother on the beach in Dieppe they had an old car he loved driving it but they would sit on the beach I'll dig up those old photos but two it's different he was with her and the sea too other people do it or fishermen by the river but him sitting there among the reeds all day and when it rained he took a big umbrella and set it over him just like a fisherman but he wasn't I couldn't get through to him any more I see him sometimes in my dreams I ask him as I never dared to do while he was alive I ask him what he's doing but he never moves he never seems to hear I turn away or wake up but sometimes there's so much pain so much in my heart I remember him as he was picking me up and throwing me in the air and at the same time at the very same time I see him there like a stone with his eyes on the river and when I called him when I went right up close and called him in to dinner he would turn and look at me and the river was in his eyes behind his eyes I don't know how to explain to you the river was flowing behind his eyes he would get up he would follow me along the bank and through the reeds and back

across the garden to the house and he would sit at the table
and eat Claude would ask him what he would answer sometimes at other times not he wasn't there he wasn't really there
for godsake I said to him for godsake don't speak to me if you
don't want to but speak to him to the boy he would turn and
look at me then and smile I didn't know what to do when he
smiled when he put his hand on my arm it was worse it wasn't
him and always the boy between us and the thought that perhaps
though we both knew better but it was the silence and –
– Do you want to stop?
Her neck hurt. She looked at him.
– If you want to stop. We're in good time.
– If you want.
– I wouldn't mind a drink, he said.
– Where are we?
– Usk. It isn't far now.
– I don't mind. I'm not tired.
– You were asleep.
– No.
– You were. I'm sorry.
– Oh Richard! she said.
– But you were!
– How much further? she asked him.
– About a hundred miles.
– I don't want a drink.
– For Godsake!
– You go. I'll wait here.
– What's the matter? Are you sulking?
– Sulking?
– Because of what I said?
– No. Of course not. I can't remember what you said.
    The wood cracked like a pistol and a red spark flew across
the room.
    – Christ! he said. Where's the fireguard?
She felt the heat of the fire on her face. He got up. She could
hear him hunting about in the pantry for the fireguard. The
wood burst again and she stretched out a leg and pressed the
red ember hard into the carpet.
    – It's ridiculous, he said. How did the wood get so dry in
a place as damp as this?

He put the fireguard in front of the fire.
– Please! she said.
– What?
– You're shutting out the heat.
– Don't be silly.
– What's the point of having a fire if you go and put something right in front of it?
– The heat comes through.
– I'm cold.
– I'm sorry, he said. I don't want the place to go up in flames.
– What made you want to study geology in the first place? she asked him.
He kept his eyes on the road, taking the corners at speed.
– I don't know, he said.
– The rocks? she said. The age of the rocks?
– I don't know, he said. I was always interested.
– And now?
– Now?
– Does it still interest you?
– Yes of course.
– But not passionately?
– Passionately?
– I thought from your tone...?
– They're rocks, he said. For Chrissake!
As Claude had said: – It's only a river. An old man sitting and staring at a river.
– Then why won't she stop talking about it?
– My mother?
– Why won't she?
– I don't know. She's crazy perhaps.
– You think that's it?
– Sure. She's crazy.
– She didn't strike me like that.
– They're all crazy. You've known her for a long time. You know how crazy she is.
I hate your American accent, she wanted to say to him, but perhaps her French was no better and it wasn't accents they were talking about why confuse the issue what were they talking about was it his mother or something else was there always something else whenever you talked it was about something

else and the answer too that was about something else never
what you had set out to say in the first place you don't understand she wanted to say, standing at the window looking out
at the moonlit fields, you don't understand you won't understand it wasn't like that it wasn't like that at all why do you
turn away why do you fight me and she knew she wasn't
speaking knew it was she who was fighting that it wouldn't be
any good that it would never be any good that it couldn't start
from her it couldn't it had to be someone else she could sense
his voice hardening at the other end as she repeated

    — It's me. Gina.

    — Gina?

    — Yes. Paul. Yes.

as if to prove to him by saying his name that she was sane,
aware of what she was doing, that he must listen, that he must
help her, waiting for him to speak, hearing the pips, pushing
more coins into the box, and him

    — But where are you?

    — At the station. I've just got in.

    — In? From Paris? What's the matter?

    — Please. Come and fetch me.

    — But why? What's happened?

And then understanding creeping into his voice: — Oh you
mean you

    — Oh Paul

    — But you said you'd

    — I didn't have time. I had to get out.

    — But

    — Please

    — All right. Wait. I'll be over as soon as I can. It may take
some time.

She should have known by his voice, by the pause in his
voice, but her eyes were shut clenched tight shut she had to
keep moving she had to keep talking if she stopped it came
back if she stopped she would fall it would be finished it would
be the end but not the end because there was no end no beginning she heard the shouts the laughter they had shouted like
that as soon as they had arrived they had overrun the place the
shouts came back to her they filled her head and the sense of
running the sense of lightness fear mixed with joy terrible fear

and terrible joy and the sense that in the end everything was
all right the trees the fields the river they found the body even
when her father told them they had found the body warned
them about the river there was no sense of danger no sense of
anything except the heat of the summer and the running and
laughter do you understand do you understand do you do you?
— And you married him because of that?
— I don't know.
— Because he had lived in that paradise before you? And you
wanted to get back to it?
— No, I —
— Not physically. I mean through him.
— I don't know.
— It sounds crazy.
— I don't know, she said.
— Then what? he said. What do you know?
— Nothing, she said.
— Then what?
— Nothing.
— All right, he said. I heard you.
In her mind's eye she could see him sitting at the table in
front of the open window looking at his stones, tapping with
his little mallet, when they walked he took his mallet with him,
this is X he said, this is Y, this is a good region for geologists.
This —
— Explain to me, she said.
But when he started, it was too complicated and she lost the
thread after the first few words outcrop bivalve loess orogeny
geosyncline cycle of sedimentation it was the stones she liked
the pebbles he kept them under his bed in a box under his bed
— I wouldn't show them to a girl.
— Why not?
— She wouldn't understand.
— There's nothing to understand. They're just stones.
— Then why are you interested?
— I'm not interested. Who said I was interested?
— You wanted me to show them to you.
— I don't care. Keep your stuffy old stones.
They divided into groups. The three girls and the two boys.
Or sometimes it was two girls and one of the boys and the

other girl and boy, there were many groupings and was it two summers or three or four?

She began to shiver, standing by the window in the moonlight. She got back into bed. He had pulled the blankets up over his thin shoulders and when she tried to get her share he wouldn't let go. She tugged and finally he turned right over with the blankets and threw an arm across her, still breathing steadily. She drew away from him but his arm kept her firmly clamped. She held her breath and tried to make herself as small and tight as possible. Gradually the shivering ceased and she lay looking up at the ceiling. Outside, the owl hooted.

She got up, making as little noise as she could. She need not have worried. He lay on his back, his mouth open, breathing heavily. In the bathroom she looked at her face in the mirror. The building shook as another train entered the station and the cracked glass on the washstand moved a little nearer to the edge. She watched, fascinated, but it slid gently back into place.

She dressed quickly. She wanted to wash her face but was afraid of making a noise. Her heart was pounding. She put out the light in the little cubicle and opened the door. He had not moved. The building shook again as another train arrived. She bent down and very slowly pulled the suitcase from under the bed, stopping guiltily at every noise, waiting, then starting again.

Outside in the corridor the blue hotel lights made everything look unreal. She hadn't remembered that her suitcase was so heavy, but she bit her lip and hauled it to the lift. Perhaps she was just overtired. She leaned against the mirrored wall of the lift, her eyes closed. The lift stopped and she opened the door, then saw the night clerk sitting, dozing, his white hair falling over his face, and quickly shut the doors again and pressed the button for the basement.

His voice was as she had remembered it – surprised, distant, but ready at any moment to become warm:

– Where are you?

– Here. Victoria Station.

– Victoria?

– Yes.

– But – ?

– The train just got in.

– In? From where?
– Paris.
– But
– I told you
– I didn't think you
– Didn't think I meant it?
– No no. That you were planning to I mean to come so soon I
– I didn't plan I just couldn't it

She waited for him to speak. The pips went and she pushed another coin in.

– Hullo? Yes??
– It's all right, she said.

Another silence.

– Please, she said.
– You want me to come? he said. Now?
– Yes, she said. Of course.
– Yes well I
– I'll wait. Under the clock on the right as you come in.
– Yes. Wait. I'll take some time. I have to get dressed.

She put out the light and eased the bathroom door open. She need not have worried. He lay on his back with his mouth open, just as she'd left him. Another train rumbled into the station and the building shook again.

She bent down and pulled the box of stones out from under the bed: red stones green stones blue stones smooth little pebbles and large knobbly flints.

– Leave them alone. They're mine.
– I want to see them.
– Leave them.
– I want to see them.
– They're mine.
– Just to see them.
– No.
– But I

The lift stopped with a thump and the doors opened. She got out, lugging the suitcase after her. At first she could see nothing. She felt her way forward and banged hard into something. She dropped the suitcase and held her knee tight to stop herself crying out in pain. After a while the pain eased and she picked up the suitcase again. It was too heavy to lift now and she started to drag it between the rows of parked cars. She went up one alleyway and then turned right down another that crossed it. But there was no sign of an exit anywhere. She stopped and looked round. A train rumbled somewhere above her. The smell of smoke and soot was worse here even than in the room. Her steps and the scratching noise of the suitcase as she dragged it along the concrete echoed in the darkness.

She left the suitcase suddenly and went forward to the end of the alley, but there was only another alley, identical, bisecting it at right angles, and no sign of an exit anywhere. She shuffled back to the suitcase, feeling her way at each step, picked it up, then dropped it again in frustration.

Now it was possible to see a little in the gloom. She ran down the alley, leaving her suitcase where it had fallen, turned left, slowed to a walk as her chest began to hurt, turned left again and caught sight of the red glow of an exit sign. When she got to it she found that the door was locked. She turned, looking round slowly for another lighted sign, thought she saw something and started to walk towards it. She lost it after being forced to turn down another alley, then all at once found herself in front of it. She pushed at the bar on the door and suddenly she was out in the London night with the stars above her and only the echo of her footsteps for company. When she turned to look back at the hotel it had merged into the other buildings in the street.

Her knee hurt where she had banged it. She bent over and rubbed it and felt the glow of the fire on her face.

– A penny for your thoughts, he said.

– No one says things like that any more.

– I do, he said.

Another log burst and a shower of sparks fell on the carpet.

– Aren't you going to stamp them out? she asked him.

– What's the point?

– You mean because I...?

– You found him? he said. In the river?

– Oh no, she said. He was found. Before we arrived. Though we kept pretending to find him. To frighten the others. But it was because of that she sold the house.

– He jumped in?

– Who knows?

– What did the police say?
– Misadventure. They always do.
– And she?
– The daughter?
He was silent.
– We didn't discuss it, she said. What did it matter anyway?
– Well I'd have thought –
– Perhaps he was drawn in. Looking so hard. Or fell asleep and dropped in. Does it make all that much difference?
– Well if he
– He was an old man.
– Yes but
– I don't know, she said.
He was silent.
– They only found him two days later, she said. Right in the reeds.
He waited for her to go on.
– They didn't want her to see him. She told me. But she did.
– And?
She shrugged.
– The air we don't breathe, he said.
And again it overwhelmed her, so that she choked and gasped, closing her eyes, opening her mouth wide, filling her lungs, trying to understand, remembering how she waited for the woman to go on, pressing her hands together on the cold table, waiting for the sun to move round, to enter the dark kitchen, to bring some warmth, some light, though the woman seemed not to notice, went on talking in her strong Southern accent, the handkerchief over her head as she had always seen it, so that she wondered if she ever went to bed or always sat there in that gloomy kitchen while the minutes and the hours and the days and finally the years etched the lines a little more deeply into her face and her voice got even hoarser than it had been, she tried to remember the first time she had talked about him was it when she came back with Claude it seemed as if she had always sat in that kitchen always talked even when they were small when they hardly noticed her, the others certainly didn't at all but she had gone with her father he had said, We must go and visit the lady who sold us the house, will you come with me? and they had gone and sat in the

kitchen the same kitchen nothing had changed the woman had
given her sweets to suck she had sat on the floor peered under
the table while her father talked to the woman two adults what
did she care what they said Claude was standing in the corridor
outside when they had left her father had bent over had told
him he must come and play with them he must use the garden
as he had always done he had stared up not talking not even
listening she remembered his face when he took her arm in the
street in Paris years later holding her arm like that so that she
tried to break free, thinking someone was after her bag that
she had to shout for help then seeing his face something clicking
remembering the way he didn't look at you, turned slightly
away and looked past you his face white but she was pleased
to see him and he too if he held her like that what was it about
that family holding and not holding you holding and pushing
away, it was as if he had known and she too perhaps it was as
if she too had always known they would meet again like that
he didn't let go of her they sat down on a bench in the street
not even a café just a bench against a tree in the street she tried
to ask questions tried to turn it into a social occasion in her
English way but he wouldn't play wouldn't talk he just held
her hand and looked at her and once he laughed she did not
remember him laughing when they were children and finally
when she had run out of things to say and her French was
beginning to falter he just said
  – I found you.
  without inflexion, as if he were recounting a story or making
a statement she couldn't tell if he meant he had been searching
after all how could he know she was there she certainly had
no idea he was but there was no hesitation on his part after all
it was many years since they had seen each other she could
have been anyone he could have made a mistake perhaps he
had because when she asked, You mean you've been looking
for me? All these years? and laughed to pass it off, he just said
again
  – I found you.
  and turned his head a little away from her as he had that
first time and later when they saw him, once or twice, in the
evenings, by the river, he never played with them, they tried
to draw him in but he wouldn't, that was when she felt for the

first time that perhaps they were intruders that the river and
the garden and the woods didn't belong to them that there was
something wrong, it disturbed her when it happened but then
she forgot about it they accepted that he would be there that
he wouldn't play with them, even when her mother tried to
draw him into the house to give him tea he stood without
moving and the winter sun was shining and the crowds were
surging past them on the pavements she tried to draw her arm
away she giggled he did look funny after all in that black coat
and the high collar and bowler hat as if he had come out of a
play or a review or something but his face was unmistakeable
the pinched look and big dark eyes

– So you're never going to let me go? she said

and he turned his head and looked at her and let go her arm
but then she felt closer to him than ever before and she wanted
him to hold her arm again so that she could pull away she
waited for him to speak but he wouldn't she didn't know what
to do she waited the crowds surged past them it grew cold she
stood up she said I must go he said no

– No?

He stood up. He was no taller than she, smaller probably
without the hat and she found herself saying

– Shall I see you again? and he

– Yes. And she

– Where? Where? but he only repeated

– I found you, using the polite form, the plural form, I
found you again, she couldn't remember if they had ever
addressed each other directly in those other times she said
quickly

– What do you do?

He shrugged. They were walking together there did not
seem to be anything else to do she said quickly

– How is your mother?

– It goes.

– She still lives in...?

– That's it.

– And you? cursing herself for chattering on unable to stop
wishing she could be silent like him and just accept walk beside
him without the need to speak to laugh to enquire

– You will see.

Then she was quiet and they were walking together, crossing the Luxembourg Gardens the sun was disappearing behind a thin film of grey the air was cold she started to shiver but he didn't seem to notice it was as if he had come out with the express purpose of finding her and now he was taking her back and perhaps it was like that he had always had that sort of taciturnity, as if speaking was painful and silence too she wanted to take his shoulders stop him turn him round look into his eyes and ask him what he was doing what they were doing where they were why he was so sure she would go with him that she had nothing else to do the day to give up to him no other friends to see or work to do that she too had just come out for the same express purpose of seeing him finding him returning with him she wanted to look into his eyes ask him to explain but what was there to explain that was always what happened always how it was there was the need to explain to understand and then nothing to explain nothing to understand but still the need persisted and it was as if this nothing was what had to be understood how it could be nothing and something both together and at the same time so that it was as if a hand had taken your heart and squeezed it and it slipped up and out of your hand like a fish you had to hold it you had to press it you caught it again and again it jumped you would never catch it and

– Open the window, she said.

– There's only soot outside, he said.

– Open it.

He sat on the bed, looking at her.

– Come and sit down, he said.

– Open it.

She went to the window and tried to push it open. It stuck.

– It's half past three in the morning, he said.

– The train was late. They had to change the engine.

She pushed hard and suddenly the window gave and swung open. A cloud of smoke and soot descended on her and filled the room. He got up off the bed and shut the window.

– I realize the train was late, he said.

– You told me to phone.

– From the other end, he said. From the other end.

– I didn't have time.

– I'm not saying you did. I'm not saying it's your fault. I'm just reminding you what time it is.

Taking her arm, putting his hands on her shoulders, round her waist, drawing her to him, saying

– It doesn't matter, it doesn't matter at all, we have plenty of time we

– I want to talk to you, she said.

– Tomorrow.

– No. Now.

– Tomorrow.

– No!

She lay still. The moon had come into view between the edge of the window and the monkey-puzzle tree. It appeared to be full, or nearly so. The sky was white, milky, and a cold white light fell on the bed. She thought of getting up and seeing what the landscape looked like in that white light but she was afraid of waking him so she just lay staring at the sky.

But he was not asleep. – What is it? he said.

– Nothing.

– Can't you sleep?

– Yes.

– What are you thinking?

– Nothing.

– Are you worried?

She got out of bed and sat down on the broad window-sill, tucking her legs inside her nightdress. It was as if a sheet had been laid across the hills. Even the owl was silent.

– What? he said again.

– Have you worked in the Olduvai Gorge? she asked him.

– What the – ?

– Have you?

– Why do you ask?

– You seemed to want to talk.

– For Christ's sake, he said. It's the middle of the night.

– Have you?

– No.

– Aren't you interested?

– I'm an industrial geologist, not a palaeontologist.

– What's that?

– Come on. Get back to bed.

– Aren't you?

– What?

– Interested.

– Christ! he said. What's got into you?

– I just wondered.

He turned over and pulled the blankets up round him.

– I suppose with stones you can start anywhere, she said.

He half-turned: – Anywhere?

– I mean they're all old.

– Some are a bit older than others, he said. By a few hundred million years.

He turned again and pulled the sheets over his head. She shivered.

– Don't let Dad catch you, Jimmy said.

– He won't.

– Just don't let him.

– He won't. Not if no one tells him.

– Who'd tell him?

– Oh shut up. Leave me alone.

– You think I'd tell? You think I'd do a sissy thing like that?

In the distance the train hooted. That was twelve o'clock. She got off the sill and crept to the door. The others were asleep. She opened the door and listened. The house was silent. She stepped out into the corridor, stopped again, listened again. Still no sound. She closed the door gently behind her and waited again. Silence. She began to creep along the corridor. A board cracked under her and she froze, her heart beating furiously, but no one stirred. Then she was out of the house and running. Her feet made no sound on the grass. She ran along the rose-hedge and through the gate, then down the field to the river. They had never lived by a river before, not by any kind of water, now she was only happy when she was beside it.

The moon was up and the sky cloudy. The river, when it loomed up in front of her, was blacker and bigger than she had remembered it. She stopped. There were many noises now, the noise of the current in the middle of the stream, the noise of the water swirling in the reeds that lined the banks, the noise of innumerable insects in the grass at her feet. An owl hooted suddenly nearby and she jumped. She moved out along the little path they had found through the reeds to where the bank rose a little and there was a sort of hollowed-out seat just above the line of the water. She sat down and closed her eyes, feeling the water running past her and the wind gently blowing at her nightdress.

– I ought to go back.

– Why?

– You're busy, I'm sure.

Why had she said that? Why hadn't she said she didn't want to go with him, at least not then, like that, so suddenly, after meeting him like that, it was only a moment ago after all, why did she have to phrase it like that in that ridiculous polite way why did

– I'm not busy. No.

He still held her wrist in his fingers, but now he let it go and felt in his pocket for the key.

– No, she said. Really. Another time.

– Come, he said.

– Another time, she said. I've got an appointment. Leave me your address. I –

– No.

She climbed the stairs in front of him. He had stepped back to let her through the front door of the building and she had gone in. Now there was nothing to do except climb up. She turned round at a bend in the steep stairs, questioningly, but he just said:

– No. Higher.

At the top there was no landing. A door opened straight onto the stairs. He fumbled with the key again, again stood back to let her pass. She went in.

It was a simple flat, barely furnished. The front door opened straight into a bed-sitting room and she could see a little kitchen beyond. The ceilings sloped steeply.

He took off his coat and hat and hung them up behind the door. He went into the kitchen and came back with a bottle and two glasses. She stood uncertainly by the table in the middle of the room. He sat down and filled the two glasses. He said nothing. Finally she took off her own coat and hung it over his. Then she pulled back the other chair and sat, facing him.

He raised his glass: – Your health.

– And yours. She sipped.

He looked past her in that disconcerting way he had always had.

– You haven't changed, she said, to say something. Because if she was going to sit there and drink his wine she would make something of the occasion.

– Oh yes? he said.

– I didn't... at first... with that hat and coat... But when you...

He looked past her left shoulder, out of the window.

– And you recognized me? she said. Straight away?

– Yes, he said.

– I haven't changed then? she said, laughing.

He shrugged.

– How is your mother?

– I told you, he said.

– Yes, she said. That's true.

He emptied his glass and immediately filled it again.

– I ought to go, she said. She stood up abruptly.

At once he was up too, facing her. – No, he said.

– No. Really.

– Sit, he said.

He sat down again himself. After a moment, feeling awkward standing there, she followed suit.

– You've been here a long time? she asked him.

– Longish, he said.

He turned his face a fraction to the left and looked at her.

– Are you studying here? she asked him.

He shrugged.

– Then what?

He poured the remainder of the bottle into his glass and looked down at it.

– What are you doing? she asked him.

– Oh...

– Nothing, she said. He was not doing anything. Or ever would, I should think. At least not anything you and I would call work.

– Then why –

– I don't know. It was as if there was nothing else to do, as if I had always known there would never be anything else to do as if I had been waiting or my body had been waiting for this moment, all those years, all those years, and when it came there was no question, I just –

– You could have returned on your own, he said. There was no need to. . . . If you felt. . .

– Not return, she said. Not like that. Physically. I mean it was waiting for me and if it hadn't been then it would have been later I –

– But–? he said. How old were you when you. . . ? How. . . ?

– I just remembered, she said. Just that time. That summer. Or perhaps it was two or three. It wasn't a particular year. It was like a different world. I suppose Father couldn't afford it in the end and so he sold it again and we didn't go any more you know the way children are they don't question or try to understand and nobody told us nobody tried to explain to us we cried I suppose and then that was it even when I went over to Paris for a year brushing up my French even then it never occurred to me to go and see it or them it didn't seem to be the same world and when I met him four years later when I was there again starting to research it had gone from my mind perhaps I dreamt about it occasionally but the thought that one could actually get onto a train or into a car and in an hour one would be there it just never occurred to me as I say it was another world so that when he stopped me like that for a moment it didn't make sense he couldn't be here he couldn't belong here in Paris in the street it was an education those few moments like learning to walk or to see again learning to make sense of space to realize that things did link up did join up that the present and the past and here and there weren't different universes but had links connections that's why I couldn't leave him that's why I stayed in a sense there didn't seem to be anything else to do I –

– But

– No. Listen. The way one learns. Not all smoothly and correctly but swinging wildly from one extreme to another so that just as I'd forgotten all those years so suddenly all that intervening time had vanished it was as if we had never sold that house only now it was different he was talking to me we were still there and yet grown up and elsewhere how can I explain how can I

– But if you

– No, she said. That was the mistake. That was what I had
to cope with later it wasn't as simple as that what I remembered
what he remembered it wasn't the same he never spoke it was
as if he wasn't interested you must talk to my mother he said
as if that was what he had got hold of me for to sit and listen
to his mother as if she needed an audience she hardly looked
at me she just talked just opened her mouth and spoke about
that time without anguish or surprise or anything just speaking
about that time as if she had to as if it was necessary for her
about how he would come in and sit absent-mindedly she
would pile his plate with food but sometimes he missed his
mouth with the fork he would press the spinach or whatever
it was against his cheek move his jaws she would have to lean
across help him like a baby it wasn't age it was something else
his eyes were so quick she said but his movements so slow
always his eyes so quick and his movements so slow she would
show me sticking her index finger out like a fork show me in
that gloomy kitchen she too had quick eyes dark eyes like her
son he had probably had them too sometimes he would sit
without moving after the boy had gone off to play she had
washed up and put the plates away he would sit without moving
she didn't know what to do with him what to say to him they
had been so close but now there was this barrier of silence as
if he had forgotten her forgotten the world she would suggest
he go to bed but sometimes she had to repeat it three or four
times even take him lift him up he would look at her and smile
so that she didn't know if he was fully conscious was laughing
at her or if it was something else if he really was elsewhere she
would move him in the direction of the stairs sometimes she
even had to undress him put him to bed he would lie there
smiling and when she looked in the next morning the bed
would be smooth, tidy, as if he had just lain there where she
had left him and then stood up some time in the early morning
and got his clothes on and walked out of the house down to
his river she would go mad sometimes scream at him or burst
into tears he would pat her head but never explain never take
her into his confidence it was as if it was no longer important
to talk to explain the doctors found nothing wrong with him
the local doctor who had always treated him she even had a

specialist down from Rouen but there was nothing wrong with him he was polite his speech was clear they could find nothing wrong with him at all and he'd always been fit, healthy, there was no history of anything just this shutting off at times she didn't mind she would herself sit with him or they would drive to the coast he had been there often with his wife her mother there were even photos she showed me yellow photos of the two of them on the beach and the grey Channel beyond he liked those drives he liked sitting at the wheel of his old car but he wasn't interested much any more now he had the river he hardly used the car eventually she sold it there was no point in keeping it and hardly ever using it she didn't need it she only wanted to make him happy to try and understand him to get through in some way you understand he wasn't antagonistic or anything like that he was just indifferent or not indifferent but unaware it was like having a rock in the family she said to me a rock a stone sitting at your table sleeping in your house and you are descended from him he carried you in his arms once he spoke to you when you were small he danced you on his knee why does it have to change to be like that what does it mean but she didn't ask me as though she expected an answer as though she were even waiting for an answer as though she were even puzzled she only repeated the words but angrily almost as though she had to and didn't want to dismissing them with a shrug then and sitting in silence in that kitchen and after a while starting again with another story another anecdote always about him as if there was nothing else to talk about as if the whole world round her no longer existed and perhaps had never existed at least not for a long time and she —

He knocked on the door: — Have you finished with the bathroom?

She opened the door of the little cubicle and stood facing him.

— It's hot. Open a window.

— They're all sealed up.

— They can't be.

— Anyway, they're filthy. I wouldn't touch them if I were you.

— Switch off the central heating then.

— I have. It's still too hot.

She sat down on the bed.

— Look, he said, you wanted to come here. Not me.

He threw himself on the bed behind her and pulled her towards him.

– I want to talk to you, she said.

– Yes, You said that on the phone. We can talk afterwards.

– No, she said. I – What do you think you – ?

– After, he said, pulling her towards him. After.

– The room was too hot, she said, keeping her eyes on the road. I felt as soon as we entered. I didn't know he would – I –

– You mean you – ?

– I had come home to see Mother. I bumped into him in the village shop. I hadn't seen him since I left school. He gave me his phone number. I –

– But

– He gave me his number. In London. I don't know. He must have sensed he must have seen me

– You mean you hardly knew him? But you

– Well I

He kept his eyes on the road, intent on his driving.

– It was easier, she said. With someone I didn't know well. I found his number. In my bag. So I rang him and he

– You rang him? From Paris?

– I had to talk I had to

– But if

– No I

– But

– No listen, she said. He wrote to me in Paris.

– And he came to see you there? While you were married to Claude?

– No we talked. I –

– And Claude?

– Claude?

– I don't understand, he said. How did he

– No, she said, it wasn't like that. I

– Like what?

And again it came to her that there was no beginning and no end, no way to explain or talk even, no way of stopping everything and looking back, stopping it and seeing where to start again you were plunged in and then you had to swim you looked up you got your head out of the water you tried to make out a direction if only you had a moment a moment of

respite to think to breathe but you had to keep going the waves
choked you blinded you your heart beat harder you knew if
you stopped you were done for you had to push you had to
keep going the waves got bigger you choked you swallowed
mouthfuls of water you

— Aren't you feeling well? he asked her.

He stepped on the brakes and pulled the car in to the side
of the road — Are you going to be sick?

— No.

— You look white.

— Let's get out and walk.

They found a lane leading up the side of the hill.

— Where are we? she asked him.

— Monmouthshire.

— Is it like this where we're going?

— No. Wilder. Barer.

They stopped half way up the hill and turned, looking out
over the undulating countryside.

— We arrived at night, she said. We were so excited we
couldn't sleep.

— I thought you said it was daytime? That you ran out of
the car all of you and swarmed over the garden?

— Well I...

— What?

— I remember both, she said. It must have been two separate
occasions.

— How many were you?

— Five of us, she said. Plus my parents. My brother and
sister and two cousins. The house was a mess. That made it
more exciting of course. There'll be plenty of work for you
lot, Father said. He told the boys he wanted them to help him.
Of course they never got half of it done. Not that summer.
He must have had workmen in in the winter because when we
came back the following summer there was another bathroom
installed and everything was clean and white.

— But that day? When you arrived?

— We had been on the ferry and then driving down to that
place. Nobody asked anything about it but somehow the
excitement mounted as we approached. My parents talked in
low voices in front. We fought as usual in the back.

She stopped.

– Go on, he said.

She shrugged.

– The next day? he pressed her.

She shivered. – Let's go back, she said.

They climbed down the hill and got into the car again. He drove in silence. The landscape started to change around them.

– Why are those hills black? she asked him.

– They're slag-heaps.

– Oh.

– You know what that is?

– Yes.

After a while she said: – Tell me how coal is formed.

– Another time.

– You mean I wouldn't understand?

– I'll give you a proper lecture. One of these days. I promise.

– Is there any rest? she said. In the earth I mean. Does anything stay still at all?

– Well, look at it, he said. Isn't that still enough for you?

– Silly.

– Well.

He got up quickly and went out. She could hear him jumping on the longer pieces of wood he had collected from the moors and left in the porch to dry.

He came back with his arms full, knelt by the fire and stoked it up.

– This'll slow it down, he said.

She was seized suddenly with the feeling that she had to get up to move to walk to do something that she couldn't go on sitting on the sofa like that with her legs curled up under her watching the fire and

– Where are you going? he said, half-turning.

– Out.

– Out? At this time of night?

– I want to walk.

– It's not safe. You'll break your leg.

– I don't care. I have to get out.

She climbed the hill outside the house. It was darker than she had realized, big clouds scurried across the sky, hiding the moon, and she slipped once and fell, got up but missed her footing and found herself on her face in the damp heather she wanted to run to scream but found some basic prudence restrained her she bit her lips turned over and lay looking up at the clouds looking for the stars but there was nothing only darkness until gradually the mood passed and she started to shiver again and got up and felt her way down the hill and so back to the house.

He was sitting by the fire, with the light on beside him, reading.

He stood up when she came in: – Are you wet? What have you – ?

– No no.

– Let me make some tea. Something.

– No no.

– But you're –

– Oh shut up, she said.

He sat again.

– You're so damned reasonable.

He was silent.

– Don't you see that?

– You're cold, he said. Have a bath and go to bed.

– I'm not a child.

– Who said you were?

– I'm grown up. I can look after myself. I don't need you to mother me.

He took off his glasses and polished them on the lower edge of his pullover, looking at her and blinking.

– I'm sorry, she said.

– It's all right.

She sat down. On the table beside her there was a piece of paper. She picked it up and read it. It said: I love you.

– Oh Richard, she said.

Her leg hurt where she had fallen. The man said: – Are you all right?

– Yes.

– I saw you limping up the road.

– No. I'm all right.

– You've come from far then? Walking all the way?

– Not very far. Up there.

– And you've walked all the way have you?

– I had to, she said. She clasped the box against her chest. The hard edges cut into her.

– Ah, he said.

She closed her eyes. The van bumped and jolted but the man didn't seem to notice. He gazed at the road out of small blue eyes, puffing at a pipe stuck in the corner of his mouth.

– I turn this way for Swansea, he said. I'll leave you at that corner then.

He pulled in to the side of the road. – You should get a lift here, he said.

– Thank you.

– Good luck then.

She sat down. They had not put on any lights in the room and she could only see him at moments, when the flames flared up in the grate.

– She talked, she said. Every day she talked. While Claude slept upstairs. But it wasn't like listening to someone speaking it was like something else, like pulling back a screen or opening a tap and listening to the water flowing away. And she showed me pictures, photos of them, her father and her mother, with the car he was so proud of and then on the beach at Dieppe, Honfleur, Sainte-Adresse, all those places along the Normandy coast there was even one of him in front of the house, before they bought the field and the wood going down to the river, after that she said he wouldn't budge for a year or two after that he stopped going anywhere it's true his wife had died but even before that he grew more silent more withdrawn they would search for him everywhere and finally she got used to fetching him from the river and –

– But she stayed? he said. When she married? I mean.

– She hardly ever spoke about it. Just that the man came and fathered the child upon her and left. They were legally married, there were papers to prove it, but it was as if they hadn't been as if he had just come there to that village for the sole purpose of fathering that child and then when he had done that when he

– But

– He just left, she said, I don't know if he disappeared and it broke her heart or if she pushed him out or if he went and she never even noticed, it was as if it had never been, she said, except for the child who was there now and hadn't been before, so that once again, as when her mother was alive, there were three of them, except that this time each belonged to a different generation, though he would laugh sometimes and say perhaps he is ours, yours and mine, and she didn't have to ask him she knew what it meant it was monstrous but what evidence was there to the contrary the other the husband might never have been there at all he might never have existed he was so shadowy he didn't belong not to their world nor perhaps to any, perhaps she had dreamt him up when she found herself pregnant she would search in the drawers for some sign of his existence for some proof that he had indeed been there but there was nothing except that piece of paper that certificate what did it prove what did it mean it said nothing to her nothing that she could understand he was a labourer she told me though she didn't speak of it much he was working on a building site on the new station I think it was she didn't know why they married the old man said nothing and then a few days later he was gone. She never tried to find him or enquire after him it was as if she too was uninterested and Claude of course I asked him after that first visit I asked him point blank but he wouldn't say anything he just shrugged said I'm here why bother about origins, and I, But you must be curious you must care it isn't as if, and he, What difference would it make I am as I am and that's that, and I, But if, and he, It wouldn't change anything to know, he wouldn't go on he wouldn't talk about it perhaps it tormented him or perhaps he didn't really think about it at all I never knew I didn't –

– Was he like her? Did he think about the old man all the time?

– I don't know.

– But

– I don't know. I don't think so.

– But you married him, he said. You should know.

– I thought he must be but perhaps there was nothing. Perhaps he just didn't like talking. I don't –

– But he caught you. That day. He brought you back to his flat.

– Yes, she said.

– He must have

– I don't know, she said. I don't know what there was behind
it. I thought there was something, you do when people act
like that, but perhaps there was nothing, perhaps he was just
all surface and I was a fool to try and look underneath to think
I would find something hidden something he –
  – But –
  – I thought he wasn't like other people, that he didn't speak
easily, didn't just babble for the sake of it, I liked that or rather
liking didn't come into it I knew I had to stay there was something that had happened I had no choice I accepted it and
thought I would grow to understand it but I didn't I couldn't
there wasn't anything behind it or at least I never discovered
what it was I was never allowed to enter to see to
  – Yes but. And his mother. Was he close to her?
  The fire was dying out. He did not bother to get up and
bring in more wood from the porch. She looked into the glow,
feeling the heat on her face, her knees.
  – Not particularly, she said.
  – But I thought
  – No. He just brought me down to see her.
  – But
  – In a few weeks I suspect I had got closer to her than he
had ever been. She was so taken up with the old man, it was
as if he had to be excluded. Or perhaps there had been a shock,
that's what I thought at first, that the discovery of the body
and it didn't look good I'm sure not after two days in the
water, that the discovery had been a shock he was only nine
then but I don't think it was that I don't think he thought
about it he certainly never talked he just
  – But what? Do you think having to get out he
  – Out? You mean out of the house? And finding other
people in it? I don't know.
  – But you must know, he said. You must have views at least.
  – I don't know, she said. It's always moving never still I've
tried to understand tried to stop to stand still and look hard
but it can't be done or at least I can't do it or perhaps there's
nothing to understand and even the old man sitting there looking at that river day after day perhaps there was nothing you
could explain perhaps he just liked it and there was nothing
more, people have different tastes perhaps he just found it nicer

than other things and he didn't have many years left perhaps
he was tired perhaps he didn't know himself and
  – And so he threw himself in?
  – Perhaps he didn't, she said. Perhaps he fell asleep and just
slipped in or his heart stopped and he slid in who knows who
can tell and anyway it
  – But she didn't tell you? They didn't have an autopsy?
  – She didn't talk about it, she said. Only about him sitting
there or them eating, the three of them at table, she talked
about him when he was alive for her he was still there after all
he was no more absent then, fifteen years later, than he had
been when he was alive if he never talked perhaps less because
when he was there and silent, withdrawn, you wanted him to
be more than that whereas after she was glad I suppose she
was glad to have him so vividly there in her mind and she
hadn't talked to anyone about it but it wasn't as if she was
waiting for me or missed talking she just told me in her flat
voice she just told me how it was and it didn't seem to worry
her or upset her it was as if she had been waiting for someone
anyone it didn't matter who or as if no time at all had passed
since I had last seen her at the age of twelve and there was
nothing more natural than to talk to me to tell me to show me
the photos it was worse than if she had been upset or anguished
she just told me how it was she didn't try to understand perhaps
it didn't mean anything more but she had to speak she had to
tell someone her voice droning on she would probably never
have noticed if I had got up and slipped out perhaps she would
have gone on talking in that deep voice she always had but
made deeper by age have gone on even if she had noticed that
I had gone that she was alone, going over it again and again,
the silence the light bringing him back from the river the meals
in the evening the way they crossed each other without talking
if they met during the day him sitting by the river and gazing
and gazing and gazing and then perhaps having enough and
letting go slipping in and always the same the
  She pressed the button and heard the coins dropping in.
  – It's me, she said.
  – What?
  – Me.
  – Oh. Where are you?

– Here. In Victoria. I've just arrived.

There was a pause. – Do you know what time it is? he said.

– Look, she said, the sea was rough. The train was delayed. It's not my fault.

There was another pause. Then he said: – Well?

– Can you come and fetch me? I have to talk to you.

– Well...

– I have to talk to you. You said if

– I'll be over as soon as I can, he said. It'll take a bit of time.

– Yes, she said.

– I have to get dressed.

– Yes, she said.

– Wait there.

– I want to talk to you, she said.

– Yes yes. Wait there.

– Under the clock. On the right as you go in.

– Yes. Hold on.

And when he arrived, bleary-eyed, she said again: – I want to talk to you.

– But what happened? he said. You said you'd phone me from Paris.

– I didn't have time.

– You walked out on him? Just like that?

– I don't know, she said. I had to go. I couldn't –

– You told him?

– What?

– That you were going?

– I had to get out, she said again. And, sitting on the too soft bed in the overheated hotel room, she repeated: – I had to get out. I had to talk to you.

– But what happened? You haven't explained what happened.

– Nothing, she said.

– Nothing?

– I couldn't breathe, she said. Then, quickly: – No. It wasn't that.

– What are you talking about?

– I told you, she said.

– I'm sorry. I understand.

– Do you?

– Look, he said.

– He watched me go, she said. He stood and watched me go.

– He didn't say anything?

– No, she said. He kept his hat on his head.

– His hat? What hat? What are you talking about?

– His hat, she said again. He kept it on his head.

She stood in the tiny bathroom and examined her face in the mirror.

– Come on, he said. Haven't you finished in there?

And again the feeling came over her, overwhelming her, dragging her down, so that she had to struggle to retain her balance, to fill her lungs, the old woman in the dim scrubbed kitchen with her black handkerchief on her head speaking, speaking, not letting up, and the old man sitting motionless and staring across the river while the sun rose and travelled across the sky and set again and the birds called out and screamed at each other in the trees and the river flowed and flowed and she called and came towards him, stood beside him, touched him on the shoulder, said, It's supper-time, and he looked at her and got up and followed her back to the house without a word and they sat down, the three of them, just as they had the day before and as they would the day after and she brought the dish out of the oven and put it on the table between them and served the boy and he bent over his plate and began to eat at once and she and the old man exchanged glances and he winked at her suddenly and just as suddenly she had burst into tears, the drops trickling down her cheeks and her body shaking as she tried to pretend that nothing had happened, shaking in its black dress and the two men or rather the man and the boy not looking at her not saying anything munching steadily so that she gradually stopped, pulled herself together, tried to eat a little but they didn't help it was as if they weren't there except for the steady munching and

Her knee hurt where she had fallen. She felt the blood forming a scab under the harsh material of her jeans. She held the box against her chest and began to walk up the road in the direction the man had indicated.

He called out again: – Come on! Haven't you finished?

She took her eyes away from that other face looking at her from the mirror.

– Come on! he said again.

She opened the door and looked at him.

He had taken off his tie and shoes and was lying on the bed, his hands behind his head.

– Look, she said, I –

– Come here, he said.

– No. Listen.

– Come on, he said.

She sat down on the edge of the bed. He moved and put a hand on her arm. She shook herself free.

– What's the matter? he said.

– I must talk to you.

– Later, he said.

– No, she said. Now.

He sat up and pulled her towards him.

– No, she said. If you

– But what

– I have to talk, she said. You told me if ever I wanted to talk I

– Yes, he said, but

– You said I could talk you said I could I

– You got me up at three in the morning? he said. To talk to me?

– Please, she said, I

– No, he said. I can't believe that. I'm sorry I can't believe that. You're just

– Please I

– You're just

The box hurt as she pressed it to her chest. Cars whistled past her, hooting at her to get out of the way. She paid no attention, moving forward in the direction the van driver had indicated. Her knee hurt where she had fallen. She shivered and tried to pull the blankets up round her but he had dragged them all over to his side.

She lay with her eyes open, staring at the moonlit window and the big spiky tree outside. And again the feeling swept over her, taking hold of her body and shaking it so violently that in a moment she had forgotten everything else, could think only of this buffeting, this being hurled from side to side and up and down, the sense of helplessness and loss, of the impossibility of speaking and the need to speak, if only she could

find the thread, the way through, if only she could stand back
and see when it all began, disentangle the memories, the events,
she felt herself carried on a current, borne on the waves, if
only she could stop if only she could hold on, tell it, tell it,
do you understand what I'm saying it's just that there's too
much for one person to say too much to have all that inside
you it runs about in my head my body it needs an outlet it
needs to find a way out a

   – You're just

   – No, she said, pushing him away, getting up, going to the
window.

   – Christ, he said.

   – Please Paul I

   – Christ, he said again.

A car pulled up and the driver leaned over and opened the
door on her side. She glanced at him and walked on. He called
out to her but she kept moving. He drove slowly alongside
her, shouting something, then, when she didn't reply, he
revved up violently and shot away from her.

The road led up a hill and round in a wide curve. She was
suddenly tired and stopped. A lorry hooted and swerved round
her, covering her in dust as it roared past. She sat down on
the side of the road, drawing up her knees and closing her
eyes, seeing herself talking, trying to explain, the fire cracking
in the grate, the moors silent outside, only his outline visible
as he sat upright in his chair, his pipe sticking out of the corner
of his mouth, taking it out occasionally and tapping it on the
floor, then sucking at it and fiddling with matches and lighting
it, saying:

   – But why did your father – ? and she

   – He just bought it. I never asked him. He heard that it was
for sale and he bought it. And he

   – But why France? I mean at that time – And she

   – I don't know. We piled into the car and drove down. We
didn't quite know where we were going but there was the sense
that it was something special there was so much excitement in
the car we couldn't keep still and the first morning we stormed
over it like ants, like ants she told me afterwards, you see she
came and looked, came and stood, looking over the wall – And
he

– But – And she

– She'd moved into a smaller house. With the boy. In the village still, but on the other side. But she knew we were arriving. Father had written to her. She knew the day. She stood and looked over the wall. We didn't notice. Or did, perhaps, but paid no attention. She must have come every day. Watched us running over the land she'd lived on for so long, tearing down the branches of the trees she'd watched grow, I don't know when I first realized she was there but I started to look out for her I wouldn't go near that wall, the others noticed nothing or perhaps like me they did but kept quiet, and even when I'd been to see her with Father in the cottage she'd bought, in that dim kitchen where years later I would come back and sit and listen to her talk while Claude slept upstairs, even then I didn't connect her with the person who frightened me by standing so still so silent looking over the wall I don't know when I realized I don't know if there was a definite moment or if somehow I knew and felt I had known for a long time, it all fitted in, I wasn't frightened any more, only a little uneasy, and then she ceased to come ceased to watch at least regularly, but it was then, I don't know if it was just coincidence or what but it was then that he started to come into the garden we tried to get him to play with us but he wouldn't he wasn't rude but he just wouldn't. Talk to him in French, Father said, practise your French on him, but whether it was because he couldn't understand us or because he didn't want to he would look at us and go on playing by himself, in our garden, throwing sticks up into the trees or squatting on the ground and looking at the ants' holes –

– You didn't talk to him then? You didn't get to know him?

– After a while we ignored him. The others did anyway, I'm not sure I did I kept seeing him out of the corner of my eye or coming on him when I turned a corner of the house, that was why it wasn't a surprise, not really a surprise, despite the funny hat and coat, when there he was in the rue des Ecoles, standing in front of me, looking at me out of those black eyes of his, saying, It's you, as if we'd rehearsed it as if it was a play or something and I suppose that's exciting, at first at any rate, to think your life has suddenly taken on the shape of a play after all, the hope is always there of course it's always

there but most of the time we try and ignore it, try to pretend
we don't believe in such things, not for ourselves at any rate,
but it takes a little thing, just a tiny accident to make all that
accumulated wisdom drop away, to make us believe that the
miracle has happened that at last it's happened to us just to us
and –
    – But –
    – No. Let me finish.
    – Then how – ?
    – What? How what?
    – How did you
    – What are you saying? What?
    – After that? You...?
    – You mean why did I marry him?
    – Well...
    – I've told you. I've told you why. Because there wasn't
anything else to do. Because we were both committed to the
past or to a vision of the past, or to a vision of one man perhaps,
or perhaps he wasn't perhaps it was only me and he had other
things in mind, on his mind, however you like to put it and –
    – But you never talked? Afterwards? I mean what...?
    – He stood there. He said: You? And it all came back. It
was as if he had to bring me back with him, as if he wasn't
complete without me, and I didn't know I didn't see I
    – But
    – Why? I don't know why. Or what he had in mind. Except
to hold me there. Apart from that he wasn't interested but
perhaps that's not the right word the right formulation nothing
seemed to interest him he didn't talk like other people he wasn't –
    A car slowed down, then pulled up a little way beyond her.
It reversed and stopped in front of her. The driver leaned across
and opened the passenger door.
    – Do you want a lift?
    – Are you going to Merthyr Tydfil?
    – Jump in.
    She got in, clutching the box, and pulled the door shut behind
her.
    – Been waiting long? he asked her.
    – I don't know.
    – Pardon?

– No. I don't think so.

The driver gave her a long look.

– What have you got in there? he asked her.

– Nothing.

– Nothing?

– Stones.

– Stones?

The car screeched to a halt. The driver leaned across her and opened the door. – Out, he said.

She got out. The car shot off, its tyres screaming.

She began to walk again. Her leg hurt where she had fallen. She sensed the general direction and hoped she would come across a road soon. Her shoes were wet from the early morning dew. She held on to the box till her chest and fingers hurt.

The sun had risen and almost at once been hidden by a bank of cloud. It was a grey morning. She didn't know how long she had been walking or in which direction she was going any longer. All she knew was that she had to put one foot in front of the other and then pull the first one forward and place that in front of the second and so on and on, putting as much distance between herself and the farmhouse as she could, hoping he wouldn't come after her, wouldn't try to talk reasonably, she knew she couldn't bear that, that she must avoid seeing him again, avoid that at all costs, avoid another of those interminable conversations, arguments, discussions, his well-meaning questions, his puzzlement, his concern.

She stumbled over a fence and found herself on a little country road. She turned right and began to walk.

A van rumbled up the hill behind her. She went on walking. There was an old man at the wheel with a pipe in his mouth. He stopped the van and lowered the window.

– You're walking then are you?

– Is this the way to Merthyr? she asked him.

– Hop in. I'll take you as far as the junction. There I turn off Swansea way.

She got in. He glanced at her. – You've cut yourself, he said.

She looked down at the blood on her trousers. – It's nothing, she said.

– Ah.

– I fell over.

— Ah, he said again.

— I'm glad you came by, she said.

— Ay, you're lucky. There's not many cars come along these roads.

He gazed steadily ahead. She relaxed in the warmth of the van.

— At the junction you just wait for a car coming in the opposite direction, he said.

She sat up: — Are we there?

— Almost.

She looked about her, rubbing her hands together to restore the circulation.

— We're coming up to the junction now, the old man said. I go off this way to Swansea then.

— Thank you, she said. I don't know how to thank you.

— That's right then, he said, pulling in to one side of the road. Good luck.

— Thank you.

Her legs were stiff from sitting so long in that cramped position. She lifted the box down after her.

— Wait here, he said. You'll get a lift soon enough.

She began to walk away from him. After a moment she heard the van start up and move off. She kept on walking.

And again it came to her that she would never be able to find a way of explaining to him, that she would never be able to start or start at the right place she had thought it would be so easy she had thought she just needed someone to talk to and all would be well or perhaps she had not thought at all perhaps as usual she had just hoped or not even that she had to go there had been no other way no other solution she didn't know when she decided when she finally made up her mind she remembered his words, Phone me if you ever need me, here's my London number, she would look at the number in her book and put the book away and then one day she just did she went down to the café at the corner and did so, hoping almost that they wouldn't connect her that he wouldn't be there that he wouldn't answer, and when he did when she heard his voice saying Yes, coldly, drily, she was seized with panic all she could find to say was, It's me, and when he waited a bit she said again, I'm calling from Paris, and heard him gasp and splutter and say What? Why? and she

·

– I don't know. And he
– But – And she
– You told me . . . And he
– What is it? Is something the matter? What is it? And she
– You gave me your number. And he
– Yes but

And then she rang off. And went back to the flat. But began again a few days later.

– It's me.
– Yes. Where are you? Give me your address. Do you know you didn't even give me your address? And just rang off like that? Are you all right? And she
– Yes. And he
– Well then what – ? And she
– I don't know. And he
– Are you here? Are you in London? And she
– No. And he
– Well then what – ? And she
– I don't know. I just wanted to hear you. And he
– Give me your number. Give me your address. Before you ring off.

And then she put down the phone again. Knowing he would be there. So that when she arrived, breathless, exhausted, in the middle of the night, she dialled his number, knowing he would answer.

– Where are you?
– Here, she said. Victoria.
– Well, for God's sake. Get a taxi and come over.
– No, she said. You come.
– Come? And fetch you?
– I have to talk to you.
– Can't we talk when you get here?
– I have to talk to you.
– All right, he said. I'll come.

And came.

– I want to go to a hotel, she said. There must be one here.
– A hotel?
– I'll pay, she said.
– It's not that, he said. It's just . . .
– I want to talk, she said. I don't want to go to your flat. Please.

Why had she said that? Why had she felt the need for that? Why had she been so sure it had to be that and then the way it had all so quickly faded and turned sour so that she didn't want to talk knew she couldn't or wouldn't knew it was no good he had misunderstood her it was her fault not his but it made no difference the room was too small too hot the trains shook the building but it wasn't that it wasn't even him holding her pulling her down it was it was

– What are you talking about? he said.

– You don't understand, she said.

They reached the edge of the outcrop above the house and stopped.

– You asked for it, didn't you? he said.

– Yes, she said.

They looked across at the mountains to the north and east.

– Which way? she said.

– Down here. We'll follow the old Roman road.

They clambered down through the ferns and boulders.

– You can't blame him, he said.

– I'm not blaming, she said. I didn't say that. You don't understand.

– What do you mean?

– Even if he had listened. Had sat and waited for me to go on. Even then I

– What?

They climbed a wall and he held out a hand for her but she jumped and kept walking. He caught up with her.

– And so you left again? he said. In the middle of the night?

– He was sleeping, she said. He didn't want to listen. I couldn't talk, anyway.

– But why had you ever thought you...?

– That he would listen?

– Yes and that you...?

– I don't know, she said. When I went home to visit Mother he was there. It was the feeling of seeing again someone one had known in the past. There was a bond between us I thought. He gave me a lift to the station. He told me he was separated from his wife. She had kept the children. He said if I ever needed help he was there. He gave me his London address. He seemed reassuring. Dependable.

– Yes but...

– I didn't want to speak to anyone close to me, she said. We'd been at school together. That was just the right distance. Don't you understand that?

– Yes, he said.

– I wanted him to talk, she said. Claude I mean. To tell me about his feelings. His childhood. After all, she did, his mother, but it was as if he wasn't interested. He laughed it off. He just said they were crazy. They lived like crazy people. His grandfather and his mother. And when I said why he just shrugged.

– Well if he thought he

– No no, she said. It wasn't that. He didn't think it was important. He didn't think it had any meaning. But then why did he stop me why did he hold me I hadn't forgotten them but it was in the past it was something in the past I no longer thought of it it was another country it never entered my head that it was only a hundred or so kilometres up the river it was another country another world it was the past a moment in my childhood perhaps all my childhood just those two summers or maybe three and as soon as I recognized him it wasn't him I remembered but the old man sitting in his stillness his silence looking out at the water she would tell my father tell how he sat there day after day how once he had seen a coffin pass by or maybe it was just a big box of wood drifting past on the river that was one of the few times he talked to her about his day one of the few times he told her what had happened what he was feeling day after day he talked to her about that coffin but it wasn't morbid she insisted that it wasn't morbid you understand she would say to my father it was just that it struck him most of the time there was nothing just the light in his eyes the light of the day the light of the river all those reflections those shadows the light broken up and thrown back reflecting the sky the clouds revealing the reeds the little flies the underwater life it filled his eyes it filled his face he was all made of light when you looked at him sometimes when he turned away from the river when he came into the house we sat here in the kitchen the boy ate I was afraid, afraid of the light in his eyes, every morning he would get up with the dawn, rain or sun he would get up and go down to the river he was

never in the house when we got up he would sit there all day
with a sandwich sometimes to keep him going or not even that,
sometimes he would come in at lunch but he wouldn't talk we
would pass each other in the garden and he would smile sometimes I would try and drag it out of him I would shout and
yell, telling him he was wasting his time that he was going mad
that he couldn't do that to me to the boy but he wouldn't
respond, only look at me sometimes and say, Where is he?
and I would say Who? and he would say, You know who, and
I, What do you mean where is he? And he, Where have you
buried him? And I, What are you talking about? And he,
Where? Don't you ever ask yourself where? And I, I didn't
bury him, neither did you, he went away, you know he went
away, and he, you buried him, And I, No, you drove him
away, and he would smile and say again, Search, Search for
the grave, if you have forgotten. And I had forgotten. Or not
wanted to think to remember they were horrible years or rather
a horrible year and when he went away it was like a bad dream
from which one wakes you understand only my belly was full
and there was no one else to blame but you see how it was just
the three of us in that house with the garden and the field and
the river beyond the poplars the willows the silence we were
caught like that in that silence nothing seemed to relate to
anything else at least that's how it seemed to me I tried to give
the boy a life tried to make it good for him but the other was
like a shadow, sitting with us and yet not with us wandering
in and out of the house and the children at school asking him
where his father was and him asking me at supper and me
saying He's gone away and Father saying, He never existed,
and the boy looking at us both, and Father winking at him
and then I flew into a rage I wanted to hit him I had never felt
like that before, while Mother was alive, never felt anything
but affection and some awe but afterwards the days seemed to
stretch so endlessly and there seemed to be such a gap between
the three of us, I don't know if the others felt it but I certainly
did, such a gap between us, as if we had just been dropped
there in that paradise, because it is a paradise, isn't it, I don't
have to tell you, I remember when you first arrived, the five
of you, running all over that garden shouting and laughing in
the sunshine, one could hear your voices right across the village

really it was paradise I daren't go near I daren't look up to that point in the river even that isn't real I still see him sitting there and turning when I drew near him turning and looking at me but he wasn't looking not really not with that light in his eyes it was as if you could still see the river flowing but behind his eyes now behind his eyes and as if he had it there and was drawn to it and had to live with it and in it just once at dinner when I was thinking of something else, he wouldn't have said it if I had asked him or if Claude had asked him or anything like that he would have shrugged or pretended not to hear but because I was thinking of something else and Claude was playing with breadcrumbs or scratching something with his knife I don't remember only that he came out with it he just said, The air we breathe, and stopped again, and when I asked him to elaborate he just smiled or giggled rather as he sometimes did he was an old man by then I sometimes forgot as you do with someone you've known all your life you've seen every day there's no real sense of how they change how they will look to an outsider but he was an old man I wasn't that young myself it was the longest period of my life it just seemed to stretch on and on forever and the boy grew up fifteen years I suppose it was from start to finish from the day Mother died to the day he fell in though even now he seems still to be there you know sitting there by that river I must show you photos of him and Mother in Dieppe, Honfleur, Trouville, Deauville, they would take the car out there he was so proud of his car the photos aren't good of course they're not but I've got them here somewhere I've kept them all he loved taking them and having taken them he filed them away but at the end he lost interest I tell you he lost interest in everything he didn't wash he didn't do anything except sit and stare, What is it you're looking at, I would ask him, What are you looking for? but he wouldn't say he would smile and say Just looking, I got to accept that afterwards I got to accept that you could just sit there and look but at first I didn't know what he was up to if he was sulking or mourning or trying to come to a decision about something but you just had to look at his eyes to know it wasn't that it lit up his face I had never seen him like that I suppose you could say in one way those last years they were the happiest of his life and even at the end who knows how he felt at the end right at the end they wanted to make a tragedy of it here in the village in the papers but why should it be a tragedy I'm not saying it was fun only how can we judge how can we tell perhaps the light drew him forward perhaps he finally grasped what it was he was after perhaps that was the only answer or something else something much simpler and he just fainted or his heart gave out and he slipped in but somehow it doesn't seem real it doesn't seem the important thing he no longer talked to me he wasn't a companion he was already dead in some sense but more alive than anyone I have ever known and Claude seemed to feel that too he would touch his coat as if it was holy or gave off power or something I'm not trying to make out he was a holy man or the hand of God was in that or anything but it felt different from other people you ask Claude when he wakes up ask him you'll see when he wakes up he –

– I've asked him. He won't talk about it.

– Ask him again. You'll see that he remembers.

– Perhaps he remembers too well and won't talk about it.

– No. You ask him. You'll see. He's a good boy.

– That's one thing he never talks about. Though he doesn't actually talk much about anything.

– Well he had an unusual upbringing. That explains a lot.

– He won't talk to me. Not at all.

– He will. In good time. You're the best thing that ever happened to him.

– But I can't go on. Not much longer.

– You will. For old time's sake. You will for a little longer.

– I don't know.

– You must. You must do that. For me. And Father. And the house.

– It's my life.

– Your life's bound up with that.

– Perhaps. Perhaps I need to unbind it.

– You can do that. But your destiny is with him. With us.

– I don't know.

– I know. I know what you will do.

– I'm not sure. Don't count on it.

– I'll count on it. I'll count on you to help him.

– Perhaps he doesn't need me. Doesn't need any help.

– I need it.

A mini-van stopped and the young woman inside made a questioning gesture and held the door open.

– Merthyr?

– Get in.

She got in. The girl engaged gear and moved off.

– Been waiting long?

– No. I don't think so.

– What have you got in there?

– Nothing. Stones.

– Stones?

– I stole them.

– You what?

– From a man.

– Oh, the girl said.

– I was staying with him. He's a geologist.

– Oh.

– But he just collects these for fun.

– Why did you take them?

– I don't know. I left my suitcase behind.

The girl concentrated on the road. It had begun to drizzle and the wipers grated against the glass.

– I thought of leaving them on the road. But it seemed silly. After all that.

– Yes of course.

– After carrying them all that way.

– How far have you come?

– Quite far. I left in the night. I mean it was early morning. I walked across the moors.

– Really?

– I don't know why.

– Why you walked?

– Why I took them. I don't want them.

– Oh.

– Do you want them?

The girl took her eyes off the road for a moment and looked at her.

– It doesn't matter. It was just a thought.

– You can leave them with me if you like, the girl said.

– Can I?

– I'll look after them for you.
– You don't mind?
– If you wanted me to send them on somewhere...?
– No no. I'd like to know they were in good hands. They're nice stones.

The car swung off the main road and over a cattle grid, then down a narrow road.

– You've come far?
– It was dark when I started.
– And you walked all the way?
– No. I got a lift in a van.

They emerged over the dirty town.

– Where do I drop you?
– Oh. Anywhere.
– Where are you going?
– To the station.
– Fine. I pass right in front of it.

She was silent, negotiating the narrow streets. Finally she stopped and switched off the engine.

– Is this it?
– Yes.
– Well, thanks.
– You're sure you don't want those stones?
– No.
– If you give me an address...?
– No no. I'd like you to have them.
– And the man?

She shrugged.

The car drove off. She watched it disappear and then went into the little station.

– When's the next train for London?
– One-fifteen. Change at Cardiff.
– Cardiff? Isn't there a direct train?
– No. Change at Cardiff.
– I see. Thank you.

She got her ticket and looked at her watch. There was more than an hour to kill. She wandered away from the ticket office, looking for the station waiting-room, but the place was tiny and there was nothing.

She went out into the street again.

The town was packed with shoppers. She let herself be carried by the tide, found herself in front of a pub and entered.

At once she knew she had made a mistake. She forced herself to go to the counter and order a cider. She took the glass to a vacant table and sat down. The old men turned and gazed after her, grinning.

She leaned back and closed her eyes. Her heart was beating quickly. Whenever she opened her eyes she saw the old men watching her, silent, grinning. She swallowed the cider in big gulps, put down her glass and went out.

She found her way back to the station and sat down on a bench on the only platform. There was no one about. She tried to concentrate, to force herself to go over the events of the last few hours and try to understand what it was that had been happening to her, what it was she had been doing, but she grew dizzy with the effort and felt sick suddenly. The station announcer blared away in a continuous incomprehensible monotone. Every few minutes a little tune chimed through the loudspeakers. Then the announcer started again. It was bad enough in England, in France she couldn't make out a word. She pressed her knees against her suitcase and looked at the crowds hurrying past her. Once she thought she caught sight of Claude and her heart leapt in terror, but nothing happened and she calmed down again.

– He won't talk to me. He won't listen even, she had told his mother.

– He's a good boy.

– But he won't listen to me. I can't get through to him. I don't know what interests him. We're strangers.

– He was always wild. You know that.

– Tell me about his father.

– I don't know anything.

– But you must. You must know something.

– I've told you what I know. He was working here in the village. On the new station. I don't know why we got married. Then he went away.

– And you never tried to find him?

– I was glad he had gone.

– Oh.

– Sometimes it was as if he had never existed, you see. Only

there was the boy. Just me and the boy and Father. Sometimes
Father would tease me. He would say Where have you buried
him? Where have we put him? So that I would laugh at first
and then I would think, perhaps it is true, perhaps we have
killed him, perhaps we have buried him, and then I would see
Father looking at me and wondering and I would ask him what
was the matter and he would say, Perhaps he was never there,
perhaps he never existed, and I would say, And the boy? and
he would shrug his shoulders and look at me so that I understood and I would grow red and turn away and then I wouldn't
know it might be possible after all who can tell he left no trace
no trace at all we had the boy that was the only proof so we
studied him carefully looked him over for any sign any detail
that could guide us we didn't know any more and one day I
would think one thing and the next another I couldn't tell any
more perhaps there was no husband perhaps he was right there
were just the three of us and before that there had just been
the two of us after Mother died you know how one thinks
about such things then I would look in the drawer and find
the marriage certificate, I would show it to him, thrust it in
front of his eyes, but he would only shrug and smile a little
then I would wonder if the other thing was true if we had
perhaps and he was in the ground somewhere I would walk
round the garden looking for the spot and he would be sitting
by the river not looking not thinking I don't know what he
did all day sitting by that river it was when we bought the field
he took to doing that before that we only had the garden before
that he would go to the seaside he always liked to sit and gaze
sometimes he took me when I was small he took me to Rouen
and we would sit and look at the cathedral for hours once we
went by train I don't know why he had that car he loved one
of the first a big one it went so slowly by today's standards so
slowly but when Mother died he began to lose interest finally
he sold it what's the use he said I don't want to go off by
myself for the day and anyway I'm happier sitting here looking
at the river I asked him what he looked at what he saw but he
wouldn't answer he wouldn't explain it was just a thing he did
I like it he would say I just like to do that there's nothing
strange about that is there? There are many things we like to
do and a few which we can manage to do you sit in the kitchen

and think I sit here and look but what do you look at I asked
him I just look he said I sit and look but what do you look at
I sit he said I sit and let the light fill the river and fill the air
and fill me too he didn't talk about it much especially towards
the end but once or twice at the beginning he let drop a hint a
word afterwards he wouldn't say anything he would go out
there with a sandwich early in the morning and his folding
chair sometimes and take up his position always in the same
spot and sit and sit I would watch him sometimes for hours
he would sit without moving his eyes open I could tell he
wasn't asleep there was a kind of concentration about his shoulders once he came back and said he had seen a coffin passing
on the water, A coffin? I said, A large box, he said, I think it
was a coffin, What about it? I said, Nothing, he said, Why
did you mention it then? I said, Because I saw it, he said, But
you must see lots of things floating by as you sit there, I said,
but he wouldn't be drawn, he was in a good mood that day
though, he chucked the boy under the chin and they had a
mock fight as they sometimes did and then he lifted him up
and carried him out into the garden and carried him towards
the river it was dark by then the boy started screaming I could
tell he was frightened but I let them be and of course he didn't
drop him in he set him upright on the bank and they went
down and stood in the dark and listened to the current and the
insects but I'm making it sound like an obsession or a fetish
or something it wasn't that at all it was just an old man going
down to spend his days in a way he enjoyed, as others sat by
the fire or drank in the local café or played cards or just talked
so he went and sat by the river and looked he wasn't –

– Why are you telling me this? he said.

– I thought you wanted to know.

– Yes but all this.

– I thought you wanted to know.

A log cracked in the grate and this time it was he who jumped
up and stamped out the ember as it reached the carpet.

– I thought you wanted to know, she said again.

– Yes, he said. You've said that already.

– Well?

– There a difference, isn't there, he said, between explaining
and . . . and . . .

– And what?

– I don't know, he said. The way you went on. As if you'd forgotten I was there.

– I'm trying to understand, she said.

– Haven't you had enough of it? he said. Why don't you leave it alone?

She was silent. Then she said: – Yes. Perhaps.

– Well then.

– But I have to understand it, she said.

– Understand what? he said. A bad marriage? It happens to everyone. A crazy old woman, an old man you've never even seen – what is there to understand?

– My childhood, she said.

– God! he said. You married him for that? Because he had been there? Had been born in that place where you happened to spend two summers in your childhood?

– Three, she said.

– Three then. Because he was connected with the place? And then when you realized you had nothing in common you left him. Why make a fuss about it?

– I want to understand, she said again.

– But what? What?

– I don't know, she said.

– Oh God, he said.

She paid no attention to him.

– Oh God, he said again.

– Something to do with that silence in which he looked, she said. And then us coming like that. I can't make sense of it. Our noise and his silence. In that same place.

– But what is there to make sense of? he said.

– Just the two things, she said.

– Any two things, he said. Any two things are odd if you put them side by side like that.

She was silent.

– Don't you see? he said.

– Yes, she said.

She closed her eyes, willing herself to sleep. But getting up to look at the moonlight on the hills had made her cold and she started to shiver.

She curled herself up tight, digging down under the blankets.

Listen, she said to him. Listen. Perhaps it was as you say. But does that make it easier to understand, to bear? She stopped, trying to see it as he saw it, trying to stand outside and look at her life as someone else might see it, to focus on the children running across the garden and the field, screaming with pleasure and fear, and then on herself and her father going to see the old woman and Paris later and the first meeting after all those years, but suddenly she couldn't do it, she felt the tide overwhelming her, she couldn't control it, deal with it rationally, she felt herself drowning in the giant wave that came from nowhere and went nowhere, which picked her up and whirled her round, tossed her forward and sucked her under, she tried to catch her breath, to hold on to the things she knew, to dates and ages and the facts about houses and flats and births and deaths and marriages but the wave was tossing her and shaking her so that she no longer knew where she was or how she had got there, only that she didn't have the suitcase with her any more and it was night and she was in the middle of London somewhere near Victoria it must be or perhaps she had wandered into quite another district she had been walking for hours it was not true that the stars were invisible above big cities that the lights of the cities drowned the sky she could see them clearly or at least one, the morning star probably, bright overhead she tried to remember where she had left the suitcase was it in the room or on the train or afterwards she had had it in the lift yes she had left it in that carpark under the hotel wandering round and round that concrete labyrinth looking for an exit wandering for hours and at one point put down the suitcase, noted the spot, decided to come back for it when I found the exit but then forgot when I found myself outside so relieved to be outside and walking down the street there was no one about it was not cold not particularly cold I could still hear the trains rumbling into the station and out as well how had they built this place when had they built it that it shook every time a train came in how could anyone sleep or were they just too tired too indifferent to notice I didn't know how long I had been wandering at one point I remembered I had been walking by the river and alongside a park another time now dawn was coming I must have sat down once or twice surely I could not have gone on without stopping like that especially after that journey after the anxiety of the day before but now I had to think I had to decide where to go what to do it was evening again and I realized I had asked myself that question once or twice before during that day and then put it aside decided to go on just to walk and sit occasionally I was grimy my feet hurt but I didn't want to stop I didn't want to decide I would have to decide I passed a phone booth and then another and finally I went in and phoned my sister.

— And she took you in?

— I stayed with her for a bit. She would have been happy for me to stay a long time. Her eldest girl was away at University and she told me I could stay as long as I liked. But I didn't feel I could and anyway I didn't want to talk and of course she wanted to know what had happened and what I was going to do and I didn't want that she was kind she was helpful but I didn't want any of that I wanted to get out I wanted to keep walking I couldn't talk to her I couldn't tell her what needed to be said I —

A train crept into the little station. She stood up.

— Is this the train for Cardiff?

— Not yet. Next one in.

— Thank you.

She went back to her seat. Suddenly she realized that she didn't have the box with her any more. She searched under the bench, stood up, looked round, started to run back to the ticket office, then remembered that she had left it with the girl in the car.

Why had she even taken it? She sat down again, staring out at the tracks and asked herself: Had she really taken it, or only thought of doing so? She remembered asking him:

— What's in there?

— Stones.

— Stones? To study you mean?

No. It hadn't been like that. She had just seen him at work and leaned over his shoulder and watched him. He had fitted a lens into his eye and examined the rock, held between a pair of pincers. He had laid it down and cut away fragments with a little chisel, then picked it up and held it to the light again.

— What are you doing?

— Work, he said.

– How? What are you looking for?

– Traces of coal. Of oil.

– Oh.

– That's one of the reasons I come here. We're on the edge of the old red sandstone and the carboniferous limestone.

– Oh, she said. I see. Then added: But I thought modern geologists worked in high-powered laboratories with the latest equipment?

– That's right, he said, examining the rock through his lens.

– Then how can you work like this?

– I can't.

– Then what are you doing?

– I'm pulling your leg.

– Oh, she said. Then: – It's not very funny.

– I do my best, he said.

– One does expect people to tell the truth when one asks a simple question, she said.

– Naturally. It would be impossible to pull people's legs if they didn't expect one to tell the truth.

He put down the piece of rock and took the lens out of his eye. He rubbed the eye and looked at her.

– It was the lens took me in, she said.

He held it out to her.

– No no, she said.

– You don't want to see? It's really interesting.

– I can see well enough as it is.

He laughed and came and sat down beside her.

– But you do collect rocks, she said. For fun.

– I like the look of them, he said.

– You'll show me your collection some time?

– We'll go out and explore.

– Now?

– This afternoon.

The train that had just crept in crept out again. A porter came and stood on the edge of the platform, staring vacantly at the lines.

– When is the train due in? she asked him.

– Any minute now.

– That's the London train?

– Change at Cardiff.

– Do you know what time it gets to London?

– Ask at the ticket office. They'll tell you at the ticket office.

He walked away down the platform, then vaulted down and crossed the tracks, clambered up the other side and disappeared round a corner.

The station started to fill up. A porter in a mechanised trolley drove slowly down the length of the platform. A very small lady in a red hat asked her: – Is this the platform for the Cardiff train?

– I think so.

– Oh dear. No one knows anything.

– They told me it was.

Another train rolled into the station and she stood up and moved towards it. But it was only a goods train. The guard in the mechanised trolley appeared again and went down the length of the train. He stopped and started to load his trolley with cases that were handed out to him.

– Is the train late? the lady asked her.

– I don't know.

She got up and went out to the ticket hall and then right out of the station.

She stood on the steps and watched the people go by. Then she went back in and sat down on another bench, at the far end of the platform.

She saw a guard and went up to him.

– Is the train delayed?

– Engine trouble.

– So it is delayed?

– They're replacing it.

– What's the matter with it?

– Engine trouble.

She laughed. – I thought it was only planes that happened to, she said.

– These new engines, the guard said, they're as complicated as planes.

– Why do they fit them then?

He shrugged. – Madam, I'm not the transport minister.

– How long do you think it'll be before we get away?

He shrugged again. – Who knows?

She looked over her shoulder apprehensively. She didn't

think he would have followed her. After all, he had stood and watched her as she packed, stood and watched as she walked away from the building. Stood and watched and said nothing.

She wondered now, sitting in the train and being carried north, how near they would pass to the village, whether it was just such a train, in which had sat people just like herself, which she had heard hooting so mournfully in the night all those years ago.

She stood up to look at the map on the wall opposite, but the carriage was crowded and she felt conspicuous all of a sudden. She went out into the corridor, but that was crowded too. She went back to her seat.

The man next to her had put his briefcase on her seat.

– Excuse me, she said.

– I'm so sorry.

She sat down.

The sky was grey and a wind beat against the windows of the train. Water clung there from an earlier shower.

– It'll be a rough crossing, the man said.

– Oh?

He shrugged.

– I don't get sea-sick, she said.

– How lucky you are.

– You do?

– Invariably.

– Have you tried taking things for it?

– I've tried everything.

– Oh dear, she said. Why don't you fly?

– I get asthma flying.

– Really?

– That's right.

– I'm sorry.

– So am I. I fly as rarely as possible.

– Yes. I can understand that. If you...

She stared out of the window. The moon must have been full because the contours of the fields and hills were clearly visible, as though covered by a huge white sheet.

– What is it? he asked her.

– Nothing. I'm looking.

She wanted to talk to him, now, to explain to him, she knew

now she would be able to talk so that he would understand, so that *she* would understand, turned, ready to wake him again, but then the futility of it overwhelmed her, the sense of hopelessness in the face of so much material, where was the start, where the finish, it had always been with her, this sense of incompleteness, of excess rather, as if it was necessary to cut down the branches, thin the forest, before she could start to understand, but how to cut, where to begin to cut, it went back and back in a never-ending spiral, so that she longed for a moment of clarity, a moment of illumination, when she would be able to look down on it all, on the mess and the confusion, the doubts and uncertainties, the thousands of half-begun and half-completed endeavours, when she would be able to look down and see, even if only for a second, what it was she had to do, how it was she had to live, but the moment never came, the instant of clarity and illumination, she felt the wind blowing through her she felt full of holes full of spaces, gaps, the wind blowing through nothing to join one part with another nothing to link to bind just moments and gaps how did other people manage where did they go to find the strength the purpose to block up the holes perhaps there were no holes perhaps it was her perhaps it had never –

– You remember nothing before that? her sister asked.

– No. Isn't that strange?

– When exactly did you...?

– The moment we were in the car. Bowling along. There must have been things before. But I only remember the excitement and Father saying: There's a river as well.

– You don't remember the house in Kent?

– You've talked about it. And Mummy. But I don't. Not personally. It's as if the other has pushed away everything else.

– And you're going to marry him because of that moment? That 'other'?

– Oh Helen.

– Isn't that it? Isn't that what you're telling me?

– I don't know.

– But we only stayed three summers. Six months in all, if that. And you were ill for half of one of them.

– Was I? she said. I remember those days so clearly. I don't remember being ill. I remember the excitement.

– It was only three summers, Helen said.

– But don't you remember the excitement? How we screamed?

– They were good times, Helen said.

– I'm not explaining properly.

– What? What aren't you explaining?

– Everything. What happened. How it happened. I'm not making it clear at all.

– Well we've got time. Why don't you start at the beginning?

– There's no beginning.

– You said there was. You said the ride down in the car.

– No, she said. It was only when I saw him again. When he seized my wrist. And then when the old woman started to talk to me about her father. And I remembered how we used to pretend to be frightened. Because we'd been told of his corpse washed ashore. All blue. And the boys would try to scare us.

She was silent. Her sister waited, glancing quickly at her watch as she pretended to arrange the carpet.

– You have the children to fetch home. I'm sorry I –

– No no. Greta is fetching them. But Angela has to go to her ballet class later and I promised I'd phone Howard and . . .

– Can I just say this?

– Please darling! I told you. Start at the beginning. I've got bags of time. I promise you.

– No. I just want to say this. Or ask rather. Don't you ever think about the old man?

– The old man?

– Him.

– Drowning you mean?

– No. Sitting and looking at the river. Day after day. As if that was the beginning. Before we came.

– That? But you didn't even know him. We never thought of him. Except as a bogey.

– Day after day. Just the three of them. Hardly talking. And her, the daughter, coming out to fetch him back in the evenings and looking at the boy and wondering who the father was, wondering if she could even remember the father, if perhaps she had imagined him and he had never existed, there had just been the two of them and then her child, wondering if perhaps, but she couldn't remember, she had a vague sense of a moustache,

a hairy hand, but she might have imagined that, there might
not be anyone else, only her and her father and the river and
the silence and then her son was there, growing up with them,
between them, she would stare at him for hours, trying to
decipher in his face, his look, if he was going mad, I suppose
it was a way of going mad, because nothing could tell her,
nothing for certain, so that at moments she brushed her doubts
aside, the whole thing was ridiculous, at others it seemed obvious, so obvious, she questioned herself but she could remember
nothing, she went over the events, went over the past, but it
was always the same, at some point information was lacking,
after the death of her mother, she brought out the photos and
showed me, she laid them out as she must have done by herself
hundreds of times, the old tinted oval photos on thick boards,
the two of them in the garden, standing in front of the car,
him with his feet planted a little apart, gripping the earth, like
a sailor, with his sailor's beard too, and the mother small and
plump, content to stand beside him, photos of them at the
beach, white photos in the white sand, the sea diffused, the
water shimmering in the background, him always so firm so
solid with that paunch those eyes that beard, she diminutive,
smiling shyly, she could barely remember her mother, I asked
her once and she said no, then ventured nothing more, as if it
was of no importance no interest there was only the father and –

– Your train Miss.

She looked up. The porter had stopped his motorised carrier
a few feet from her.

– Your train Miss. On the other platform.

– For London?

– Change at Cardiff.

– Oh. Thank you. Thank you.

– Have a good journey Miss.

She got on to the train. There were hardly any other passengers in the two carriages. She sat down by the window and
looked out at her reflection.

What had she done with the box of stones? Jimmy was always
pulling it out from under his bed and inspecting it, ranging the
items, labelling them, dusting them. When they tried to see
what he was up to he would put his arms protectively round
it and tell them to go away.

– Do you remember that? She asked him, but he shook his head.

– You don't remember your passion for stones? You collected them wherever you could. You'd wade into the water and feel about for them for hours on end.

– You're sure it wasn't Mark?

– Of course, she said. Of course I'm sure.

– Well I don't really remember that period, he said. I have memories of the very early years, in the house in Kent. Flashes of memory. And then when I started going to school. I remember the school.

– Not the house in Normandy or the river or anything?

– Quite frankly, only what you and Helen have told me.

She stared at him.

A train pulled into the station and the building shook.

– You said if I ever needed you, to phone.

– Oh yes?

– That day. In the garden. With Mother. You said.

– Of course. And haven't I come?

– I want to talk to you.

– Afterwards. We'll talk afterwards.

– No. Now.

– Afterwards. Come on. It's three in the morning. You haven't dragged me all this way just to. . .

She lay in the room in the middle of the silent fields. Outside, the moon passed behind the absurd monkey-puzzle tree that someone had once planted in front of the house and which now dominated the place. She clutched the blankets and the feeling was upon her again that she had to talk, to tell it all, to start at the beginning and not stop till she got to the end, to tell it all, leaving nothing out, to let it unwind, unwind, but how to start, where to start, there was only the image of the old man with his paunch and his beard and his fierce gaze sitting in the sunshine staring out over the river, and then the sense, she could feel it now as she had felt it then, the sense of them rushing across the garden, the field, tearing down to the river, shouting, laughing, climbing the trees, chasing each other through the undergrowth, such excitement, her heart was almost jumping out of her mouth, her legs were weak but she was still running, still running, and –

– You married him to find that again? he said.

He got up and went out to the porch. She could hear him jumping on the wood to break it. He came back with his arms full, then knelt and laid two more pieces on the fire. Immediately it flared up, lighting his thin bony face, his intent eyes behind the spectacles.

– You think so? she said.

– Isn't it obvious?

– Would one do a thing like that?

– People do odder things.

– I don't know, she said.

– They do. I assure you.

– No. I mean me. I don't know if that's the reason.

– You've only talked of that, he said.

She was silent.

– As if you had to remind yourself, he said.

– Remind myself?

– Of that time.

She was silent.

– You don't agree, he said.

– No, she said slowly. You don't understand. I see us from the outside. I look down on us arriving, going wild, taking over that place. But it didn't belong to us. It belonged to him.

– Him?

– He had bought it. He –

– And then you bought it in turn from his daughter. I don't see that –

– He had lived in it, she said. Really lived. Do you understand? He had looked and looked and it was his. How could we do that to it?

– That?

– How could we? Screaming and shouting. It's the gap between that and his silent watching that I can't get over, that I can't make sense of.

– Make sense of? What do you mean?

– I don't know, she said.

He was silent, sitting on his haunches, looking into the fire.

– The impossibility of the two existing side by side, she said.

He was silent.

– It's funny, she said. I must have sensed it at the time. I must have felt something. Seeing her watching over the wall perhaps. Or the boy scurrying about and refusing to talk to us. Don't you see, I must have felt something? Even then I must have wondered.

    – About his death?

    – No, she said. Not his death.

    – But you said you were –

    – Of course we were frightened. And because we were frightened we pretended to be even more frightened, and showed as clearly as we could that we were pretending.

    – Well then if –

    – But no, she said. It wasn't that. It wasn't the fear. It was the sense of his presence, not his death.

    – But you –

    – What?

    – It was only after. Only –

    – Yes, she said. I must have sensed there was something wrong. But not been able to give it a name, and so forgotten it. Because she didn't talk then. At least I don't remember her talking to Father. Not when I went there with him. After all, he had bought the place from her, she was polite, she told him what he wanted to know, but she didn't talk about the things that mattered to her. Why should she to a stranger? But when I went back, when I arrived with Claude, I don't know, it was as if she had been waiting for me all those years, as if no time had passed at all, and I must have known too, I must have come prepared for something like that, at least it was no surprise to me, just a kind of shock, as if I was being shown a space, a hole in my life, in life itself, as if it was being shown to me and I couldn't get away from it, couldn't make sense of it and couldn't understand it – do you see what I mean?

    – No.

    – But you –

    – I still think what I first said was right, he said.

It was then that she felt the weight of what she had to say, and wanted to cry out, to hold him, to force him to listen, but she knew that she couldn't and wouldn't, that she had to go back, to go through, to find the thread and follow it forward, that all was confused again which had seemed so clear a moment before and that she had lost it but it was there, somewhere,

somewhere, staring at her reflection in the window now, as the train jerked and began to move slowly out of the little station, seeing again the porter who had been so nice to her, he waved as she went by, but whether to her or to someone else she could not be sure, would never know, waved back anyway, and they were out of the station and the town, chugging along into the greygreen countryside with the mounds of slag rising above them and the dirty sheep browsing on the slopes for all the world as if on hills that god and not man had made, thinking I won't stop, I mustn't fall back, I must think it through this time, her knee hurting where she had fallen in the night scrambling over the moors with that ridiculous box in her arms or did the box belong to another time, another place, Jimmy kneeling over it and refusing to show, Mark kicking it angrily and then in the night sneaking it out from under the bed, opening it up and peering at the serried ranks of stones, dragging it out without his waking up, getting the door open, slipping out into the corridor, the hideous blue hotel lights shining dimly, dragging it to the lift and waiting interminably while the cage of the lift crept up, half expecting him to open the door, to come out and confront her, walking now under the stars, the city silent, her steps echoing, the lights starting to go out street by street as the sky reddened into dawn, remembering her sister's voice when she told her where she was, You? Here? And Claude? and then waiting and listening, But you must come here, and then sister and brother and trains and more trains and London again and a bed with this friend and that friend and then a room here and a room there, how many days was it or months, she seemed to have been on the move forever and then Richard in the street and lunch and her urgent need to talk again, holding herself back, saying the minimum, and him looking at her intently, asking her to lunch again and then her sense that she had arrived, that she had finally arrived, rest at last, driving down to Wales, it's not much further now, this is the Head of the Valleys Road, these are the Beacons, not much further now, and the sense, engulfing her again, as she knew it would as long as she lived, of the weight of it all, like a river, a dam bursting, a river flooding her, so that she had to struggle to get her breath back, gulping in air, trying to fill her lungs, feeling herself swept along,

thinking, This is life, this is what life is, what it does to you,
you want to stop, stand back, get your breath, but it knocks
you down and flows and flows and there is no way of escaping
but if you let go and float you will drown, dragging at the air,
her mouth opening and closing in the empty compartment,
the grey countryside gliding past her, thinking, It must stop
some time, it must stop, there must be an end to this, remembering again the trains and the room, the endless streets and
all the faces that had turned and listened to her or pretended
to listen, the eyes distant or glazing, flicking past as if she were
glancing through an album, her mother, her father, her
brother, her sister, and the others, all the others, all turned
politely towards her, all smiling, if only she could have stopped
and looked, if only she could have listened, if only there had
not been this rush of the seconds and the hours and the days
and the weeks, was it like this from birth and would it not end
till death, were there no moments in which it was possible to
stand outside, above, to look down on it all, to draw lines
round it and across it, was everyone like this, hurtled forward
into nothingness, their faces turned towards the past, where
had she read this quoted recently, something about the angel
of history, someone had quoted it, someone had written it,
the angel of history, something about chaos and history and
the rush of a mighty wind, other people looked so calm, seemed
unaffected by this, and she too, there had been a time when
she too was like them, or had she always felt the rush, never
known where to turn and how, never known – but that wasn't
true, there had been a time, the time of the garden and the
river, the sense of the sun glinting on the water and running
through the trees, that had been a time untainted by the other,
by the sense of everything passing, changing, nothing staying
still, though even there a shadow had fallen, the shadow standing by the wall and looking in, even there it was she who had
noticed and not the others, and noticed again when her father
had taken her to see the old woman, the previous owner, Why
are you frightened why are you silent, the woman knew she
knew they looked at each other, each knowing the other knew,
her father saying, Why don't you speak to her, why are you
so rude, excusing her, saying she was shy, knew no French,
and they went on looking at each other, so that later, when

she came back, married this time, and to this same woman's
son, she would sit in that very same kitchen and the old woman,
just the same, no older, old enough, though twenty years had
passed, sitting in that same gloomy kitchen, the old woman
would tell her she had felt from the start, from the moment
their eyes met across the wall, five children playing in her
garden, the garden she had owned, so the ex-owner and the
daughter of the man who had bought it stared at each other,
keeping their gaze steady, neither willing to turn away, until
her brother jumped out of a bush, started to chase her, and
she had to run, looking once over her shoulder though and
seeing the woman staring after her still, not moving, from that
first moment then, it had not only been herself who was
affected, though she had tried to exorcize it, or perhaps only
to prolong it, by coming to the same corner of the garden every
day, but the other, the old woman, as she told her later when
she returned, all those years later, with the son, now her husband, and they sat in that gloomy kitchen, in the half-light of
an early morning in October, the mist rising off the river, the
hills all round covered in the white haze, the sun trying to
pierce through, but the room was dark anyway, would be dark
in summer too, even on a bright summer afternoon, as they
sat there in the gloom, the old woman telling her she had
known from that first moment when their eyes met across the
wall, had known that their paths would cross again, that the
knot would be tied, and tied again, and she wanted to say,
What knot, what are you talking about? but the old woman
was not listening, only talking, or sitting staring into the
gloom, turning to her suddenly and saying, I still see him,
sometimes I still see him, sitting there looking out at the river,
and I go out and prepare to call him in to supper, and she
thought suddenly, Is this what life is about, trying to fathom
the ridiculous father-fixation of an old French peasant? but
knew at once that she was getting it wrong, that it was not like
that, more complicated, less clear-cut, what did these words
mean anyway, how did they touch her as she was, now, the
person she was, moulded by who knows what mixture of accident and design, heredity and environment, none of that made
any sense, that was what she had to hold on to, that whatever
had happened or would happen one was oneself and other

people and what they said or wrote were only marginally helpful, or helpful perhaps in ways you neither expected nor
perhaps even wished, looking at the old woman sitting very
upright, her black dress draped loosely round her thin prim
form, her white face shining out in the gloomy kitchen, those
bright eyes her son had too and which no doubt they had both
inherited from the old man, had his eyes seen more than other
people or was he just more receptive or simply more tired,
lazier, unwilling to pass the time in drinking or playing cards
or reading or even watching the flickering shadows of the television screen, if they had had television in those days, she
couldn't remember, not at first anyway, but he wouldn't have
watched, he was after something else but what was it what
kind of a private god could it be who would satisfy an old man
or was it the river did it act like a drug, hypnotize you, draw
you in, so that once you had crossed a certain line there was
no escape, nothing else to do except go back as often as possible
for as long as possible and drink it in drink it in if that wasn't
too ridiculous a term to use, what had he seen though, she
often asked herself, what had he really seen, and what did
seeing mean in a case like that, when it was no longer a question
of identifying an object but something else, something altogether different, she didn't know what but it was the whole
self that was engaged then, the whole body, not just the eyes,
the eyes were the focus but the whole body came alive, vibrated
in the light, and then what did it mean, where did it lead, what
was the secret of the light, she remembered the old woman
telling her about a day of her childhood when her father had
taken her to Rouen and sat with her in front of the great grey
cathedral, unmoving, unblinking, she had run off, would run
back to make sure he was still there, and he always was, sitting
without moving, his eyes on the grey stone building, his lips
firmly closed, prominent and fleshy through his greying beard,
and when she returned in the evening there were tears in his
eyes, he had not budged but his eyes were moist, why would
he not talk about it, why would he not try to explain what he
saw, it was as if he had lost interest in words early on, had no
need for them himself and could not see that other people
needed them, that if he was to function at all in the world he
would have to make an effort, have at least to tell his daughter

why he was crying but he wouldn't he didn't even try to wipe the tears away he just let them remain, glistening in the corners of his eyes, so that she grew frightened herself, began to cry in turn, and he just held her hand in the little train as they chugged back, and she sobbed, wanting to speak to him, wanting to beg him to tell her, to explain to her, but he wouldn't, not even at the end, when she would come and stand beside him in the evening, and they would gaze in silence at the river flowing past, and finally she would put a hand on his arm and he would get up, still not looking at her, and follow her back to the house and sit down, still not looking, not talking, between her and the boy, breaking the bread, eating with his head bent over whatever she put in front of him, then, towards the end of the meal, at the fruit perhaps, or the cheese, looking up, catching the boy's eyes fixed on his face, winking at him so that the boy blushed and turned away and she got up quickly and removed the plates and made him his cup of mint tea and he lit a cigarette and then, finally, finally, though even this did not invariably happen, spoke to her, asked her a question, or perhaps just said:

– Good. And she
– Yes. And he
– Listen. And he, turning his face in her direction:
– What? and she
– It can't go on. And he
– What? And she
– It can't. I can't. And he
– Has the cheque come? And she
– No. And he
– You must take the matter to the authorities. And she
– We've been into that. Listen. I want to talk to you. It can't go on. And he
– What does that mean? And she
– I don't know. And he
– We must bear our burdens. And she
– Burdens? Burdens? And if you bore your own for a change? And he
– Oh? and She
– Let me finish. Let me finish. And he
– I'm letting you. Aren't I? And she

– You won't help me? And he

– Help? And she

– Oh, oh, oh, bringing her hands up to her face, unable to go on, and him getting up, standing at the window, then tramping up the stairs, and her with her head on the table, her face in her arms, then looking up, finally looking up, seeing the boy standing, looking at her, saying

– Go and get on with your homework, and when he didn't move, stood watching her, turning away from him then shouting suddenly

– Go on! Leave me alone!

but he wouldn't move and she had to turn finally and face him, ask him what he wanted, what he was looking at her like that for, feeling the accusation in his gaze, the bitterness and anger, wondering if perhaps she wasn't imagining it, then looking again and feeling sure she wasn't, that it was there, snapping out at him

– Go on! Leave me alone!

and he, not moving, looking at her with those big black eyes they all have, and she suddenly standing up, pulling him to her, unyielding, but resisting too, pulling him towards her and holding him close, wondering again at the miracle of his presence, his flesh, the head against her breast, wondering again where he had come from how he had got there what it all meant the clocks had stopped in the house she had ceased to wind them up it was many years since a clock had ticked on the mantelpiece or in the hall, feeling time had abandoned her, had left her behind, a small bundle, in its wake, washed up on an empty shore while time receded, never to return, and the three of them were there in that space, timeless, silent, waiting for God knows what, at first she didn't realize it, didn't see anything was amiss, and even afterwards it wasn't that anything actually *was* amiss, it was only that suddenly she was aware of the three of them as they must seem not from outside, no, but from another planet, from God's own point of view, though she had never believed in God but it was as if everyone in the world had vanished, leaving just the three of them in that house, that garden, the boy going to school in the morning and coming back in the early afternoon, those long Spring afternoons, but no friends, no one visiting, no one disturbing

the silence, a silence that felt as if it had always existed and
would last for ever, only her heart beating a little faster as she
climbed to bed after washing up the supper things, or coming
out to fetch him in after helping the boy with his homework,
and then the three of them would sit, each bowed over his
plate, at lunch she brought him out a sandwich and a glass of
wine, he didn't look at her, didn't thank her, if it was raining
he had his umbrella up like a fisherman, sheltering him, watching the drops pucker the river and if it was bad, really bad, he
would stand in his room, at the window, looking out, wouldn't
eat with her, wouldn't touch the food she brought up to him,
would glare at her on the stairs as he went out, enveloped in
his hat and oilskin cloak to take the air, to tramp through the
fields, I could feel the rage in his eyes, the sullen rage against
everything, everything, himself included, and a kind of fierce
pleasure in that rage, as if it was that that kept him alive, that
kept him going, as if once that was taken away from him there
would no longer be any reason for him to live, but usually he
was at peace, he would sit by the river, even smile when I
arrived, when I called him in, he would wink at the boy and
even ruffle his hair and I would look at the two of them and
suddenly the old horror would come over me, I knew it wasn't
rational, I knew what its roots must be, I knew there had been
a father but that he had come and gone and left me this, I
remembered his voice, his neck, the hairs on his hands, though
not his face and his name only with an effort, he had talked a
great deal, at first I liked to hear him talk, he had worked up
and down the country, on the railway in Carcassonne and across
to Mulhouse he had so many stories he would sit at the table
staring straight into my eyes, seeing me less and less clearly
the more he drank, but always gazing into my face, and telling
his stories, interminable stories, he had plans for us he wanted
to give up all that to settle down, Father didn't say anything,
he eyed him narrowly and got up when the stories went on
too long I don't remember when I began to feel they went on
too long myself anyway one day he wasn't there he had got
up in the night and left, taking his things with him and even
a few of ours, quite a few of ours, although we didn't have
much, but what we had that was easy to take he took, I said
nothing, I laid his place at the table, Father said nothing, and

again at lunch and dinner and so for three days, but he didn't
come back and I stopped laying the extra place and my stomach
swelled we didn't talk about it and when the time came Father
started doing the cooking and looking after me and suddenly
there were three of us again the boy was growing up was going
to school I don't know if it was then that the thought struck
him, struck Father, perhaps he too was as uncertain as I was,
wondered if there had ever been anyone, apart from the two
of us, Look for the place, he started to say to me, What place?
I said, The place where we put him, he said, the place in the
ground, and for a moment I thought I had forgotten it I
remembered so little of that time it was possible that I had
done that, The evidence must still be there, Father said, the
evidence in the earth, I laughed and turned the conversation
to other things but it started to work on me, I began to walk
round the garden, the field, with my eyes on the ground, I lay
in bed at night and tried to remember exactly what had happened, when I had first met him, when he had kissed me, when
we married, and then what happened, what happened after
that, but I couldn't, I couldn't remember a thing, it was blank,
empty, anything could have happened, You dug the hole, he
said to me, you dug it with your own two hands, you chose
the spot and dug the hole don't you remember? and when I
wouldn't listen any more he said, Perhaps he was never there,
and I, How do you mean? and he, There was no one, perhaps
there was no one, and I, But the boy? and he, shrugging his
shoulders, turning back to his food, and I, still not getting it,
But what do you mean? and he shrugging, and I, But the boy,
as if that was proof, final proof, and then, when he didn't
answer, when he bent over his plate again and didn't answer,
I understood, the food just came up, my stomach must have
turned right over, I couldn't hold any of it down I must have
rushed away from the table I remember waiting for my heart
to slow down my mind to focus I wanted to empty myself
right out I couldn't think about it and I couldn't not, it was
there, like a weight pressing down on me, I must have been
sick again I could feel the stuff coming out of my nose my ears
I thought of that old play you know that old story about the
king whose brother makes him eat his children and then tells
him what the dish he enjoyed so much consisted of, how he

brought up, how he tried to empty himself, to cleanse himself out, I felt like that, I think it's a bit what happens to us all, in one way or another, life makes us eat and then we try to pretend it never happened, we torment ourselves and brand ourselves to purify ourselves and find a way of living with the body that has done these things, anyway, I got through it I survived as we always do but the weight wouldn't go, he didn't repeat it only smiled at me some more but whether in pity or sympathy or perhaps he was laughing at me I don't know I went back over it all in my mind I tried to remember every detail but was I imagining it all now, remembering only a dream, a possibility, to block off what had really happened, or was this monstrous thing itself something I had imagined and had he perhaps not even spoken was I imagining that how could I ask him I thought of doing so several times, perhaps he had not spoken, nothing had changed, I was only hearing what I wanted or didn't want to hear who knows who can tell where is the truth nothing had changed life went on as before I tried now to remember his voice when he said that but then something happened, the same sense of unreality, how could I ask him if he had not said that, or even the other, about the grave, I began to doubt that too, I looked at the boy I studied his features I hunted in all the drawers there was nothing nothing except that piece of paper that certificate what did it prove he might have gone just after decamped with the few bits of silver we had and the other might still have happened I tried to recall my mother to test my feelings against the things I best remembered but all that came to mind were the photos of the two of them, of him and Mother smiling in the sunlight on the beach at Dieppe, I knew it was that because it said so on the back, Dieppe, 9 July 1911, there were others but that was the clearest, the stony beach and the light so bright that everything came out whitish and the two plump middle-aged people sitting smiling vaguely at the camera as if not quite sure what it was they were supposed to do, or it might have been because of the sun, two people caught anyway at a precise moment in time, there were others, of them standing, hands on hips in front of the house, or of them at the head of a group of friends at a long trestle table in the garden, it must have been Mother who was the social one after she died no one ever came to the house again, or perhaps it was her death that shocked him into solitude, I don't know, I don't think so nothing seems clear nothing seems important any more except the three of us or perhaps it is only him, sitting on his stool staring out at the river and then turning, the river in his eyes, do you understand what I mean, running past his eyes, behind his eyes, the water rippling and the flecks of light appearing and disappearing, something hypnotic about that light that river the play of reflections on the moving water always moving always the same perhaps it was just hypnosis like looking into a log fire I don't know I think it was something else it was active there was an energy in him I could sense that energy it was there when he woke up there when he walked when he sat when he ate I –

The train had stopped. They were in a station and everyone was getting out. She stood up, looked round for her suitcase, remembered, and stepped out onto the platform.

– Where's the London train please?

– Platform three.

The porter pointed. She thanked him and walked down towards the exit.

– Where's platform three please?

– What do you want? The London train? Over there.

– Thank you.

It was already filling up. It must have been standing at the station for some time. She walked down the length of it, then slowly walked all the way back.

She got in and sat down. A young man with a small black beard was reading a thick black book. She sat down opposite him, with her back to the engine. His nose twitched as he read. She closed her eyes, waiting for the train to move. But the delay on the Channel must have thrown the time-tables out of gear because for a long time nothing happened. She thought of taking her book out of her suitcase, but it was wedged tightly between the many bags and cases of the other passengers and she let it be. Though it was over an hour since they had got off the boat she still felt queasy. She closed her eyes and tried to sleep, but she knew she would never be able to. Her mind raced and her heart thumped in her chest at such a rate that she felt she would only be able to relax when the train was rushing along at a similar speed. Night had fallen quite suddenly and when she looked out of the window all she could see was her own reflection and the crowded, brightly lit carriage behind her.

– Excuse me.

She stood up abruptly and clambered past the other passengers, ignoring their looks of disapproval. Even the corridor was crowded, but she managed to get to the toilet. It said 'Vacant', but when she pushed the door wouldn't yield. She tried again and a grunt warned her that someone was inside. She turned and tried the other and mercifully it was empty. She locked herself in and pressed down the cold water tap with a sense of relief.

Nothing happened.

She tried again. Still nothing. She tried the hot, but there was no water there either. She pressed her finger against the tap and found that a drop had formed on the rim. She wiped her forehead slowly.

The train had started to move. The bearded man looked up and past her, out of the window, the tip of his nose twitching more than ever. She found that he was staring straight at her and turned her head away quickly. When she glanced at him again he had gone back to his book. He took a packet of French cigarettes out of his jacket pocket without looking up, took one out with one hand and stuck it in his mouth. He let the packet lie on the table beside his book and fumbled in his pocket for the lighter. She feared for his beard, but no disaster occurred. He laid the lighter down next to the cigarettes and turned a page of the book.

She made a movement to get to the door but he held on to her wrist.

– I want to go, she said.

– No, he said.

– I must go, she repeated.

He stood in front of her, looking down at her with his dark eyes. She remembered his gaze. He would never join in their games. Father asked us to include him and we tried but he shook his head. He doesn't understand your French, Father said, but it wasn't that, anyone could see that he had made up his mind, whether out of pride or fear or a mixture of both, he had made up his mind and nothing would budge him. Well then, Mark said, he should get out of here, it's our garden and if he doesn't want to play with us he should get out, but he wouldn't do that either and when Jimmy suggested we throw him out by force I protested, not that I didn't mind his being there, on the contrary, I was more aware of it than anyone else, I felt his eyes following me about I didn't know if he was resentful or unhappy or bitter, what I knew was that there were demands, his eyes made demands, demands I didn't want to meet, he wouldn't speak wouldn't answer questions and it was just the same all those years later except that I didn't want to go away I didn't want to leave him now I had found him again or rather he me, we had found each other anyway, and he stood now before me in that room and looked at me and I said again, I must go, and he, No, and I, But –, and he again, No, as if that was the only word he knew and it was stronger than all my words, than anything I could or would ever say or have to say I turned then I remember I turned and walked to the door and he didn't move he must have known I would turn back that I couldn't go there was something unfinished we both knew it or at least he seemed to know it I no longer knew what he thought or thinks how can one tell it seems at one moment as if

– Weren't you just fixated on your childhood? he said.

– No, she said quickly.

– But you were, he said. Are. It's obvious, isn't it?

The wood cracked and a spark flew past her foot into the room. Automatically she got up and stamped on it.

– Yes, she said. Perhaps.

– It's obvious, he said again.

– I don't know, she said.

– All you wanted from him was to lead you back to the magic garden, he said.

– All? she said. All? How can you say all? What right have you to say all?

He shrugged. And again the feeling overwhelmed her that she would never be able to explain, to tell, to get it out, all of it, the way it was, the way it had been, would be, would never be able to free her lungs, to rise above the waves, the waters overwhelming her, hurling her backwards, sweeping her feet from under her, so that she came up panting, spitting and

choking, needing air, only air, if she could get air into her
lungs it would be all right, she would survive, she didn't ask
for anything else, only survival, and she knew then that she
would, indeed she would survive, that the tide would recede,
she would be able to look down at the river, not be forever
hurled forward by that intolerable pressure, as the train hic-
cuped, slowed and eventually stopped in the middle of the
countryside, the sky grey no movement in the fields and now
the engine too had cut and she was aware of her breathing, of
the hum of the carriage, of the man sitting opposite reading in
his black book as if nothing had happened, she said:

– The train has stopped.

He looked up, his nose twitching more than ever, and looked
her over, slowly.

– It's stopped, she said.

– Yes, he said.

He selected a cigarette from the packet on the table and lit
it, then turned back to his book.

The train began to move slowly forward again and then, as
if the effort had been too much for it, stopped again.

The primeval soup, he had explained to her. It all began with
the primeval soup. She could imagine it, the three of them
silent, bent over their bowls, the spoons going in steadily and
then up to their mouths, and even when they had finished, the
boy first and then the woman and finally the old man, even
then no one spoke, no one looked up, until she made a gesture,
a movement, collected the bowls, removed them, brought the
next dish to the table.

The train gave a splutter which jerked her forward in her
seat, then stopped again. The primeval soup. It all began with
the primeval soup. Then gradually a crust formed, but the
centre of the earth was unstable. There were eruptions. The
earth bulged, cracked, rocks were pushed up and pressed
against each other continents drifted apart, seas rushed between
land masses, one huge sea stretched from Mexico to Siberia,
ice lay over the earth, it melted, forming valleys, it vanished,
it returned, even now the earth was unstable, was always in
motion, the balance changing, shifting, only we couldn't see
it, he explained, our lives were too brief, if we lived a thousand
years, a million years, then we would notice what was going

on, look at this piece of rock, he said, tapping it as they passed, look at it, it seems inert, the most inert bit of the universe there is, but it has been fashioned by pressure by fire by water by more pressure than you ever –

– It doesn't frighten you? she said.

– Frighten?

– I don't know. The thought of all this...

– It's not frightening, he said. It's just how things are.

– But if life is

– Does it change how you live from day to day?

– It must do, she said. If you know that, if you

The train had started to move. Slowly, then with gathering speed, it left the empty field in which it had come to rest.

– We're moving, she said.

He looked up from his book and studied her.

– Pardon?

– We're moving, she said again.

He went on looking at her. She shrugged at him and smiled, suddenly embarrassed.

– I just said it like that, she said. I didn't mean to disturb you.

– That's all right, he said.

He bent his head again and was absorbed in his book.

She stared out of the window. The fields were white in the moonlight. She wondered if the sheep were taken in at night. She thought she could make them out, little mounds here and there in the fields. Her feet were cold. She turned back to the bed. He had pulled the blankets up round him and was all hunched up, with his back to her. I want to explain to you. You must understand. All those words we use, love and hate and despair and the rest, they don't correspond. Perhaps I was tied to the past but what does that mean? What gives things their meaning? Who says it is just this and not something else? Who decides it means this and not that, who decides the explanation must go like this and not like that, I'm trying to be reasonable to be rational I look back at my past at all my life suddenly I can look back and where does it start who decides where it will start who decides even that an explanation is needed? I'm trying to keep calm but I want you to understand I want you to see that there are just certain things that happened they happened to me I don't understand what they mean but they mean something and unless I talk about them I won't be able to sleep not ever again it's all in movement it won't stay still if only there was a moment when it stopped when I could pick up the threads take my bearings but it won't I can't you've got to help me where is the beginning where is the end only trains and more trains and talk and more talk if there was a silence if there was a space you've got to help me I

– Haven't you finished in there? he called out to her.

She closed her eyes, holding on to the washbasin.

– Haven't you finished? he said again.

A train rumbled into the station and the building shook.

She opened the door and looked out into the narrow hotel room.

– Are you all right? he asked her.

– Yes. I'm sorry. That crossing.

He moved towards her.

– I must talk to you, she said.

– After, he said.

She moved away from him and round the bed till she was standing at the window.

– I must tell you, she said. I must explain.

– It's three in the morning, he said.

– Yes, she said. Listen.

– Come on, he said. Let's get into bed. Tell me after.

– No, she said. Now.

She turned away from him and began to try and open the window.

– What are you doing? he said.

– I just –

– Leave it alone. It's filthy.

– I need some air, she said. It's stifling.

– Look it's not by –

She gave a final heave. The window swung open and the air was filled with soot and dust. She fell back, coughing.

– I told you, he said, came forward and closed it with a bang.

Abruptly, she began to cry. She sat down on the bed and put her face in her hands.

He sat down beside her. He touched her shoulder. – Come, he said.

– No, she said. You don't understand. I must tell you.

About the river. I've never understood. How he sat and
looked. And the corpse was blue, floating in the reeds. How
he held my wrist. Please. I must tell you. I came all this way
to tell you. I have to speak. Please.

– All right, he said. Go on.

She looked at him.

– Get it over with, he said.

She stared into his face.

– I thought you wanted to speak, he said.

Now he lay on his back, breathing evenly, his mouth open.
Every few minutes the building trembled as a train entered or
left the station.

– I like the sound, the woman said. The sound of the train
in the middle of the night. Hooting. You must have heard it
as a child. When you were here. One hears it better by the
river. I heard it better in the other house. Do you know who
owns it now? Do you want to see what they have done with
it? You did well not to return before. There is filth in the river.
Filth from the factories outside Paris. It washes up at the bend,
there, where everything gets washed up. It was there they
found him. Do you remember? I never knew what went on
in his head. Why should I bother? Do you want to see photos
of him? I have them here. Here. On the beach. In the garden.
With a hat, looking down at the river. With my mother. With
me. On the terrace. On the porch. That's him with friends.
They had come up from the South. Friends of his youth. After,
nobody came. He didn't even go to the café any more. Or
even into the village. I did the shopping. I got what we needed.
He sold the car. He got up at five and went down to the river.
Every morning. And in the evening I went to fetch him. He
had no need of company. He was content as he was. Here is
one of him in a bathing suit. He was younger then. Mother
must have taken it. He grew a beard later. Of course everyone
wore them then but his was especially fine. And here's one
among the boats at Le Havre. He had wanted to be a sailor
when he was young. Did you know that? But when he married
he decided against it. He liked to stand and look at the boats.
Here's one of him in Rouen, by the cathedral. I went with him
once. He stood outside and looked at it. I wanted to go in or
do something else, but he just went on looking at it. I didn't

know what he was doing. Like when you see someone reading without moving their lips and you're still too young to read, you can't understand why they should be sitting hour after hour with this thing in their hands which they move every few minutes. I've never had much patience with books. My mother was keen on work, on school, but Father didn't particularly encourage me. His hands were large. Look at them hanging at his sides. Large and powerful. I often felt he could pick me up with just one hand. He was so gentle. I would look at him and wonder. The other, my husband, he was quite different. I hope Claude doesn't take after him. Sharp and hard. He came into my life like that and then went again. Nobody said a word. Afterwards it was as if it had never been, as if he had never existed. But my stomach swelled and then there was Claude. But it was difficult to remember what he looked like. You understand that, don't you? Perhaps I got into bad habits. Father was so silent. Afterwards there was nothing to say to the child. You must try to understand that. It wasn't that we had nothing to communicate but we had grown unused to words. There was very little need of them. Perhaps he is the same with you. That is not a reason to turn against him. He means well. He doesn't mean you harm. He needs you, believe me he needs you. How can you leave him after such a short time? Surely you should try and understand him. I will help you to understand him. To accept him. To accept your life with him. I understand you too. I have always liked you. I knew you would return. That one day you would return. Because you were the one who came with your father. You were the one who saw me looking over the garden fence. You were the one who sat and listened when I talked to him. I knew you could not be gone for ever. And he is not gone for ever. It is just a question of adjusting your sights. Of ceasing to think of time as always moving forward, to think of it as moving sideways or backwards or not moving at all. And you can do that. I know you can do that too. Why did you marry him if it was only to leave him at the first smell of trouble? Accept him the way he is. As one has to learn to accept life. He will talk to you. In time he will talk to you. He has a great deal to say. He has talked so little in his life that he is out of practice, but when he starts you will have difficulty in stopping him. If he had not wanted you he would not have stopped you that day. He would not have brought you to this house. He needs you. He needs only you. And you need him. Otherwise you would not have gone through with it. Perhaps you have forgotten. But you need him too. He gives back a meaning to your life. He returns you to your childhood. You can live here if you like. Until some understanding is reached. You can live here with me. You can run in the wood. Go down to the river and look. You can peer into the garden and see the house. They are not often there. They spend their time in Paris. The house is boarded up. The garden has been allowed to run to seed. You can climb over the wall and find the old paths again. Life should not always be lived simply forwards. We need to go back. We need to take strength. Here he is in shorts and sandals. Even when he was very old his body was that of a young man. His face was reddened by the wind. Behind the beard it is tanned and hard. I couldn't sit still after a while. I had to get up and peer into the shop windows. I would dash away and come back quickly to see if he was still there. As he didn't move I grew bolder. I explored to the end of the street. I ran right round the old cathedral. He was always there when I got back. He had not moved. Look, he would say. Look at the light. I didn't know what he was talking about, I looked but couldn't see anything. I expected something else, you see, something extra. I wandered round the town, once I got lost but it was not difficult to find ones way back. I began to feel cold. I told him I was cold. He patted my head. He took me on his knees. Finally, when the sun had gone down, he lifted me up and carried me to the railway station. I was afraid to look in his eyes. His body was hot. I am telling you this so that you will understand. So that you will have patience. The early years are the hardest. You must learn to bear them. You must not talk again of leaving. Because that would be leaving for good and you cannot do that. Not now that you have returned. You can never leave this place. You can never leave him. But for the moment you can come and live with me. For the moment you can think of it as yours. Then you can go back to him. You will see. He will come and fetch you. He will come and he too will understand. What you have done will be good. Will be good. Don't talk the way you have.

Don't talk like that again. It is not a way to talk. You did not marry him for his sweet temper. Remember what you did it for. Even if you never knew, you knew. Somewhere inside you, you knew. Don't let the trivialities of the present blot out that knowledge. Make it part of you. Listen to the trains. Listen to them. Even here they can be heard. Why is the sound so mournful? I remember nothing before we came here. And practically nothing of the time when my mother was alive. Just these photos. I have more. Upstairs. One day I will show you. Let me put these away and then we can eat something. At your age one needs to eat. Even if one is English one needs to eat. Give me that photo. There. Give it to me. Here is the box. I will put them away. One day I will show you the others. There are many more. Before my mother died. She was the one who took them, who liked them. Afterwards he sold the car. No more trips to the seaside. There was no need. I didn't expect it. And there was the boy. Sometimes he looked at him as if he didn't know him. As if he didn't know where he had come from. I was afraid. I started to tremble. I looked from one to the other. They ate with their faces down low over their plates. He wouldn't come out of his room when I told him they had found the body. Not for three days. Perhaps it was love. Perhaps it was guilt. Perhaps he wanted to push him in. Who knows what goes through a child's mind? Perhaps nothing. Perhaps we make too much of their silences. I bought him a ball. I had to sell the house. Not to anyone. Not to any of the villagers. When your father said he had three children, when he showed me the photos and I saw you, I told him he could have it. I knew it was the right thing. I told him it was his. He didn't understand. He thought I wanted to bargain. I told him I accepted. I was happy for him to have it. Suddenly he realized what it was I was saying. He turned away from me. He went to the window. He thought perhaps he had been rash. That if I gave it to him so easily there must be a hitch. That the river flooded perhaps. Or the roof was ready to fall in. But then he looked out of the window and I could see he felt it didn't matter. He drew his shoulders back, I knew he would turn round smiling, that he would hold out his hand to me I knew in a moment it would be over I wouldn't have it any more I closed my eyes to concentrate I opened them again he turned towards me and he was smiling. I took his outstretched hand.

— Why are you telling me this?

— I don't know I

— Why don't you leave these things alone?

The wood exploded in the grate, but though she waited for the sparks to fly, this time they didn't.

— A nail, he said.

— Yes, she said.

Outside, the owl hooted. She looked round.

— Why don't you put curtains in the windows?

— I haven't got round to it. Besides, no one goes past. What's the point.

— I don't know. One feels vulnerable here in the light. It's so dark outside.

— If someone wanted to break in and kill us a curtain wouldn't make any difference.

— No, but the thought of being seen without being able to see, I suppose it

— Why don't you leave these things alone? he said again.

— I can't, she said. I have to I

— Or else go back to him.

— It's not that, she said quickly.

— One or the other, he said.

— I can't go back, she said. You know I can't go back.

— Then don't think about it any more.

— I have to, she said. I have to start from the beginning. I have to.

— It doesn't do any good, he said. You won't clear up anything by talking like that.

— It's not a matter of clearing anything up, she said, and again the weight of it hit her and submerged her and for a moment she lost sight of the room and the fire and his thin body arched over the chair.

— You can't get out of it like that, he said.

— Then how? she said. Then how?

— It's just there, he said. It's happened to you. You've got to accept it. Why should it make sense?

— Why? she said. I don't know why. But don't you see that if it doesn't I can't go on? Don't you see?

— What does that mean, he said, I can't go on?

– It means – it means –

He drove expertly, taking the bends with the minimum of deceleration, his eyes fixed intently on the winding road.

– I don't know what it means, she said.

– We've all got our lives to cope with, he said.

– You're so wise.

He bit his lip and drove faster.

– I'm sorry, she said.

– We're in Monmouthshire now, he said.

– Is that Wales?

– Border country.

– How far is it still?

– An hour. Not much more.

– I don't mind, she said. I like cars.

They crossed a bridge and drove along a little river.

– I want to help you, he said.

– I know.

– I told you. From the beginning.

– I know. I knew you would help.

– When you saw me?

The man was staring at her. His nose twitched once and he scratched his right ear with a little sharpened pencil.

– What? she said.

– No. I thought you said something.

– Perhaps I did.

– Are you travelling far?

– No.

– London?

– I suppose so.

He laughed. – You're not sure?

– I don't know.

– Why? Is someone supposed to meet you?

She stared at him. – I'm sorry, she said.

– Sorry? Why?

– I interrupted your reading.

– Oh. That. It's interruptable.

She looked out of the window.

– Would you like a drink? he asked her.

She turned from the fields slipping by and stared at him.

– There's a bar on the train, he said. I could get you a drink.

I'm getting one for myself.

– No. Thank you.

– Coffee? Tea?

– No, she said. Thank you.

He shrugged, turned back to his book.

– What is it you're reading? she asked him.

He held it out to her.

– Business management? Is that a textbook?

– I don't read it for fun. I assure you.

He held the packet of cigarettes out to her. She shook her head. He tapped it, extracted one, stuck it in his mouth and lit it.

– Where have you come from? he asked her.

– Far, she said.

– Very far?

– Uhuh.

– Well, he said.

– I mean I've been travelling a lot recently, she said. All over the place. I seem to be on the move all the time. I don't know what you mean by far.

– I just –

– I don't know what you mean.

– Nothing, he said. It was just an idle question.

She turned back to the window. Their eyes met in the reflection and then he was reading his book again.

She said: – I came by car. Someone drove me down by car.

He glanced up. – Oh really?

– We left the motorway after the Severn Bridge and drove through Monmouthshire, she said.

He looked at her.

– Through Usk and along the Head of the Valleys Road, she said.

– Look, he said, getting up, are you sure you don't want a drink?

– No no.

– You never drink?

– Yes I drink. I just...

– Not at the moment, eh?

– Well...

The compartment was empty now. She could not remember

if he was coming back or not. There was a suitcase on the rack above the seat opposite her so presumably he was. Her knee hurt where she had fallen. She lay under a bush, her heart beating wildly. The others ran to and fro, looking for her.

– We know where you are Gina. Come on. Give yourself up. Come on Gina. Give yourself up or we'll come and get you.

She pressed her face into the damp grass and kept her eyes shut tight.

– Come on Gina. We know where you are. We'll give you a minute to come out. One two three four five six seven eight nine ten eleven

Her knee hurt. It was bleeding. She was sure it was bleeding but if she moved to look they would spot her.

– We can see you Gina. We can see right where you are. If you don't come out of your own accord we'll come and get you.

She could hear them talking excitedly together, then the voices retreated and she couldn't hear them any more. She went on lying there for a long time, afraid to move, her heart beating hard, her mouth dry, her knee stinging. Then, very slowly, she turned round and twisted out from under the bush.

Their voices came to her, very faint, at the water's edge.

The train braked suddenly and began to slow down. It entered a station and drew slowly to a stop. The loudspeaker grated out a message and people hurried on and off. She felt around the spot to see if there was blood on her knee but it was difficult to tell through the jeans.

The train started to move again. The man came back and slipped into his place opposite her. Their eyes met but there was no sign of recognition on his part.

Once or twice he got up to fetch more wood, but he always came back and sat down in the same place, on the right side of the fireplace. It seemed to her that she had been talking all her life, at least for as long as she could remember, and there was a sense that she would have to go on and on, on and on, until it was all said.

– What all? he said. What are you talking about?

– Just this sense, she said, that he was looking and looking and even the stone, the hard stone, was dissolving under his gaze, it was not there any more, even the cathedral was not there it was only light specks of light and the light changed

he forgot words nothing stayed in place any more the stone
the streets the town the river when he looked down, looked
down from his place in the reeds everything turned into specks
of light and bits of sky and weeds and light you couldn't separate the sky from the water any more the light from the surface
the specks of light dancing on the water among the colours the
world the whole world dissolving that was why he didn't listen
to her didn't hear her even when she called it was a long way
he had to come back a long way and the fields the sheep nothing
except the white light I am not there is nothing all is caught
up in that light that silence don't you see he couldn't he didn't –

– What are you talking about? he said. What light?

– When I went out, she said. When I walked in the night.
It was all –

– But it's him, he said. We're talking about him. Why do
you bring in the light?

– Nothing, she said. Not stones not rocks not trees all dissolved in that light don't you see he had to fall he had to go it
was the end or rather it didn't make any difference not any
more not to him there was no him and each day to come back
to have her there to have to talk how could he bear it how could
anyone bear it I can see what it meant I can see why he did it
when I went out it was like milk it was thick the air was thick
it was all air he must have had that sense one day it must have
come to him that sense and then he couldn't leave he couldn't
move nothing meant anything any more don't you see he –

– But what – ?

– Don't you see? she said. Don't you?

She sat in silence, closed in on herself in the dark room.

– What? he said. What are you talking about?

The wood exploded again and the embers flew into the room.

– You can't stop like that, he said. You must go on. You
must talk. You must explain to me. What do you mean? Why
do you say that?

She could feel the heat of the fire on her face, her knees.

She said quickly: – Nothing any more. Just emptiness. You
only have to look at those photos. I felt it when she showed
them to me. It was the light in his eyes. And now I understand.
How everything would dissolve. Turn into light, which means
into nothing. You and me. Nothing. Held up by our ideas of

what we are. He left that behind. He let the light penetrate him and then it was too late. He couldn't turn back

  – Back? he said. Back how? Where?

  – Yes, she said. He couldn't. Not after that. Not turn back.

  – But from where? he said. I still don't –

  – Back. After that. Talk to her again. As he had before. It was too much. Everything dissolving. He couldn't hold on to anything again. And then he let go completely.

  – Are you saying he dropped into the river? Because of something he'd seen?

  – I don't know what I'm saying. Not any more.

  – But how – ?

The train had stopped. The man had gone. She looked out of the window. They had reached the outskirts of the city.

The ticket collector came down the carriage, tapping on the backs of the seats to attract attention. She handed him her ticket and he took it and put it away.

  – Don't I get it back? she said.

  – No.

  – Are we nearly there?

  – Another twenty minutes.

  – And I don't need it when we arrive?

  – No.

He moved on, tapping methodically as he went.

The train started again, then stopped. Everyone in the compartment was silent. A child asked a question, then it too was overcome by the silence and stopped.

  – I don't feel anything any more, she said. I don't hear anything any more. I don't know where I'm going any more.

She started again: – I don't have. I don't know. I have almost arrived.

Still the train did not move. She stared at her reflection in the window.

  – Hold on to that, she said, looking at her face, watching her lips, seeing them motionless, like the train.

  – Hold on to that, she said. Why don't you speak to yourself as you know you can speak? Why do you speak as if you were talking to someone else? All those words rushing to get out. As if by speaking them you might be able to say something to yourself. Send yourself a message.

The train gave a sudden jerk, then started to inch forward. She thought it was going to stop again, but after a moment's hesitation it went on, gathering speed.

– Nothing, she said. Nothing any more. After so many years in the world and here I am at last with nothing. Where am I going? Why? And after I have arrived? Arrived where?

The train was hurtling through the suburbs. Cold figures huddled on bye-line platforms. She felt well all of a sudden. Felt less of a need to speak. She knew she was coming to an end.

– What end? she said.

She closed her eyes. The words were coming between her and the feeling, but the feeling seemed to call forth the words. That was it. First there was the feeling, then there were the words. But the words came between her and the feeling. Yet the feeling without the words was incomplete.

The seat opposite was empty. When had he got off? Had she been asleep? Had he been there at all? The empty packet of French cigarettes lying on the table in front of her gave her the answer.

A world without names. A world of light. No more fathers and daughters and grandsons, no more cathedrals and cars and railways. If the cathedral is different at twelve from what it was at ten then there is no such thing as a cathedral. It is just a convenient shorthand. Look, and it dissolves.

When we ran through the garden there were no houses and cathedrals and fathers and mothers. Only light and the nerves round the heart. Swarming over the place like locusts. Screaming and laughing. Do you remember?

– Yes, her sister said. We had a good time.

– I'm not talking about that. It was a special feeling. The sun shining on the water. On the trunks of the willows, the poplars. On the leaves. It was as if we were in a state of over-excitement all the time.

– They were good days, her sister said.

– You don't remember? That particular feeling? When we went there. Special. Of all places.

– I remember the gooseberry bushes, her sister said. You hid under one once and came out all scratched and bleeding.

– When we leapt out of the car. When we swooped down screaming. That first moment.

– Yes. They were good times.

She said: – I met Claude again recently.

– Claude who?

– The boy. Whose mother sold us the place. I met him in Paris.

– Was that his name?

– Yes.

– What's he up to?

– Up to?

– I mean how did you meet him?

– In the street. He wouldn't let me go.

– Wouldn't let – ? What do you – ?

– He held my wrist. He wouldn't let me go.

Her sister was sewing a cushion for the living-room sofa. She peered shortsightedly at the needle, her glasses perched on the end of her nose. – I'm afraid I don't have a very clear memory of him, she said.

– I did. I knew at once it was him.

– And he? He too?

– We're getting married, she said.

Her sister put the cushion down and looked at her. – What? she said.

– Yes.

– But –

She waited.

– What does he do? her sister asked at last.

– I don't know.

– You don't know? And you're...?

She shrugged.

– Do you know what you're doing? her sister asked.

– We went back, she said. To the place. To see his mother.

– Oh?

– You remember her?

Her sister pretended to think. – No, she said finally.

– You never came with Father when he went to call on her?

– I can't remember. I don't seem to have much memory of those times you know Gina.

– We went down to see her anyway.

– And so?

– Nothing had changed. Much. I walked in the garden.

Her sister sighed. – I don't think it meant as much to me as it did to you, she said.

– The house was shut up. The owners live in Paris.

– We lived in London.

– All right. I'm not saying...

Her sister was staring at her: – How long has this been going on?

– We sat in the kitchen and talked. She told me about her father.

– Her father?

– Don't you remember?

– What?

– He drowned.

– Oh yes. Of course. I remember.

– His body floated up two days after.

– That was before us, wasn't it? her sister said.

– Yes yes. That's why she sold us the place. That's why we were there.

– Yes of course. Why did she talk about him?

Her sister pushed the glasses back up her nose and began to sew again.

– She thinks about nothing but him.

– What's she like?

– The mother?

– Yes.

– She talks about him.

Her sister put down the cushion she was sewing and took off her glasses. She said: – And this – you're serious about it?

– Isn't one usually?

– Yes but I mean you –

– What?

– What does he do? You haven't told me what he does.

– Is that important?

– Well it gives one some idea.

Her sister waited, then said: – You're so cagey one would think he was in the white slave traffic or something.

– I don't think so, no, she said.

– You don't think so?

– I'm almost sure not.

Her sister shrugged. – Suit yourself, she said.

– Yes.

– And what's he like? Physically?

– He hasn't changed much.

– I told you, her sister said. I don't have a particularly good memory.

– He's hungry.

– Hungry?

– Yes.

– How do you mean?

– It's in his eyes. As it always was. When he looked at us. He has her eyes. The father probably had them too.

– He was there? I mean... We played with him?

– No. He wouldn't play. Father urged us but we tried and he wouldn't.

– Are you sure? I don't remember any of that, her sister said.

– It doesn't matter.

– And when are you going to marry him?

– I don't know. Soon.

– And your work?

– What work?

– I thought you were researching into something. Ronsard or something.

– Not really. No. I never had much faith in it.

– So you're throwing it up to marry him?

– I'm not throwing anything up. I thought you'd like to know.

– Thank you. Have you told Mother?

– Not yet. No.

– Hadn't you better?

– I will. Yes. I intend to.

She looked at the packet lying on the table. The cellophane wrapping had been removed from the top to allow the packet to be opened, but had been left round the bottom. One edge was torn and the whole had a crumpled look, as though it had been carried about for a long time.

She glanced at her watch. – I must go, she said.

– Wait, her sister said. Try and explain to me.

– What?

– Well, what this is all about.

– I don't know.

– But you must know something. You're not a baby.
She was silent.
– I just thought it would help, her sister said.
– Thanks. I understand.
– But you won't try?
– There's nothing to explain.
– You're in love with him?
– I'm going to marry him.
– Yes. So you said. I asked if you were in love with him.
– I don't understand what such words mean.
– Well then, why are you doing it?
– Who knows?
– You have doubts?
– Doesn't one always?
– But you want to get married?
– No.
– Then I don't understand you.
– It's just one of those things. I have to do it.
Just one of those things. She couldn't understand.
– And? he said.
– Nothing. I said I had to.
– And now?
– I don't know. I don't know any more.
– You still feel you had to?
– I tell you I don't know. I had to get out. I know that. It
wasn't –
– Wasn't what?
– It wasn't . . . I had to. To get out, I mean. It wasn't anything
he did. I just –
– You made a bit of a mess of things, didn't you? he said.
– Perhaps.
– You don't think you did?
– Perhaps, she said.
– Anyway, he said, you're out of it now.
– You see, she said, he had been there. He had known the
old man. He had watched him at meals. And then we came.
We were outsiders. We took their property. We –
– Don't talk rubbish, he said.
– We didn't know, she said. There was all that we didn't
know.

– So you're a guilty colonialist? he said. Don't give me that.

– I didn't say that.

– Didn't you?

– I suppose I wanted partly to make up for that, she said. For not having known. For the noise we made. And –

– For being happy, he said.

– Yes, she said. Perhaps... The noise... After the silence...

– For God's sake, he said. Do you think they even realized?

– Perhaps, she said.

– Then what are you going on about?

– I don't know.

– You don't know? Why you're acting like this? Why you've done what you did?

– You're talking like my sister, she said.

– God forbid.

She looked out of the window. The moonlight lay across the fields like a sheet.

– Listen, she said. I will try to explain. Because I have to. I have to make you understand. I can't shake free of it. If you could see his face you would understand. And when Father took me to see her...

She put out a hand and pushed the packet a little way along the table. The cellophane glittered in the light.

When Father took me to see her.

When Father took.

– What happened to him? he asked.

– To him?

– To your father.

– He's dead. He's been dead for some time.

– And you don't think...?

– You don't understand, she said.

The train started to slow down. The wheels screamed as the driver applied the brakes.

People stood up in the carriage and started to put on their coats.

– I don't know, she said, fixing the empty packet of cigarettes.

The train drew into the station. It crawled along the platform. People crowded the aisle. The train stopped. She sat and waited, looking at the packet of cigarettes in front of her, looking out of the window, looking again at the packet of cigarettes.

The passengers filed past the window. Then the tumult died down and there was silence.

She looked at the packet of cigarettes on the table in front of her.

She got up. Her knee hurt momentarily, then she forgot about it. The sun shone down into the gloomy station. She walked down the platform towards the exit.

Taxis lined the ranks. They took off, one by one, with their passengers.

She stood, not waiting for anything in particular, in the middle of the crowded station. Then wrapped her coat tightly round her and walked slowly out into the street.

Her hands were free. She had nothing to carry. The evening sun shone down warmly. She crossed the street, walked, then crossed into another street.

She entered a pub. It was big, airy. There were few people about at this early hour of the evening. The sun shone in through the yellow windows and made patterns on the red carpet. She walked through the patterns and stood at the bar. She ordered a drink and took it to a seat in the corner.

She sipped her drink, closing her eyes. How can I explain? How can I?

– Try, he said.

– There's so much. I don't know where to start.

He was silent. The fire cracked again. Mechanically she stretched out a leg and stamped on a burning ember.

– I don't know, she said.

His silence unnerved her. She turned from the fire to the uncurtained windows. Outside the moonlight lay on the hills like a great white sheet. She opened the door and stepped out. She knew the general direction and the moon was so bright it was almost like walking in broad daylight. She was holding the box of stones in her arms. She looked down at it and wondered what it was doing there, but it seemed right, even necessary, and she walked on, down the wild garden and through the gate, down the road in the direction of the village, and then right, to cut across the narrow valley and up into the hills on the other side.

– If you stop you are lost, he said.

She laughed. – If I go on I am lost, she said. I feel I'll never

be able to stop, ever, talking or running. I don't know when
it began, perhaps that day he saw me there in the rue des Ecoles
or perhaps later, yes, later, when I packed my suitcase and he
watched me without saying anything, but I've been running
ever since, catching taxis, trains, buses, boats, dragging suit-
cases into stations and hauling them into lifts, leaving them
behind and picking up others, as if there's always something
holding you back, something you'd like to get rid of but that
you also need, a kind of animal inside you that roars and roars
and you give it meat and more meat but you know too that if
you stop, if the roaring ceases, then something has died, it's –

– What animal? he said. What are you talking about

– Do you know those paintings by Magritte? she asked him.
With men in suits and bowler hats? He wore suits like that.
And a hat. I swear. Old ones. Like a circus act only it was his
clothes. Why? Why?

– Who? he said. What?

– Claude, she said. Those kinds of shiny suits that don't
seem ever to wear out, like plastic, only break in the end.
Break, not tear. Do you know what I mean?

– He wore those?

– I was in the middle of one of those Magritte paintings. I
swear. I don't know why he did it, I asked his mother, with
a watch in the waistcoat and a chain across the chest, I swear
it I swear it, I asked her why and she just shrugged I –

– All right, he said. All right. Tell me after. Tell me after
we've had a little sleep.

– I don't want to sleep, she said. I want to talk to you.

– Yes, he said. Yes. It's three in the morning. Tell me about
it later.

– Stop saying that, she said. Just listen to me. Please.

Leaving the road now she found the bridge at the bottom
of the valley and crossed over. The moon was gradually disappearing but the dawn was grey and misty. She climbed up the
other side and struck out across the foothills. She had a sense
of where the main road would be and headed in that direction.
The box hindered her and she caught her foot in a root and
suddenly found herself lying on the ground with a sharp pain
in her knee.

She got up, retrieved the box and carried on. The leg of her trousers was soaking, but she wasn't sure if it was blood or water or both, and she didn't want to stop and look. The great thing was to keep moving, to keep moving.

She realized now that this was no longer true, that she seemed suddenly to have lost the desire to keep moving, to keep talking, it was her and yet it was someone else, she could hear her voice, she could see herself walking through the fields, the country roads, the city roads, the light was changing, the mist was lifting, the train had stopped and everyone waited, without speaking, without moving, looking out at the silent fields.

Her glass was empty. She got up and crossed the red carpet again. The bar was still quiet, except for one man talking in low tones to the barman.

– A glass of water please, she said.

She put her empty glass on the bar and waited. He didn't ask her why she wanted it or if she wanted something stronger. He just threw the cloth over his shoulder and swilled out her glass and let the tap run and then handed it to her across the shiny metal.

– Thank you.

As she crossed the room again the evening sun touched her face for a moment as it came through one of the high windows.

She sat down. The sun formed a pool of light on half the little round table in front of her.

Two men came in, talking loudly. She looked up for a moment, then it was as if they had never existed. Her voice rose in her throat, it filled her ears. Then it was gone.

The light fell on the glass of water in front of her. Light is the lion. She heard the words, clear, quiet, inside her head. Light is the lion that comes down to drink. Yes, she thought. Light is the lion. Light is the lion that comes down to drink.

6

Volume IV, pp. 167-169

She was born in a small Austrian village a few miles from Salzburg. Her father was a baker and the smell of warm bread stayed with her to the end. It was not a good time to be born: 1928. She was the only child. Her mother died during the war, of fear and malnutrition. Her father went on baking. In 1946 she entered the University of Vienna. Obscurely, she already knew what her life would be like.

She took a degree in modern languages and then found a job in a big cement factory, dealing with the foreign correspondence. She saw the refugees pouring through Vienna but made no comment. Her stories had begun to appear in student papers, and then in the more adventurous literary magazines, in Berlin as well as Vienna. They were quiet stories, impersonal, level in tone. But their quietness masked an unease; or rather, affected the reader with unease by their very freedom from all sense of it. At the time they were described as 'pure', as 'classically calm', but their very purity seemed somehow to throw doubt upon even the possibility of classicism. All in all a surprising literary venture in the hectic climate of those post-war years.

After only a few months she left her lodgings near the factory and went to live with a painter. They had known each other at University. He was older than she was and had been married. Shortly after this she gave up her job, but the greater freedom this allowed her did not seem to affect her writing one way or the other. Her stories continued to appear, at the rate of one, or at most two a year. Quietly, they made their mark.

Four years, almost to the day, after she had moved in with the painter, she paid a visit to her father, the baker. She sat in the back of the shop, as she had done as a child, and watched him at work. Afterwards, they shared a meal. Then she went back to Vienna, packed her bags, and caught the train for Rome.

The painter did not try to follow her. He knew it would not be any use, felt even that somehow, somewhere, he had always

361

known it would happen. From Rome she wrote to him, saying that the absence of German in the air soothed her. 'My words on the white paper always look so unreal,' she wrote. 'Now their unreality is justified.' He would have liked her to say 'at least' – 'is at least justified' – but that of course she would never do. 'Is justified' was all he could expect from her. Indeed, he would perhaps have been disappointed with anything else.

Her stories grew simpler, purer. As though she would force reality to manifest itself by isolating the very essence of that which it was not. She lived alone, in a small but comfortable flat in Trastevere. Her stories had been published in many countries now. In the German edition they stood, three slim volumes in elegant off-white covers, on the shelves of all the libraries and bookshops. No one asked if they provided a sufficient income for her to live on, and, if not, for it seemed unlikely, how she managed. Her life, like her writings, was as it was. There was no room for questions.

One day there was a fire in the flat. Flames shot out of the windows and on the other floors women screamed in terror. When the firemen eventually succeeded in putting out the blaze very little damage had been done to the building. But in her flat nothing remained but a heap of charred and sodden ruins. And she too was found, burned almost beyond recognition.

Her stories sit on the shelves, four chaste volumes in off-white covers (the fourth was published after her death). In their simplicity and purity they give nothing away. Did she feel the impossible strain of that purity, that calmness? She always knew exactly what she was doing, no one had any doubt of that. She would know when there was nothing more to be said. Some of her friends maintained that violent action went against the whole tenor of her life and beliefs. They pointed to the fact that accident often played a role in her stories, yet accident so calmly rendered as barely to disturb the smooth sequence of seemingly inevitable events which her stories seemed less to create than to coax into visibility before our always myopic gaze. There is no such thing as a dead end, they liked to quote her as saying. When all the roads are blocked there is always another way round. It is merely a question of patience. Patience and attention.

For days, though, the smell of burning hung over the building.

Steps

He had been living in Paris for many years.

Longer, he used to say, than he cared to remember.

When my first wife died, he would explain, there no longer seemed to be any reason to stay in England. So he moved to Paris and earned his living by translating.

He was an old-fashioned person, still put on a suit and tie to sit down to work, and a raincoat and hat when he went out. Even in the height of the Parisian summer he never went anywhere without his hat. At my age, he would say, I'm too old to change. Besides, I'm a creature of habit, always was.

He lived in a two-roomed flat on the top floor of a peeling building in the rue Octave-Mirbeau behind the Panthéon. To reach it you went through the dark narrow rue St. Julien and climbed a steep flight of steps on the right, which brought you out into the rue Octave-Mirbeau opposite the building. There were other ways, of course, but this was the one he regularly used: it was how his flat joined on to the world outside.

From his desk, if he craned, he could just see the edge of the Panthéon. Every morning he was up at 6.00, had a look to see if the big monster was there, made himself a light breakfast and was sitting down to work by 7.15. He kept at it till 11.15, when he put on hat and coat and descended. He had a cup of coffee in a bar at the corner, did what little shopping was needed, ate a sandwich with a glass of beer at another nearby bar, and was back at his desk by 1.30. At 4.00 he knocked off for the day and made himself a pot of tea – he kept a supply of specially imported Ceylon tea in a wooden box with a red dragon stamped upon it, and was very precise about the amount of time he let it stand once the boiling water had been poured into the pot. Afterwards, if the weather was fine, he would take a stroll through the city. Sometimes this took him down as far as the river, or even the Louvre, at others he made straight for the Luxembourg and sat on a bench looking

up into the trees. He was always back by 7.00, for that was
the time a table was kept for him in a nearby bistro. He ate
whatever was put in front of him and paid by the month without questioning the bill. After supper he would return to the
flat and read a little or listen to music. He had a good collection
of early music and his one indulgence was occasionally adding
to it – Harnoncourt he particularly admired.

Sometimes you went to concerts, his wife – his second wife
– would interrupt him. He seemed to need these interruptions,
was deft at incorporating them into his discourse. Not often,
he would go on, too expensive and, really, after London, live
music in Paris was always a disappointment.

We listen a lot here too, his wife would say. Friends who
came to stay and neighbours who dropped in on them in their
converted farmhouse in the Black Mountains, up above Aber-
gavenny, were indeed often entertained to an evening of
baroque music. His wife, a handsome woman still, with a mass
of red hair piled up on her head, would hand the records to
him reverently, dusting them as she did so with a special cloth,
leaving the final gestures – the laying of the disc on the turn-
table, the setting of the mechanism in motion, the gentle
lowering of the stilus – would leave all that to him. I'm so
uneducated, she would say. When I met him I thought a
saraband was something you wore round your head. You had
other qualities, he would say.

In between records he would often talk about his Paris years.
After his wife's death what he had needed most of all was
solitude. Not that he wanted to meditate or brood: just that
he didn't want to have to do with people. He took on more
work than he could easily manage, needed to feel that when
one piece was done there was always another waiting for him.
Sometimes, in the early morning or evening, the light was
excessively gentle, touching the tea-pot. I wouldn't ever have
known moments like those if I hadn't been alone, he would say.

As he strolled through the city in the late afternoons he
would occasionally have fantasies of drowning: a vivid sense
of startled faces on the bank or the bridge above him, or perhaps
on the deck of a passing boat at sea, and then the water would
cover him completely and he would sink, shedding parts of
himself as he descended into the silence and the dark, until in

the end it was only a tiny core, a soul or knuckle perhaps, that lay, rocking gently with the current, on the sandy bottom. He knew such feelings were neurotic, dangerous perhaps, but he was not unduly worried, sensed that it was better to indulge them, let them have their head, than to try and cut them out altogether. After all, everyone has fantasies. In the one life there are many lives. Alternate lives. Alternative lives. That's the foolishness of biographies he would say, of novels. They never take account of the alternative lives we live alongside the main one. Like Shiva with his arms. In their converted farmhouse in the Black Mountains his wife would serve chilled white wine to anyone, friends or neighbours, who had dropped in to see them, always making sure that no glass was empty. You thought of alternative lives as you climbed the steps, she would say in her excellent English.

Steps are conducive to fantasy, he would say. Going up and down steps lets the mind float free. How often we run up and down the steps of our lives, like scales on a piano.

And always with his hat, his wife would say.

Yes. Always with my hat. On my head. I'm a creature of habit. I would have felt naked without it.

He had to explain to me that a baroque suite was not something you had at the end of a fancy meal, she would say.

And certainly she made life comfortable for him, saw to it that he had everything he needed, was not disturbed by any of the practical details of daily living. He for his part looked up to her, would do nothing without her consent, wanted her to say when he was tired and ready for bed, when he was hungry and ready for a meal.

He had been happy in his Paris flat. His desk was under the window and as he worked he felt the sun warm the top of his head and then his neck. If he gave his alternative lives their head he also knew how to keep them in check. Most of the time I lived just one life, or less, he would say. When he poured tea into his cup in the early morning silence it sometimes seemed as if all of existence was concentrated in that one moment, that one act. Could he have wished for greater happiness?

But do you always know what it is you want? What it is you really feel? Sometimes the tediousness and unreality of the novels he had to translate was too much for him. It was an

effort to keep going till 11.15, and then he couldn't bring himself to face the afternoon session. One day, indulging his
drowning fantasies more than usual, he did not go back to his
room after lunch. Instead, he walked down the hill and across
the river to the Island, and then across again and up in the
direction of the Bastille. He must have walked for two or three
hours, his mind a blank, because he suddenly realized that he
felt utterly exhausted, could not walk another step. There was
a café across the road, so he crossed and went in. It was empty
at that time of day, except for the patron in his shirt-sleeves,
polishing the counter. He eased himself on to a stool and
ordered a coffee. When it came he swallowed it in one go and
ordered another. This time he toyed with it a little longer,
dipping a lump of sugar into it and watching the dark liquid
eat into the white, letting it drop into the cup and stirring
slowly, gazing down at the spoon as he did so.

By the time he had drunk this second cup he felt restored,
wondered how he could have reached the stage of exhaustion
he had just been in.

I want to make a phone call, he said to the patron.

The man stood in front of him, separated by the counter of
the bar. He was a large man with a red face, bald but with a
bristling moustache and large amounts of hair on his arms.

Could I have a token please. For a phone call.

He thought the man had not heard, then saw that he was in
fact holding out his hand, palm upward, and there lay the
token on the creased red skin.

He looked up into the man's face again. The man was grinning, holding his hand out across the polished counter. He
lowered his eyes again and looked at the token. There it was,
waiting to be picked up. Gingerly he stretched out his own
hand and reached for it, but just as he was about to pick it up
he realized that it was no longer there. The large hand was
open, palm upwards, but it was empty.

He looked up quickly. The man was still grinning. He lowered his eyes again, and as he did so the man slowly turned
his hand over, and there was the token again, a small silver
circle, lying on the back of the hand. The man thrust his arm
forward again, as if to say, Go on, take it. So, once again he
watched his own hand going out to meet the other, and this

time the fingers closed round the token and he lifted it off the
hand and drew it back towards him. As he did so he saw the
hole. It was a small round black hole in the middle of the man's
hand, just where the token had been. It was smoking gently.

He must have walked a lot more after that. He didn't remember where or for how long, but towards the end of the afternoon
he found himself by the river again. He tried to look at the
books for sale on the quays, but his mind wouldn't focus. He
didn't want to go back to the flat, but his feet were hurting
badly and he felt he had to take his shoes off or he would start
to cry. He found some steps and staggered down them to the
level of the water. There was a patch of grass at the bottom
where a tree grew under the high wall. He sat down slowly,
leaning back against the tree, closed his eyes, and fumbled with
the laces of his shoes. When his feet were at last free he opened
his eyes again and sat motionless, staring down into the water.

When the girl came it had grown almost dark. He couldn't
make out her face clearly, only the mass of red hair that fell
down to her shoulders under a little green beret. For a moment,
in the half-light, she reminded him of his dead wife.

He must have spoken because she said at once:

You are English.

How did you guess?

I guess.

He couldn't place her accent.

It's hot today, she said in English.

Are *you* English?

She shrugged.

I too will take off my shoes, she said.

He wanted to talk about the token but checked himself.

She took off her beret: Hold it please.

She brushed her hair hard, moving her head in time to the
strokes. Then the brush vanished as abruptly as it had appeared,
and she took the beret back from him and carefully put it on,
though this time at rather more of an angle than it had previously been.

He was looking at the lights of the city reflected in the river
when she said to him: Do you mind if I put my head on your
lap? Without waiting for a reply she did so, quickly settling
into position and tucking her legs under her skirt.

Her eyes were closed and he thought she had gone to sleep, but then she began to move her head on his lap, slowly at first, as though trying to find the most comfortable position, then with gathering violence. He stroked her hair; the beret fell off; she began to moan.

They must have got up together. He could remember nothing except that her room was red. Like fire, she said.

He found himself walking again, swaying like a drunkard. His trousers felt too tight, his thighs itched where they rubbed. His body seemed to have been scraped raw from neck to crotch. When he finally stumbled home he was so tired he could hardly get the key into the lock. He fell on the bed fully clothed and was asleep at once.

When he woke it was dark. He didn't know if he had slept for eight hours or thirty-two. To judge from his hunger it was probably the latter. He found some food in the fridge and wolfed it down. Then he got into his pyjamas and crawled into bed again.

The next time he woke it was early morning. He groped his way out of bed and to the window of his study for his daily look at the Panthéon. It was as he was doing so, craning a little to the left as usual, that he suddenly remembered that all had not been entirely normal in the past few days. Alternative lives, he thought to himself, made his breakfast and settled down to the novel on his desk.

It was only that evening, as he was having a bath, that he saw the wound in his thigh. It was a long straight cut, like a cat's scratch, and it ran all the way from the top of his thigh to his knee. He touched it but it didn't hurt. He dried it carefully, examined it again, and decided that there was nothing to do but let it heal and disappear. In fact though it never healed. Years later, in Wales, whenever he talked of his Paris days he would point to his leg and laugh and say: It never healed.

You didn't want it to, his wife would say. Friends who had known him in the old days would comment on the resemblance between his two wives. Especially when she stood in the middle of the room like that, dusting a record before handing it to him, saying: You didn't want it to, really. No, he would say, looking up at her. No I didn't did I?

He's so superstitious, she would say. He never went to a doctor about it.

What could a doctor do?

Maybe give you something to get rid of it.

We've all got something like that somewhere on our bodies, he would say. Maybe if we got rid of it we wouldn't be ourselves any more, who knows?

Who knows? his wife would echo.

He would tell of his fantasies of drowning, vivid images he experienced at that time, when he was living in Paris after the death of his first wife. As I sank I would feel quite relieved. I would think: There goes another life – and know I had not finished with this one.

One sprouts many lives, he would say, and look at her and smile. One is a murderer. One an incendiary. One a suicide. One lives in London. One in Paris. One in New York.

One, One, One, she would echo, mocking him.

With his soft grey hat pulled low over his eyes, he climbs the steps out of the rue St-Julien.

That Which is Hidden is That Which is Shown; That Which is Shown is That Which is Hidden

One day they found him under the bed, curled tight, pressed against the wall. For as long as they could remember he had been in the habit of hiding objects in boxes, in drawers, in holes he dug in the garden. Sometimes, when they sat down to a meal after calling for him in vain, he would suddenly appear from under the table. But when they found him that day under the bed it was different. He wouldn't come out and they had to pull the bed aside and haul him to his feet. His pockets were stuffed with objects: pebbles, a rusty spoon, two pen-nibs, a half-sucked sweet. When they asked him what he was up to he wouldn't reply. They pleaded, threatened, cajoled. When they finally gave up he went back to his place under the bed.

He was no trouble at school, did his homework, bothered nobody. But he began to spend more and more time in cupboards, sitting in the dark, or crouched in a corner of the pantry, behind the potatoes. In the attic they found an inlaid mother-of-pearl box with a cricket ball nestling inside. When they tackled him about it he only shook his head, so they desisted and hoped the fad would pass.

No one ever complained of him, but he was not interested in his work at school and left as soon as he could. He was never a burden to them, was never out of work, though he rarely held down any job for very long. One day he disappeared, and when he turned up again he told them he had found a room nearer his work.

In his new room he fitted out a workbench and began to make little boxes for himself out of bits of wood he found lying on dumps, and then more elaborate things, cupboards, boats, mysterious contraptions with shelves and holes and little passages and conduits linking one part of the interior to another.

Inside these spaces and holes stood little wooden men, sometimes with trays in their hands, staring straight ahead of them,
birds with beady eyes, giraffes. The door into the dark spaces
was always half open, so that the figure was both concealed
and revealed. Look, he said to his mother. Look, look inside.
And closed the little door.

The objects proliferated, grew more complex. He gave up
his job and concentrated on his craft. He spent hours walking
the streets, looking for likely pieces of wood. Sometimes he
took trips to the seaside and collected hard grainy driftwood.
Back in his room he sawed and chiselled and sandpapered. He
used no nails, only wooden pins he made himself. The objects,
looking like a cross between old butter-churns and complicated
toys, stood in rows against the walls of his room. There is
nothing inside them, he said to his father. And held the little
doors closed. Nothing inside.

The room is empty now. He has gone, taking his possessions
with him. In a derelict house, not far from the station, the
police have found a number of strange objects: little cabinets
with multiple divisions and, here and there, behind half-open
doors, tiny wooden figures, round-eyed, staring straight ahead
in the dark. The house is crumbling, deserted. The police take
away the objects and then, when no one claims them, smash
them up and throw them away.

There are no objects any more. There were never any objects.
Now you know. Don't look for me. By the time you read this
I will be far away. You will never find me.

In the Fertile Land

We live in a fertile land. Here we have all we want. Beyond the borders, far away, lies the desert, where nothing grows.

Nothing grows there. Nor is there any sound except the wind.

Here, on the other hand, all is growth, abundance. The plants reach enormous heights, and even we ourselves grow and grow, so that there is absolutely no stopping us. And when we speak the words flow out in torrents, another aspect of the general fertility.

Here, the centre is everywhere and the circumference nowhere.

Conversely, it could be said – and it is an aspect of the general fertility here that everything that can be said has its converse side – conversely it could be said that the circumference is everywhere and the centre nowhere, that the limits are everywhere, that everywhere there is the presence of the desert.

Here, in the fertile land, everyone is so conscious of the desert, so intrigued and baffled by it, that a law has had to be passed forbidding anyone to mention the word.

Even so, it underlies every sentence and every thought, every dream and every gesture.

Some have even gone over into the desert, but as they have not come back it is impossible to say what they found there.

I myself have no desire to go into the desert. I am content with the happy fertility of this land. The desert beyond is not something I think about very much, and if I occasionally dream about it, that contravenes no law. I cannot imagine where the limits of the desert are to be found or what kind of life, if any, exists there. When I hear the wind I try to follow it in my mind across the empty spaces, to see in my mind's eye the ripples it makes in the enormous dunes as it picks up the grains of sand and deposits them in slightly altered patterns a little further along – though near and far have clearly a quite different meaning in the desert from the one they have here.

In the desert silence prevails. Here the talk is continuous. Many of us are happy even talking to ourselves. There is never any shortage of subjects about which to talk, nor any lack of words with which to talk. Sometimes, indeed, this abundance becomes a little onerous, the sound of all these voices raised in animated conversation or impassioned monologue grows slightly disturbing. There have even been moments when the very abundance of possible subjects and of available directions in which any subject may be developed has made me long for the silence of the desert, with only the monotonous whistling of the wind for sound. At those times my talk redoubles in both quantity and speed and I cover every subject except the one which obsesses me – for the penalty for any infringement of the law is severe. Even as I talk though, the thought strikes me that perhaps I am actually in the desert already, that I have crossed over and not returned, and that what the desert is really like is this, a place where everyone talks but where no one speaks of what concerns him most.

Such thoughts are typical of the fertility of our land.